Praise for *The January Dancer*

"A picaresque tale with intriguing and colorful characters set in a complex and fully developed far future. *The January Dancer* is Flynn's most ambitious novel to date, and overall the most successful." —*SciFi Weekly*

"A fast-moving space opera . . . Flynn has a keen ear for dialect and a deft hand with characterization. . . . Fascinating." —*RT Book Reviews*

"Flynn puts his world-building skills to good use, creating a context that begs to be further explored." —*Booklist*

"A full and detailed story arc, a fabulous future galaxy to play in, and a race of humans who are trying to save what they can remember of ancient Earth. If you enjoy space operas told from many points of view, you might get a kick out Michael Flynn's *The January Dancer*." —*SFRevu*

"Reminiscent of the tall tales and cautionary stories of Mike Resnick and revealing the talent of a master storyteller, this SciFi Essential book belongs in most libraries and should appeal to fans of SF adventure and space opera." —*Library Journal*

BOOKS BY MICHAEL FLYNN

*denotes a Tor book

THE
JANUARY
DANCER

MICHAEL
FLYNN

TOR® A TOM DOHERTY ASSOCIATES BOOK • NEW YORK

THE JANUARY DANCER

Map by James Sinclair

A Tor Book
Published by Tom Doherty Associates, LLC
175 Fifth Avenue
New York, NY 10010

www.tor-forge.com

Tor® is a registered trademark of Tom Doherty Associates, LLC.

ISBN 978-0-7653-5779-3

First Edition: October 2008
First Mass Market Edition: July 2011

Printed in the United States of America

0 9 8 7 6 5 4 3 2 1

To Hari, Bikram, Sandeep, Yash,
and the rest of the gang down in Old Chennai

contents

those of name

A Harper	
The Scarred Man	
Amos January	captain of the tramp freighter *New Angeles*
Micmac Anne	his Number One
Maggie Barnes, Bill Tirasi, Johnny Mgurk, Slugger O'Toole, Nagaraj Hogan, Mahmoud Malone	crew of *New Angeles*
Handsome Jack Garrity	a Certain Person on New Eireann
Little Hugh O'Carroll	The Ghost of Ardow, assistant manager of New Eireann, a.k.a. *Ringbao della Costa, Esp'ranzo*
Sophia Colonel Jumdar	commanding the 33rd IC Company Regiment
Major Chaudhary	her second in command
na Fir Li	a Hound of the Ardry, commanding Sapphire Point Station
Greystroke	Fir Li's senior Pup, a.k.a. *Tol Benlever*

the Molnar khan Matsumo	chairman of the Kinlé Hadramoo, Cynthia Cluster
the Fudir	petty criminal in the Terran Corner of Jehovah, a.k.a. *Kalim de Morsey*
the Memsahb	leader of the Brotherhood of Terra on Jehovah
Olafsson Qing	a courier from the Confederation of Central Worlds
Bridget ban	a Hound of the Ardry, a.k.a. *Julienne Lady Melisonde*
Grimpen, Gwillgi	Hounds of the Ardry
Donovan	a sleeper agent of the Confederation of Central Worlds
Konmi Pulawayo-Schmidt	STC Director on Peacock Junction
Fendy Jackson	leader of the Brotherhood of Terra on Die Bold
Radhi Lady Cargo Dalhousie	Chairman of the Interstellar Cargo Company
the Other Olafsson	a Confederate shadow agent
Bakhtiyar Commodore Saukkonen	commanding, vanguard, 3rd ICC Peacekeeper Fleet

Barflies, pirates, merchants, traders, rebels, 'Cockers, sliders, servants, thieves, Terrans, and sundry lowlife

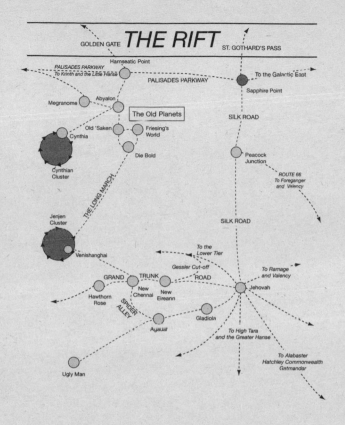

THE RIFT

GOLDEN GATE   ST. GOTHARD'S PASS

Hanseatic Point

PALISADES PARKWAY
To Krinth and the Little Hanse   PALISADES PARKWAY

To the Galactic East

Sapphire Point

Megranome   Abyalon

The Old Planets

SILK ROAD

Old 'Saken   Friesing's World

Cynthia

Die Bold

Peacock Junction

Cynthian Cluster

ROUTE 66
To Foreganger and Valency

Jenjen Cluster

THE LONG MARCH

SILK ROAD

Venishanghai

To the Lower Tier

Gessler Cut-off

GRAND   TRUNK   ROAD

To Ramage and Valency

New Chennai   New Eireann

Jehovah

Hawthorn Rose

SPIDER ALLEY

Ayaufr   Gladiola

Ugly Man

To High Tara and the Greater Hanse

To Alabaster Hatchley Commonwealth Gatmandar

souch-cencral district,
united league of the periphery

Two-dimensional projection of the South-Central Spiral Arm, United League of the Periphery. Not all systems and clusters are on the same level and the connecting roads are not always proportional to the travel time required.

peripheral time equivalents

The Old Planets use dodeka time, based on multiples of twelve, while the rest of the Periphery uses metric time, based on multiples of ten. Both systems are based on the heartbeat. In addition, planetary governments also use local times.

1 beat = 0.83 seconds

METRIC TIME	APPROX. TERRAN TIME
100 beats = 1 hektobeat = 1 metric minute =	1.39 minutes
100 mminutes = 1 hektominute = 1 hora =	2.31 hours
1 kilominute = 10 horae = 1 metric day =	0.96 days
10 mdays = 1 dekaday = 1 metric week =	9.6 days = 1.38 weeks
40 mdays = 1 metric month =	38.6 days = 1.29 months
1000 horae = 1 hektoday = 1 metric season =	96.5 days = 13.8 weeks = 3.2 months
360 mdays = 1 myear ≈	347 days*

(*) The metric year is shorter than the dodeka year by about 13.5 mdays. The League Bureau of Standards mandates what is known popularly as "Catch-up Week," although it is longer than a metric week.

Dodeka Time	Approx. Terran Time
12 beats=1 doozybeat =	10 seconds
24 beats=1 case of beats =	20 seconds
144 beats=1 grossbeat=1 dminute =	120 seconds=2 minutes
24 dminutes=1 case of dminutes=1 are =	48 minutes=0.8 hours
360 dminutes=1 circle of dminutes =	12 hours
2 circles of dminutes=1 dday =	1 day
144 ares=1 gross of ares = 1 dweek=	4.8 days
half doozy week=6 dweeks = 1 dmonth=	28.8 days≈1 month
360 ddays=1 circle of ddays=1 dyear =	360 days

Dodeka multiples are 12 (doozy), 24 (case), 144 (gross), and 360 (circle)

Colloquially, a dodeka day is called a do-dah day; dodeka time in general is often referred to as "doozy-days."

THE
JANUARY
DANCER

*E*verything in the universe is older than it seems. Blame Einstein for that. We see what a thing was when the light left it, and that was long ago. Nothing in the night sky is contemporary, not to us, not to one another. Ancient stars exploded into ruin before their sparkle ever caught our eyes; those glimpsed in glowing "nurseries" were crones before we witnessed their birth. Everything we marvel at is already gone.

Yet, light rays go out forever, so that everything grown old and decayed retains somewhere the appearance of its youth. The universe is full of ghosts.

But images are light, and light is energy, and energy is matter; and matter is real. So image and reality are the same thing, after all. Blame Einstein for that, as well.

The Bar on Jehovah needs no other name, for it is the sole oasis on the entire planet. The Elders do not care for it, and would prefer that the Bar and all its patrons drop into the Black Hole of ancient myth. But chance has conspired to create and maintain this particular Eden.

The chance is that Jehovah sits upon a major interchange of Electric Avenue, that great slipstreamed superhighway that binds the stars. Had it been a small nexus, some bandit chief would have taken it. Had it been a large one, some government would have done so. But it is the Mother of All Nexi, so none dare touch it at all. A hundred hands desire it, and ninety-nine will prevent the one from taking it. Call that peace.

Consequently, it is the one Port in the not-so United League of the Periphery where a ship's captain and crew can rest assured in their transient pleasures that cargo, ship, and selves are safe. The Bar is thus an Eden, of sorts. There, one may take the antidote to the fruit of the Tree of the Knowledge of Good and Evil, for a man in his cups seldom knows one from the other. The Elders know a cash cow when they see one, even if the cow looks a lot like a serpent and money is the root of all evil.

She has come to Jehovah because, sooner or later, everyone does. The Spiral Arm is a haystack of considerable size and a particular man a needle surpassingly small, but Jehovah is the one place where such a search might succeed, because it is the one place where such a man might be found.

She is an ollamh, as the harper's case slung across her back announces. She is lean and supple—a cat, and she moves with a cat's assurance, not so much striding as gliding, although there is something of the strider in her, too. The Bartender watches her wend the pit of iniquity with something like approval, for no one carries a harp in quite that way who cannot make it weep and laugh, and frighten.

As she crosses the room, she gathers the eyes of all those conscious, and even a few fallen comatose turn blind gazes in her direction. She has eyes of green, and that is dangerous; for they are not the green of grass and gentle hillsides, but the hard, sharp glass-green of flint. Her hair is the red of flame, complementing the color of her eyes; but her skin is dark gold, for the races of Old Earth have vanished into a score of others, and what one is has become, through science, a projection of what one would be. Yet there is something solitary about her. Her heart is a fortress untaken; though from such a fortress who knows what might sortie?

When she reaches the corner the men sitting there drag the table and their less mobile mates aside and make a place for her. She does not ask permission. None of her kind do. Minstrel and minnesinger; skald, bard, and troubadour. They never ask, they simply appear—and sing for their supper.

She opens her harp case and it is a *clairseach*, as those watching had known it would be: a lap harp of the old style. She plays the cruel metal strings with her nails, which is the only true way of playing. The truest songs have always a trace of pain in their singing.

In self-mockery, she plays an ancient tune, "A wand'ring minstrel, I," to introduce herself and display the range of her music. When she sings of the spacefarers, the grim jingle of the Interstellar Cargo Company runs underneath the freewheeling melody: mockery in a minor key. When she sings of the Rift, the notes are empty and lost and the melody unremittingly dark. When she sings of Old Earth, there is unrelieved sorrow. When she sings of love—ah, but all her songs are songs of love, for a man may love many things and anything. He may love a woman, or a comrade. He may love his work or the place where he lives. He may love a good drink or a good journey. He might get lost—on the journey, or in the drink, or especially in the woman—but what is love without loss?

Matters are different for women. They generally love one thing, which is why the love of a woman is like a laser while that of a man is like a flood. The one can sweep you away; the other can burn you clean through. There is One Thing that the harper has loved and lost, and the memory of it aches in all her songs, even in the cheerful ones; or especially in the cheerful ones.

For her set piece, she sings "Tristam and Iseult," the cruelest of the songs of love, and with its ferocity she holds her listeners' hearts in her hand. When she plucks out the strokes of war, their hearts gallop with the thundering strings. When she caresses the gentle tones of trysting, they yearn with the lovers in their bower. And when her fingers snap the sudden chords of betrayal, a shiver runs through them and they look at their own comrades through lowered lids. She plays with her audience, too. The music suggests that this time, somehow, it will all end differently, and in the end she leaves them weeping.

Afterward, the Bartender directs her to a dark corner, where a man sits before a bowl of *uiscebeatha*. The bowl is empty—or not yet refilled, depending on the direction of one's thoughts. He is one of those lost men, and it is in this very bowl that he has become lost. So he stares into it, hoping to find himself. Or at least some fragment of what he was.

He is a man of remnants and shadows. There is a forgotten look about him. His blouse is incompletely fastened; his face concealed by the ill-lit alcove. It is a niche in the wall and he, a saint of sorts, and like a statue'd saint, he makes no move when the ollamh sits across the table from him.

The harper says nothing. She waits.

After a time a man's voice issues from the shadows. "We thought it was a potion that seduced Tristam from his duty. We thought he fell in love unwillingly."

"It's not love unless it *is* unwilling," the harper answers. "Otherwise, why speak of 'falling'?"

"Your eyes remind us . . ." But of what he doesn't say. It may be that he has forgotten. She might be one of those ghostly images that haunt the berms of Electric Avenue, crawling along at the laggard speed of light, only now arriving from some distant past.

The harper leans forward and says, with unwonted eagerness, "They tell me you know about the Dancer, that you knew those who were in it."

Mockery from the shades. "Am I to be a seanachy, then? A teller of tales?"

"Perhaps, but there is a song in the tale somewhere, and I mean to find it."

"Be careful what you look for. I think you sing too many songs. We think you sing more than you live. It all happened so long ago. I didn't think anyone knew."

"Stories spread. Rumors trickle like winter snowmelt down a mountain's face."

The shadowed man thinks for a time. He looks into his bowl again, but if he intends another as the price of the story, he does not name that price and the harper again waits.

"I can only tell it as it was told to us," the man says. "I can weave you a story, but who knows how true the threads may be?" His fingers play idly with the bowl; then he shoves it to one side and leans his forearms on the table. His face, emerging from the darkened alcove at last, is shrunken, as if he has been suctioned out and all that remains of him is skin and skull. His flesh is sallow, his cheeks hollow. His chin curls like a coat hook, and his mouth sags across the saddle of the hook. His hair is too white, but there are places on his skull, places with scars, where the hair will never grow back. His eyes dart ever sidewise, as if something wicked lurks just past the edge of his vision. "What can it matter now?" he asks of ghosts and shadows. "They've all died, or gone their ways. Who can the memories hurt?"

The shadows do not answer, yet.

GEANTRAÍ: SAND AND IRON

It began on an unnamed planet, the scarred man says . . .

. . . around an unnamed sun, in an unnamed region distant from the Rift. That was a bad sign to begin with, for what can come from nameless places but something unspeakable? It was a bad place to break down, a bad place to be, far off the shipping lanes, on a little-used byway of Electric Avenue known as Spider Alley. But it was just the sort of place where a baling-wired, skin-toothed tramp freighter might find itself. When there is little to lose, there is much to gain, and the secret shortcuts of the Periphery have a way of finding profit.

And this at least can be said about such forgotten corners: It is in such places that the flotsam and the jetsam of the galaxy wash up.

One such bit of flotsam was the free trader *New Angeles,* out of Ugly Man and bound for the Jenjen Cluster with a cargo of drugs and exotic foodstuffs that the folk there do not make for themselves. The jetsam had been there much longer. How much longer, no man could say.

There were contractual dates, penalty clauses, maintenance budgets. It was the sacrifice of the latter on the altar of the former that had brought the ship to this place. Something had blown—it doesn't matter what—and *New Angeles* had drifted into a side channel and into the subluminal mud.

. . . and alfvens aren't really designed to entangle at Newtonian speeds. One hard yank on the fabric of space to slide off the ramp of Electric Avenue without becoming a Cerenkov burst, a few more tugs to get below the system's escape velocity. Past that, they tend to smoke and give off sparks. Here on the edge of nowhere there was no Space Traffic Control, no magbeam cushions to slow them, and the unwonted deceleration strained *New Angeles* to the limit. The twin alfvens screamed like tormented souls until the ship finally entered the calm of a Newtonian orbit.

By the grace of physics, every strand of Electric Avenue is tied to a sun, but there is no guarantee of planets to go with it, or at least of useful ones. As the ship shed velocity circling the star, the crew imaged the system from various points, searching anxiously for parallax, until . . . There! A planet! Hard acceleration to match orbits; and a long, slow crawl across Newtonian space, during which each crewman could blame another for everything that had gone wrong.

The planet was the sort called a marsbody: a small world of broad, gritty plains and low, tired hills that barely interrupted the eternal westerlies. The winds blew at gale force, but the air being thin, the storms were but the ghosts of rage. Orbiting the planet, the ship's instruments detected sand and iron, and with silicon and heavy metals, a man could make most things needful. So a downside team was assembled, equipped with backhoe and molecular sieve, and sent below in the ship's jolly-boat while the engineers and deck officers waited above in various states of patience.

In one state was the chief engineer, Nagaraj

Hogan, who whiled his time in certain recreations based on the laws of probability—to the benefit of his assistant, who had found those laws highly malleable.

In the other state fidgeted Captain Amos January, who, like a sort of anti-Canute, spent his time not sweeping back the tide, but urging it forward. He was the orifice through which all the pressures of budget and schedule were concentrated and directed at the crew—though with little more consequence than the spiritless wind on the planet below. January owned that most treacherous of countenances, for he was a hard man with a soft man's face. Who could take seriously anything he said? The lips were too full, the cheeks too round, the laugh lines too prominent. They belied the harshness with which he often spoke.

There comes a time when fatalism conquers logic and conquers even common sense, and the crew of *New Angeles* had reached that point, and perhaps had reached it long before. They *ought* to have worked with more passion on the repairs, but why hustle to meet the next disaster?

Because the ship would miss the delivery date, January fumed. Micmac Anne, his Number One, thought that if the folk in the Jenjen had sent all the way to Ugly Man for the drugs, they would hardly return them because they were a trifle stale.

January turned to her from the ship's viewer, his cherub's face flushed with anger. "The groundside party has shifted the dig!"

Anne verified the mining party's location. "Two hundred double paces to the west-southwest," she acknowledged. She did not see that it much mattered, but the captain was given to fits of precision. "I'm sure they had a good rea—"

"They're digging in the wrong place! The mass densitometer showed the ore closest to the surface *here*!" His finger stabbed the map projection on the viewer. "Greatest benefit, least work."

"The least work," she reminded him, "was to cannibalize part of the ship. That's what Hogan recommended."

"Cannibalize the ship! Oh, that's a wonderful idea!" January cried, and for an instant Anne almost believed he meant it, so happy was his countenance. "And after a few rounds of that," he continued, "there'd be no ship left to repair."

Anne thought it might also mean less ship to break down, but she forbore expressing that thought.

"Someone should put a bug up their asses," January said. "Hogan can't spend his whole life playing cards."

Anne sighed and turned away. "Alright . . . I'll just . . ." But January stopped her.

"No, you stay up here, keep on top of things. I'll have Slugger take me planetside in the gig."

His Number One, who had been turning toward the radio and not toward the boat davits, hesitated. Amos had decided that the Personal Touch was needed. This was a mistake, in her opinion. On the radio, his voice, pure and hard, might have transmitted some of his urgency. Delivered in person, it never would.

Slugger O'Toole grounded the gig near the jolly-boat, and January was out the hatch before the sand beneath had even cooled. It was the sort of planet where skinsuits will do. The air was thin and cold, but could be gathered into breathable quantities by the suit's intelligence. The breather made talking difficult, and gave the voice a squeaky texture—not a good thing, under the circumstances.

Striding across the gritty plain, he saw that the

work party had moved the backhoe and sieve over into the lea of the low ridge that bordered the sea of sand. Further, having seen the gig land, they had stopped to watch the captain's approach. This was one more straw on January's personal dromedary. Did they think they could dally here forever?

The backhoe had been digging in a drift just below a cleft in the face of the ridge. Atop it, half-turned in her seat, Maggie Barnes waited. The engine hummed in idle. Every now and then, its insolators twitched a little to follow the world's sun. Maggie—she liked to be called Maggie B.—was a short, thick woman with unwomanly strength in her shoulders. Her skinsuit was a sky-blue, but of a different sky on a far-off and almost forgotten world. Here, the sky was so pale it was almost white.

Tirasi, the system tech, tall and thin and with the look of a cadaver awaiting its tag, stood by the smelter with his arms crossed. The molecular sieve had already processed the needed silicon—mining sand had been no problem—and awaited now only some heavier metals. Occasionally, he tweaked a knob, as if fearful that the settings would otherwise all run amok. The deckhand Mgurk waited with a shovel planted in the sand, hands draped over the handle tip, and his chin resting upon the hands. His dull red skinsuit nearly matched the oxide sands, and he wore his hood pulled so tight that the goggles and breather mask were all that could be seen.

The sight of so much work not being done further aggravated January, who greeted them by squeaking, "You were supposed to be digging over there!"— indicating the vast open and featureless expanse of the desert.

Maggie B. had not known why the captain had dropped planetside. Anne had stayed out of it, and

New Angeles was now below the horizon. A variety of possible reasons had suggested themselves, chief among them that Hogan had aroused himself and found another source of metal and, therefore, no further work was needed by the surface party. To be told she was digging *in the wrong place* was so unexpected that she laughed aloud.

It must be a joke, right?

No, it wasn't. So she threw up her first line of defense. "Over there, it itches!"

Itches! Yes. The constant winds carried fines of sand, and while the air was too thin to carry much force, the continual spray on the skinsuit tickled.

"Tickled," said January, suspecting some trick.

"Over here, we're in the cliff's wind-shadow."

"But the ore body is buried deeper here!"

Now, by this time, it would have meant more work and more time to return to the original site and start over. The hole was by now already half-dug. Maggie snapped at him. "Makes no damned difference where I dig!"

Now, that may have been the last moment of sanity in the universe, because it should have occurred to all of them that if it made no difference, why had she moved in the first place? In fact, it did make a difference, and a damned one at that. But that came later. In truth, she had simply felt an urge to move the machine.

"You're wasting my time, Captain," she snapped, and as if to prove this point, she put the backhoe into gear.

One more scoop and the claw tips of the bucket made a peculiar, almost musical screech that set their teeth on edge. Even Mgurk roused himself, lifted his chin, and peered into the pit.

Something dull and metallic lay beneath the sand.

"The ore body," said Maggie in quiet satisfaction, and gave January a triumphant look.

"Must be a meteorite," said Tirasi. But January knew immediately that was not right. This close to the surface? With no sign of an impact crater?

"Who cares?" Maggie said, and drew the backhoe for another scoop. Again, that singing note called out. Mgurk cocked his head as if listening.

"It's smooth," said January when more of the body had been revealed.

"It's bloody *machined*," said Tirasi, who had abandoned the smelter to kneel at the pit's edge. Maggie Barnes hopped off the backhoe and joined him.

"Nonsense," January said. "Rivers will smooth a stone the same way."

Tirasi swung his arm wide. "See any rivers nearby?" he demanded. "Water ain't flowed here in millions of years. Nah, this here's a made thing." He pulled pliers from his tool belt and tapped the object. It rang, dull and hollow, and the echoes went on longer than they should have.

January squeaked, "Johnny! Bring that shovel over and clear this out a bit. Johnny? Johnny!" He looked up, but Mgurk was nowhere in sight. "Where has that lazy lout gone now?"

It was a fair question, given that for many leagues in any direction lay nothing but gritty, open desert. Johnny had an aversion to hard labor and showed wonderful imagination in its avoidance; but where in all those miles could he have hidden himself? January used the all-hands channel on his radio. "Johnny, get your lazy carcass over here and help us dig!"

He heard static on the bounceback—a burst of noise that might have had a voice in the center of it. It seemed on the very edge of forming words.

O'Toole answered from the gig. The sudden excitement of the group at the site had attracted his attention. "Johnny's after wandering off t' the cleft," he told them. "What's going on?"

Maggie Barnes told him. "We found us a prehuman artifact!"

What else could it be, a machined object, buried under the sand on a forgotten world? The works of man are wondrously diverse and widely spread, but where you find them you generally find men as well; and none had ever ventured here. "Let's not count chickens," January chided them. But for once his Santa Claus countenance did not lie. There might be riches here, and he knew it as well as they did. Yet caution led him to say, "Not every prehuman artifact—"

But he was talking to the wind. O'Toole was already clambering down the ladder from the gig, and Tirasi had leaped into the pit to brush sand away from the buried object. "Big," the system tech muttered. "Big."

Too big, January noted of the portion thus far revealed. The boats would never lift it, not all of them combined. "Not every prehuman artifact," January tried again, "has made money for its finders. House of Chan had the Ourobouros Circuit for most of a lifetime and could never make it do anything. After Chan Mirslaf died, they sold it as a curio for half what they spent experimenting on it."

"Hey," said Tirasi. "This thing's translucent!"

"And the Cliffside Montage on Alabaster sits in the middle of a plain, visible for leagues, so the Planetary Council can't even fence it off and charge an admission fee." January sighed and crossed his arms.

"Well, Cap'n," said Maggie B., proving someone had been listening, "we won't know till we know what it is, will we?"

O'Toole arrived from the gig and paced round the

circumference of the pit, whistling and exclaiming. A big, blocky, thick-fingered man, he always moved with unexpected grace and dexterity, even when—or especially when—he had hoisted a few pots of beer.

"So let's not get our hopes up before we know what we have," January said. "How many prehuman discoveries have been nothing more than empty chambers or the shells of buildings?"

"There was an entire city on Megranome," Maggie recalled. "And near as we could figger, it was formed as a single structure, with no seams or joints. We used to go over there when I was a kid and play in the ruins, pertending the prehumans was still there, hidin' 'round the next corner." She laughed, then turned suddenly, as if startled, and her gaze swept the open desert. "Wonder where they all went to. The prehumans, I mean."

January shrugged. "Who cares? No matter."

"We usta call 'em 'the folk of sand and iron.' Nobody knew why. Makes our reason fer stoppin' here a little weird, don't ya think?"

"Stuff and nonsense," said January. "They were gone long before humans went to space."

O'Toole had finished his circuit of the pit and had returned to where they stood. "Don't ye believe it, Cap'n," he said. "They tell stories. On Die Bold, on Friesing's World, specially on Old 'Saken. Hell, half the Old Planets have stories o' th' prehumans."

Maggie B. nodded vigorously. "Some of them old legends are so old they been forgot."

January snorted. "Myths, you mean. Legends, fables. I've heard them. If any two of them describe the same creatures—if any two stories even fit together logically—they'd be the first two. We don't know when the prehumans were around, or for how long. We don't know if they ruled this quarter of the galaxy or only roamed through it. There's probably a tall tale to cover every possibility. People can't tolerate the inexplicable. So they tell a story or sing a song. All we've ever found were their artifacts. No human ever saw them in life."

"They mayn't been even life as we know it," said Maggie B. "Mebbe, they was fluorine life or silicon life or somethin' we ain't never figgered on."

"Silicon, eh?" said O'Toole. "Now, I'm not after hearin' that one. Hey, maybe they nivver disappeared. Maybe, they just crumbled into sand and"—he waved his arm over the surrounding desert—"and maybe that's all what's left o' th' fookin' lot uv 'em." The quickening wind stirred the sand, lifting and tumbling granules as if they were dancing.

"And maybe," said Tirasi from the pit, "you can jump down here, Slug, and help me dig the bloody thing out!"

Tirasi always managed to slip under O'Toole's skin, not least of all by abbreviating the man's nickname. Physically opposite, they were much alike in spirit, and so repelled each other, as a man spying himself in a fun-house mirror might step backward in alarm. From time to time, they debated whether "Slugger" or "Fighting Bill" were the weightier epithet, with the question still undetermined. Slugger was a bull; Fighting Bill a terrier. The pilot leapt into the pit with the system tech, and they both dug and brushed the sand off the artifact using their hands.

January shook his head. "And Mgurk has the shovel, and he's not about. Maggie, you dig some more around that thing. See how big it is and—maybe—you'll find that ore body while you're at it." This last was intended sarcastically, to remind them why they were beached on this forsaken world in the first place. The artifact wasn't going anywhere, and if they didn't complete the repairs, *New Angeles* wasn't either.

Maggie moved the backhoe a little farther off and began to probe for the edge of the artifact. Her digger came down too hard into the sand and struck a still-buried portion of it. It rang like a great bass bell, a little muffled, but loud enough that the two men in the pit clapped their hands to their ears. January, who had been searching for some sign of Mgurk's dull red skinsuit, noticed the sand vibrate into ridges and waves half a league away.

About where the mass detector had located the "ore-body's" closest approach to the surface.

January had a sudden vision of the artifact as a buried city, all of one piece, honeycombing the entire planet, and that Tirasi and O'Toole would grub about it forever, brushing the sand from it, inch by inch.

"We ought to go look for Johnny," he began uneasily, and then stopped with his words in his throat, for three dull clangs reverberated from within the buried shell. Tirasi and O'Toole started and scrambled back from it. Maggie made the sign of the wheel across her body and muttered, "The Bood preserve us!" After a few moments, the clangs were repeated. "Ye turned it on somehow," O'Toole told the system tech.

"Or you did," Tirasi answered. He began to brush furiously at the sand that covered the thing, clearing a space. Then, shading his eyes with his hands, he pressed his face to the translucent surface. "I can see inside, a little. There are shapes, shadows. Irregular, ugly. Can't quite make them . . . Aah!" He scrambled back in alarm. "One of 'em moved! It's them! This is where they all went to! Holy Alfven help me!" He began to clamber out of the pit, but O'Toole grabbed his arm. "You were right about the 'ugly,' " he said, pointing.

And there, with his face pressed to the inner surface of the shell, was Johnny Mgurk and the shovel with which he had been beating the walls.

The entrance was in the cleft, of course, obscured by the shadows in a fault in the southern face—a darker opening in the darkness.

New Angeles had come back over the horizon by then, and January informed Micmac Anne what had happened, cautioning her not to tell Hogan and Malone lest, transfixed by visions of easy wealth, they abandon ship and drop planetside in the lighter.

January thought at least one of his crew should stand guard outside the entrance. In case. In case of what, he couldn't say, which did nothing to win their assent. The others thought he wanted to cut them out of a share in the treasure, which by now had in their minds achieved Midas-like proportions. All was decided when Mgurk appeared in the entry and said, in his execrable Terran argot, "Hey, alla come-come, you. Jildy, sahbs. Dekker alla cargo, here. We rich, us." And so they all hurried after him.

January was the last to enter, and the clambering footsteps of the others had faded before he reached the point where the cave became a tunnel with a flattened footpath. He passed an enormous white stripe on the wall, three man-lengths high and a double arm's-length wide. January had barely registered the peculiar dimensions when it struck him that it was the edge of a sliding door nestled into a slot in the rock. Yes, there was the matching slot on the other side of the passage. Pulled out, the door would seal off the entrance. January was impressed. That was one thick door.

And made of marshmallow.

No, not marshmallow, he decided, pressing it experimentally, but some highly resilient material. He pushed, it yielded. He released, and it sprang back. Elastic deformation. He pushed as hard as he could, and his arm sank into the door up to his elbow. It would submit to a chisel or a drill bit in exactly the same way, he decided. A jujitsu material, strong because it yielded.

As soon as he relaxed, the material snapped back, ejecting his arm with all the stored energy with which he had pushed and nearly dislocating his shoulder. Jujitsu material, indeed, he thought, rubbing his shoulder. Best *not* try chisels, drills, lasers, or explosives. It would absorb all the energy, and then give it back. His curiosity ran high; but not that high.

Whatever had required such a barrier must be of inestimable value. He rubbed his hands in anticipation of the wealth waiting below.

Yet, one thing troubled his mind. A door so thick had been meant to bar entry against the most determined explorer. He could not imagine that little Johnny Mgurk had simply rolled it aside. Perhaps the lock had failed over the eons and the system had been designed to fail open.

But why design a "fail *open*" mode into an impassable barrier?

As he continued deeper inside, the rough rock walls smoothed out into an off-white ceramic. Faint veins of pale yellow ran through it, though whether decorative or functional, he couldn't say. Here artistically sinuous, there fiercely rectangular, they could be either, or both. But if decorative, he thought, prehuman eyes had been attuned to finer color contrasts than humans.

Or they'd had lousy interior decorators.

The passage wound down a spiral ramp and some freak of geometry cut off the sounds of the crew's voices, leaving a radio silence within which a persistent static hiss rose and fell irregularly, like a snake trying to speak. The dry air, the constant, sandy wind . . . the planet must be an enormous ball of static electricity.

He came at last to the chamber that the backhoe had uncovered. Through the translucent ceiling drifted the light of the pale sun. It was an oval room of gray sea-green accented with undulating curves of slightly darker shade. The walls seemed to swirl about in unending stillness. Had the effect been meant for beauty, January wondered, or just to make people dizzy? But if prehuman technology was unknowable, their aesthetics were unfathomable.

Arranged irregularly about the room, eleven pedestals emerged seamlessly from the floor. All but one were faerie-thin, and all but four were empty. In a separate chamber, entered as through the languid petals of a fleshy white lotus, a twelfth pedestal, also empty, swept in a graceful exponential arc from the floor. Amid this peculiar cornfield his crew darted with great exclamation.

At the farther end of the room, but offset from the tip of the oval, another white, spongy door sat half-open. Through this opening, January could make out a long, dim corridor receding into the blackness.

"You try lifting the bleeding thing, you think you're so strong!" That challenge, issued to O'Toole by Bill Tirasi, drew January's attention. His four crewmen stood before the first pedestal, upon which a single jet-black egg the size of a clenched fist balanced precariously.

The egg seemed made of glass, but glass so deep that light could not make it to the center, for it appeared much thicker than its size would warrant. Myriad pinpricks gleamed within. Perhaps light had tried to penetrate the blackness, had given up, and scattered into its component photons.

O'Toole was not given to such fancies. Smirking over Tirasi's failure, he laid hold of it and lifted. His muscles bulged, his eyes stood out. But it did not move. He grunted, gripped it in both hands, and still it would not budge.

Yet the balance was so delicate, it ought at least to roll.

It did not. Pushing and pulling had no more effect than lifting. Tirasi scoffed. "Heavier'n it looks, eh, mate?" O'Toole's glower deepened. "Sure, it must be bolted to the fookin' stand."

"I'd bet your whole year's share of profits," Terasi said, "that thing's made of neutronium. Compressed matter . . ." He sighed. "Imagine the profit potential in *that*! A bloke could get stinking rich once he learned the secret."

"Then he'd have to spend his life here," January said, and the others started, for they hadn't seen him enter. "There's not a ship on the Periphery that could lift a neutronium egg."

"That egg, big-big," said Mgurk.

"Nah," O'Toole mocked him. "That egg, small-small."

"That egg, full of galaxies," Mgurk answered. "Yes, yes."

"Oh, right," said O'Toole. But Tirasi scowled and, because he was an instrument tech and carried on his person a wide and wonderful assortment of instruments, pulled out a magnifier and studied the egg with it. "Bloody hell," he said after a few moments. "Those light spots are made of millions of smaller lights." He upped the magnification. "They must be the size of molecules, arranged all in swirls and clusters to look like galaxies. You got good eyes, Johnny."

Maggie B. borrowed the magnifier from him and studied the egg. "That's right purty. Those prehumans must've had eyes as good as Johnny here to enjoy something so hard t'see."

"If they had eyes," said Tirasi. "Maybe they had other senses to appreciate it."

Maggie B. scratched her head. "So, this here place was what, a museum, an art gallery?"

Behind vault doors thick enough to defy all creation? January did not think this a gallery, though it might have been a vault to safeguard priceless treasures. The proudest possessions of the prehuman empire? Assuming the prehumans had had empires, or possessions, or pride. Four treasures only, and one too heavy to take away. Yet the building seemed to extend far out into the sea of sand, and might penetrate deeper into the world. Treasures beyond number might lie elsewhere in the complex.

And they could spend a lifetime searching for them.

January turned to the pedestal beside him and studied what at first seemed to be a pale red brick sitting on end, about a forearm high and just over a handgrasp around. Of the many things which on this world might be rare, January did not think to number sandstone. Unlike the Midnight Egg—they had named the first treasure already—this was nothing more than a geometric slab whose proportions were, to human eyes, the least bit off. Yet, what made one combination of height, length, and breadth pleasing, and another unsatisfactory? The prehumans may have apprehended matters from another perspective, and esteemed this the most beautiful object in the room.

He rubbed the side of the stone and was surprised that despite its rough appearance, it was smooth, and cool to the touch.

"Maybe," said O'Toole, "if we can't lift the fookin' thing, we can chip off a wee slice, something small enough to take. Even a chip could make us all rich."

"Hey," said Mgurk. "You-fella, no break him. No diamonds, those." And the Terran put his left hand in front of his face and wagged it side to side three times quickly, a gesture that the crew had learned to read as vigorous defiance.

O'Toole balled a fist. "You gonna stop me, Johnny? You and what Management Company?"

"Johnny," said Maggie B. "If them ain't diamonds, what are they?" O'Toole rolled his eyes. As if a Terran would know!

"Galaxies," the deckhand answered. "Whole universe in a ball. Story, they tell ut in Corner of Abyalon, when me a kid. King Stonewall, he want alla-alla galaxies, *jildy*. So his bhisti science-wallahs press universe small-small. But Stonewall fear touch ut. An he smash ut, universe ends." Mgurk pointed to O'Toole. "You chip, you break sky. Big trouble." And he arced his arm over his head.

"Aaah! Those old stories ain't worth shit." O'Toole was unimpressed by tales of an imaginary prehuman "king." But he stepped away from the pedestal.

January raised his eyebrows. "A whole universe compressed into a ball that small? No wonder it's so heavy."

Tirasi snorted. "Rot! It's too damned *light* to be a whole universe. I don't know what stories they tell in the Terran Quarter on Abyalon, Johnny, but that just doesn't make sense."

Mgurk shrugged. "Pukka tale. Here ball; just like tell story."

Maggie B. pursed her lips. "How can the universe be inside a ball inside the universe? That's like finding *New Angeles* inside a cargo hold of *New Angeles*! It ain't . . ." She hesitated, searching for a term to express the *ain't-ness* of it. "It ain't *topological*!"

O'Toole made a disgusted sound. "I thought we come down here to get rich, not stand around discussin' kiddie stories and fookin' philosophy. C'mon, Bill, there's three more things to check out here."

Tirasi took one more look at the Midnight Egg, captured an image of it, and folded his magnifier. "If we can't take it with us, it doesn't matter what it is." He announced this as if excuses were needed, and followed the pilot to the next pedestal. Mgurk said something about foxes and grapes that January did not catch.

January was about to follow the others when he noticed that the sandstone block beside him seemed now twisted into a half spiral. Curious, he took it off the pedestal—it proved lightweight and comfortable to hold—and tried untwisting it; but it was "rock solid" and had no give to it. And yet, imperceptibly, the thing had altered its shape, like a dancer turning his upper body while leaving his feet planted.

Whatever, it wasn't moving now. He increased the sensitivity of the skinsuit's perceptors, but could detect no movement in the thing. January took some comfort that the stone was not actually squirming in his hand.

The next artifact was what they finally called the Slipstone. It seemed to be a chunk of blue coral, irregularly shaped into tendrils and cavities, and about the size of a man's head. Like the Midnight Egg, the Slipstone seemed to go on forever: each tendril, each cavity, when magnified, resolved into further tendrils and cavities. "Fractal," was how Maggie B. described it and, since she was the ship's astrogator and Electric Avenue was a fractal network, they accepted her word for it.

They could not pick it up, either.

It proved immovable, not because of its weight, but because it was frictionless. They could get no grip on it, not with hands, not with tongs, not even by first covering it with the sandy grit that they had tracked with them into the chamber. How could something so irregular be so slippery?

"It doesn't make bleeding sense," Tirasi complained. "If it's frictionless, how does it stay put on the pedestal?"

Maggie B. shrugged. "Same way that other pedestal could support an entire universe."

A joke, thought January as he watched their hapless efforts with a growing sense of his own frustration. (Had they forgotten there was also a ship to repair?) The Slipstone was a joke like the Midnight Egg was a joke. One was very small, but very big. The other was very rough, but very smooth. Was this place the repository for prehuman practical jokes? A collection of alien whoopee cushions and joy buzzers?

Even the door was a paradox. Soft and yielding, but impenetrable.

Neither Maggie B. nor Johnny could recall a prehuman legend involving anything like the Slipstone; and the others came from worlds where such fables were never told, or at least never mentioned. "Oh-for-two," Tirasi grumbled, finally conceding defeat in his effort to grasp the Slipstone. "What's the point of finding a bleeding treasure trove if"—he waited out a burst of static on the radios—"if you can't pick any of it up?"

His answer was a sudden howl of pain from O'Toole, who was dancing away from the third object, holding his right hand. "Sunnuvabitch!" he cried. "Sunnuvabitch, sunnuvabitch, sunnuvabitch!"

"Heard you the first time." Tirasi laughed, reaching for the golden object, cupped on a pedestal of pure white. "But we've known that about you for . . . Bloody son of a bloody bitch!"

Now it was Tirasi nursing his hand and dancing a little. Mgurk cocked his head. "Hey, that piece one Budmash Lotah."

Maggie B. pursed her lips. "I wouldn't touch that, Cap'n, was I you."

January bent close to study the artifact. It was shaped like a discus bisecting an oblate sphere. "Saturnoid" was how he would describe it. Many gas giants were saturnoid, some with quite spectacular rings. January wondered if this was a compressed gas giant. *At least it won't be as heavy as the Midnight Egg . . .*

The surface had a cool metallic look, whether actually metal or not, and was smooth and shiny and golden. It seemed to glow from within, and waves of yellow and red and orange passed through it. "Those look like flames," January said. "Was it hot?" he asked the two men, but another static discharge covered his words. "Did it burn you?" he asked when he could.

O'Toole had calmed down somewhat. "Like a million needles sticking my hand." Tirasi pulled a pyrometer from his scrip with his left hand and gave it to Maggie B., who examined the object's surface.

"Ambient temperature," the astrogator announced. That made the object rather more cold than hot. "It looks like it's burning up inside," January mused aloud. But fire was a chemical reaction. It could not have continued for eon upon eon without consuming eons of material. *Of course, maybe this pot is all that's left.* There were chemical reactions that oscillated between different colors, and the appearance of roiling flames might be a consequence of such a reaction. But could such oscillations remain undamped over so long a time as these objects must have sat here?

They called this one the Budmash Lotah, which Johnny explained meant an evil-doing brass pot in the Terran patois.

January gave up. He could not grasp the nature of these objects. There was nothing in his experience from which he might analogize. Each was beautiful in some manner, but the only other thing they had in common was that they could not be moved.

That's why all the other pedestals are empty, he suddenly realized. Whatever else was once here could be removed, and so they had been. (But when? And by whom?) Leaving, what? A display of . . . immovable objects? Earth, water, fire . . .

He wondered where the irresistible force was.

"Hey," cried Mgurk, "come-come, look-see." The Terran was standing by one of the empty pedestals and passing his hand slowly through the air above it.

"Now what?" Tirasi complained. He and O'Toole joined the Terran.

Maggie B. turned to the captain, who had not moved. "What is it?" she asked.

January waited out a growl of static. "Something's missing."

"Holy Alfven!" said Tirasi, and O'Toole turned to the captain. "It's a fookin' ghost."

"You have to look at just the right angle," Tirasi explained when the captain and Maggie had joined them. "Johnny, stand away. The light has to be . . . *There,* do you see it?"

January nodded slowly. He could make out the billowing of yellowed clouds against a ruddy background, as if a slice of orange sky many leagues deep had been captured and set on a pedestal. "It's a whole-gram," he guessed.

"Yah?" said Tirasi as he viewed his gauge in disgust. "A projected image *with mass*?" He showed January the readout. "*And* with a temperature *and*"—passing his hand through the image—"with a texture. Cool, smooth, and I can feel that it's hollow."

"You can feel it," Maggie B. said, "but you can't pick 'er up." Tirasi nodded. "Like grabbing smoke."

"Why am I not fookin' surprised," said O'Toole. He was answered by another outbreak of static.

The second chamber was right beside the pedestal and January idly felt one of the soft, spongy leaves that ringed the entry. It seemed made of the same material as the door of the vault.

At that point, Tirasi and O'Toole noticed their captain's possession of the sandstone block. "Well, now," said O'Toole with a glower. "And are ye cutting us out on the only bit of loot we can actually walk off with?"

January, surprised, looked at the sandstone block in his grip. It had fit his hand so comfortably that he had quite forgotten he was holding it. The stone was thicker at the ends now, and curved in a slight arc—and he had not felt even the smallest movement.

It was an exceptional piece, he realized. An exception not only to the beauty of the other items, but also to their immobility. A cuckoo in the nest. *And why wasn't it taken when the rest of this vault was plundered?*

Tirasi nudged the pilot. "Greedy sod, ain't he? C'mon, Slug, let's explore the rest of this place. Might be there's more stuff in the next room."

January suddenly knew. Those fleshy "leaves" were not the petals of a decorative flower that ringed the entrance to the second chamber. They were segments of another of those marshmallow doors. Something had pierced the door in the center, and it had peeled outward in pie-slice sections. From the arrangement of the pieces, the door had been pierced from *inside* the chamber. And there was nothing inside the chamber but an empty pedestal.

"Wait!" he said, and to his surprise the others stopped and turned expectantly. January looked again at the shredded door. What had sat on that pedestal, sealed off from the other objects? The irresistible force? How long had the door resisted it? Millennia? Eons? But it had failed at last.

Where was it now? It could not have gotten off-planet, surely. No, it must still be loose somewhere on this world.

Waiting for a ship to happen by.

"You're absolutely right, Bill," he said. "There may be other relics somewhere in the complex, but for all we know that corridor"—he pointed toward the half-open door at the end of the room, half enticed by the dark at the end of the tunnel, half expecting *something irresistible* to come pouring through it—"for all we know that corridor leads nowhere but to a dead end deep inside the planet. That would fit, somehow. But we need to get off this world, now."

O'Toole scratched his ear, cast an uneasy glance at the corridor, and said, "Sure thing, Cap'n. But I hate to leave without getting *something* out o' this."

The lack of objection surprised January. "Something's happening," he told them. "Have you been listening to the static on the comm channels? It's getting stronger. There's a storm brewing, and a big one. Look." He wanted desperately for them to understand. "We can't take these other things with us, but we can still cash in. Think what people would pay to come see them. They have to come through the tunnel, so we can control admission. But . . ." And here his voice became lower, more urgent. "We must leave *now*. We don't have the supplies to stay and explore every pocket in this entire complex. We need to get a stake, so we can come back and do this proper and controlled."

Maggie B. pursed her lips, thinking. "Who you thinking might stake us?"

January took a deep breath. "The Interstellar Cargo Company . . ." He hesitated, waited for the objections; then, when none were forthcoming, stammered on. "The ICC's a damned pack of jackals, and ships like ours only get their leavings; but we may be able to work out a deal with them. If we're going to do a seismic survey, map the complex, conduct a grid-by-grid search in an orderly manner, document our discoveries, we're going to need more resources than the poor old *Angel* can earn in our lifetimes."

A moment of silence passed. Then Maggie B. said, "Right, then. There'll be time between here and the Jenjen to cook up a plan to protect our rights."

Tirasi nodded. "An' we'll be able to show 'em that thing"—he indicated the now S-curved sandstone block in January's hand—"and the videos we took of this place."

"But if ye show 'em yer rock," O'Toole warned him, "be fookin' careful, or they'll be taking it off ye. That bein' yer honor's very own stone."

The display of unanimity and agreement was so unexpected that January waited a moment longer for the objections. Then Johnny Mgurk cried, "Chop and chel, sahbs. We go jildy. Hutt, hutt! Big dhik." And the spidery little man led them up the tunnel.

January half expected to find the main door now shut, trapping them inside, but it was still rolled into its slot in the wall. The five of them tumbled out into the rocky cleft, blinking at the light, noticing that it was already dimmer.

Through the growing static on the radio, he heard Micmac Anne calling, ". . . swer me! *Angel* ca . . . Jan . . . ! C . . . in, Amo . . . !"

January flipped the responder. "Tell me thrice," he said three times. The ship's intelligence could create a coherent sentence by splicing the fragments that got through the static.

"Amos!" said the reconstructed Anne. "There's storm coming your way, a big one. It started over your eastern horizon, and we've been tracking it since . . . There's lightning. Lots of lightning. Lots of *big* lightning. I've never seen anything like it. It's coming right down on you. Amos, get out of there now!"

They had already reached the excavation site. Maggie B. began to mount the backhoe, but January said, "Leave it. You heard Anne. The wind won't be much at this pressure, but the sand can clog our breathing masks. And the lightning . . ."

He could hear it now. Thunder like galloping hooves. Underneath—a steadier tympani of deeper booms, like the lumbering gait of a giant. Black dust clouds loomed on the eastern horizon and lightning flashed within them like fireworks. The clouds seemed a-boil, rolling toward them. Johnny began to run toward the jolly-boat. "Shikar storm!" he wailed. "Hutt, hutt!"

"Shut yer food-hole, ye Terry slob!" O'Toole cried, bounding past him to the gig. Tirasi had fallen behind, staggering with the molecular sieve in his arms. "Drop it," January ordered him. "Drop it and run for the jolly-boat." The system tech threw his precious machine to the sand and sprinted.

Maggie was already firing the jolly-boat's engines when O'Toole and January reached the gig. O'Toole

popped the hatch and clambered in. January paused
at the foot of the ladder and looked behind. Tirasi
and Mgurk were sealing up the jolly-boat. He nodded and entered the gig.

"We'll worry about our orbit after we have one,"
he told O'Toole as he slid into the number two seat.
"Lift! And lift now!"

So, they did.

Both boats reached the stratosphere ahead of the
advancing storm front. Lightning crackled below
them. Yet part of the storm had broken through the
tropopause—dour thunderheads looking for all the
world like billowing giants made of smoke. A tremen-
dous bolt arced *upward* into space. O'Toole cursed.

"Climb, Slugger," January told the pilot. "Climb as
fast as you can. Climb, even if you dry-tank the gig.
Annie will pick us up in the lighter if she has to."

"Aye, Cap'n." Sweat was pouring off the man. His
fingers might leave dents in the pilot's yoke. "We're
heading east to west, an' that's a bad climb f'shure;
but we're stayin' ahead o' those sand clouds. 'T isn't
ourselves I'm worrying over, y' follow, but what that
jolly-boat is a slow climber."

"Where are they now?"

"So far, so good." O'Toole gusted a sigh and seemed
to relax microscopically. "But that's what Wheezer
Hottlemeyer said whan he was after passin' the second
floor, and him falling out av a noine-story buildin' at
th' toime."

And a skybolt turned the viewports blue. The gig
shuddered, and one of the panels sparked and died.

"Are we hit?" January cried, half rising in the two
gees. "Did it get us?"

O'Toole laid a beefy hand on January's wrist, touching the sandstone as he did. "Don't ye be worryin',

Cap'n darlin'." And January relaxed, weirdly comforted, confident now in the pilot's abilities to see
them through. "Aye, an' there's the jolly-boat, too!"
the pilot cried, a triumphant shout, finger stabbing the
360-sensor display, piercing its ghostly green wire-
frame images. "Hoígh, th' *Roger*. All bristol, down
there?"

"Hoígh, *Aloe*," Maggie replied. "Skin of the teeth
here, Slugger. There was one bolt, I thought it was
gonna peel the paint right off the skin, and leave its
autograph. Hell, mebbe it did. Storm's well below us
now. Looks like we made it, you damned Paddy!
Now we gotta find the *Angel*."

"Shure," said O'Toole, "an' ut'll be a story for to
tell our grandkids."

"I don't even have kids yet," Maggie said.

"Well, then, let's you an' me make some while
there's still time!"

The pilot and the astrogator instructed their re-
spective boats to lock on to the *New Angeles,* plot a
suite of orbits, and report back with projected transit
times and air and fuel usage. When the engines cut
out and the gig entered low orbit, O'Toole grinned
and turned about to face January.

And the smile faded. Slugger clasped his fists together into a ball and shuddered. "*She* can joke, but I
know how close that was." He sucked in a deep breath.
"It weren't normal, Cap'n. That storm. It was coming
at us east t' west, an' that's aginst th' prevailin' winds.
Yessir, 't was, and I nivver heard tell uv a storrum doin'
that. An' maybe a planet dry like that an' all can work
up a monster static charge, but, Jaysus, Cap'n, that
storrum was bigger'n the planet, I'm thinkin'."

January glanced at the prehuman artifact in his
hand. It was twisted along its length like a screw. He

had ordered the others to abandon backhoe and molecular sieve, but he had hung on to this. It really was
quite pretty when you got used to it.

"I'm guessin' th' toorist attraction notion is off th'
table now."

January laughed with nervous release. "By the
gods, yes. But, maybe we can sell this . . . this dancing
rock for enough to replace the gear we abandoned.
Looks like Hogan'll have to cannibalize the ship after
all. I don't think we should go back and try to sal-
vage the equipment."

"Jaysus, no! I'd ruther be back home on New Eireann awaitin' for th' Big Blow. Our equipment'd be all
lightning'ed over by now, anyways, the backhoe and
Bill's toy. Nothing lift uv thim but slag. But I shure
hope the storrum didn't hurt those other things—the
Midnight Egg, the Slipstone, the whatever heathen
name Johnny gave the pot . . ."

"The Budmash Lotah."

"Yeah. I don't know for why Johnny don't speak
fookin' Gaelactic like th' rist uv us."

"I don't think they were hurt, the Unmovable Objects. And, Slugger? I don't think that was a natural
storm, either. I think the prehumans made something
they had second thoughts about and they locked it
away forever, but . . ." The gig's orbit, looping around
the planet had brought them back up over the site,
but January saw nothing out the viewport but a black,
writhing mass covering a quarter of the planet. Maybe
it was fading, settling out now. He couldn't tell.

"But?" O'Toole prompted him.

"But even forever ends." And he relaxed in his har-
ness, stroking the lovely sandstone, thankful that
they had escaped the Irresistible Force.

*I*t's to be a geantraí, *then*," the harper says. "A joyous stain. A triumphant escape from the unknown—and with *the prize in hand!*" She has uncased her harp, and setting it upon her lap, it sings the happy tune her fingers pry from it. About the room, men, half listening, smile without quite knowing why; and one (a woman, of course) frowns and turns toward the darkened alcove, as if seeking the source of such unwonted delight.

The scarred man grins, though the rictus is joyless. It is the smile more grieving than sorrow; the delight that is dark as despair. "Beginnings often are," he says. "Otherwise, who'd go on? Sorrow is for conclusions, not commencements."

The geantraí grows hesitant, pivots from the third mode into the darker fourth, hints at sorrow underneath the joy. But, then . . .

She lays her palm flat across the strings, silencing them, and those in the room—other than the scarred man, who is impervious to all music—sigh a little from apprehensions released. Music has charms, but it is not always charming.

"No," says the harper. "That's a cheat. That's seeing the past with the eyes of the future, which is why the past is never quite seen correctly. Let them have their gaiety. No one ever knows it's only a beginning they have. Let them be in their moment. The past must be seen as if it were still present, and the future all possibilities."

The grin of the scarred man is not pleasant. "As if Tristam might yet succeed? But it's over. It's done. What happened, happened and you can't change it.

There is no moment without a future in its gravid belly. No tragedy issues but from the womb of the happiness that bore it."

The harper's smile is brighter, more pleasant, more deadly. "And ulta-pulta," she answers. "Topsy-turvy. Yin-and-yang. Sorrow births joy." Her fingers tickle the harp, which laughs in reprise of Tristam's theme. "He did succeed. Tristam's death was his triumph."

The scarred man grunts. "He might liefer have failed, then."

The harper forbears to argue the point. The scarred man has confused triumph with survival and she has no wish to antagonize him, not before she has sucked the wellspring dry of its story. Her fingers evoke January from the harp, and the discovery of the Dancer. It is all fragmentary, only motifs and themes. It is not yet a song. She limns the forlorn wastes of the unnamed world, the mystery of a city under the sand, the curious beauty of the Chamber and its unmovable Contents—earth, water, fire, and air. The relentless approach of the Irresistible. And the figures end in a dance of danger and escape—wild reel and stately quadrille, whirling waltz and graceful ballet. That much is true, at least. Waltzes and reels are dangerous, and she suspects there is dancing yet to come.

"And so, they cannibalized part of the ship anyway," she says over the fading chords. "It's what they should have done in the first place."

"Yes," the scarred man answers. "That's something to keep in mind. And you've made the same mistake that January made."

"What mistake is that?"

But the man shakes his head. "That's for the ending, and it's a poor end that has but one beginning."

GOLTRAÍ: WEARING OUT THE GREEN

It began on New Eireann, the scarred man says . . .

. . . a world of black volcanic glasses and uplifted basalts. What little green the world owns is in its name and in a narrow winding valley that ends in a small glen just below the summit of Ben Bulben. Like all the worlds, it has been terraformed; but it is too young for such maturity and only this one high valley had been conquered before seed and stock and will gave out. The world was barely weaned from its molten infancy, and still threw tantrums of molten rock and pyroclastic ash, and the Vale remained a great green wound upon the planet's sullen red-and-black flesh. Little by little, to those who measure these things, the boundaries of the valley contract, as basalt and granite and diorite win back what they had long ago lost.

("But let them have their moment," the scarred man sneers. "For now, they live in a green paradise and the black igneous reality lies out of sight, beyond the crest of the Reeks. All the eruptions, all the steam and lava, burst forth in the Barrens below, where the plates are thinner and the core breaks through. So their future doom is yet to come. Unless . . .")

. . . unless one day the Vale of Eireann, too, erupts. The Big Blow, they call it, making it a joke. There are hot springs in the glen below Ben Bulben . . .

And so it is a world of sad songs (*which should please you, harper*). When they want to make merry, the *Eireannaughta* don't sing. They fight. And that they do often enough to lighten the mood that surrounds them.

They have little enough in the Vale. They can feed

themselves and make the most basic things, and they have far more power than they need from thermal stations, but there's little to do for diversion and their arts are ordinary. Drinking is one (and there they do show considerable talent) and conversation is another (and that they class as a martial art). Orbital factories, built by companies from better-endowed worlds, have come in search of cheap power. New Eireann makes most of its off-world exchange by beaming excess power to them, and a little more by supplying them with fresh food. ICC ships come and go with other supplies for the stations and haul away their products. Very little finds its way to the world below.

The other major source of off-world income is the tourist trade. People have come from Agadar and Hawthorn Rose, from the Lesser Hanse and Gladiola, from even High Tara itself. They come to climb the Western Reeks and stare at nature raw, at the great geysers and fountains of lava, at the rivers of molten rock and the basalt glaciers. "An' d'ye be seein' the wee pyroclastic cloud there? Sure, an' I hope 't isn't blowin' our way . . . Ah, mind the drop here, yer honor; wouldn't want ye t' fall into yon lava pool." Oh, they play it up, the Reek Guides do: a great mouthful of the blarney and just enough hint of the danger to make the tourists shiver in delight.

("An' shure 'tis only an image," the scarred man mocks the accent. "They are no more Irish than you or I are Tibetan. Nor any less. Across so many centuries, everyone on Old Earth was our ancestor. It takes more than eponymous settlers or carefully contrived archaisms to resurrect something that long dead. But what can a people do when they have no future, save reconstruct some storied past?")

Then the tourists ride the gondolas back down into

the Vale from which the rest of the planet, out of sight behind the Reeks, can seem a bad dream. They stay in Da Derga's Hostel or in quaint tourist cottages in the Mid-Vale or sample the excitements (such as they are) in New Down Town. They spend some more money and remain until they grow bored (which happens soon) or frightened (which happens sooner). One morning, the tourist throws open the shutters in the terribly cute guest room, and takes a deep breath of the bright green grassy Vale—and the breeze is just a trifle too warm and bears just the tiniest acrid wisp of molten stone. And "terribly cute" seems suddenly more than merely "cute." So they think, *Who in their right minds would ever have settled here?* And *then* they think, *Who in their right minds would* stay *here a moment longer?*

So the tourist numbers aren't very great in the wider scheme of things. Far more people flood Alabaster to see the Cliffside Montage. But enough of the curious come to satisfy a small world like New Eireann. They bring hard currency—the Shanghai ducat, Gladiola Bills of Exchange—and they bring something near as important: news of the great wide world. Messages travel only so fast as the ships on Electric Avenue, and only to where those ships touch orbit, and so news arrives in snatches and batches at irregular intervals and often from unexpected places. The Eireannaughta were tolerably well informed of doings on New Chennai and Hawthorn Rose, and somewhat less so regarding Jehovah or the Jenjen Cluster. But High Tara? The Hatchley Commonwealth? Far Gatmander? Oh, those were magic names and faraway places! At times it was easy to believe that there really was a sprawling United League of the Periphery out there, and itchy youths like Slugger O'Toole might ship

out on a passing tramp and go searching for the planet
crusted with gold.

A number of years earlier the Eireannaughta had
hired the Clan na Oriel to manage their government
contract and the Clan sent in an honest administra-
tor, who took the office-name of Padraig O'Carroll,
though his real name was Ludovic Achmed Okpa-
laugo. By all accounts he ran a clean and honest administration, though at first the Eireannaughta didn't
realize that because they didn't know what one looked
like. When they did, they revolted, because an administration that won't take bribes generally won't hand
out favors, either.

There are appetites that ought not be fed, for they
grow on their feeding. As an extra inducement to
potential renters, New Eireann had invited the Interstellar Cargo Company to service those orbiting factories. ICC ships ranged throughout the ULP, "from
Gatmander to the Lesser Hanse," as their slogan had
it. And they had the magic touch: uncannily anticipating where each good would demand the best price.
It worked well for everyone: customers received goods
they wanted, producers found greater profit, and the
ICC pocketed a handsome fee. So the ICC pretty much
owned the traffic for everything in New Eireann space.

Except the tourist trade.

There was a nice cash flow in that pipeline. Not
much compared to what the ICC already had; but
consuming all that wealth had only made them hun-
grier. And when a fat man feasts, there are always
those who gather the crumbs. Oriel wouldn't kick
back or fix contracts, but the ICC was more flexible
in that regard. They did not consider buqshish to be
wrong. They were not bound by the moralities of

ancient religions and made no secret of it. They believed in sharing the wealth, too, so long as they had the larger share.

Neither did they lack for corporate ethics. When you take a bribe, you give good value in return. If you kick something back, you make sure of performance. One time on Agadar, the ICC let a contract to build a road along the Inkling Ocean. The contractor skimped on the materials and the road washed out in the first monsoon. So the ICC factor called up his house militia and they found the contractor and put him to work on the repair gang, out in the hot sun with a tar-brush in his hands and a *terai*-hat on his head. And they gave the repair contract to his biggest competitor. There's something charming about such an honest corruption. The kidnapping and forced labor weren't legal, not until afterward when they had bought the Assembly; but it was poetic. You can't argue that.

So when Certain Persons approached the ICC factor on New Eireann and suggested that a change of administration might be to the benefit of all, the factor—whose name was Vandermere Nunruddin—replied that while he could not condone such a thing, he saw no reason why the ICC could not do business with whatever administration held Council House. He may even have suggested a few management corporations that might bid on the job, one of which was, in the spirit of open competition, not an actual subsidiary of the ICC.

No one expected what happened.

Nunruddin probably anticipated a quiet coup, with Clan na Oriel offered a golden parachute and an ICC subsidiary brought in. Cynics often think that everyone else is just waiting to cut a deal, and that even saints are selfish. The Certain Persons who dined with him probably thought the People were behind them. But if an honest administration that gives no special favors and taxes at a reasonable rate for matters palpably in the public good engenders a certain loathing in the hearts of some, it evokes genuine fondness in the hearts of others. Most of the Eireannaughta would likely not have minded dipping their snouts in a government trough, but most of them didn't believe that Certain Persons would ever let them anywhere near that trough. So if it surprised the cabal and the ICC factor when so many people rose up against the coup, it surprised everyone else how many backed it.

A war is always ugly, and a civil war the ugliest of all. An invader may be expelled and sent back to where he came from, but a neighbor remains a neighbor after the fighting is over.

New Eireann had no army. The Vale was too narrow and too rugged to support contending states. The nearest other state was the Maharaj of New Chennai, three days hard streaming down the Grand Trunk Road; and New Chennai had no interest in nor even much awareness of the Vale of New Eireann.

Consequently, there were no tanks or warplanes or artillery on the planet. But New Eireann had a police force—the gardy—and the gardy was armed because there are plug-uglies in the slums of any world and even a small world has its share. When the cabal rushed the Council House to seize Padraig O'Carroll and his ministers, half the gardy and a third of their commanders raised the Oriel banner atop the Hotel Wicklow in New Down Town. At this signal, the Spacedockers Union defied their own bosses, stormed Union Hall, and announced a general strike in support of The

O'Carroll. The revolutionary cabal was utterly stunned by all this.

The farmers out in County Meath, in Mid-Vale, went the other way. They had always grumbled about the "off-world managers" from Oriel. So they formed up a militia, burnt out a few neighbors who wouldn't go along with them, and sent a company's worth of eager youth to the City to support the "Revolution."

When the Loyalist gardies tried to retake Council House, some of the Oriel household troops took heart and fought back against their shocked and distracted captors. A fire was started—by accident, everyone says—and The O'Carroll and three of his ministers died of smoke inhalation. Terrance Sorely, who was a Certain Person, became a little less certain after that. He hadn't expected deaths. He told the others he wanted out, and they told him it was too late, "the die was cast," and all that, and he said he was out anyway, and so Handsome Jack Garrity shot him dead right there at the boardroom table, and he got his wish.

A war is always ugly, and never more so than this one. Planes and tanks and precision munitions at least keep things sanitary, and most everyone you kill is out of sight. But pistols, rifles, gelignite—they called it "jolly good-night"—are up close and personal. You can make a peace with someone you've fought at a distance; but it's harder to do that with someone whose stinking breath is in your face and his knife an inch from your throat.

And it did get down to knives and swords and pikes. New Eireann had not much of a munitions industry. Just enough to keep the gardy better armed than the plug-uglies. There was no hunting because there was no wild game in the Vale; and target shooters used harmless infrared "beamers." It didn't take long after the Burning of Council House to use up the stocks, and whatever might have been in production at Reardon and Harrigan's munitions factory was denied to both sides by the partners, who set fire to the Works, created a crater of impressive dimensions on the outskirts of Galway Town, then shook hands and went their separate ways, Reardon to join the Revolution, Harrigan to the Loyalists. There was something admirable about that small gesture, something even gentlemanly. They limited the magnitude of the war, even at the expense of their profits and everything they had ever owned. That aura of self-sacrifice made Reardon a poor fit in the cadre of the Revolution. The other Persons distrusted him just the smallest bit.

A few people made "jezail" rifles and "zip" guns, but these were regarded as the weapons of barbarous folk, and the Eireannaughta much preferred the cutlass, the dirk, and the two-handed claymore sword. Why send a high velocity slug of lead ripping through someone's organs when you could cleave him from collarbone to groin with a well-aimed stroke? You can shoot a man by accident, but you need real commitment to lop his head off.

War is always ugly. It is guts streaming from opened abdomens. It is a head trying to speak its last few words as it stares in astonishment at the body it once topped. It is learning the ghastly meaning of the term "human remains" in the ruins of Da Derga's Hostel, after some boyo has used up the last of a dwindling supply of jolly good-night.

So there had better be a damned good reason for it, because even if it is good, it is still damned. Yet, better to fight over liberty and loyalty than over tuppence difference in the tariff on lace. Bigger wars have been fought for a great deal less. And if a man will not fight to keep his liberties, he is a slave to the first tyrant who would kill to take them. That doesn't make things less ugly, but it might mean that in later years, when a man wakes in the dead of night in a cold, shivering sweat, he can, at length, go back to sleep.

Now the Revolution did not set out to be tyrants. They only wanted to dip their beak in the tax money flowing through Council House. But events, once unleashed, consume their makers. Certain steps became "necessary." After two weeks' fighting, none of the original cabal were still alive, except Handsome Jack, who, though crippled, still directed things from the Broadcast Center. Even the ICC factor was dead. The rumor had gone out that he had instigated the coup, and the Loyalists bid Nunruddin a jolly good-night in his ground car one spectacular evening.

The Loyalists had never had a leadership, as such. The counterrevolution had been spontaneous, and The O'Carroll and most of his henchmen had perished in the Council House fire and in the fighting that followed. But by the end of the second week, The O'Carroll's *tainiste,* his assistant manager, emerged from hiding in the Glens of Ardow, where he had been conducting public hearings over the school curriculum when the fighting started—an activity that sounds so sweetly normal that a man might weep for the innocence of it. He and his bodyguard took to the hills when the trouble broke. The Revolution had not known he was out of town when they sprang their coup—they might have waited another week if they had—so they failed to sweep the Southern Vale to capture him. By the time they thought of anything beyond taking Council House and the Broadcast Center, the *tainiste* was nowhere to be found—and everyone in the County Ardow had blank, innocent looks.

He spent the two weeks gathering intelligence and assembling forces. He had only his personal guard at first; but he located and mobilized other Oriel troops scattered about the Southern Vale, pockets of native Loyalists, and natives who had bid into the Clan na Oriel. He even used, though with some reluctance, the Magruder Gang. For a price they were willing to stool and that gave the *tainiste* his intelligence arm.

The *tainiste*'s office-name was Little Hugh O'Carroll, though he had been born Ringbao della Costa on Venishànghai in the Jenjen Cluster. What Little Hugh discovered was the value of a legend and a hitherto unsuspected capacity in himself for mayhem. Little Hugh became the "Ghost of Ardow." No leader of the Revolution was safe from his death squads. His people struck quickly and silently and, after some experience, fearlessly and competently. The Magruders had ears in every city and knew people who knew people. They could always finger the target, could always find or bribe an entry. In contrast, the Ghost always eluded Handsome Jack's men, and many were the storied adventures and hair's breadth escapes.

Some Loyalists, especially the remaining gardies, objected to his methods. It was dishonorable to strike from ambush, to backstab, to bushwhack. A man should meet his enemies face-to-face. Little Hugh told them to meet the enemy face-to-face—and keep them distracted while he picked off their leaders. After a while, as the Revolution became more and more disorganized, the Loyalists began to see the logic of it, although they never did learn to like it.

The Revolution was on its second or third round of leaders by then and finding it hard to recruit a fourth. The only one that Little Hugh ever failed to hit was Handsome Jack himself, who had turned the Broadcast Center into an impregnable fortress. Three teams tried to penetrate, two succeeded, one reached Handsome Jack's office. His guards dispatched two of the assassins and Handsome Jack himself took out the other, which was not bad for a man with one arm.

This was the stuff of legend. Handsome Jack and the Ghost of Ardow locked in a titanic twilight struggle. Men began to sing songs—and the war was four weeks old.

There were missteps. One time, a death squad "took out" Krispin Dall, the Revolution's District Leader in Coyne Village, while he was in bed with his mistress, and the mistress was taken out, too. That was bad, because there was an unspoken rule about noncombatants. Another time, Handsome Jack lost the whole of County Meath when his men wiped out the last of the gardy in a well-planned ambush. The Meath farmers had had a genuine affection for the old peacekeepers and the end of it was a dash of cold water in their faces. They looked at their bloody swords, at each other, and wondered what had come over them. They set out as a body for the Mid-Vale and Handsome Jack's forces tried to stop them. That compounded the mistake, because first of all, everyone knew that the Meathmen had had a stomachful and only wanted to go home; and second, they were going home with their swords in hand, and four weeks of fighting had taught them how to get the use of them.

The Revolution had been driven back to New Down Town Center, Fermoy Village, and a few other pockets when two ships entered orbit carrying a rump regiment of ICC house troops. With guns. And helicopters. And satellite surveillance capabilities.

They had been bound for Hawthorn Rose, where

the ICC expected to win a bid to provide border protection for the small but wealthy state of Falaise. They had departed Gladiola Depot, three weeks up the Grand Trunk Road, anticipating R&R at New Eireann, and found themselves a civil war instead of a rest stop. Sophia Colonel Jumdar, commanding the two companies, thought civil wars bad for business—power beams to the orbitals had grown intermittent—and downright fatal to the tourist industry that ICC had hoped to acquire. The Guild of Power Engineers and the Reek Guides Association, who had stood by appalled while they watched their livelihoods destroyed, begged her to intervene before the factories refused to stay and the tourists refused to come.

The final straw was the news that the Loyalists had killed the ICC factor—in her view, an innocent bystander.

Such terrorism must not stand. She ordered her two companies to prep and drop and sent a swiftboat back to the Regimental Depot with the news of what had happened and with a call-up of the other two companies. "I will end this rebellion in a week," she swore, perhaps forgetting that the Loyalists were not the ones who had rebelled.

So, she did.

What can you expect? The colonel had brought a gun to a knife fight. Her satellite recon could spot even small groups infiltrating through the Glens of Ardow and either orchestrate their capture or drop something on them from orbit. The latter, she did once, for demonstration, and never had to do it again. Afterward, something remarkable began to happen. People began to inform on the Ghost of Ardow.

And that set up the last act of the tragedy. Little

Hugh had men and women about him now who loved him more than they loved the Vale, more than they had loved the old administration; men who would die for him, if only he would live and carry with him their hopes for "the Return of the O'Carrolls." Red Sweeney. Maeve the Knife. Voldemar O'Rahilly. Names uttered with only a little less awe than that of Little Hugh Himself.

And die they did. Rear guard after rear guard perished to ensure his escape. Hugh moved like a fish through the water. Once as a tinker, another time as a priest, a third time as a woman. In the latter incident, he was exposed when an ICC corporal lifted his skirts with another objective entirely and received a great, and final, surprise. Colonel Jumdar almost caught him in Fermoy Village, where he was disguised as a common laborer rebuilding Da Derga's Hostel, but he slipped the net and vanished. There was a fight in the Mid-Vale where, remarkably, he was *organizing* the reconstruction of the burned-out farmhouses of the recalcitrant neighbors. He was using an assumed name, but it wasn't much of an assumption, and the people he was organizing had fought long and hard for the Revolution until the Massacre of the Gardies had shocked them out of it. When the ICC squad swooped in by jet-copter, a trio of hardened Meathmen rushed them with swinging claymores and in the time it took the squad to shoot them down, the Ghost had disappeared. Colonel Jumdar wondered what sort of man could command loyalty even from his enemies. When she asked Handsome Jack Garrity, the one-armed man thought for a long moment before he finally shook his head and told her, "You wouldn't understand."

Nor did she. Tips on Little Hugh's whereabouts began to slow and, as often as not, began to prove false, running her squads up and down the length of New Eireann and once even to the tiny glade at the very head of the Vale below the crest of Ben Bulben.

Finally, after several days of hide-and-seek, union dockworkers at the spaceport packed Little Hugh into a crate equipped with amenities sufficient for nine weeks, addressed it and labeled it FRAGILE, and sent it up by lighter to the transshipment station in High Orbit. There, it would await the next interstellar freighter passing through. They got all teary-eyed just before Little Hugh stepped into the crate and there were many embraces and kisses on the cheek and Sweeney the Red said, "Will ye no come back again?" And the Ghost of Ardow did something he should not have done. He swore *on his father's name* that he would come back one day and redress the treachery that had been done New Eireann.

A week passed at Upabove Station and those who knew held their breath, wondering if the ruse would be discovered, and let it out only when a passing tramp freighter took the crate (and Little Hugh with it) on consignment.

Colonel Jumdar watched *New Angeles* depart with mixed feelings. She was not one to entertain romantic thoughts of revenge, and she had secured something of inestimable value from the hapless freighter crew for little more than an ICC promise to remit the proceeds later. Perhaps she was feeling good about that when she ordered the watch to stand down. Her mission was to restore order, and she thought Little Hugh's escape would achieve that more effectively than his capture. Legends cause problems, but martyrs cause more. Without the Ghost of Ardow to lead them, the last Loyalists were gathered up almost as an afterthought.

In the end, no one achieved what they sought. The Loyalists did not get the old administration back. An ICC subsidiary quietly bought the management contract from the Clan na Oriel, which accepted a payment of wergild to square the accounts; and Colonel Jumdar generously allowed O'Carroll employees to leave the planet at ICC expense. But neither did those Certain Persons who had started the whole thing gain the power they had sought. They had died to a man, save only Handsome Jack. And even Handsome Jack found himself marginalized. His side had won, but Jumdar did not trust him and the prize was hers, not his. She suspected, too, that he had taken a hand in the Escape of Little Hugh, and she could not understand a man who would do that.

People went back to their lives under the wary eyes of the 33rd Guard Regiment of ICC's peace enforcement corporation. They looked at one another with horror and with pity and at the wreckage they had created and bit by bit they began to build things back up again. That suited Jumdar, who assumed the Civil Office of Planetary Manager in addition to her colonelcy, because until order was restored and the tourist trade recovered and power broadcasts returned to normal, "Sèan Company" would see no profit from this contract—and profit they desired above all else.

What she never did understand was when erstwhile Loyalists and Rebels began to meet in pubs. That they joined hands in public to encourage rebuilding efforts was expected. She herself, as Governor-pro-tem, had pleaded with them to do so in live broadcasts and personal speeches down the length of the Vale. Also, they knew that, in case of disturbance, the 33rd was instructed to "step in the middle and shoot both ways." But that they gathered privately in pubs in the evenings to retell stories of the Burning of Da Derga's Hostel or the Massacre of the Gardies and sing mournful songs of the Storming of Council House or the March of the Meathmen, impartially celebrating the feats of each side . . . this eluded her entirely. When her lieutenant-colonel told her of one song—"Little Hugh Has Gone Away"—in which one verse revealed her own last-minute forbearance and ascribed it to a secret admiration for the Ghost, she thought for a moment of suppressing it. But Handsome Jack advised otherwise. "We sing and dance at wakes out here," he explained. And later she heard him humming the selfsame tune at his desk in the Trade Office.

All of which convinced her that the Eireannaughta were mad.

Meanwhile, she had this clever little prehuman statue. A stone that somehow danced. She would stare at it for hours, trying to catch it in the act of changing, only to realize after some time had passed that it *had* changed. She knew she would have to surrender it to the Central Office on Old 'Saken, because there would be no profit from it until it went on auction, but in the meantime it was hers. She had January's sworn affidavit of provenance, chopped by his crew as well, and embellished by a clever little story, undoubtedly fabricated to frighten off would-be claim-jumpers. To this, she added her own affidavit to attest to the chain-of-custody.

And all this in exchange for a chit for maintenance-and-repair at the ICC Depot on Gladiola plus the promise of a share in the eventual auction proceeds. It was a fair percentage for a finder's fee; but January had not even asked whether Jumdar had the authority to offer it. Privately, she hoped the Board would honor her promise. The ICC could be generous when it didn't cost much; and January would get a ship almost like new; so he had no complaints coming.

The sandstone fit so comfortably in her hand that she took to carrying it with her. *Like a scepter,* some pardoned Loyalists in New Council House grumbled, and their Rebel coworkers agreed, for they hadn't fought to make a Queen.

Yet, the proclamations she issued seemed reasonable, even inspired, and the people who heard her threw themselves into the Reconstruction with a fervor equal to their previous fury. There was even talk in some quarters, admittedly brief, that having a Queen was not so bad an idea. Jumdar seemed to get things done, and although some of the Guides in their remote Reek-side cabins grumbled about the "kiss-ass" of their fellow citizens regarding ICC dictates, everyone agreed that the dictates made good sense in the wake of what had gone before.

The wake of what came later was a different matter.

AN CRAIC

A goltraí, *then," the harper says. "A Lament for Hugh O'Carroll." And her harp sings so mournfully that half the patrons in the room grow inexplicably teary-eyed.*

The scarred man listens for a while, but without visible effect. "They are *mad, you know," he says. "The Eireannaughta are. But what can you expect from a folk who live on a raft upon a sea of seething magma? The Big Blow can come at any time, so it's not surprising that they themselves erupt now and then."*

"Did Jumdar intend to keep the Dancer, or did she really mean to send it to Old 'Saken?"

"Not at first, I think; and in the end, it wasn't her decision to make. What happened to Jumdar is of little interest, except to Jumdar. No, if you must have a lament, the truly tragic figure in the story is Handsome Jack Garrity."

The harper is surprised and her fingers hesitate and still. "Is he? Why?"

"Because he was a man who won everything and gained nothing, and what worse fate is there than that? He found himself a deputy commissioner in a minor office. Small beer for the Hero of New Down Town. That's why his struggle with the Ghost came to consume him. It was the one time in his life when he had mattered."

The harper strums a mockingly conventional military march. "I'd not call him a hero."

"No? What is a hero, then? Surely, a man larger than life, who acts with courage, who controls his contending emotions—his anger, fear, and despair—to achieve his goal. Handsome Jack did not succumb to despair until after he had won. Can only those be heroes who show courage in causes you favor? The Ghost of Ardow, maybe?" The scarred man gestures broadly with his arm, as if the Ghost has entered the Bar and the scarred man is introducing him.

"No." And her earlier Lament turns twisted and jangled, and she sets the harp down at last and balls her hands on the table. "But I had thought he was a better man. Not an assassin, not a murderer." She seems much affected. There are, it appears, emotions whose music is silence.

The scarred man laughs hideously. "But give him this much: at least he excelled. We suppose there is a difference between killing a particular man quickly and efficiently, and killing many men wholesale on a battlefield. Maybe you can explain the difference to us."

"The heroic man," she says quietly, "conquers himself."

At this, the scarred man falls silent for a while. Then he takes his uisce bowl and spins it toward the far side of the table, where the harper snatches it before it falls off. "That's a struggle," he suggests darkly, "in which some of us find ourselves outnumbered." He looks at the bowl and then at the harper.

The message is clear. She signals to the Bartender, and shortly, the "water-of-life" has been replenished. The harper receives unasked a bowl of her own, and she raises it to her lips. It is an awful, numbing liquor with the one obvious purpose of numbing something awful.

"Do you know what's funny?" the scarred man asks her. But he doesn't wait for an answer. "Hugh O'Carroll was a schoolteacher by vocation. That was why he was in the Southern Vale when it all broke out. All he ever wanted to do was teach children."

"Where did he go?" the harper asks. "Where did his men address the crate?"

The scarred man grins like a skull. "Where does any such residuum wash up?"

"Ah." The harper turns and looks out at the Barroom and studies the men in it. "Not a very glorious end for a legend."

"Who says that was the end? It wasn't the end of the man, nor even of the legend, though legends are always harder to end. We spoke, he and I, at that table there by the window"—a bony finger points—"and we got the whole story out of him."

The harper reaches for her instrument. "So, then it's to Jehovah next."

"No. There is one more beginning."

SUANTRAÍ: BREAKING ON THE
PERIPHERAL SHORE

It began near the Rift, the scarred man says . . .

. . . a region where despair has become a feature of the sky. A place where some ancient god had drawn a knife across the galaxy's throat and left a black gaping flow of blood. In this void there are no suns—or no living suns, an emptiness made all the less bearable by the surrounding shores of light.

On the farther shore of this hole in the sky gleam distant suns with magic names—Dao Chetty, Tsol, the Century Suns—stars whose worlds are storied in antiquity: strange worlds, ancient worlds, decadent worlds, worlds of peculiar and exotic customs. From the hither shore, they appear as they once had been: antique light hundreds of years on the journey, the lamps of the Old Commonwealth before it crumbled. A telescope subtle enough might still glimpse those halcyon days in the tardy images just now breaking on the Peripheral shore.

A happier time, the stories said; a time before the Great Cleansing. Now the Confederacy of Central Worlds—tightly ruled, patiently waiting, watching the Periphery with hungry eyes—squats upon that distant shore across the gap of stars.

Thankfully few roads cross the Rift, for the electric currents that crease space into superluminal folds depend on the plasmas of roaring suns, and there are no suns in the Rift. Those that do cross are as tenuous as rope suspension bridges across a gaping canyon, their end points snubbed to stubborn blue giants. The crossing points have been carefully mapped by the fleets of High Tara, the Greater Hanse, and the Hatchley Commonwealth. Their survey ships have pricked each on their charts and noted the speed of space—the local-c—and other such qualities of space-time; and by each such crossing they have positioned a squadron of cruisers and swift-boats. These check the bona fides of the trade ships that venture out and of those that venture in; and await the day when Confederate corsairs pour across the Rift in a wave of conquest. Then they will die—for what is a squadron against a fleet?—but the swift-boats will stream out and spread posthumous warnings to all the nearby suns.

The High Taran squadron commanded by the Cu na Fir Li guards the crossing known as St. Gothard's Pass. This current curls in from a frontier province of the Confederacy and, on the Peripheral side of the Rift, entangles a blue giant called the Sapphire Point Interchange. From there, short Newtonian crawls reach the Palisades Parkway, which skirts the edge of the Rift toward the Old Planets, and the Silk Road, which winds its way around two dozen stars before reaching the great interchange at Jehovah, whence to Gladiola, and Ugly Man; to New Chennai and Hawthorn Rose; to Alabaster, and far Gatmander. A third current flies off from Sapphire Point to the Galactic East, whose worlds are as yet unsettled and unexplored.

It was, in the reckoning of Fir Li, the obvious invasion point. No other crossing offered such ready access to so extensive a volume of the ULP. He had said so, and often, to the Ardry of High Tara, Tully King O'Connor, until, tiring of this Jeremiah in his court, the King had ordered Fir Li to take personal command at Sapphire Point.

So Fir Li had taken his "Pups" and his personal ships, and heighed off to stand the watch. Yet, where his enemies at court saw defeat and exile, Fir Li tallied a triumph. He was a Hound, and Hounds usually get what they want. Since then, captains and men and ships had come, and served their rotations, and gone, but the Hound of Fir Li stayed on—an exile from the court, or a sentry on the wall, depending on one's point of view.

Over time, some courtiers had whispered, the sight of the Rift, of such an emptiness in the midst of light, could break a man, and drive him mad.

A Hound of the Ardry could be many things and any thing. Loyal for a certainty. Relentless on the scent. The High King had no more loyal servants than the Hounds. They were resourceful; skilled in all manner of arts, both politic and martial; without pity or remorse when what had to be done had to be done. They could use words the way the Meathmen of New Eireann used claymores—often with the same decapitating results—but they were no strangers to other weapons. A single Hound, dropped at dusk into the Vale of New Eireann, could have stopped the civil war in a night and a day.

Na Fir Li, in his youth, had not been the least of this company. He had overthrown the Fourth Tyrant of Gladiola with a few well-placed rumors dropped in the bars of Florentz City. He had for five years managed the planet of Valency, where his name is yet revered, ending their awful Interregnum. He had directed the reconstruction on Ugly Man after the earthquakes there. He had assassinated fifteen men and women who had deserved death; and rescued twenty-seven who had not. He had even crossed the Rift, to walk the fabled streets of the Secret City on Dao Chetty, where none but Those of Name may tread.

Messenger, spy, ambassador, saboteur, assassin, planetary manager—a Hound could be whatever the Grand Seanaid desired when the Ardry spoke "with office" in the name of the ULP, for no one loved the ULP more than the Hounds of "The Particular Service." It might fairly be said that the League existed as something more than a theory only in the convictions of the Hounds; and if ever there was anything that could drive a man mad, it was not the Sapphire Point Station, but devotion to a thing that was not quite real.

But there is something enervating about a duty in which for the most part nothing happens and where success can be measured by nothing continuing to happen. It was a period of détente, and the border was supposed to be open, so there was a steady, if slow, volume in trade, and this made for an occasional customs inspection, but not often enough or varied enough to counteract the ennui of the long watch. Routine dulls the wits; so the Hound of Fir Li called random security drills and mounted exercises, neither too few to ensure readiness, nor so many as to dull it. It was a fine tuning, like stretching the strings on a harp, seeking the proper pitch without snapping the chords.

And so most time was spent in relaxation—in sports, in games of skill and chance, in debate, in reading and writing and painting and the creation of music. In romance and in quarrel. In all those things with which, since the Caves of Lascaux, human beings had decked their lives. It fell to Greystroke, Fir Li's deputy, to manage these things, to arrange the concerts and the bounceball leagues and suchlike— and also to apply discipline when the music became too loud, the debate too physical, or the games of chance too certain; to adjudicate all those frictions that develop when those who have been trained to act on a moment's notice must wait for that moment not to come. Greystroke was journeyman enough to chafe at such mundane duties.

Fir Li's flagship, *Hot Gates*, was a faerie castle set loose in space. Never intended to enter an atmosphere, it lacked even a pretense of streamlining, and might have seemed more a small village to the ancients than what they had imagined a spaceship to be. It was Greek and Gothic and Tudor and Thai, and Fir Li, who had never heard of any of those folk, had managed to incorporate all the most monstrous aspects of each. *Hot Gates* was a chimera, odd even by the standards of its kind—blocks and spheres and tubes and causeways were all a-jumble, protected within a spherical field and given a whimsical variety of ups and downs by an idiosyncratic use of gravity grids. The faeries had been mad. It would have seemed out of place anywhere—save here on the ragged edge of space.

Fir Li himself had chosen midnight for his skin and moonlight for his hair. He was blacker than the gap he guarded, and in his dim-lit rooms, the white cascade of his mane could be the only visible sign of his presence. When he moved, it was swiftly and silently. Bridget ban, a colleague, had once compared him to a panther; others had compared him to the Rift itself.

He sat in a light-framed swivel chair in the center of an otherwise empty sitting room, one wall of which was an image screen kept tuned to the Rift. *He can see the Point,* some in the Squadron whispered. *He got these funny eyes and he can see deep down into the currents. When the 'Feds come, he'll spot them afore our sensors do.* It wasn't true, or maybe it wasn't true; but the Rift drew him, possessed him; and the sight of it had impressed itself upon him like a signet impresses the wax, and a bit of its emptiness had invaded his soul.

Perhaps that was why he kept his sitting room dark at most times. The chair he occupied was an octopus, whose flexible arms caressed the Hound with controls and inputs and outputs. Using them, he could hear what the ship heard, see what the ship saw, speak with the ship's voice—but he had muffled all but two for the moment. On one, he scrolled through a novel by the great Die Bold writer Ngozi dan Witkin, who had lived in the early days of the Great Cleansing and had written most poignantly of the loss and confusion of those first generations. But because Fir Li was paraperceptic, a second reader displayed statistics for traffic through the Rift. This did not divide his attention, for each called upon different faculties of his intellect. A third faculty, the one that touched on icon and myth and image, contemplated the great rift displayed upon his wall.

Not all the trade ships came back.

So the statistics said, and although Fir Li was aware of the shortcomings of all statistics—"They are first written down by the village watchman, and he writes what he damn well pleases!"—he found the figures troubling. *As troubling as the cruelty of Those of Name, who had uprooted entire peoples of the Old Commonwealth and scattered them beyond the edge of space, Ngozi's grandparents among them.*

Nothing compelled a ship departing Sapphire Point to obtain her return frank there, save the commercial regulations of the League. But the Hound of Fir Li had obtained the customs information from all of the crossings and had cross-tabulated them, and . . .

. . . not all the ships came back.

Many of the crossings were narrow, and a ship ill-piloted might run afoul of the shallows and beach catastrophically into the subluminal mud. The god Ricci, who caresses each point of space, had graced the roads with a "speed of space" far greater than flat space, and a ship might slide down them comfortably below local-c yet far above Newtonian-c. A ship at translight speeds that found itself suddenly in Newtonian space would become a brief but spectacular burst of Cerenkov radiation. Such mishaps were not common, but they did occur. Yet models existed that related that probability to the local properties of space, and the number of disappearances exceeded the expected value at the five percent risk level.

The Dao Chettians had exiled their defeated foes with deliberate disregard for cultural homogeneity. A Babel of exiles could not combine and conspire if they could not even understand one another. Like all the others finding themselves far from home in the company of strangers, Ngozi's grandparents had tried to maintain the old country customs—but there were too few compatriots and they were scattered too widely and over too many worlds. "The center cannot hold," an ancient poet had written, and so things had flown apart. Ngozi herself had lived at just the right moment in history and could look back upon her grandparents' struggles to maintain the old, and forward upon her grandchildren's struggles to create the new.

How to explain the *excess* in the number of lost ships? Those of Name had become decadent—Fir Li had seen this for himself—and they had forgotten many things; but they had not forgotten how to be cruel. The code that had allowed them to disperse whole peoples, to dissolve living cultures into artfully re-created and inward-looking archaisms, would not forbid the seizure of an occasional ship for no better reason than the joy of it.

And so each faculty of his attention came to rest upon the same object. From settlement days on the Old Planets to the disappearance of ships in the present to the sight of the starless abyss, the menace of the Confederation ran like the drone note of a bagpipe.

"Yes, Pup," he said, for three channels did not exhaust his paraperception. "What is it?"

Greystroke always stumbled a bit when he entered his Master's quarters. It was not so much the three-fourths' gravity as it was the sight of the Rift. The span of the wall screen played with one's peripheral vision and so it seemed as if the ship's hull had been stripped off and the emptiness without had poured within. Fir Li's quarters were deep within the vessel—no architect was so foolish as to put a commander's suite at the very skin of the ship—but the illusion always caught some part of a man's mind off-guard, and no one ever entered the suite when the screen was active without a sudden and unwitting hesitation in his step.

Greystroke was no exception, and the momentary stumble was a source of great vexation to him, for he tried to school himself against it. It irritated him that an illusion would catch him up.

He was a young man the color of his name, so average in appearance and demeanor that he had achieved an operational sort of invisibility. This could be advantageous for a journeyman Hound. When he desired so, he could remain unnoticed for a very long time. "Cu!" he said.

Fir Li scrolled a page on his viewer. "Something unusual." Fir Li's voice was a bass rumble, something between a growl and the grinding of rocks.

"Aye, Cu."

"But not an emergency at the crossing, or I would have been summoned by the alarms."

"Aye, Cu."

The Hound scrolled another page on the reader. "Traffic control, then. A ship on our side of the Rift approaching the Interchange, but not a typical merchant or you'd not disturb my rest at all."

"Cu, the pickets have detected the bow waves of a large fleet coming up the Palisades."

The Hound was about to turn another page, but paused in thought for a moment. "A fleet," he said. "How many ships?"

"The swift-boat counted twenty. All corvette class."

The Hound bobbed his head side to side. "Too small for a colony fleet; too many for a survey expedition. A war has started somewhere." He turned off his viewer and stood gracefully from his chair. "I will be in the command center shortly. Such a grand fleet, I must dress for the occasion."

The command center in the heart of *Hot Gates* was a broad, ovoid room, the dome of which was a display screen of impressive and subtle scope. Staff were arranged by units and sections around the room's circumference—clerks manning the consoles, department heads standing inboard from them at podiums.

Greystroke entered, fastening a red-and-gold dress jacket. "Point Traffic," he said, "alert me when you spot Cerenkov glow from the Parkway exit. Swift-boats are fast, but that fleet won't be too far behind."

The supervisor in charge of Sapphire Point Navigation and Tracking Section acknowledged. "Timer says four metric minutes until arrival."

"I assume they're heading for the Silk Road. Communications, hail their commodore as soon as they are subluminal. And Fire Control?"

"Aye, Pup?" The captain of Battle Management Section turned at her podium.

"We've gotten no swifties from Hanseatic Point, but we cannot discount the chance that a Confederate fleet has forced the crossing west of us. If so, they'll come off the ramp firing. Be alert."

"On it," said Fire Control; and she directed her staff to key off Traffic's bearings.

"Customs," Greystroke said dryly, "prepare for maximum likelihood."

The supervisor of Customs Section grinned as he set his screens. "Maximum likelihood; minimum impact. Boring."

"Boring," said the Hound of Fir Li as he entered through his personal door, "but preferable to the more exciting alternatives." He wore a tight-fitting suit woven of thread-of-gold, bearing no insignia of rank and but a single decoration: the red-and-blue lapel ribbon of the Appreciation of Valency. It was the only one he ever wore. He strode through a chorus of greetings to the dais in the center of the room and stood behind the rails, gripping them with both hands. "Status?"

"Two metric minutes," said Traffic.

"Cu," said Greystroke. "Squadron is dispersed and all ships on amber alert."

The Hound nodded. "Sensors, dome view. Palisades at focal."

The ceiling dome darkened to the outside night. To the right and rear of the command station: the emptiness of the Rift. To the left, the frontier stars of the League with the haze of the Periphery beyond them. At the forward focal point, enclosed in red-line crosshairs, the exit from the Parkway. Invisible, an anomaly in n-space, limned in false colors so as to resemble the mouth of a tunnel.

"Ninety beats," said Traffic. "Sir, a swifty exiting the Parkway."

"Message from incoming fleet," said Comm. "Screening for viruses. Clean."

"Play it."

A window opened on the dome display just to the right of the crosshairs, revealing a flat-faced man with thin black moustaches and hair done up in greased braids that fell past his shoulders. His skin was pale with a greenish cast. Studs, rings, and gems graced every feature of his face, though effecting no discernible improvement on any of them. A golden torque encircled his neck. A ruby was set in the center of his forehead.

"G'day, to youse, yer honors," the apparition said, with an easy confidence and a predatory smile. "Don't be a-frightened at our little outing here, youse. We're just passing through Sapphire Point. Welcome to it, sez I. Oh, yeah. I hight the Molnar khan Matsumo, me; chairman of the Kinlé Hadramoo out of th' Cynthia

Cluster. We've twenny ships exiting th' Parkway, an' makin' cut-off to th' Silk Road. No reason to go waving yer weapons all about, youse. Oh. And nothing to declare," he added with a smile.

"Fleet exiting!" called Traffic.

"Hold all fire," ordered the Hound.

"He didn't say where he was bound," Greystroke murmured to his chief.

"I noticed, Pup." Then, louder, "Comm, put me through. What's the time lag?"

"A grossbeat."

"Metric time, if you please, Mr. Lazlo."

"Sorry, sir. One-point-um-three, now."

"Compress and squirt, then. 'Intruder fleet, this is His Majesty's battle cruiser, ULS *Hot Gates,* Sapphire Point Squadron; Cu na Fir Li commanding. This is interdicted space, and authorization is required for transit. Do you have a visa?'" A wave of laughter rippled across the bridge.

"Let me blast them," said Fire Control. "Please?"

Na Fir Li shook his head. The Cynthians had twenty ships, all corvettes. *Hot Gates* and her support ships could take any one of them easily, perhaps any five of them; but she could not take all twenty. The Squadron expected to die when the Confederacy crossed the Rift; but there was no reason to die to enforce League commercial regulations on some back-cluster pirate fleet.

The reply packet came, and once more the Molnar showed his teeth. "I'm impressed such an important boy as yourself is standing by to wave at me as I pass through. And dressed so pretty, youse. Sorry 'bout th' visa, me. Nobody told me, not even th' late ICC factor. An' I thought he told me everything he knew before he passed on. Ha ha!" Muffled laughter was heard in the background.

"Where away?" Fir Li asked.

The reply came sooner, as the Cynthian fleet's trajectory brought it nearer the Squadron. "Oh, some folk need a civics lesson, and we're to be th' tutors." The Molnar had a diamond stud embedded in his top right incisor. When he grinned, it flashed. "There's been a bit of a dust-up there and they need a strong hand to set them right."

"You're going to raid a planet!" Fir Li said.

"Well, we won't stay longer 'n we need to make our point! Oh. And to tell the ICC people there that they need a new factor on Cynthia Prime. Poor fella's heart gave out. Cracking on and blinding, he was, how the ICC would settle things in Cynthia, now that they had the Twister." The Molnar sat straighter in the viewscreen. "Maybe he didn't know th' insult was mortal, him bein' an outlander, and all; but that don't excuse him saying it. He learned better. Ha ha! So, I figger, once we have this Twister thing, we'll be safe from th' ICC. Don't know why you doggies don't go barking after *them* and their threatening free folk and all."

"If you need to tell the ICC anything, you could go straight to Old 'Saken. It's closer to Cynthia."

The lag time had begun to increase again as the Cynthians accelerated toward the entrance to the Silk Road.

"Ha ha," said the Molnar with apparent delight. "That's a good one. Wait'll I tell my wives. Old 'Saken, she's like a lion's den. Lotsa tracks go in; not many come out. You don't beard a lion in his HQ, Fido. All we want is the ICC should leave free men be."

"Free men!" said Fir Li. "Free to pillage! While across the Rift the Confederacy waits to scoop us all up. To travel so far . . . What profit in that?"

The Molnar's reply this time came through grim

lips. "Hear me, Fido. A man pleasures only in battle. Everything else . . ." He spit to the side. "Money? Love? Power? The stars care nothing; and death ends all. I live. I eat. I have women and boys. I kill. 'The bright madness of battle,' say the holy books. You know how th' world works, Fido. 'The strong take what they can; the weak suffer what they must.' I do it better, me. I live, make sons. The weaklings, their seed is lost. You fear the 'Feds, you? Then be happy some men here know how to *fight*!"

"And . . . he's gone," Traffic Control announced. The pirate fleet had vanished down the Silk Road.

"I live," said Fire Control. "I eat, I fart, I stink."

"I have women and boys," said Comm, "and sheep and small mammals!"

Fir Li said nothing amid the laughter, for the lawlessness endemic to the Periphery was no laughing matter. *Would that the Ardry smite them as they deserve* . . . But it took too long for the Ardry to learn of matters remote from High Tara; too long for the response to follow. In practice, the will of the Ardry and the Grand Seanaid extended no more than a week's streaming from High Tara. And wherever his Hounds might find themselves. Each planet or planetary combine kept the peace locally as best they could. And some of them were the worst offenders.

"What was that 'Twister' he mentioned?" Greystroke asked. "If the ICC has come up with some new weapons system, the Ardry ought to know of it. Whatever it is, this Molnar is willing to take an entire flotilla on a long trek to grab it."

Fir Li looked over his right shoulder, at where the Rift spread across the ceiling. "It's a distraction from our duty. Send a swifty to High Tara and pass this Twister rumor on to the Little One. Let the Master of Hounds decide."

"Aye, Cu," Greystroke said and turned to the supervisor of Auxiliary Vessels and Drones; but Fir Li held him back with a word.

"Pup," he said. "Hear me. No effort is the greatest effort. You stumble because you try too hard not to stumble."

AN CRAIC

A lonely duty," the harper says and her fingers evoke the loneliness of the Rift, empty, echoing chords that seem to sound from very far away. The scarred man watches her play for a while, then he tosses off the remainder of his drink in one long swallow. His face screws up and his fists clench.

"There's no pleasure in that draught."

"Then why drink such slops?"

"Because there's less pleasure in not drinking it. You need a different mode for that. Something mad. Something off-key."

The harper introduces a dissonance into the vacancy of the Rift and proceeds in diminished sevenths, inverted. "You think na Fir Li mad?" The strings laugh, but the laughter is a little off.

"Don't you? He believes in something that doesn't exist."

"The threat from the CCW."

"No, the ULP."

"Ah. The gap between theory and practice. He's obsessed, not mad. There's a difference. It's the man who cares for nothing who may be mad. The root meaning of 'care' is to cry out, to scream; and what sane man is careless?"

The scarred man grunts without humor. "You caught the irony, of course. On the one hand, Fir Li regretted the Molnar's power to pillage; but on the other, he wished his Ardry had the power to crush him. What is the difference between a pirate chief and a king but the number and quality of the ships at his command?"

"The pirate butchers; the king milks. On the whole, I'd rather be milked. Fir Li knew the difference."

The scarred man runs a hand through the remnants of his hair. "I hate Fir Li. We hate the very thought of him. He thinks too much."

"Normally," the harper answers, "thinking would be accounted a good thing."

"No, we mean his paraperception, his multitasking, or however your milk-tongue puts it. For a man so single-minded, he's had too many minds."

"I don't know how the encoding works for parallel perception, but . . ."

"You don't want to know. Beside, Fir Li doesn't matter. He wasn't a player, except on the edges. A fit role for a man on the edge of the sky, and perhaps on the edge of his own sanity. Although being of more than one mind, he might be edgier than most."

"Who was the player then . . . ? Ah. Greystroke."

"Yes, the man no one sees. He could be sitting here at this table with us, and you'd not mark him, so well does he blend in."

The harper laughs. "Surely, an exaggeration!"

The scarred man smiles, and his smiles are not pleasant. "Surely. An exaggeration. But what sort of music would you play to limn a man like that? Music wants to be heard, to call attention to itself, and that is the very opposite of the Grey One.

"I can hide a melody in the chords. It's not always the top notes that sing, you know."

"The trick," the scarred man says, as if to himself, "is for all the notes to sing in concert."

"January, Little Hugh, and now Greystroke. We're for Jehovah now?"

The shrunken head dips, the smile turns bitter. "For now. There are a few others who aren't in it yet. But we have enough to start with."

GEANTRAÍ: BREAD AND SALT

It began on Jehovah, the scarred man says . . .

. . . because this is the place where everything begins or where everything ends, and we are not yet at the end.

The Bar of Jehovah hums like a bagpipe. All those private conversations blend together and couple with some curious resonances due to the architecture of the room. There is a permanence to this sound. Like those eddies that form in flowing water, it persists independently of the men and women who flow in and flow out. It is said that there are conversations still going on, long after their originators have passed away. The hum seldom changes in pitch, though it will rise and fall in volume and even, by random chance, drop into momentary silences.

The Bar is a place where the dispossessed take possession. The skyfaring folk—freighters and liners and survey ships and military vessels—come and go, but there is a substrate beneath these transients, a more permanent population for whom the Bar is less a refuge than a home. Here, old grudges are endlessly rehashed and new plans continually laid. Here, the past is always remembered and the future never comes.

There were five at the table, speaking in that desultory way of chance acquaintances. Drink and smoke and crowding and craft had placed them together. They spoke of ship arrivals and departures; of the quality of the drinks or the inhalations. The weather came in for much debate, not only the electric potential around the Jehovah Interchange and the local speed of space, but also the mundane weather planetside. It looked like rain.

"I saw a storm once," Captain January told his companions. "A dust storm. Maybe seven, eight weeks back, it was. It covered half the planet, and the lightning flashed like popcorn." It was a big Spiral Arm, with a lot of planets, and nothing has ever been seen or heard but that someone else hasn't seen or heard a bigger. No one disputed January's bragging rights; but Micmac Anne, sitting beside him, recalled that the storm had covered only a quarter of the southern hemisphere. How long, she wondered, before raconteurial evolution produced a version that blanketed the entire world?

She could not recall that escape without a shudder. She had seen the lightning spike upward five or six leagues from the cloud bank, to ground in the solar wind itself. It had licked each of the boats like the tongue of an indigo snake. She studied Amos under lowered lids and sought refuge from what-might-have-been in a tankard of beer. *He* could laugh about it; but he had only *lived* through it. He hadn't had to *watch*.

The man on January's left had entered a world where none could follow, his face nestled in his arms on the table. From time to time, he roused himself and spoke. "Had me 'n ancestor on Die Bold, praise be," he announced in a local accent, and the table chuckled. Who did *not* have an ancestor on the Old Planets?

"Lef' me a legacy," he went on. "Got a 'ficial notice, an' all. Lord knows I could use ut." His hand snaked out and pulled to him the hose from which he sucked the smoke of his own particular fantasy. Air bubbled through the huqa, cooling the smoke, lying to the lungs. He exhaled slowly, contentedly, and the table filter gathered in the brume and it was no more. "There's this guy there, on Die Bold," he explained. "He can sennit t'me, God willin', but he needs two thousan' 'n Gladjola—'n *Glad-i-o-la*—Bills t' file th' right papers." The man's fingers moved restlessly, playing with the hose. "Fren's 'r helpin' raise th' bills." He paused hopefully, then added, "M' fren's can share the 'heritance whennit comes, God willing."

The others looked to one another and grinned. He had no friends here. Not for so transparent a ruse as that.

Another of the tablemates, a woman as thin as a willow branch, mahogany-dark with blue eyes and bright yellow hair, wondered aloud how many "gladdys" the enterprising Die Bolder had already snared from fools such as this one. "It doos not take mooch," she assured the others, her Alabaster origin revealed by her accent. "He oonly needs to fool soom o' the pipple soom o' the time. Small change, boot he meks it oop in voloome."

"Someday," said the fine-featured man who wore a shirt of many colors, "there really will be a legacy discovered, and none of the heirs will believe it." Lamplight glittered off his jewelry as he waved a dismissive hand.

Their banter was interrupted by a giant. Twenty-one hands tall with shoulders broad to match. Red, shoulder-length tresses entwined with glass balls of various colors. The scar that crossed his face should not by rights have left as much nose behind as it had.

This apparition leaned his fists on the table. "I'm looking for a man," he said without preamble.

"Aren't we all," said the mahogany woman to general laughter.

The fine-featured man studied the newcomer with interest. "Any man in particular?" he asked.

The smoke-drunk native began to snore gently.

The giant looked around the room, studied the people at the table, leaned closer, and lowered his voice. "The O'Carroll of New Eireann."

The fancy man and the mahogany woman shook their heads. January scowled and Anne, who had picked up some notion of Eireannaughta politics in their brief stopover there, said, "Who wants to know?" She had it from Colonel-Manager Jumdar that this O'Carroll had been an assassin and a rebel whose death was sought by many.

"Sweeney. He'll know the name—aye, an' the nose. Should ye be runnin' into him here . . ." And the giant again scanned the Bar. "If ye be sayin' him, tell him the clans o' th' Southern Vale wait his retarn an' th' overthrow o' the ICC tyranny. Those wards, exactly."

As Sweeney straightened, January muttered, "I'd overthrow the ICC myself, if I could."

The giant cocked his head. "And what foight is it o' yers?"

"They took something of mine. A dancing stone. They'll sell it for me, they said. I'd get a finder's fee, they said. I've got a paper signed by Jumdar. But I don't trust them."

Micmac Anne laid her hand on his arm. "Hush, Amos. They fixed our ship."

"They do have a way," the giant said, "of coming into things that don't belong t' them." And so saying, he departed to inquire at the next table.

The fancy man watched the departure. "He's not going about his quest very discreetly. Or is a loud whisper what passes for stealth on his simple world?"

"The Eireannaughta," said Anne, "are rather a straightforward lot."

The mahogany woman raised her brows. "A dancing stoon? What iss this tell?" The others clamored to hear the story and January recounted, with relatively little embellishment, his discovery in Spider Alley. "And I signed it over to Jumdar," he concluded. His ruddy face beamed as if happy that he had done so. "I don't know what came over me, but it seemed like a good idea at the time. Now it sits in the ICC vaults on New Fireann."

"Or it's oon Gladioola by now," said the Alabastrine.

January shook his head. "No, they'll send it all the way to Old 'Saken. I hear Lady Cargo is a collector of antiquities. Gladiola's in the wrong direction, and there hasn't been time yet for a message to reach 'Saken and a courier ship arrive."

"Woodn't this Joomdar send it right oof?"

"I don't think she could spare a ship. She'd already sent two troop carriers on to Hawthorn Rose just before we got there, and needed the other two to keep order on the planet."

The man in the colorful shirt asked, "Do you plan to go back for those other . . . What'd you call them? Immovable Objects?"

January turned to him. "If I could, they wouldn't be bloody well *immovable,* now would they?" His vehemence surprised the others. He finished his ale and set the pot down with emphasis. "I shouldn't have made that deal," he said again. "I've good mind to go there and demand the Dancer back. Damned thieves, that's what the ICC is." He said that a little too loudly, for several men in ICC uniforms at nearby tables frowned in his direction.

"I think we're well shut of it," said Micmac Anne, but she wouldn't say why.

"Maybe with better equipment," said the fancy man thoughtfully, "they'd not be so immovable."

"They're guarded by the Irresistible Force," January reminded him.

The fancy man shrugged, as if to say that irresistible forces were a ducat the dozen and he dealt with them handily every day.

"A friend oov mine from Friesing's World," said the mahogany woman, "he mentioned a stoory from Oold 'Saken aboot a Twisting Stoon. I wonder if that's the same oobject."

Anne asked how the story went, but the woman didn't know. "It was joost in passing. I think he said it was a scepter, maybe."

"The scepter of King Stonewall?" Anne named the prehuman king that Johnny Mgurk had mentioned.

The other woman shook her head. "He never sayd."

"What difference," grumbled January, still intent on his own grievances. "It's all fantasy anyway."

And yet the stone had moved and turned and twisted. That much was no fantasy.

Evening had gotten on and the streets outside the Bar had dissolved into patterns of darkness broken only intermittently by streetlamps or the cyclopean headlights of auto-rickshaws shuttling between the Bar, the Hostel, and other, less comfortably named places.

The Corner of Jehovah was a ramshackle collection of buildings sprawled behind the Bar and permeated by a circulatory system of narrow and twisted alleys. It was here that the First Ships had landed and eco-fast dwellings had been built for each of the crew on half-acre lots. There had been a river running through it at the time; but it was an underground sewer now, and acted the part. The original crew housing had been modified over the generations with additions and extensions and sublets as the population grew. Each addition was more slapdash than its predecessor, and it seemed as if a building were a growing thing anxious to maximize the area into which it would one day collapse. It was said that every building in the Corner was in the process of going up or coming down, and the only way to tell which was by the degree of entropy in the construction materials piled beside it. The Corner was a warren now, a topological network of unknown connectivity. The original lots were buried beneath the jumble. Boards and runways coupled rooftops; tunnels linked basements—and not always the ones expected. Occasional flyovers leaped across street or gulli from the mid-story of one building to a mid-story of another. To enter one edifice in the Corner was to enter all.

Not that entering was a good idea.

From the rooftops, the lights of Port Jehovah and of the capital itself seemed a distant galaxy. The man who called himself the Fudir danced along the skyway of planks and rickety bridges with a squirrel's cunning, tracking the figures stumbling through the moonlit alleys below. "Big dikh," he muttered to himself, "but the man's my key."

Sweeney the Red had stopped at the alleyway's entrance and, pushing his charge deeper into the narrow street, turned to face the way they had come.

"Murkh," the watching man said. "Fool. That's Amir Naith's Gulli. A dead end." And it would be a dead end, too, he saw. The red giant pulled a long knife from his belt. "I wonder if that was the least conspicuous man they could have sent."

Or had he been sent with his conspicuousness in mind? There were layers here.

The Fudir scurried to the corner of the meat-dukān that overlooked the intersection, and from it he studied their back-trail. Yes. *There* was the third man, minus now his colorful shirt and flashy jewelry, moving easily from shadow to shadow past the shuttered shops and kiosks that lined Menstrit. This late in the evening, there was little traffic, only an occasional auto-rickshaw to momentarily spot-light the hunt. At each cross street and gulli, the pursuer paused and looked briefly into the deeper shadows of the narrow lanes.

The watcher considered the red-haired giant. "If you don't want him to know which gulli you've gone down," he whispered, "don't stand in the mouth of it like a hotel doorman."

The pursuer came finally to Amir Naith's Gulli. He and the giant made eye contact, and the giant gestured into the alleyway with a toss of his head.

"So, it's like that," the Fudir decided as Sweeney stepped aside. "I hope you were well paid for the treachery."

The fine-featured man turned a little as he passed Sweeney, and the redhead jerked three times and slumped to the ground.

"And paid quickly, too," the watcher muttered, not without some satisfaction. Sweeney had been a fool to expect any other coin. The Fudir pulled a whistle from his cloak and gave three short blasts. Then, throwing his hood up, he clambered down a ladder affixed to the side of Stefan Matsumoto's pawn-dukān. As he descended he began to sing.

*"As I came home on Monday night, as drunk as
drunk could be,
I saw a ground car by the door where my own car
should be . . ."*

Hunter and prey had frozen alike at the sound of
the whistle. Now, seeing a drunk stagger out of the
dim end of the alley, the latter retreated into a darkened archway, while the former resumed his stalk.
Dropping the song, the Fudir closed with him, one
clawlike hand outstretched. "Bhik, bhik," he pleaded.
"A few coppers, tide me over?"

"Off with you," the man snarled. "I've a debt to
pay." Then he took a closer look. "What, your inheri-
tance hasn't come yet?" He laughed.

The Fudir affected to notice the teaser in the man's
fist. "Ayee!" he cried. "Cor! Thief! You bad man. No
gelt b'long me. Very poor, me. Very poor. No shoot,
please!"

There are several ways to deal with an armed man.
One is to drop heavy objects on him from a great
height. Another is to disarm him, and there is more
than one way to be disarming.

"I've no interest in you, you filthy beggar." The
man reached out with his left to brush the Fudir
aside, and in doing so, he lowered his teaser.

As fast as a black mamba striking, the Fudir seized
the assassin's right wrist and gave it a sudden turn.
The man howled and the teaser dropped from nerve-
less fingers, to be kicked quickly into the shadows.
There, a smaller shadow detached itself, swooped
upon the gun, and ran toward the gulli-mouth.

"You broke my arm!" the assassin shouted and
hauled back to punch the Fudir with his left.

A brick splashed into the mud beside him. Looking

up, he saw along the rooftops on either side, silhou-
etted by the city-lit skies, men and women standing
in unnerving silence, brandishing bricks and other
objects. His gaze sought the gulli-mouth. Too far.
However fast he ran, he could never escape the gulli
before that deadly rain of brickbat struck. He'd
chance a teaser or even a needle gun, he'd laugh at a
pellet gun; but stoning was another matter.

"Not nice, call names," the Fudir said mildly, drawing the assassin's now-uncertain attention back to
him. "No filthy, me," the Fudir said. "No gandā. This
place no b'long you-fella. You go now. Jehovah police
come. Punish sinners. Swift retribution. You budmash
fella. You kill man. We see. We tell him, police-fella.
Lucky I no break arm, you. Only numb. Go! Jāo-jāo!"

Another brick splashed into the mud to punctuate
the command.

"Who are you people? What is this place?"

The Fudir laughed. "This 'die Ecke,' the Corner of
Jehovah. No one lives here but Terrans or by Terran
permission. Go, now, while you yet live."

Perhaps it was the sudden shift into Standard Gaelactic that finally broke the man's nerve. He stared at
the Fudir a moment longer, then bolted, splashing
through the dank puddles and kicking empty cans
and bottles and the foul detritus of rotting food from
the stinking raddī-piles. Fudir watched his flight, contented. The Jehovah rectors used no sirens. They
would be waiting at the mouth of Amir Naith's Gulli
with the body of Sweeney the Red and the gun that
Harimanan the street urchin had delivered up to
them. The Fudir did not like loose ends.

He turned and, strolling casually toward the back
end of the gulli, called sweetly in a singsong voice,
"Oh, Little Hugh! Come out, come out, wherever you
are!"

The Ghost of Ardow had managed many a hair's-breadth escape during the end-game of the New Eire-ann coup. He was a master of disguise and a knower of byways. But the byways he knew were light-years distant, and the disguises had depended heavily on the willingness of a great many people not to pierce them. He had, however, already pried partway open the grate in the archway and was himself halfway squeezed through the narrow crack thus wrested when the Fudir found him.

It was a bad position from which to make a fight. Like a fish caught in a weir, he must accept capture and await the proper moment to wriggle. All he needed was a nearby stream. He might be Little Hugh O'Carroll, but he was also Ringbao della Costa, and the slum-boys of New Shanghai did not grow up stupid, when they grew up at all.

The Fudir studied this unlikely catch, wondering how to play him. He finally decided on the approach direct, and said without the patois, "The assassin is caught. The Jehovan rectors have him."

Little Hugh had not secured a senior executive position with Clan na Oriel—nor for that matter survived Venishànghai slums or Handsome Jack's ambushes—without the ability to gauge people. Hugh sensed that the man spoke the truth; but that was all he sensed.

"And Red Sweeney?" he asked.

"Dead. The assassin burned him with a teaser. That was to be your fate as well."

"Dead." O'Carroll repeated the statement slowly as if the repetition itself were the confirmation. "Aye, there went a true friend, to give his life for The O'Carroll."

It had not exactly gone down that way, but the

Fudir did not hesitate. "Aye, he did that." And in a way, the treacher *had* saved the fugitive by his death. Had the assassin not paused, the Fudir might not have intercepted him quite in time; at least not without enough "Terran confetti" from the rooftops as to prick the interest of the Jehovan rectors, an interest every entrepreneur in the Corner was anxious to avoid.

The Fudir helped extricate the younger man from the grating in which he had gotten trapped. "Sweeney had a word for you," he said. "I suppose he must have told you. He said that the southern clans in the Vale await the return of The O'Carroll."

The Ghost gave him a sharp look. "And ye know this, how?"

"I was in the Bar when he came looking for you." He tossed his head. "And so was the assassin."

O'Carroll nodded. "Was he? Sweeney was careless. The assassin must have found my trail by following him."

Which would not have been the most difficult of feats. But the Fudir wondered if he gave the red giant too little credit. The fox-faced man may indeed have gotten the scent through Sweeney's less than subtle inquiries, and may indeed have offered the thirty pieces of silver. But Sweeney may have decided that the assassin you know is better than the one you don't, and taken the bribe as a ruse. In the mouth of the gulli, he had stepped aside; but who can say but that he meant to strike as the killer strode confidently past? It seemed an obvious enough maneuver, as was most every maneuver Sweeney had made, and the assassin was not thick. A man whose basic tool is treachery will see it wherever he looks.

It had made no difference in the end, least of all to Sweeney. What corpse remembers how nobly or ill it perished?

"And yourself," said The O'Carroll. "I saw you climb down from the rooftops, so I know you are no drunk and this was no chance encounter. Why should you be taking sides 'tween me and Handsome Jack?"

"Two things," the Fudir replied. "We Terrans hold a monopoly inside the Corner. Your assassin did not have our leave to ply his trade on our home ground."

"And second?"

The Fudir looked around at the ramshackle buildings, at the stinking midden heaps, at the shuttered and barred shops across Menstrit, visible through the mouth of the gulli. "Second? You are my ticket out of here."

The Fudir led him inside the warren of buildings and Hugh found himself quickly disoriented. Down these stairs; through that tunnel; take this branch; up this ramp. Doors opened to special knocks. Even on the flyovers, where he could at least glance through the windows at the streets below, he could get no bearings. In the dark, those fitfully lighted lanes seemed all alike, and he suspected that even daylight would make no difference. He wondered at the sudden impulse that had joined him to this stranger, for he had not missed the significance of his rescuer's name.

The Fudir. The Stranger; the outlander. Obviously an office-name.

My ticket out of here, the old man had said, in as affectless a voice as if he had merely commented on the weather. On New Eireann, folk said "on the run." Perhaps it was that tenuous bond, and not simple gratitude, that accounted for his agreement to follow the Terran's lead. The older man was, after all, Hugh's "ticket out of here," as well.

He was not so naïve as to suppose that everyone who did him good was a friend; but at least for now his interests and this "Fudir's" ran in parallel. Little Hugh did not believe that today's assassin would be the last that Handsome Jack would send. "An arrow must be stopped at the bow," ran an old Shanghai proverb and from time to time he remembered wisdom he had learned on the streets there.

Like rats in a maze, they scurried through the Corner. When they paused in the lobby of a long-vacant building, the Fudir broke silence. "There may be a way to restore the rightful government to New Eireann," he hinted, "without more bloodshed."

Hugh, wondering why a Terran should care who managed the Vale, made no answer. Who could say if words poured in this man's ear might spill from his mouth? He thought the promise was meant as an enticement to return to New Eireann rather than report to Oriel headquarters on Far Havn. But Oriel would probably cut its losses, sell the contract to the ICC, and reassign Ringbao to another project. Neither they nor this Fudir could know that he had sworn *by his father's name* that he would return. He needed no enticement, bloodless or otherwise.

The Committee of Seven were five in number, one of its members having been apprehended by the rectors and another being by direct consequence "in the wind." The chairman was a hard-looking woman, thin of face, white of hair, pallid of hue. Her eyes were a bitter hazel. Those flanking her, two on either side, sat in shadows, as befit those who, though sought so much, were seen so little. They had regarded Hugh with brief indifference before demanding of his guide by what right he had brought a stranger into their presence. There was something in their question that caused Hugh to dread the answer; for should that an-

swer prove unsatisfactory, both he and the Fudir
might suffer. Yet, the Fudir's response, when it came,
surprised and puzzled the erstwhile *tainiste* of New
Eireann.

"I can give us back the Earth."

Delivered with confidence, that statement was the
only one Hugh had yet heard the man utter that was
accompanied by any depth of emotion. Almost as
one, the Committee turned to a hologram painting
that hung on one of the walls of the small, dark audience room. It portrayed a large, white, domed building with towers at its four corners, sitting behind a
long reflecting pool.

The chairman, who alone had not turned, continued to study the Fudir with steady gaze.

"Can you now?" she said.

"Do you know the story of the Twisting Stone?"

That drew the attention of the other committeemen, one of whom expressed his opinion in a snort.
"We are layink now hope on altar of fable?"

"What means this fable?" another asked, but the
chairman put her hand on his forearm.

"I tell you later, Dieter. Explain, Fudir. I know you
have always a great mouthful of words, but this
should be one of your better efforts. I was not happy
that you called us out tonight. What should the rectors have taken alarm?"

The Fudir pressed his palms together and bowed
over them. "Nandi, Memsahb. Certain things have I
learned . . ."

But again one of the committeemen interrupted.
"No pukkah, bukkin' Standard," he said, pointing at
Hugh. "That fellah no fanty, him." At that, all of them
descended into the patois, words running too thick
and fast for Hugh to follow. They began to shout at

one another, all talking at once, gesturing, voices rising in pitch as well as volume. Hugh studied the room and its exits, thinking that he might need one soon.

And then, as suddenly as it had begun, the commotion died. Everyone was bobbing their head side to side and smiling. "Very well," the chairman said. "We are agreed. New Eireann lies but two weeks down the Grand Trunk. The proposal may be a fantasy, but so is our Hope. If the one may win the other, it is worth the shot. And should it prove to be nothing, the cost is minimal. Sahb the Fudir, you will have your certificates at this time tomorrow. See Cheng-fu at the seal-maker's dukān. You know the man. We will secure you the vacancies you require. The rest is up to you."

"Mgurk is one of us," the Fudir told them. "He will do as we ask. The other, let it be the woman, Micmac Anne. She is at the edge of knowledge, and might guess too much too soon. We can be thankful that January did not know what he had; we can only hope that Colonel-Manager Jumdar has not yet discovered it."

The chairman struck the table with her knuckles. "Bread and salt," she called out. The Fudir bowed over his folded hands as a servant scuttled in bearing on a silver tray a plate of naan and papad. Then, when small cups of thick, creamy tea had been served out, they all rose but Little Hugh and faced the picture and, bowing over their hands, chanted in a rough unison, "Next year, the hajj upon Terra."

The harper has grown steadily more impatient, and when the scarred man pauses for another drink, she strikes the table with the flat of her hand. "Is this to be all beginnings and no ends? Who is the Fudir? What is this story of the Twisting Stone?"

But the storyteller taunts her with his smile. "All things in their season, harper. You do not strike all your chords at once or it would be naught but noise. How can there be ends without beginnings? Besides there are more than seventeen different versions of that Twister story, and not all of them support the Fudir's plans."

"This Fudir, who was he? What was his interest in the Dancer? Why did he favor Little Hugh over Handsome Jack?"

The man looks into a distant corner of the room, and perhaps beyond it. "The Fudir cared nothing for either," he says finally. "He told the Committee that the Dancer would regain them their lost Earth. He told Little Hugh that it would regain him New Eireann. What he told himself, he never told another; and that was the egg from which much later hatched. Perhaps he hoped to regain a world, too; or maybe his hopes were more modest than that."

"You speak of him in the past tense. Is he one of those who died?" The harper's fingers trace the beginnings of a goltraí, but the scarred man stops her.

"Don't mourn him yet. There will be mourning enough when that time comes. After all, we are all dead men. Our younger selves have died, and yet we live. If some of them live on in my stories or your

songs, *why, that is the greater immortality. For now, 'let them have their moment.' Little Hugh escaped the assassin. The Fudir secured his* "ticket outta here." *Perhaps the Committee had their moment, as well, for the Fudir was not to their taste, we think, and they may have been happy to see the back of him, fables and a madman's chance notwithstanding.*"

The harper considers his words while aimless notes drift off her strings. She wonders if the scarred man is making the whole thing up in the hopes of cadging more drinks. But if he is, what recourse has she? Against what other touchstone might she rub the tale to test it? Her one other source is gone. Finally, she asks, "Are all the players in place now? I've heard other names mentioned. When does this thing finally start?"

"Oh, the ballet is already begun. The dancers are whirling and turning, but they do not all step off at the first bar. What sort of dance would that be? Yet the *prima ballerina is halfway to her goal. There is a* telos, *if you've been following. There is a direction. And it all lies implicit in January's initial error.*"

"January's error . . . You've mentioned that before. What was it?"

"We need to bring another dancer in. You've met him before, but have forgotten him already."

SUANTRAÍ: DISPATCHES FROM
THE EDGE OF NIGHT

*Na Fir Li exercised in the old Greek style, though
he did not know that he did.*

Sweat gleamed on his torso, his brow, his thighs, so
that he seemed to embody the glittering blackness of
the sky itself. He moved lithely from bars to rings to
bags to weights across the gymnasium of *Hot Gates*
in an intricate ballet impossible to remember save
that the body had a memory of its own—which is
just as well, because his mind was engaged, as always, on three or four other matters.

On the floor mat, Fir Li executed a series of mo-
tions that were half dance and half combat; pleasure
and threat combined, though it was the dance that
threatened. "Pup," he said at the top of a twirling
leap, "would you care to walk on the ceiling with
me?"

Greystroke had entered quietly and was standing
by the edge of the mat. Fir Li was the only person he
knew who could be aware of his unannounced presence. "Aren't you too old for that?" he mocked. "The
swift-boats report a monoship approaching."

"I can reduce the gravity in here, if you think the
ceiling out of your reach." The Hound whirled to rest
in the center of the room and made a gracious bow.
"You may strip, too, if you think it would help."

Greystroke grunted and went to his master's side
in his coveralls. "In what combat do we pause to
strip? The blue wall, then?"

"It offers fewer obstructions. Go!"

The two raced across the gymnasium floor toward

the chosen wall. As they neared it, they leaped, as nearly simultaneously as made no difference, and landed feetfirst about halfway up. Two more steps up the wall and . . . the gravity grid won. Both men back-flipped to the floor again, landing on their feet side by side.

"I don't recall raising that ceiling," Fir Li complained. "Whence this monoship? Go!"

Another dash at the wall. Two, three, four steps up. Na Fir Li grinned whitely and touched the ceiling with the ball of his left foot before back-flipping once more to the floor. Greystroke did not quite make it and landed a split second later. Fir Li clapped him on the back.

"At least you landed on your feet, Pup. Some don't. Perhaps when you are as old as I am, you will run higher."

"It comes from the Galactic East."

The Hound, who had bent into his cooling off exercises, paused and gave his full attention. "I knew you were saving a surprise for me. Excellent. I was growing bored since the little incident with the Cynthians. Your conclusion?"

"Cu, there is another crossing, farther east. One that has never been mapped."

"The scientists say the Eastern Rift is too wide for a sustainable road. But never mind. The scientists are always right until they're wrong." He resumed his cooling down exercises. "Your reasoning?"

"As yours, Cu. The ULP has no worlds in that region of space and none of our ships have ventured there; so this cannot be one of our vessels returning. Further, I think it unlikely that a lost colony could have reachieved starflight since the Diaspora and yet remained out of touch until now. Radio signatures would foretell them, if nothing else. Of course," he added slyly, "it could be a ship of the prehumans, hiding out in the wild east and returning now at last."

The Hound snorted. "Ah, 'the Great Returning.' You don't believe in that, do you?"

"Nor would I look forward to it if I did. Sequels always disappoint."

"What of another nonhuman race, achieving starflight at last?"

"There is a first time for everything, I suppose. But for a nonhuman race to achieve starflight, one would first need a nonhuman race. There have been only the prehumans and us."

"It's a big Spiral Arm."

"So it is, but it is far more likely that—"

"That there is another Crossing, that the CCW has recently discovered it, and has sent a ship to learn where it leads, which—fortunately for us—is into my lap. Now you see my wisdom in placing drones along that road?"

"A low probability, many thought . . ."

"There was great amusement in the kennel," Fir Li said. "The old dog has lost his mind." His laughter was very like a bark. "But of course it was far better to put the drones out there and never need them."

Greystroke glanced at the chronometer. "The interceptors will have secured the stranger by now. We start the interview in about three days, after they get down here."

The Hound smiled grimly, revealing another band of white. "The curse of Newtonian space. We slide across light-years in mere days, but a few million leagues reduce us to a crawl. Learn what you can while he is in transit. Are any competent inquisitors on the interceptor?"

Greystroke shrugged. "Your apprentice, Pak Franswa-ji."

"So. He will have to do. Perhaps we have plucked only a merchant-adventurer. They talk readily enough, if the price is right."

"In a monoship? More likely, a Confederate agent."

Fir Li resumed his exercises. "They can be brought to talk as well. It is only the price that differs."

Bones can be broken, whips and screws applied, and a man may wear such scars with honor, because he will know he bore the pain, and can brag, even if he broke on the other side of it, that he had endured as much as he had. But there is another sort of breaking and other sorts of scars, and they reduce a man only to an object of pity, because he cannot even recall what courage he showed before courage found its limit.

Greystroke reported at the Squadron staff meeting, attended not only by Fir Li's kennel, but also by the naval officers and department heads. And so amid reports on stores, on fuel consumption, on disciplinary hearings, on traffic and customs, was one on a pithed man. The department supervisors looked away and the naval officers threw their heads back in a gesture of distaste. They knew such measures were used, but they liked to pretend they were not necessary.

"He was sent to contact an agent of theirs on Jehovah," Greystroke said.

Fir Li was reading three other reports and discussing with the commodore ship dispositions for the coming metric week. "What name was he told to find?"

"'Donovan.' His contact is via the Terran Brotherhood."

"Yes. Well, all Terrans are Confederate spies. Are the ship dispositions satisfactory, Leif?"

The commodore bowed his head, and suggested two changes. "Because *Shree Anuja* will leave the Squadron as soon as *Victory* arrives."

"Positioning them for a quicker departure? Surely, the *Anujas* are not bored with this duty?" Several men and women around the table laughed. "Pup! What message was he carrying to this 'Agent D'?"

Greystroke paused for effect. That na Fir Li was paraperceptic and could handle multiple information streams simultaneously was known to all. *Why keep the eyes from reading,* the Hound had once complained, *simply because the ears are hearing?* His interlocutors made a certain allowance for his seeming deficit of attention; but at the moment Greystroke wanted the whole thing.

His pause could have been measured in microbeats, but achieved its intent. Fir Li held a palm out to silence the commodore and the traffic control director (who had his other ear) pushed the reports forward, and balled his hands on the tabletop. "Am I going to like this or not?" he asked Greystroke.

"It could go either way, Cu. What do you call it when you pierce a mystery only to find an enigma behind it?"

"A delaying tactic by a subordinate. What was the man's message?"

"That Those of Name wish Donavan to report on the detention of CCW merchant ships by ULP forces."

The silence spread to the whispered side conversations around the table. Leif Commodore Echeverria blinked his large, owlish eyes. "But we aren't . . ." The Hound hushed him.

"*They* have been detaining and impounding *our* ships," Fir Li said.

"Cu, the *fact* is only that some ships have entered the Rift and there is no record of their return. The reason for this has yet to attain the lofty stature of 'fact.' It may be no more than faulty record-keeping;

but now we learn that the enemy has the same concern. We never thought to ask how many of *their* ships disappear."

"Or we learn that They wish us to *believe* they have the same concern," said the Hound. "Couriers have been used before to spread disinformation."

"Cu, which of the two evident paths should I follow?"

"Oh, the second, of course. You are not weaned for the first. For *that* task, I will call to Hounds."

The other Pups smiled, and the commodore threw up his hands, looking for support among the rest of the management team. "Oh, that was clear!"

"Perhaps as clear as need be for one rotating out on the next duty cycle." Fir Li had gathered the reports to him and his eyes, ears, and mouth parted company once more. "But, to humor you, Leif. My journeyman wishes a journey. We know that ships enter the Rift and do not return. The obvious explanation is that Those of Name have seized them. But as my Pup has pointed out, we do not yet know if they actually reach the other side. There may be some unknown hazard in the Rift itself. One way to learn that is to dispatch a man into the Confederacy. Greystroke-ji believes he is ready for that. He is wrong, but the confidence does him credit. The second way is to complete the courier's mission for him. You *do* have his passwords, Pup."

"Of course, Cu. And the encrypted bubble. I assume it contains the names of the missing Confederate ships and that Donovan possesses the dongle to decrypt it."

"And that being the shorter journey," Fir Li continued to the commodore, "and the one more likely to bear fruit, I have instructed him to pursue it."

"But . . ." interjected Traffic Control, "but you told

him to take the 'second' course before you knew which one he meant!"

Fir Li grinned and turned full face to Greystroke. "I knew. One who'd not dare *that* journey first is no Pup of mine."

When Greystroke had reached the door to the boardroom, Fir Li stopped him with a word. "Pup?"

"Aye, Cu?"

"They send them out in pairs, so that if one is caught, the other might get through."

Greystroke nodded. "Of the second courier, we learned nothing."

"See that you do," the Hound said as he read the report on sick call, "before he learns of you."

Two days out along the Silk Road, near the approaches to Last Chance, Greystroke realized the full depth of his master's humor. He had entered the pantry to make a cup of his favorite blend—a tea from the slopes of Polychrome Mountain on Peacock Junction, where the variegated soils and the judicious splicing of selected fruit genes had achieved the nirvana of teas. There, he paused and reflected.

One who'd not dare that *journey first is no Pup of mine.*

Indeed. Had Greystroke's mind numbered the two choices otherwise, his master's orders would have sent him across the Rift into the CCW, in cold likelihood to his doom.

And, so, no longer a Pup of Fir Li.

He completed the preparations and secured the tea canister in the cabinet. Then he threw back his head and laughed.

Greystroke's mobile field office, *Skyfarer,* was a comfortable vessel, streamlined for atmospheric flight, and as gray a ship as he was a man. Her name was unremarkable; her appearance, ordinary. A hundred thousand other private yachts possessed the same lines, the same colorings; some, indeed, the same registration number on the hull. And yet, beneath her ordinary exterior lay an extraordinary ship. Her sensors were of surpassing fineness; her Newtonian engines of matchless power. Her intelligence was more supple than that of many of the passengers—and prisoners—she had carried. Her alfvens could brake her unaided by any ground-based decelerators. She contained facilities for exercise and recreation, storage rooms, a refectory and library, a bay for the dūbuggi, another for the collapsible flitter—but all of it so cunningly laid out that no interior volume was wasted.

More extraordinary still—and despite or because of this utilitarianism—her furnishings were richly decorated. No comfort had been neglected; nothing plain had been permitted. Art filled odd spaces; color emblazoned panels. The decor extended from the visual to the audible to the other senses. Intricate ragas and concertos played subtly over speakers. Incense burned; the larder bulged with the most savory of fauxcreatures. Nor were the inner senses neglected: the library, both physical and virtual, was of unsurpassed variety. The most ordinary of fittings had been milled and chamfered and routed into elaborate vines and grotesques. Control knobs bore the heads of beasts. The ship's interior was as ornate as its owner was not, as if every bit of ostentation that had been squeezed from his person had been applied to his vessel.

In this comfort, Greystroke spent the twenty-two metric days from Sapphire Point to Jehovah Interchange. He planned a brief respite at Peacock Junction to secure more of his preferred tea, but otherwise he settled into his shipboard routine. He read from Còstello and other favorite philosophers; he enjoyed—and sometimes participated in—simulations of great battles or great fictions; he sparred with the onboard intelligence in games of thought. He sparred, too, in his gym, which, while smaller and less well appointed than Fir Li's, provided ample scope to hone his skills.

He researched the various costumes of the Terran Corner in *Benet's Sumptuary Guide to the Spiral Arm,* and programmed his anycloth to emulate them. A flick of the wrist, and the plain, gray bolt became a tartan mantle that he draped around his shoulders. A shrug, and the microfibers shivered into a knee-length kurta with embroidered borders; a tug at the collar and it opened into a dhoti, which he tugged down to his waist. A whispered command and the colors faded and the edges grew ragged. Satisfied, he pinched the seam and it opened up once more into a simple bolt of gray fabric.

From time to time he scanned the yellow-white blur that marked the shoulders of the Silk Road, and tried to tease out the images of long-gone ships from the subluminal mud. The walls of a Krasnikov tube consisted of lamina whose "speed of space" decreased steadily from the channel itself outward toward the Newtonian flats. Where the lamina were thin and "packed close," the shoulders were said to be "steep" or "tight," and no ship could pass through them without some portion of her structure crossing a contour line faster than the speed of space on the other side. The resulting Cerenkov "blink" could rip the vessel asunder or destroy it completely. Even at rest in the channel, a ship might be traveling many times faster than Newtonian c. Elsewhere, usually at certain resonance distances from suns, gravity broadened the lamina into "ramps" more easily negotiated. The Silk

Road was well charted, but Greystroke and the ship's intelligence kept a wary eye out when the shoulders grew tight by sounding them at intervals with a molecule or two.

But one curious consequence of the lamination was that the images of passing ships were trapped, for they moved always at the speed of light and so the deeper into the shoulder one peered, the older and slower those images were. There were ships that had passed by centuries before whose fossil images were only now reaching this point. With luck and skill and with instruments of exquisite fineness, one could sometimes tease these images from the blur of countless others. It had become something of a hobby with Greystroke. He had secured a picture of *City of Chewdad Roy* just as it was breaking up along Sweet Love Road to New Tien-ai. He had captured another of the Great Fleet that the Second Tyrant of Gladiola had launched against Ramage. Once, but only once, and this was years before, he thought he had seen a prehuman ship, an odd, misshapen vessel unlike any other he had ever seen. But *those* images, thousands of years old, were like pictures left too long in the sun, bleached and faded and indistinct. They had had millennia to sink through the shoulders of the road and now wafted pale and ghostlike across the New-tonian flats.

The ancient god, shree Einstein, the scarred man says, has not forbidden that two things might happen at the same time; but he has clouded men's minds in such a way that they can never know that they have. There is no universal time, nor even absolute space. Even if one clocks off the revolution of the galaxy, as men once clocked off the revolution of Old Earth, that motion seems different from different parts of

*the Spiral Arm. The Constant Clock on Friesing's
World is no more than an agreement and ships and
worlds synchronize with it through complex incanta-
tions prayed to Lorenz and Fitzgerald and Rudolf.*

So if synchronicity has any meaning on worlds so
far apart, Greystroke left the Rift at about the same
time that the Fudir rescued Little Hugh in the back
alleys of the Corner, and was still en route when the
Brotherhood arranged to smuggle the pair off-planet.
A cargo was booked on *New Angeles* for delivery on
New Eireann, realistic certificates of competency were
provided to Hugh and the Fudir, Mgurk dropped from
sight in the Corner, and a debilitating substance was
introduced into the mulligatawny consumed by Micmac Anne in the Restaurant Chola. The stomach
cramps might not have prevented her from shipping
out with the others, but the frequent and odious diar-
rhea proved too great an obstacle for her shipmates.

So it was that January was two hands short with
departure imminent. Maggie B. could move up to
Number One and Tirasi was qualified to sign the articles as astrogator; but that still left a hole for an
instrument tech. There were worlds from which he
could have departed shorthanded—January thought
that Maggie and Bill between them could cover all
three berths, and Malone could double up on the scut
work—but Jehovah was a stickler for the literal in-
terpretation of texts, legal texts no less than others.

What joy then, when two properly certificated individuals presented themselves and signed the articles!
Maggie B. and Bill Tirasi interviewed the one—his cert
named him Kalim DeMorsey—and judged his skills
acceptable for system tech. Nagaraj Hogan examined
the second man—one Ringbao della Costa—but this
consisted mostly of verifying that he could lift or move
objects of the required mass. Little more was required

of a deckhand, and it gave his mate, Malone, some-one to look down on.

"The berths are only for this one transit," January warned the two with his cherubic smile. "But good work, Ringbao, can earn you the berth regular. Be here—awake—at oh three hundred Sixday morning, or else."

Or else *New Angeles* could not depart on time; but January judged that such a threat would have little leverage over either man, and so he left the conse-quences ominously unspoken.

Once outside the hiring hall, Little Hugh spoke up. "So it's a common laborer, I'm to be?"

"Deckhand," the Fudir told him. "Or do you hide skills under your bushel?"

"I'm a schoolteacher."

"Wonderful. Wide scope for that on a tramp freighter."

"And I do a fair job at running a guerilla campaign."

"Same objection. What's your complaint? This will sneak you back to New Eireann without fanfare."

"No complaint. I've done scut before. But I noticed you wound up as a deck officer."

The Fudir shrugged. "I prayed to Shree Ganesha and was answered."

Hugh snorted in derision. They turned their steps down Greaseline Street along the Spaceport's bound-ary fence. At the far end of the Port, nearly to the horizon, a heavy lifter was pushed skyward on a pil-lar of light. Nearer by, a crew in dark green coveralls and straw terai-hats struggled over a balky tug pull-ing a ballistic commuter flight toward the passenger terminal. "Put a little more prayer into it!" the crew chief exhorted them. "Line it up, line it up. Insert the pin . . . Oh, God *bless* it! Back it up and let's try it again, my brothers . . ."

The Bar stood at the corner of Greaseline and Chalk. From the outside, the black building was broad, featureless, and multistoried (in both senses of the word). Behind it, the Terran Corner lay like construction debris left over from the Bar's erection. Dwelling upon dwelling filled the low land and jostled up the slope of Mount Tabor—despite its name, a steep but unimpressive ridge. "I never knew that about Terrans," Little Hugh said, pointing to the hodgepodge of buildings. "That they lived in such wretched conditions."

The Fudir grunted. "Oh, you didn't."

"No. There was no Corner on New Eireann . . ."

"Even we aren't crazy enough to want to live *there*."

O'Carroll said nothing until they reached the doors of the Bar. There was no sign to mark it. The Elders reasoned that for those who knew, no signs were needed; while for those who did not, the lack might save them from falling into evil ways. "Are all Terrans like you?" O'Carroll asked as he grasped the door handle.

"Kalim DeMorsey is from Bellefontaine on Redmount Araby. We eat Terrans for breakfast there."

"No, I'm meaning in truth . . ."

The Fudir gripped him by the arm and his hand was like a vise. The other door swung open and a skinny, pale-faced man in green spiked hair staggered out, glanced at them incuriously, and went his way. "When you wear a mask, boy," the Fudir said when they were alone, "that *is* the truth. And ditch that flannel-mouthed accent of yours for the duration."

Little Hugh pried the Fudir's fingers off his arm. He bowed from the shoulders. "So sorry, signor." And he brushed his chin with his fingertips.

Inside the Bar, talk still raged over the unknown fleet that had passed through Jehovah Interchange a few days earlier. As in all such cases, the very lack of information manured the conversations (in both senses), and the number of origins, destinations, and purposes of the fleet had increased until it exceeded the number of speculators. The Fudir approached the Bartender, who bore the unlikely name of Praisegod Barebones, and passed him a Shanghai ducat. "Greet God, friend 'Bones. Private room 2-B?"

"God bless you," the Bartender replied. "Not 2-B; it's taken. You can have 3-G." He glanced at Little Hugh. "So. Changing anatomical preferences?"

"It's not like that—and you never met me before today." Another ducat appeared by magic, and disappeared the same way.

"Would that I never had."

"We need a wake-up call for an oh three hundred departure."

"So. Is the Transient Hostel filled?" 'Bones passed him the key to the room. "At least, you leave Jehovah's World a better place than you found it."

That puzzled the Fudir and he paused before leaving. "How's that?"

"Why, by leaving it, God willing, you improve it."

The Fudir laughed and gave the Bartender another ducat "for the widows and orphans."

He led Hugh to a small room on the fourth floor of the building. "This isn't a hotel, strictly speaking," he told him. "But public drunkenness is a crime—they call it a 'sin,' but it amounts to the same thing—and they provide rooms to 'comfort the afflicted.' They think of it as a sort of hospice."

The corridor was dimly lit; the doors anonymous save for the number inscribed on each. From behind one door, they heard a woman's voice crying, "Oh, God! Oh, God! Don't stop!"

"She must be praying," Little Hugh suggested.

Room 3-G was small, containing only a bed, a small stool, and a table. They threw their carryalls on the bed, which complained at the sudden weight. The floor was swept, however, and the walls were clean and brightly colored and decorated with tranquil scenes depicting sundry Jehovan provinces. Little Hugh looked around. "Not what I expected."

"Why?"

O'Carroll did not answer. He pulled the curtain aside from the window. "Ah so. Lovely view of the Corner," he remarked. "So picturesque." He studied the slum for a moment longer. "And have those people no pride in themselves?"

"No, sahb," the Fudir answered, sitting on the bed and then leaning back with his hands locked behind his head. "We very lazy fella. You much buddhimān to see so."

Little Hugh let the curtain drop. "You can turn that blather on and off whenever you want. Why can't they?"

"Don't make assumptions to suit your conclusions."

The younger man returned no comment, but explored the room. As the room was only two double-paces each way, and most of that was occupied by the bed and the writing table, this was accomplished by no more than turning his head. He sat on the stool and opened the drawer. Inside he found a tablet with letterhead embossed with a hologram of the building and reading, *Greetings from the Peripherally Famous Bar of Jehovah!* A rather grim illo for such a cheery salutation. "So who gets the bed; or do we take turns?" He found an envelope of condoms underneath the tablet.

"These rooms weren't planned with double occupancy in mind," the Fudir said.

Hugh held up the condoms. "Weren't they? What hypocrites."

"You're letting your assumptions outrun your conclusions again. What do you know of Jehovan doctrines? As it happens, they celebrate beauty as the greatest good, and hold the human body as beautiful. God is Love, they say. It's irresponsible procreation they regard as a sin."

Hugh dropped the envelope into the drawer and shoved it shut. "So." He folded his arms and stretched his legs out, and this was sufficient to nearly touch the door. "Tell me how this Twister will help me reestablish the legitimate government in the Vale."

"You want reassurance? You've been willing enough to come this far without it."

The younger man managed to shrug without changing his posture. "Let me see . . . Assassin in the alleyway. Check. Terran criminal gang. Check. Lost in a tangled warren of hallways and tunnels. Check. Committee of Seven, with power of life and death. Check. Up to now, Fudir, I don't see where my being willing has mattered very much."

The Fudir closed his eyes. "If you don't want to go back, you can stay here. I thought I was doing you a favor."

"Fudir," said Little Hugh, "if I thought you were doing me a favor, I'd be out that door."

The Terran opened his eyes and looked slantwise at the other. "Aren't you too young to be so cynical?"

"You're using me to get off-planet. That's fine. You're probably only a step or two ahead of the rectors—"

"Five steps. What am I, an amateur?"

"—so I can see what's in it for you. Me, I vowed to

return to the Vale, so I've got it to do. But I'd like to know if that will mean anything more than another hopeless go-round with Jumdar. Set me down in the Southern Vale and I'll have the *guerilla* up and running in a metric week—and Jumdar's spy satellites and air-cav will shut it down in another. I'm as willing as the next man to make a heroic but doomed gesture—the New Eireann influence, I suppose—but you promised me something a cut above hopeless."

"Fair enough," the Fudir said. "Have you ever heard the story of the Wish of the Twisting Stone?"

"No. A bedtime story? Really?"

"They tell it on Old 'Saken and a slightly different version on Friesing's World, and other variants circulate on Die Bold and Abyalon. All in and around the Old Planets, you see. Once . . ."

". . . upon a time . . ."

". . . there was a prehuman king whose scientists presented him with the Twisting Stone, saying it would grant him one wish. 'Cutting to the chase,' as we Terrans say, the king brandished it like a scepter and said that he wished only to be obeyed."

"Isn't it supposed to be *three* wishes?" Little Hugh suggested.

The Fudir propped himself up on his elbows. "Once the wish for obedience is fulfilled, what other wish can matter? In most versions, two prehuman kings struggle to possess it. 'Stonewall,' 'Hillside,' 'Cliff' . . . The names of the kings vary from one world to another, so maybe there were more than two; but that doesn't matter. Whichever finally gains possession finds himself obeyed without question. So if we gain you the possession of it . . ."

"I'll find myself obeyed on New Eireann. Charming. You know what I think?"

The Fudir hesitated. "What?"

"That prehuman fathers chastised their children by hitting them with bricks, and that's how the story of a stone conferring the power of obedience got started."

The Fudir lay back down again. "Maybe it's the wildest of fables. But isn't it worth a two-week trip to find out? Did you have something better to do with your time?"

"How do you know what January found was this Twisting Stone?"

"In the stories, the stone is never the same shape twice. January said that the artifact he found changed its shape imperceptibly, like a very slow dance."

"I'd think that a folk that could make stones twist could also make them dance without them being the same stone."

"And as long as he had it, his crew followed his instructions. When he gave it away, they reverted to their normal squabbling."

O'Carroll snorted. "You mean the crew we're shipping out with? Wonderful. Why'd he give it away, then?"

"Because he didn't know what he had. He thought the crew had finally pulled together because of the common danger they had faced on the world of the Vault, and they've now fallen back into old habits. He doesn't connect it with having the stone and not having it. And you won't tell him any different."

"Oh, believe me, I wouldn't dream of telling him anything like that. Who has it now?"

"Jumdar. She promised January that the ICC would auction it off and January would get a percentage of the profit."

"Ah! So, Jumdar possess sigil of absolute obedience, and you and I go overthrow her. Everything now clear . . ."

"Don't give me that Venishànghai crap. She doesn't know, either. Or at least we hope she hasn't learned in the meantime. She and January both think it's an art object, potentially valuable because it's prehuman; but that's all. Any further questions?"

"No, a quixotic quest for a magic token seems about the right way to end the day. One thing does occur to me, though."

The Fudir raised an eyebrow to the question. "What's that?"

"If this gadget, or whatever it is, gives its owner such power, then why are *you* helping to gain it for *me*?"

The Fudir snorted. "There go your assumptions outracing your conclusions again. Not everyone yearns for power. Some of us yearn for justice. You were ill-used; and the ICC are crooks. That's enough for me. Come on, there's room on this bed for two even without intimacy."

"No thanks," O'Carroll said. "Harder beds than this floor greeted my back when I was on the run."

"Have it your way," the Fudir said, turning his face to the wall. "Just remember you'll be stowing cargo most of the morning, starting at oh three hundred."

AN CRAIC

A stone scepter that compels obedience to its holder?" The harper allows incredulity to speak for her.

"So the Fudir thought at the time. A flimsy notion built from half-believed myths. He might not have crossed the Spiral Arm to check it out; but New Eire-

ann wasn't that far from Jehovah, so what the hell? If he was wrong, what was lost but a little time?"

"Another short, hopeless civil war among the Eire-annaughta?" the harper guesses at other losses. She leans forward over the table and adds in a harder voice than she has used up to then: "But what matter is that if absolute obedience might be won?"

"Don't be a fool, harper. Little Hugh was going back to the Vale. Nothing could have stopped him short of death. He had promised on his father's name. *So the only real question was when he would return, and how."*

"That's two questions."

"No, *because the* when *dictates the* how. Had the Dancer been a myth, it would have made no difference to what happened. But if it were true after all, there needn't be blood at all."

"No. Only blind obedience. I'd rather see the blood."

"Yes, so long as it's someone else's."

The shot tells. The harper falls silent and her fingers touch idly the frame of her clairseach. Ideals in the abstract may be held abstractly, but the devil is always in the details.

"None of which," the harper says at last, "tells us why the Fudir decided to help Hugh."

The man leans back into the alcove and laughter emerges from shadows even as he recedes into them. "You don't get answers this soon in a tale, even if you had the question right."

"This is an intermezzo then," she says, "a bridge." She plays an aimless conjunction of music, a strain that summarizes what has gone before and promises newer tropes to come after.

"If you wish," the scarred man says. "But there is a

*notion that nothing ever happens on a bridge, and
that is wrong. People jump off them."*

The harper places her instrument once more upon
the table and the silence, now that her fingers have
ceased their continuo, is louder than her music had
been. "Now you mock," she says. "Word games. Do
you mean that O'Carroll trusted the Fudir too much?"

"Or that he trusted him too little. That's a delicate
point, don't you think? But—and maybe you haven't
noticed this, either—the Fudir had to trust O'Carroll,
too. Up to a point. The question is, was it to the same
point? But, come, drink!" He raises his uisce bowl on
high. "Drink to the quest!"

The harper disagrees. "The quest itself means nothing. The heart of the matter is Jason—and Medea—
not the Fleece. The Argonauts could have sought
anything, and their fates would have been the same."

The scarred man strikes the tabletop with the flat
of his hand, and the bowls and the tableware—and a
few nearby drinkers—jump a little. "No! What you
seek determines how you fail. Had Jason sought a Tin
Whistle or an Aluminum Coffeepot instead of a
Golden Fleece, the failure would have run quite differently."

"More melodiously in the first case," the harper allows, "and with greater alertness in the second. But,
must it always end in failure?"

"Always."

"Your cynicism extracts a price. You can never
know the thing in itself, because you always look past
it for a hidden reality. I would think all failures alike.
Coffeepot or Golden Fleece, failure means you
haven't obtained what you sought."

"No," the scarred man answers mockingly. "Each
failure is inevitably, enormously different from all the

*others. Each man who seeks does so for a different
reason, and so can fail in a different way. Hercules
failed in the quest for the Fleece; but his failure was
of a different sort than Jason's."*

"Jason secured the Fleece," the harper points out.

"That was his failure."

GOLTRAÍ: SHIPS PASSING IN THE LIGHT

*any an interchange carries more traffic than
Jehovah Roads, the scarred man says* . . .

. . . but none is ever quite so busy.

Here, ships may shift from the Champs Elysées to
the Yellow Brick, from the Silk Road to the Grand
Trunk, and to and from several lesser roads beside.
They slide in from Alabaster and far-off Gatmander,
from Agadar and Hawthorn Rose, from Peacock
Junction and New Chennai, from Megranome and
Valency, from Abyalon and Die Bold and Old 'Saken.
Here grand liners mingle with humble freighters,
with peacekeepers and survey ships and pirates, with
commercial carriers, and tourist cruisers and private
yachts, with savvy Chettinad merchants from the
Lesser Hanse.

All this riot of voyagers—high and low, desperate
and indifferent, jaded and eager and matter-of-fact—
is tossed and juggled by the magbeam "lighthouses"
spotted about the Jehovan system. Drawing their
power off the sun, off the wind, off the two superjo-
vians spinning like dynamos in the outer system, and
even off the electric currents of the roads themselves,
they push outbound ships toward their portals, cush-

ion those emerging, and coordinate the arrivals, departures, and transits in an intricately choreographed opera of words and deeds.

If the League lives anywhere other than in the secret devotions of her Hounds, it is in this bustling interchange.

New Angeles leaped into this kaleidoscope, burning off HOJO just behind a Hadley liner plying the inner circuit and just ahead of a Gladiola terraforming ark outward bound for the Rim. At cutoff, when the legendary god Shree Newton would otherwise have seized *New Angeles* and whirled her 'round in endless ellipses, HOJO Platform Number Two shook hands with the onboard target array and its beams accelerated the ship steadily toward the coopers.

Old spacehands call this traverse of Newtonian space "the crawl," and it generally consumes more time than slipstreaming from star to star. It is a slow lazy interval, for most of the grunt work happens portside and most of the skull sweat on the ramp. The crawl passes in boredom and the troubles consequent thereto.

Portside, there is cargo to load, and although the stevedores handle most of that, the ship still wants a deckhand for the orbital transfer, and no damned *outsider* is going to settle the stowage on a captain's ship. Little Hugh O'Carroll learned that, in practice, this meant that Maggie told engineering the balance along each axis, Hogan then told Malone to rectify that balance accordingly, and Malone told "Ringbao" to shift containers within the cargo hold. This struck Hugh as rather more chieftains than clansmen, but he had put up with more tedious labors during the Troubles, and so he did the work willingly, if not happily.

Mahmoud Malone, his immediate boss, had been born on Gehpari and proved not a bad sort when there was no work to pass along. In unguarded moments he would revert to a Gehparisian accent, in which stresses showed up tardy and final vowels arose like resurrected saints. He was a man of great depth but of limited breadth, so that while he knew very little, he knew a great deal about it. Women, distilled spirits, distilled spirits applied to women, the laws of probability applied to games of chance, and the mulishness of alfven engines could spark endless conversations. Outside this range, his interests dropped off in inverse squares. The easiest way to shut him up was to change the subject.

"I hand it to yew, Ringbao," Malone had said, once *New Angeles* had settled on the hyperbolic trajectory to Electric Avenue, "you air certainly a better workair than that Mgurk. We made the trim of the vessel say bone." He made a circle of his thumb and forefinger, pressed it to his lips, kissing it. Hugh did not tell him that on several worlds of his acquaintance the circle of thumb and forefinger signified an asshole.

Of course, "we" meant that Malone had given orders and watched while Hugh sweated cargo containers into place with hand truck, crane, and old-fashioned block-and-tackle—by the end of which Hugh had gained a certain sympathy for the storied Johnny Mgurk.

"Good," he answered. "Then *we* can relax until we reach New Eireann," with just the lightest ironic emphasis on the "we."

Malone's shrug was eloquent. Who knew what tasks might await the unwary deckhand in his idle moments?

————

The deck went on watch-in-four, and the Fudir found himself assigned the third watch, sandwiched between Maggie B. and Bill Tirasi. For the first several rotations, Maggie motherhenned the deck after being relieved, and Bill strolled on early, so that Kalim's shoulder was never entirely unlooked over. He signed the log and the responsibilities were his, but the other officers were not yet comfortable with him.

Any crew that has worked long together wraps itself snug into a little society—a culture of shared beliefs, customs, legends, and practices. A newcomer never quite fits in, at least not easily and not right away. There are things that went without saying that now must be said; unspoken accommodations that could no longer be accommodated. Like a jigsaw puzzle piece, the newcomer must turn this way or that until he can nestle comfortably.

So the acting first and the acting astrogator posed problems to this unknown in their midst. They ran him through the gamut of the instrument tech's art, from magbeam targeting to Doppler readings to parallax imaging. It wasn't *exercise*, of course. This was a for-profit voyage, not a bleeding nursery school—as Tirasi pointed out—and the problems Kalim worked were all relevant to *New Angeles*'s progress. If, over the first week or so, the results were double-checked by others, the Fudir didn't mind. "They just want to make sure," he told Little Hugh afterward, "that I am what I say I am."

"Sure, there's comfort for you," O'Carroll replied, well aware that the Fudir was not what he said he was. "I suppose when you counterfeited the certificates, you counterfeited the skills that go with them."

"The best disguise," the Fudir told him with a wink, "is yourself."

———

Past the orbit of Ashterath, Jehovah Space Traffic Control passed *New Angeles* on to Platform Number 18 cupped in Ashterath's L5; then afterward to others, until finally the push was taken over by the platforms feeding off Shreesheeva, a superjovian in the outer reaches of Jehovah Roads. Each time the direction of the push changed, Maggie B. took her astrogator's cap back from Tirasi and adjusted the ship's deflection to maintain the flight plan. Artificial intelligences were all well and good, but they weren't the natural sort, and there was always that one percent that could not be left to thoughtless algorithms.

The intelligence perceived only abstract mathematical objects and theoretical approximations. It believed the data it was fed. But magnetic bottles and steering jets and parallax imaging cameras were real objects made of composites and metals and fields, and subject to all the ills of nature. Models only approximate the physical world, especially at the extremes; and the extremes were precisely where *New Angeles* was bound.

By the time she passed the orbit of Shreesheeva, she had achieved a sizable fraction of light speed, and was homing for a hole in space. You can't get much more extreme than that and stay inside the universe.

Which, of course, they would not.

"We call it 'threading the needle,'" Maggie B. told Ringbao one day in the wardroom when she had come below for a bite before turning in. Ringbao had just finished an overhaul to the portside air-scrubber under Hogan's profane direction, and he and the engineer had also come to have a supper. O'Toole was present, too, a shwarma pita in one hand, a small beer in the other, and a flatscreen propped on the table before him which he studied intently.

"Course, both the thread and the needle's eye are

fookin' invisible," the pilot said without lifting his eyes from the flatscreen.

"He means the ship's trajectory and the entrance ramp," Hogan explained to Ringbao.

"Surely, entrance well known," the deckhand said. He had to take care, especially around O'Toole, not to use an Eireannaughta accent, and consequently had been falling more and more into the rhythms of his childhood.

"Well, now, 'tis and 'tisn't," O'Toole told him. "I'm only the pilot. It's Maggie who has to find the fookin' hole in space."

"All them stars," said the ship's hole-finder, "are a-movin' relative to each another, which pulls on the currents connecting them—changes what we call the speed of space—and that means the entrance ramp is movin', too. So, we have to take dopplers and triangulations during the run-up to pin down the position. You gotta hit the dang thing just under light speed, and at just the right angle."

"Otherwise, ye skid," said O'Toole, giving Maggie B. a significant look.

"Skidding isn't good," Hogan added helpfully.

"Not if ye don't have a top pilot t' compensate, it isn't."

"*One* time," said Maggie B. "*One* time!"

"Twice." O'Toole tapped the flatscreen with his nail. "That's why Jehovah Traffic is after giving us the current parameters here—electrical potential, plasma direction, flow rate of space. Your boyo, Kalim, takes the readings, Maggie checks with the astrogation program, and the intelligence computes our heading and speed."

"We'll be on the alfvens by then," Hogan interjected, to show that the power room had everything in hand.

"The square-head there"—O'Toole wagged a thumb at Hogan—"thinks *he's* flyin' the ship."

"Piece of pie," said Hogan.

"I don't know why they were telling me all that," Hugh said to the Fudir later, when relieved by Tirasi, the Terran had come down to the wardroom. The two of them were now alone. "Sure, and I'll never be astrogatin' a starship."

"You were a new pair of ears," the Fudir said, shoving a readymeal of *gosht baoli handi* into the cooker. "Each of them was trying to impress you with how skilled he was, and how he had things well in control. There's a Terran word for it: 'upsmanship.' "

Hugh sniffed the meal's aroma and made a face.

"It lacks the True Coriander," the Fudir said, without even looking up.

"It lacks *something*. What's the 'true coriander'?"

"No one knows for certain. We find it called for in many recipes, but whether a vegetable, a spice, or the flesh of some rare Terran beast, who can say? It was found only on Old Earth and the secret of it has been lost for centuries." With a distant look, he added, "It is all that we have lost, and all that we hope once more to have." He nodded toward the spiral stairs. "On Old Earth," he added, "the intelligence could have handled everything, with no human needed to take bearings or make piloting adjustments."

"Sure, and it must have been a wonderful age, the age of Old Earth," said Hugh.

"It was. We had *true* AI. We had nanotech. A lot was forgotten during the Cleansing."

"Coriander," Hugh suggested.

"We had *science*. Not just engineering, but the real thing. There hasn't been a new discovery in centuries.

Back on Old Earth, we discovered seven impossible things before breakfast."

"It does make you wonder," Hugh said, "how the Dao Chettians managed to overthrow it all."

The Fudir looked disgusted, but the cooker chimed and the Fudir took his lunch to the table and sat across from Hugh. He looked about the wardroom to check that no one else had entered. Then he leaned across and lowered his voice. "January may give us trouble. Upstairs, we were talking about his little adventure. He wants the Twister back."

"Wants it back . . . ?"

"As in, '*you* don't get it.'"

O'Carroll bowed, striking his breast. "So unworthy, signore. Ringbao only simple deckhand. Not understand deep thoughts of elder."

The Fudir looked disgusted, again checked the wardroom, listened for footsteps on the spiral stairs leading up to the control deck. "You know what I mean. If he gets the Twister—the Dancer, he calls it—then there goes your chance to restore the rightful government to New Eireann without another civil war."

O'Carroll turned thoughtful. "I don't know. The first one left a few things unsettled." When the Fudir said nothing, he sat back, very square, and tucked one hand under his other arm, cupping his chin with the latter. "It's like chemistry. Jumdar stopped the reaction before it had gone to completion. Matters hadn't fully precipitated. Jack Garrity already sent one man to kill me. Am I supposed to let that go unanswered?"

"Why? Do you take turns?"

"If I restore the rightful government, Jack has to understand that and accept it." Hugh said "rightful government" without the slight irony that the Fudir usually gave it. Things were always clear in his mind. There was a bright line dividing right from wrong and you were on one side or the other. Yet, as a Terran proverb states, "Ultimate justice is ultimate injury." Justice is metaphysical, more abstracted from the reality of men and women than even the mathematical objects the ship's intelligence pondered, and what is bright and clear in that realm may become muddy and approximate in the lower. To the Fudir, that "bright line" was rice flour drizzled in complex patterns, like the kolams that Terrans drew on their doorsteps. It was not always clear just where the other side was, or even if there was one.

"Are you so certain it was Jack who hired the assassin?" he said.

The hand fell from Hugh's chin. "Who else then?"

The Fudir shrugged. "There's a Terran proverb: 'Absence makes the heart grow fonder.' Sometimes the exiled leader is a better rallying cry than the one who comes back. Prince Charlie was a lot bonnier while he was awa'."

The younger man leaned forward, so that his face and the Fudir's were inches from each other. "My Loyalists . . . !"

". . . may have gotten used to your absence. If you come back, *someone* has to step down." The Fudir was surprised that the scenario had not occurred to O'Carroll. He sat back and, after a moment, O'Carroll did, too. "Don't worry," he said. "With the Twister in your hands, it won't matter what they *or* Handsome Jack think."

"Although it may matter what Jumdar thinks."

The Fudir spread his hands. "Legally, you are Planetary Manager. Jumdar was confused by the chaos she stumbled on, but she's had a chance to sort things out by now. If you press a demand for January's

'Dancer,' she may hand it over, even if it's just to buy
you off. The law is on your side, remember. We'll have
to wait and see."

"That's your plan? Wait and see? Somehow, I imagined something more . . . devious."

"We can try devious; but I'd rather not make plans
before I know the situation. 'A plan is blackmail lev-
ied on fools by the unforeseen.' It's a barn door for
absent horses. It's always based on what you know,
and what you know is always out-of-date. The situation on New Eireann when we get there may be very
different from when you left. If Jumdar's discovered
the Stone's power, that's one thing. But if not . . ." He
reached out and turned the viewer around. "What've
you been reading? *Bannister's Treasury of Prehuman
Legends*. Forget it. Bannister's not reliable. He doesn't
take the stories seriously."

"I found it in the ship's library. If we're going wild
goose chasing, I want to know what the goose looks
like." He pointed to a fanciful drawing of a dun-colored
crystalline creature brandishing a macelike scepter in
its claw.

"The scepter actually looks like a brick," the Fudir
said, "so I don't suppose the prehumans looked like
faceted gems."

O'Carroll turned the viewer back. "Ah. You mean,
legend not true?"

The Fudir nodded to the screen. "Bannister doesn't
have the story of the Twister."

"I know. So far, have only your word legend even
exist, let alone that it true."

The Fudir spread his hands. "Thus raising the subtle matter of trust."

O'Carroll logged off the viewer and put it away.
"Not really. It doesn't matter if I trust you or not.
Either way, I'll be back on New Eireann. Look, Fudir,

I'm grateful you helped out in the alley back then, but you are living a childhood fantasy. Those legends tell us nothing of prehumans, only what we made up *after* we started finding artifacts. The stories don't even fit together. No wonder Bannister doesn't take them literally."

"That wasn't my complaint. I said he didn't take them *seriously*. Think about this: Twenty years *after* Bannister collected those stories, rangers on Bangtop-Burgenland discovered the Grim Chrysalis in a chamber in the Southern Troll Mountains. And a generation later, recreational divers found the Finespun in Lake Mylapore on New Chennai. Half a dozen artifacts described in Bannister's collection were discovered *after* publication. Explain that."

O'Carroll smiled coldly. "Old sage say: 'What man expect, man see.' 'Kalim,' those artifacts were found by people who'd read Bannister, so they saw what Bannister prepared them to see. You're on a fool's errand. And so am I. The difference is: I know it."

Kalim was on deck when they finally lost the push from the magbeams, and Malone, back in the power room, engaged the alfvens.

"Very well," said Captain January, when Kalim had taken dopplers of the beacons in the cooper belt and the intelligence had verified *New Angeles*'s vector and position. "We shall go on watch-and-watch. Remember, it's a ballet out there and the dance is chaos. Bill, go fetch us some sandwiches and drinks. Kalim, go grab some shut-eye. You'll take the second watch with Maggie."

Kalim left the deck with Tirasi. "Remember, it's a ballet out there," the acting astrogator muttered as they climbed down the spiral staircase to the wardroom. "Every bleeding time he says the same bleeding thing!" Of course, it *was* a ballet, and all of the bodies, including the cooper beacons, were in constant motion and ultimately influenced by every other body in the universe—and the equations really were unsolvable. But Kalim did not point that out. It was the iteration that irritated Tirasi, not the fact. "Sleep tight, ye bleeding heathen," he told Kalim in the wardroom. "You're up in four—and don't you bollix my instruments." With that, he grabbed a basket of sandwiches that Ringbao had prepared, two cups of coffee, and climbed back up to the control deck.

Four hours later, Kalim relieved Tirasi and, shortly after, Maggie B. relieved January. The captain glanced pointedly at the chronometer, but said nothing. Maggie handed Kalim a cup of coffee and settled herself into the command chair, sipping a second. "Get me a position," she said when the first watch had gone. "Let's see how far off true Old Two-face let us drift."

Kalim did not react to the gibe. From what he had seen so far, January was a rather competent shiphandler. He checked the log to find what benchmarks Tirasi had shot—Larsen's Star and the Giblets—and set up the parallax cameras to take fresh images for comparison. He ran the diagnostics, judged the results acceptable, and downloaded them to the stereograph so the intelligence could calculate the parallax, and from that their direction relative to the fixed sky.

Maggie queried the intelligence, which recommended a slight course correction. "Not too badly off," she admitted, entering the correction in the astrogator's log. "Maybe because Annie isn't here to distract him."

Kalim sensed alien ground involving the captain and the two women in the crew. He and Ringbao were aboard for the free—and anonymous—passage to

New Eireann, not to take sides in the crew's internal squabbles.

"Adds up, y'know," Maggie told him, perhaps responding to his silence. "The divergence. The least bit off'n true at this point and we'd miss the entrance. Or worse, we'd go in at too dang sharp an angle. It's gotta be normal to the cross section. Better to miss and come back 'round than to skid going in, an' . . ." She came to a halting stop, then fiddled unnecessarily with the log. A furrow formed on her brow, a deep fold between her eyes, as if someone had struck her with a chisel.

"I understand completely, ma'am," Kalim said.

"Do you," Maggie B. said curtly. She shook off the study into which she had fallen. "Get me a Doppler shift on the Eye of Allah—and let's check our speed."

During the last day before entering Electric Avenue, the watch was continuous and the crew took catnaps when they dozed at all. January was always on the deck, although he deferred to Maggie B. for the astrogation. She, for her part, switched from screen to screen on the computer as fast as Kalim and Tirasi could feed her the data. The stellar spectra had blueshifted as the speed of the ship approached the speed of the medium whereby they measured it. The stars in the forward viewscreen crowded together and actually seemed to recede the faster the ship moved. Visible light slid off the scale, and the sensors shifted to infrared. Ringbao, with no specific duties, ran food and drink to the deck and to the power room, where Hogan and Malone tended the alfvens.

An hour before entry, Slugger O'Toole appeared, fully rested and sober, and took his place in the pilot's saddle. "How's the fookin' groove?" he asked of no one in particular. "Ringbao, d'ye have any more o' that tay?"

Maggie B. told him that the trajectory was within five degrees of normal to the entrance. O'Toole nodded and placed an induction cap on his head. Ringbao handed him the cup and he took a long swig of the hot liquid. "I'll see yez when I see yez," he announced, then inserted his earphones and pulled down a pair of black goggles. Ringbao, who had always traveled as a passenger before and had never seen an entrance actually being made, stood in the rear and watched everything with fascination.

Tirasi took a final set of parallax views of the weirdly distorted sky. The intelligence computed the ship's bearings and Maggie ordered a final course correction. Her hand hovered over the red slap-button, ready to snatch the last string in the fabric of space and yank the ship over the threshold should the intelligence fail to act.

The chronometer clicked, Ringbao glanced up at the sound, and—he missed the transition. When he looked again at the forward screen he saw nothing but a blur of xanthic light. January called out, "Status?"

"In the groove," said Maggie.

"Alfvens spinning sweet," reported Hogan from the power room.

O'Toole, cocooned in his headgear and in rapport with the ship, said, "Minor skidding. Nothing I can't handle."

And as slick as that, they were sliding down the Grand Trunk Road.

Now, Shree Einstein once said that nothing in the universe could move faster than light; but like many gods, he spoke in oracles. On one hand, nothing could be *seen* to travel faster than light; for such an object was moving faster than the medium by which it was seen, and an ancient superstition holds that "out of sight is out of mind."

On the other hand, if the universe is composed of all those parts that can be perceived, a superluminal ship is no longer *in* the universe. Instead, it voyages in those blank regions of the map in which men once wrote "Here there be dragons."

So just as a world includes parts unseen as well as seen, the universe is more manifold than subluminal instruments reveal. Yet, the limits still apply. In the superluminal creases, the ship did *not* move faster than light, *relative to local space*. It was space itself that was moving. After all, space is not itself a material body, and so not subject to the limits placed on matter. Not even Shree Einstein could tell Shree Ricci to hold still.

January hosted a dinner in the wardroom to celebrate their entry onto the Grand Trunk Road. "Here's to a successful slide!" he announced, holding aloft a glass of Gladiola Black Saffron, otherwise known as Old Thunderhead, because it delivered maximum impact at minimum cost.

"An' the end o' th' fookin' crawl," O'Toole seconded him.

Tirasi twirled the stem of his wineglass between thumb and forefinger. "How smart is it to leave the bleeding control deck unwatched?" he asked. By the roll of the eyes around the table, Ringbao judged this was not the first time he had raised such an objection. He wondered if anyone on this crew ever said anything that the others had not heard unnumbered times before.

O'Toole favored the Queensworlder with one eye. "We're in the fookin' groove, boyo. Dead nuts center in the tube. Won't need a tweak for another tin watches, by th' drift."

Tirasi sighed elaborately. "We have to trust your judgment then . . ."

O'Toole reddened. "My judgment *and* the intelligence's!" Too late, he saw the trap. The words were flown!

All innocence, Tirasi turned to January and said, "As long as an *intelligence* concurs."

January snapped, "Enough of that!" And Tirasi sat back, puzzled and hurt; for in spite of many years in which he might have learned better, he had thought the captain smiling at the joke.

Neither Ringbao nor Kalim had joined in the laughter at Tirasi's trick. Little Hugh thought there was too much malice in it, and he preferred to save malice for when it was genuinely needed. The Fudir, for his part, preferred no distractions from his quest, and becoming embroiled in these petty squabbles was no part of his plan. But Tirasi had heard the two newcomers' silence, and since he could not chide his own captain, turned to the deckhand. Kalim was sitting between Tirasi and Ringbao, so Tirasi had to lean past him to address Ringbao.

"You disapprove, Ring-o?"

"So sorry," the deckhand answered. "Queensworld humor so subtle."

Tirasi made a fist. "Do you know why they call me 'Fighting Bill'?"

Little Hugh studied the fist, looked in the acting astrogator's eye. "Because you cannot control temper?"

O'Toole burst into laughter. Hogan and Malone traded smirks. Captain January smacked the table. "I said, Enough!"

"Do you want a piece of me, mate?"

Little Hugh shook his head. "Too many pieces remain when done. Not able to choose."

Both O'Toole and Malone went blank, but Maggie B. understood right off. So did Tirasi himself, who clenched his teeth and glared at Ringbao. But he hesitated. Perhaps he saw something in the deckhand's face. Perhaps he saw the Ghost of Ardow, for there is a gulf between those who brawl and those who kill, and the Ghost waited on the far side of it. Tirasi backed off, glancing at Kalim, who had been calmly eating his stew the while. "Aren't you going to help your mate?" he asked with belligerency false in his voice.

The Fudir blinked and looked up as if in surprise. "Why? Does he need help?" There were little knots of anger at the corners of his jaw, and a certain unexpected hardness had crept into his voice. The others at the table fell quiet.

And January, in particular, regarded his two new hands more thoughtfully.

Later, the Fudir visited Little Hugh in his cabin, and shutting the door on them both, he grabbed the younger man by the front of his coverall. "Don't ever do that again!" he said in a whisper more terrible than a shout. "Don't ever let them see anything more than a simple deckhand!"

O'Carroll pried the Terran's fingers loose. "I didn't like the way Tirasi was picking a fight with Slugger."

"You didn't like it?" The Fudir shook his head. "*You* didn't like it? Did anyone ask that you should? The only one who had to like it was O'Toole, and in case you didn't notice, *he did*! He and Tirasi have gone round on round since the cows came home. It's a ritual with them. Malone takes bets, and everyone clucks in disapproval. So you keep your nose out of their business."

Little Hugh shook his head. "No, there was a meanness to it. You're making it out less than what it was."

The Fudir shoved him on the chest. "This from a man ready to throw an entire world back into civil war because he lost his job in a hostile takeover."

Little Hugh seized the Fudir's wrist. "Careful, old man, or I'll break you in two."

But the Fudir only relaxed and said mildly, "We shouldn't quarrel with each other." The words were meek enough, but they sounded oddly like *Do you really think you could?*

Now *there* was a new and sudden thought! Little Hugh released the Terran. "You're not as old as you look," he said in wonder.

The Fudir grunted and turned to the door. "Don't get in any fights with Tirasi. January may have sensed something. Try to be a bit more invisible. That was your specialty wasn't it? Didn't they call you the Ghost?"

"I know disguises."

But Hugh's response was ambiguous and the two parted company, and each considered what the other had revealed.

Electric Avenue lay along the geodesics, and so was straight as a rule. It was the rule that was warped and twisted. In the groove, everything was always dead ahead. O'Toole checked the ship's centering at intervals, but the only exciting moment came a week and a half out, when Cerenkov turbulence signaled the bow wave of a vessel sliding down the road in the opposite direction.

Since a ship on the Avenue was, in a certain sense, nowhere in the universe, no two ships could ever occupy the same place. There was thus no danger of superluminal collisions, only a slight buffeting by ships passing in the light. Now and then, O'Toole corrected for the slight deviations these caused. "But this time," he swore, "it musta been a fookin' *fleet*." The wake had slewed the ship to the side of the channel, close to the subluminal mud.

Nothing he couldn't handle, however. O'Toole dismissed the turbulence offhandedly, although Little Hugh found him afterward in the wardroom with a strong drink in his hand and a disinclination to conversation. Even January appeared almost concerned, his perpetual smile flattened nearly to horizontal, and something long and extremely angry had been entered in the ship's log.

"They ain't supposed to enter the Avenue so close together," Maggie B. explained when Ringbao had asked her. "Creates a passel of problems for the oncoming traffic." But when he pressed her on how close things had gotten, she only smiled and told him not to worry. That worried him.

"Why?" the Fudir asked when O'Carroll brought the matter up. "'A miss is as good as a mile.' Always a lot of traffic on the Grand Trunk and sometimes it just bunches up. No point worrying over it. January will file a squawk with STC New Eireann."

But when they exited the slipstream and yanked themselves into Newtonian space, they found STC New Eireann off-line, and the magbeam cushions failed to catch them.

Hogan swore mighty oaths and shifted the alfvens into reverse, braking the ship by snatching at the strings of space as they fell inbound from the exit ramp. The whine rose to a teeth-rattling pitch that filled the ship and put everyone on edge. Despite the refit at Gladiola, waste heat made the power room nearly unbearable and Hogan and Malone could take only an hour inside before emerging, sweat-soaked, to pant in the corridor outside and worry whether the containment field would take the strain.

"How bad is it?" Ringbao asked Maggie B. as she headed for the control deck to relieve January.

"Not now, Ringbao," she answered him.

New Angeles had braked without magbeams before, but this time they hadn't been expecting it and hadn't been prepared for it and could ye get out o' th' fookin' way, Ringbao!

It was hours before the tension eased, a little; and days before anyone relaxed. By then, Kalim had harvested enough off the radio to understand what had happened to the world they were approaching. A fleet of rievers had overwhelmed Jumdar's planetary police, pillaged New Down Town, and looted everything they could break open.

"Aye, that's bad cases, that," January said, but his mind was on the difficulties of shedding velocity without the magbeam cushions. Lacking the ephemeris from New Eireann STC, Maggie B. and Bill Tirasi and Kalim extrapolated from the ship's previous visit to identify the markers on which to take their bearings. They cursed the rievers for their troubles. Several days passed in this manner, during which time a few magbeam platforms did come back online. But the world toward which they fell was too busy binding up its wounds to worry much over an inbound tramp. Passing below the orbit of the Dagda, *New Angeles* secured her first long-distance visuals and they could see orbital factories tumbling like children's toys broken and flung aside.

O'Toole fretted, for he had been "bread-and-buttered" in the Vale, and though he had gone and flown, the places in his memory did not lie quiet. "There was a girl there," he said to Ringbao over a brooding bowl of uiscebaugh. "In Fermoy, it was, and I fancied her some; and I wud av married her but that she didn't 'prove me dhrinkin' av the creature. Ah, 'tis the wimmin an' not the alfvens what drive a man to space. An' now Kalim sez Fermoy's been . . ." He did not finish the thought, but took a drink while Little Hugh O'Carroll fought to stay within the shell of Ringbao della Costa. He laid a hand on the pilot's forearm.

"Maybe girlfriend okay," he forced his persona to say, his words wrung out of any hint of how deeply he himself felt about the world he had once helped manage.

O'Toole shook his head. "That was years ago . . . She's long forgotten me. I thought I'd long forgotten her."

AN CRAIC

The harper frowns in dissatisfaction. "And what is the point of that tale? That to journey hopefully is better than to arrive? I hadn't thought you capable of such banality."

It is difficult to know when the scarred man smiles. His lips hang down the curve of his chin like an old sock thrown across a chair-back. "Why do you think anyone has arrived, or that they have journeyed with any hope?" He laughs. "But let them have their moment."

The harper says nothing, but her mouth hardens. "Your humor is too cruel," she says at last. "I think it has poisoned the story." She stands to go, but the scarred man's words, projected somehow by the geometry of the alcove, seem to whisper by her very ear.

"Where can you go to get the story, poisoned or not? Those who were in it are scattered, gone, or dead. It's our version you'll hear, or none at all."

She picks up her harp case and slings it across her back. "Don't be so sure, old man. I did not come here unschooled. Your lips are not the only ones that tell this tale."

The scarred man lifts a clawed hand, as if begging. "Don't go," he says. It might have been a plea had it been said with more feeling; but there is little of feeling left in him and so it sounds more like a command. "Stay a while longer, for our loneliness."

The harper shifts the burden on her back and half turns. But there are things she wants to know, questions she still needs to ask, and so with ill grace, she relents. "I will stay awhile longer—for your madness," she tells him, and resumes her seat.

"Play me the journey through the creases," the scarred man says. "I want to see what you make of it."

The harper remains silent for a time. Then she bends over and retrieves the harp from its case. "The slide down Electric Avenue has been played before," she says, "but perhaps there is one more variation on that theme." Her fingers dance and notes swirl with almost superluminous speed. "I've always liked the image of the alfvens plucking at the strings of space," she says over the glissando. "Space travel is rather like playing the harp."

"Perhaps," says the scarred man, "but the alfvens move the ship and . . ." He pauses, then smiles. "Ah."

The harper shows her teeth and the arpeggio rushes into a desperate decelerando, slowing into a steady orbital rhythm whose measure is the "long line" of an ancient island poetry, and finally settles into a La-ment for the Vale of Eireann so broad as to blanket a world. A drinker nearby cries out, "Oh, God!" and turns himself weeping aside. Others there are who hang down their heads or brush away tears at their cheeks.

The Bartender leaves his post and crosses the room to confront them. He says, "People come here to for-get their sorrows, and not to have new ones added." He gives the scarred man a sour look. "How long will you sit there? People think you're part of the staff—or part of the furniture."

"I'm waiting for someone," the scarred man says.

"Oh, you are? Who?"

A shrug. "Don't know yet."

The Bartender purses his lips, but the amount of disapproval he can muster is as nothing to that nor-mal to the scarred man's countenance. "Another round," the harper says, and the Bartender turns his gaze on her. "Try to play something more cheerful," he tells her.

"I'd think that music that moves a man to drink would be more welcome here."

"You'd think wrong." And he turns away and re-turns to his post with large strides. Shortly after, a serving wench arrives with fresh bowls of uiscebaugh.

"I'm surprised he hasn't thrown you out long ago," the harper tells the scarred man. She sips from her bowl, then frowns and regards the bowl with disbe-lief. "Either he is serving better whiskey now or I've lost the tongue for the difference."

"He serves the worse drinks first, hoping to dis-courage the drinking. But most who come here can't tell the difference anyway. Ol' Praisegod won't throw

us out. I'm one of the afflicted he's supposed to comfort." His laugh is rough and broken, like shale sliding down a high mountain slope. He raises his bowl
in salute to the Bartender, who affects not to notice.
"Ah, he wouldn't know what to do with himself if we
weren't here every day. I'm his freakin' touchstone,
I am. The one constant in his life. We're—"

The scarred man falls suddenly silent and his eyes
widen. "No. You can't," he says between clenched
teeth. He grips the table edge, first with one hand,
then the other, and seems to vibrate like a plucked
string of the harp. The harper watches with alarm and
turns in her seat to see if the Bartender has noticed.

The harper's sudden movement has drawn his attention. He looks at her; then past her to the scarred
man; until, with a mirthless smile, he shakes his head
and returns to his business.

He has seen this before. Ill-comforted by that
thought, the harper turns once more to her companion,

And he is preternaturally calm. "Ready for the rest
of the tale, darlin'? I warn you, there are parts of it
that can't be spoken of, even yet. But those are the
parts I like best telling."

The harper frowns. There is something strange about
the withered old man. Something odd in his voice, as
if he has just remembered something important. Or
forgotten it.

"The thing to remember about a pursuit," he says
easily, "is that it always takes longer when you're
chasing. 'A stern chase is a long chase.' "

The harper grunts without amusement and plays a
few lines from a courtship dance on Die Bold. Sur-
prisingly, the scarred man recognizes the tune and
recites a few words.

"I fled him down the labyrinth of my mind
And hid from him with running laughter . . .

"*'The labyrinth of my mind,'*" *he repeats more
slowly.* "Aye, maybe *courting* is the answer." *He looks
at the harper and his smile is this time almost human.*
"It wasn't always a courting song, you know. It's
from an old poem from ancient Earth."

"You were speaking of a chase," *the harper says a
little abruptly.*

*The scarred man appraises her, as if wondering what
she* is *chasing down the labyrinth of his mind. Then,*
"A chase. Yes. Though no one quite knew it." *He
slouches in his chair and waves an arm.* "Come then,
harper, attend my tale."

GEANTRAÍ: THE STERN CHASE

T he Corner of Jehovah is a bad place to be," the
scarred man says.

. . . since one must find his way in and find his way
out, and neither is an easy thing to do; although more
do manage the first than the second. Without the aid
of the Terrans, it is close to impossible. But help need
not be voluntary, nor even witting, and to each rule
there is an exception.

The exception stepped into the bubbling activities
of the Tarako Sarai, that broad open market space
where Menstrit curves off shamefacedly toward the
reputable parts of town (shedding its name in the
process and becoming born again as Glory Road).
The monorail, three streets, four winding alleys, and
twelve decidedly twisted pedestrian walkways con-

verge there. To the west, Port Jehovah stretches nearly to the horizon, and tall, graceful ships gleam ruddy in the early-morning sun as if wrapped in goldbeater's foil. In every other direction, the topsy dwellings of the Terran Corner teeter over the edges of the market.

Cubical stalls made of dull composite disguised with bright pastels line three sides of the sarai. Each stall abuts its neighbors, save where walkways from the Corner squeeze between them. The west side facing Menstrit and the Port is open, and there are situated the monorail station and a carpark for ground vehicles. Before the sun has even angled into this plaza, the dukāndar-merchants have, in a rattle of chains and counterweights, heaved up steel stall-front doors, calling to one another and wishing good luck or ill as their competitions dictate. The stalls are openfront, with chairs and benches and racks within arranged as required for the best display of their wares.

Overnight, lighters and bumboats from Port Jehovah off-load the orbiting ships and bear groundside exotic arts and jewels and foodstuffs from far-off worlds. Much of this cornucopia makes its way to the Tarako Sarai, some of it legally; there, to be snatched up by eager, early-rising Jehovans, anxious for a taste of the foreign. Eager enough indeed to dare the very edge of the Corner to get it.

Later, ferry boats drop and off-load the travelers— the sliders, the world-hoppers, the touristas—gawking and pointing and capturing images and pawing through the merchandise for bargains and native handicrafts. They dress wrongly—for the climate, for the world, for the time of day—and their bodies throb off-synch to the tock of shipboard time and not to Jehovah's sun. As they enter the sarai, the bustle increases, and with it the markup on the goods. Isn't this *cute*, couples and triples ask each other. Those booths look like storage sheds or little garages. Is that a *magician*? How does he do that with the *snake*? Oh, I didn't know the human body could *bend* like that! Is that a legtrikittar they're playing over there? How strange! How strange!

The market speaks to them. Ah, yes, sahb, this is the True Coriander, known no-but else place! Seven ducat only, and that is that my children go hungry. See, here, come into my stall, when you see ever so fine 'shwari, look good-good on memsahb. Oho, *not* memsahb? Then, here you find special double-throw silk, made only on J'ovah, think how this feel on her skin . . . ! Hutt! Hutt! No mind his silks. See here my drizzle-jewels, how they sparkle so? Genuine from Arrat Mountains.

In the center of the market, push-carts peddle, performers sing and juggle, and food vendors hawk their smoking barbecues and searing tandoors. Is hot day, you like kulfi-kone, eye-said krim, most excellent! Pull-pork! Koofta kabob! Hoddawgs! Winnershnizzle! Pukka Terran food, you find him nowhere else!

But *you*, sahb, I make it five ducat fifty.

A wink, a lowered voice, a proffered discount, and Gladiola Bills and Shanghai ducats waft magically from purse to poke. And if the promise "Product of Jehovah" is no more genuine than the discount, little harm is done. Even in the ricochet ruckus of the starport sarai, some things are never said. Some of the "Jehovan" wares that leave with the tourists on the upbound ferries had arrived but a short while before on the downbound lighters. Why pay duty for so short a stay?

"Mango kulfi-kone," one of the thinning horde asked of the sweets vendor, who heaped a waffle-cone with two scoops of the rich iced-milk, holding it out and saying, "Half ducat, sahb."

"For two such paltry balls? A quarter ducat would be too much."

The vendor's eyes lit. *This* sahb was no "slider" but, by his long, fringed kurta brocaded with yellow and red flowered borders and with the amber prayer beads wrapped round his wrist, a Jehovan merchant from the City. No Terran, to be sure, but he knew his manners. "It grieves me that I cannot offer it for less than forty-three. The fruit alone costs such much, and I must pay the women who cut it."

"Thou pay'st them too much. See how small they have diced the pieces! Thirty might be generous for such slovenly knife-work."

"Bakvas, shree merchant! The smaller the pieces, as all men know, the greater the flavor. Forty." Their voices had risen, as if in argument, and some of the sliders looked at them askance and edged away. *You never can tell about* those *people*.

"Thirty-five!"

"Done!" the vendor cried in vehement agreement. He extended the cone with one hand and offered the other.

"There can be no handclasp with only one hand," his customer recited, and offered the firm grip of a Jehovan, rather than the limper Terran grip. A few coins changed possession, neither man so boorish as to visibly count them. As God is One, a man who cannot count his money by the heft and feel of it should seek another work!

The vendor watched the merchant reenter the crowd, pause at the kabob-maker's stall, and—and another customer asked for a kulfi-kone, and paid the half ducat without banter—aye, as if the vendor were but a *bisti* worker—and when the vendor looked again, the Jehovan merchant had vanished.

Each market day, after the sliders have gone and the dukāndars have twice tallied their accounts—once for themselves, and once for the men of the Jehovan Purse—and the shutters have rattled into place and lock-bars dropped home, the collectors of the Terran Brotherhood drift into the market. A man watching could not say at any moment, "They have come," but suddenly they were there. Men and women, plainly dressed, mingled with the vendors and whispered a few words here and there, and a portion of the ducats and bills and Jehovan shekels were transferred to the coffers of the Terran Welfare and Benevolent Fund. The food vendors donated also such of their goods as remained at the end of the day; and these were carried off immediately to shelters and kitchens in the Corner. What happens to the hard currency no one has ever asked.

One such collector was named Yash. He had entered the market first, using a crack in the back wall of the vacant handi dukān through which a lithe man could slip. Old Nancy Verwalter had made the finest hand-phones in the Corner, but she had died two years before and the back wall of her dukān had been opened with picks and pry bars.

A few loafers squatted about the plaza, and these Yash studied with grave interest. It was not unknown for agents of the Jehovan Purse to audit the market in the hope of squeezing one more shekel from the dukāndars. Their grooming and clothing usually marked them out, but some were more clever and knew how to blend in.

A few men, disinclined to visit the charity kitchens,

had begged cuts of meat or a few samosas or a sandwich from the vendors sealing their coolers and boxes and extinguishing their fires. One such man lounged against the wall of the shoe-dukān, where he nibbled on a pita. His kurta was a plain, dingy white, lacking any brocade or fringe. Satisfied that the market was unwatched, Yash spoke a few words over his handi and soon his runners emerged from a variety of waypoints to circulate among the merchants of the Tarako Sarai.

Yash did not leave his post while the runners gathered and brought him the harvest, but continued to monitor the market. At a few quick signals, his people could vanish.

The sliders thinned out, anxious to catch the next ferry up. The bum with the pita must have finished, for when Yash glanced that way again, he was gone. A hand signal: *Hutt! Hutt!* If the market thinned too much, his collectors would stand out too prominently, should any Pursers be about.

Finally, the take was complete. Yash counted it quickly and inconspicuously, then divided it into four equal parts, giving the other three to Bikram, Hari, and Sandeep. "By different routes," he reminded them. On the other side of the hole in the back wall of the handi dukān, a wonderful array of options presented itself.

Yash himself took to Jasmine Way, which wound crook-legged past the Mosque of the Third Aspect with its prominent rooftop observatory and where "the Submissives" prayed standing with their faces turned to the sky. There, a bare-chested man squatted in a ragged dhoti and Yash dropped a dinar in his cupped hands, careful to pull it from his own scrip and not from the bundle hidden under his blouse. Dividing the take into four parts ensured that all would not be lost if a courier were robbed or arrested—much of a muchness, in Yash's opinion—but it also ensured against a pettier form of thievery: The four parts must still equal one another when they were delivered to the Committee of Seven.

Yash's path to the Seven was not straightforward, but the starting point and ending point were fixed, and there were certain theorems in topology, unknown to Yash, that could be solved by a man learned in such things. Thus, as he made his way past the Fountain of the Four Maidens, through the narrow colonnade beside Ivan Ngomo's pastry-dukān, and even up Graf Otto's Stairs, of which none but those born to the Corner know, Yash did not particularly remark the variety of men he chanced upon: beggars, holy men, idlers gazing in display windows, a customer at a knife-kiosk, a man signaling in vain to an auto-rickshaw, a messenger brushing briskly past him only to turn back sharply at some forgotten task. Yet, a closer inspection might have noted a curious resemblance of feature among some of them.

The Seven—who were now six in number, one having found it safe to emerge from the wind—had expected four knocks upon their door, as each runner arrived. The fifth took them by surprise. Eleven knives slid quietly from their sheaths, Bikram being ambidextrous, and the Memsahb nodded to Sandeep, who was closest to the door.

The heavy wooden portal was thrown open and bounded against the wall and—

There was no one there but an old sweeper garbed in a grimy dhoti tucked up at the waist, and brushing with a hand-jharu at the leaves that littered the outer colonnade. He blinked at the sudden opening of the door and pushed erect. "Ah," he said easily and with none of the deference expected of custodians. "Those of Name greet the Seven of Jehovah."

And he smiled with all his teeth.

The Seven were disturbed by this unexpected advent. "It's been long since the Secret Name has called on us," said the memsahb chairman. Yash and his crew had been dismissed and only the Committee now sat. The courier looked around the room with studied disinterest. He seemed more at ease than he should have—there were the lime pits by the Dunkle Street ghauts, after all—but those of the Confederation were an arrogant folk and even their servants strutted like masters.

"So long that ye have forgotten your duties?" the courier asked. He styled himself Qing Olafsson, but no one in the room supposed it his true name. Years of silence—and now two had come in as many weeks, each bearing the same office-name. The Memsahb knew some unease over this, as of raindrops quickening before a coming storm.

"Dere gifs no dooty," one of the Committee said. But the Memsahb placed a hand on his arm and he fell silent. Qing thought her a hard woman, and all the harder for her pale appearance. White hair, white skin—she wore a white chiton, too. Such a hue betokened something soft and gentle, like snow or cream, not this hard-edged ceramic.

"What my colleague means," she said in a grandmotherly way, "is that our homeworld is your hostage."

"And thus your obedience more assured," Qing answered, and he noticed how eyes narrowed and lips pressed. No more than two of them might be willing servants of the CCW, he thought, had willingness any weight.

"But not our love," said another member.

A shrug did for the old proverb. Let them hate, so long as they fear.

And what was asked was a simple matter, a mere nothing. No betrayals were required; no deaths demanded. "I have an ears-only message for Donovan," he said. "You need only point me in his direction. A handshake, an introduction, that is all."

"An' why air ye needing this Donovan?" asked another council member. "Sure, he swims deep, and does not surface for trifles."

Qing smiled. "That is a matter between him and the Secret Name. Best if none know what is to pass between us."

The Memsahb placed her hands in a ball on the table before her and leaned slightly over them. "There is a problem."

"I am grieved to hear it. Does this problem come with a solution, or must the Secret Name speak with the Dreadful Name?"

Oh, they flinched at that! And some looked to the door. Couriers oft traveled with companions should their messages be ignored. If the servants of the Secret Name were the Confederacy's eyes and ears, those of the Dreadful Name were its hands and fists.

"Tscha!" said a dark-haired woman who had not spoken previously. "What are we owink to League? We live in corners, like rats. Tell him of Donovan."

The Memsahb had not turned to look at the speaker, one of those Qing had previously noted as genuinely sympathetic to the Confederacy. Now she said, "Yes. Donovan lives deeply, as I've said. His world is tangent to ours at only one point: a petty scrambler. He uses this man to contact us, and we use him. There may be further links in the chain. This man—he calls himself the Fudir—may only know someone who knows someone." She smiled with a tight horizontal smile. "I understand contact is more secure that way."

And indeed it was. One cannot betray a man unknown. Qing shrugged. "If it is a tangle of yarn and Donovan is at the other end, thy duty is to hand me the loose strand that leadeth to him. Where may I find this 'Fudir'?"

"That's the problem," the Memsahb told him. "He's gone off-world. A small misunderstanding between him and the Jehovan rectors. He's 'in the wind,' we say, and set no date on his return."

"And where might this wind have blown him? Those of Name have little patience. The longer the path to Fudir, the longer the path to Donovan, and the shorter our patience. It is only the end of the skein that matters. Thou art of no account. The Fudir is of no account. Other links are of no account. *Thou art nothing*; Donovan is everything. The sooner thou sendest me on my way, the sooner I cease to vex thee, and thou may'st return to thy petty thievery and scrambles."

"If we are servink Names faithfully," the dark woman said, "they allow us return to Terra?"

Qing waited without speaking.

Finally, the Memsahb bobbed her head. "He's gone to New Eireann."

"A small world," Qing said, "yet big enough. There is no Corner on New Eireann, but a man in hiding finds no shortage of holes."

"He has gone with another, the former Planetary Manager, overthrown by the ICC."

Another of the Seven spoke up. "Dey hope to find . . ."

But the Memsahb cut him off again. "The Fudir always has his plans, but they do not interest *shree*

Qing, here. But however hard the Fudir may be to find, the return of the O'Carroll of Oriel will surely create a storm, and at the epicenter of that storm, you will find what you seek. O'Carroll will lead you to the Fudir; the Fudir will lead you to Donovan—or to the next link leading to him."

The Memsahb seemed to derive some amusement from this. The courier had heard the ancient and obscure Terran phrase—*make him jump through hoops*—but there was no help for it. A metric week out and another back; but with no firm date for this Fudir's return, waiting here would take longer. The Fudir must be sought where he had gone.

Qing decided that the Seven knew no more than they had told him. He rose and bowed over his folded hands, as Terrans were wont to do, though it was a shallow bow to indicate his estimate of their status. "I thank the Memsahb for her assistance in my task and assure her that the Secret Name will learn of her devotion to the Guardians of Terra."

"Guardians!" said the first man in a voice of contempt.

"You are tellink them of our help," said the second woman, "and our yearnink."

Qing said, "The Powerful Name undoubtedly has His reasons for what He does or refrains from doing. Wise men are merely thankful for His wisdom." He bowed again, this time a sardonic nod of the head, and was out the door.

When the Seven hurried to the door and threw it open, the colonnade was empty. There was no sign of the courier, neither straight ahead, nor to the left, where the portico turned and ran down a flight of covered stairs to another level. Crisp leaves rattled across the paving in the autumnal breeze. A hand-broom stood propped against the balustrade.

"Dat makes two," said Dieter. "How many more messengers have the Names sent?"

"May he never come again," said another, who spit on the paving stones.

"Fool," the dark-haired woman scolded him. "Co-operation is our only hope of beink allowed to return."

The Memsahb shook her head almost imperceptibly. "No, perhaps the Fudir was right about the Twisting Stone. Longer chances have won the game. Come. Back inside. There are still the accounts to review, and it grows chilly out here."

Greystroke emerged after they had gone and, brandishing his anycloth, became once again a pilgrim seeking the Mosque of the Third Aspect, to be guided unwittingly out of the Corner by helpful Terrans. As he hurried off down the covered stairs, he wondered what the Memsahb had meant by "the Twisting Stone." There was something familiar there, a passing phrase, a similar term; but it did not come clear to him.

At Graf Otto's Stairs, he paused. He was being watched—an odd feeling, one he was unaccustomed to. But the sound of footsteps echoed his own. He bought a kebab from a street vendor, and took the moment to gaze idly about. He did not expect to see anyone, and his expectations were granted.

The Other Olafsson, he thought. The Seven had mentioned a previous visitor. The second courier's duty was to monitor the first, and if he failed to carry out his mission, execute him and take his place. The servants of the Dreadful Name were quite as skilled as any Hound, and more so perhaps than even a senior Pup. *Interesting*, he thought. If the Other knew that he was not in fact Olafsson Qing, he might never reach his ship alive.

He quickened his pace, and turned an unexpected corner, reconfiguring his anycloth as he did into a different pattern and cut. He wore once again the brocaded kurta of a prosperous dukāndar-merchant.

Shortly after, he heard the footsteps again.

While Greystroke simultaneously sought one trail while trying to lose another, Little Hugh O'Carroll tried to grasp the Rieving of New Eireann. The physical damage was simple to inventory; the psychic damage, more difficult.

There is a subtle difference between a world that has been ravaged and a world that has been ruined. There are no physical parameters for it; there is nothing that can be measured or tested. It can be seen not in the manner and extent of the devastation, but in the faces of those devastated. The Eireannaughta had gazed once before on a burnt and gutted Council House; but before it had been with grim determination. Now it was with slumped shoulders, and something seemed to have receded from behind their eyes.

Unlike the Rebels and the Loyalists, the Cynthian rievers had come neither to change the world nor to preserve its hallowed institutions nor even to suck the teats of its commerce. Even the ICC owned that much interest in the worlds they managed. One of their corporate maxims was: *If the people get rich, you can steal more from them.* The Cynthians had come only for "pleasure and treasure." They took as much of both as they could, and not all the ruins they left behind were buildings.

A surprise attack across Newtonian space has a paradoxical feature: The defenders receive plenty of warning and yet can do little but wait. Once off Electric Avenue, the attackers must brake to co-orbital speeds, and even with the outsized alfvens all warships carry, this requires several days. But the same cruel dictates of Shree Newton limit the defenders' ability to intercept the incoming fleet. Long before the Cynthians reached New Eireann, Colonel-Manager Jumdar knew there was nothing she could do to stop them.

Not that she contemplated surrender. Her database assured her that among the pleasures the Cynthians sought was the pleasure of combat. They were a folk for whom adjectives like "brutal" and "ruthless" were accounted compliments; and nothing so outraged them as a foe who would not fight. Those who surrendered were treated more harshly than those who were defeated—which is not to say that either was treated very well.

Jumdar's two ships—troop transports for her rump-regiment—were only lightly armed; and no help could be expected from their home base at the Gladiola Depot, or from Hawthorn Rose, where the remainder of the regiment had gone to complete the original contract. Long before help could arrive from either system, the pirates would be done and gone.

So it would be the Eireannaughta police boats and Jumdar's two battalions, presently scattered in peace-keeping posts the length of the Vale of Eireann. At her urgent broadcast plea, veteran Loyalists and Rebels stepped forward to defend the Vale and were issued arms from the ICC armory. Handsome Jack was brevetted Major, First Battalion of Volunteers, and given charge of this ragtag group. He immediately advised the colonel to strip the Mid-Vale of troops and to concentrate them in Fermoy and New Down Town. There was little to attract loot-hungry rievers outside the two large cities. They hadn't come to milk the cows in the Ardow.

"And put your troops under cover," he added.

"These Cynthians will put their own surveillance in orbit and will drop steel rain if they see anything needing it."

"We must be," added Voldemar O'Rahilly, who was senior-most of the Loyalist contingent, "as hard to spot from orbit as was the Ghost of Ardow."

To Jumdar's surprise, Handsome Jack Garrity had nodded and said, "If only he were with us today." But he and the O'Rahilly were still thinking in the old tropes, in the old fashion of a wild and wonderful donnybrook. They were still thinking of fighting *for a cause*. They were not prepared for the utter careless-ness of the Cynthians.

After they had left, Jumdar sat at her desk, stroking the Dancer and calling orders to her two battalions—one to gather in Fermoy, the other in New Down Town. Her staff identified map coordinates where each company could take cover, parking garages and groves of trees under which armored cars could hide. (The heavies had gone to Hawthorn Rose.) Units were placed close enough together for mutual sup-port, but not so close that their mobilization would be evident to overhead surveillance. Compliance was swift and unquestioned.

Then, all there was to do was to wait for their doom.

"And so it went," Tomaltaigh O'Mulloy explained to Little Hugh as they stood before the smoldering skel-eton of Council House. Around them clustered the leaders of the Loyalist underground, the remaining Rebel leaders, and Major Chaurasia of the 2nd Bat-talion, 33rd ICC. The fires had cooled, though there was still a residuum of heat from somewhere deep within the ruined structure that revealed itself in streamers of dull gray smoke. An evil smell shrouded the place, a heavy body of bad air composed in equal parts of metal, wood, plastic, and human flesh.

"I've never seen the like," the ICC major said. "I've never seen the like." He had said this several times already, and Little Hugh wished he would shut up, say something useful, or at least something different. The wind shifted and the thin, foul smoke wound around them. Kerchiefs emerged to cover nose and mouth. Men and women coughed, backed away.

"If only ye'd come back sooner," O'Mulloy said. He was an old Oriel supervisor who had taken Eireannaughta citizenship before the coup.

Little Hugh didn't know what possible difference that would have made; but he did not rebuke the man. He did notice that Voldemar O'Rahilly stood a little to the side with his beefy arms crossed over his chest and his golden hair flowing past his shoulders. He had been remarkably cool to the sudden reappearance of the Ghost of Ardow, and Little Hugh remembered what the Fudir had said on Jehovah before their departure.

"Sure," said Handsome Jack, who stood to Little Hugh's left. "He waited until it was all over, and now he comes in to pick up the pieces."

"Here, now," said the ICC major. "We'll have none of that." But the threat was spiritless and he no longer had two hale battalions with which to enforce it. Eventually, that would occur to both Eireannaughta factions.

"The only thing," Handsome Jack growled at the ICC major. "The only thing you were supposed to be good for was protecting my world—and look what you've let happen!" The injustice of the charge showed in the major's basset-hound gaze, and Hugh quite suddenly desired to take him in his arms for comfort.

"Not quite the triumphal homecoming," said Voldemar, as if speaking directly to the ruins, as if Hugh were not standing beside him. Hugh remembered how he and Voldemar and Sweeney the Red had spent a long, rainy night in a tumbledown ecologist's station on the Crooken Moor, where basaltic granite thrust up through the terraforming bogs, and a Rebel death squad had combed the countryside for them. It hadn't seemed possible then that three men could grow closer than they had that night. Sweeney moaned softly on a cot, his head wrapped in bandages where a sword cut had lopped off half his nose. Voldemar stood by the hut's door, glaring out over the trackless black waste. They had not dared strike a fire. *We'll make it*, Voldemar had said then with fierce conviction. *The Glen's just past the end o' these bogs.*

And so they had. But now . . . What had happened? *Have ye grown too fond o' the leadership, brother Voldemar?* Or had the Fudir's cynicism wriggled like a worm into his own heart, so that he saw treachery now where there was only anger and despair.

"They split her chest open," Major Chaurasia said, again speaking as if to ghosts. "Down the breastbone with a cutting laser, and then they pried the rib cage apart and spread the lungs out over them. They looked . . . I saw her later, after. They looked like wings . . ."

Two in the knot of people around Little Hugh covered their mouths and ducked quickly aside to retch.

"Called the Blood Eagle," said the Fudir, who had not been present a moment ago. He had gone off to the field hospital on some purpose of his own. Now he was back.

The ICC major looked at him. "Blood Eagle," he repeated witlessly.

"It's an art form among the Cynthians. They even have special instruments to perform it."

"Art." The idea was incomprehensible. The major shook his head. "Why punish her for defending the world as best she could?"

"It wasn't punishment," the Fudir explained. "It was tactical, to take the will out of their enemies." Looking around at the Eireannaughta, he added, "I'd say it worked." Then, in a lowered voice, he whispered to Hugh, "I found what she did with the Dancer."

"They used it more than once," Handsome Jack murmured. "That . . . Blood Eagle." He was a one-eyed man, now, as well as a one-armed one. "Not only on Jumdar . . ."

Little Hugh turned away from Council House and looked down the slope of Council Hill to the smoldering ruins of New Down Town.

"They set fires," said O'Mulloy. "Sometimes, they didn't even loot a house first. They simply torched it. For no reason."

"They had a reason," the Fudir told him. "It was fun."

"But," said the major, "what profit was there? To come, what, fifty days' travel from the Hadramoo? And for what?"

"They didn't come for profit," the Fudir told him. "They came for honor and glory."

The major drew himself up. "Honor . . ." But then he seemed to deflate. "There's no profit here anymore. That's a certain thing. The orbitals the Cynthians didn't smash and loot are being abandoned. O'Carroll, would you take some of the factory personnel back to Jehovah on your ship? I've sent a swift-boat to Hawthorn Rose to call back the rest of the regiment, but . . ."

"It's not my ship," O'Carroll told him. "Ask January." But that sounded too callous, so he added more kindly, "I'm sure he'll take as many as he has room for."

Later, Hugh met privately with Handsome Jack. No one was quite sure who held the management contract anymore. The ICC was going to break it—both men had read that in the major's eyes. *There's no profit here anymore.* But did that mean automatic reversion to House Oriel? Or was the contract, as some said, "up for grabs"?

They sat across from one another at a broad table in the old ICC factor's residence. Cargo House had been looted along with most everything else in the capital. Pale outlines on the walls marked where paintings, watercolors, and digitals had once hung, and Hugh thought he remembered, from an earlier visit in another era, a chemical sculpture in which substances of changing hues and various densities had writhed snakelike in a tank in the corner. But the ICC building had not, withal, been burned, as so many others had. And there were even a few chairs that had not been reduced to splinters and scraps of fabric. The table had once been polished to mirror-finish—it was red gristwood from Nokham's World—but too many boots had scuffed it in the looting and a twisted, puckered scar ran where a laser had burned a vulgar word in the chief language of the Hadramoo.

This had been the factor's dining hall, Hugh remembered. *Imported Gatmander salmon on plates of Abyalon crystal. Candlelight and sandalwood, and in that corner, a blind Terran pandit had played an evening rag on a santur.* There had been no factions then. Or at least the factions had not yet made themselves known.

Earlier that morning, a larger meeting had sat around this table. The United Front for the Restoration of the Vale—a grand name, but no one had wanted to defer to another, and so it had been less full of decisions than of discussions. Hugh had kept silent throughout most of the proceedings. On-planet only a few days, he did not know enough about the current state to say anything useful. That had not impressed the Loyalists at the table, who had expected that their legendary leader would sweep away all problems with a few wise words. And on those few occasions when he did speak up, the Rebel faction had expressed their utter lack of confidence. Major Chaurasia had tried to impose order, but lacked the will to do so effectively.

"One thing I'll say for the old bitch, Jumdar," Handsome Jack Garrity said, now that the others had left. "She could lead. People hopped to when she spoke, not from servility, but because she inspired." He ran his hand through barley-brown hair. "Chaurasia knows how to carry out orders, but damn me if he knows how to give them."

Little Hugh steepled his fingers. "It will take me a while to get 'up to speed,' but . . ."

"We don't have the time for your fookin' learning curve, lad. People are hurting *now*."

"I know that! We need to get a clear picture of the As-Is state and a vision of the Should-Be state and imagine the change-path that will get us there. Jack, we heard a report today on milk and grain from County Meath—but how accurate was it? Will there be enough to feed New Down Town? How will we get it here? Has anyone worked out the logistics, mobilized lorries and floaters, set up an Action Plan?"

"Mebd's teats!" Jack slapped the tabletop, earning a splinter for his pains from the broken wood. He sucked at his palm as he spoke. "This isn't one of those fookin' management exercises they taught you at boot camp. There were relief lorries on the High Road out of the Mid-Vale before the rievers had jumped down the Avenue. The rievers didn't touch the farm counties. They hadn't come to rape sheep. Or maybe they just didn't have the time. Maybe the lorries hadn't been fookin' *mobilized* and nose-counted by the fookin' authorities, *but they were on the fookin' road!* What would you do if there weren't enough of them? Send them back? Pick volunteers to starve? My people will send all they can spare, and a little more—and they didn't need the Planetary Manager to tell them how much and where. *Damn* this splinter!" He sucked again on his palm.

Hugh rose and crossed the room, coming to stand by Jack's side, where he drew a knife. Jack regarded him with quickly suppressed alarm; but Hugh seized his hand and spread it flat, palm side up, and with the point of his knife worried out the splinter. He handed the slice of wood to Handsome Jack. "*Now,* can we focus on the subject?" He spun the knife one-handed and it slipped neatly into its scabbard.

"Am I supposed to feel all warm and grateful, now that you've pulled a splinter from my paw? Thank you, but it doesn't work that way."

"I don't care if you're grateful or not. We shouldn't have a disputed leadership when there's a world needing reconstruction."

Jack picked up the splinter and studied it. Hugh watched how dexterous he had become with only one arm, and wondered that he didn't wear a bionic one. Or maybe he did, but preferred to use his infirmity in public. "We didn't have one," Jack said judiciously, "until a few days ago."

"He means before you came back."

Handsome Jack and Little Hugh turned to face the back of the room, where a bookcase had slid aside to reveal a hidden doorway in which the Fudir stood. Behind him, a flight of stairs spiraled downward.

"Who in Lugh's name are you?" Jack demanded. "You keep popping up, but . . ."

"It's gone," the Fudir told Hugh.

"He's a Terran I met on Jehovah," Hugh said. "He helped smuggle me back here."

Jack took in the Fudir's worn, dun-colored clothing, the stoop-shouldered stance. "I've you to thank, then."

The Fudir bowed and tugged his forelock. "I point out, sahb, that zero divided by two is no less than zero divided by one."

Jack's face puckered up as he considered that; then he laughed. "You've a lot of nerve for a fookin' Terran." Then he pointed a finger at Hugh. "Keep in mind what I've said. What you and I had, that's history. It's all songs now. We don't need you showing up now to add a discordant note. I liked you better as an enemy than an opportunist. And tell your *Terran* friend, we shoot looters."

The Fudir grinned. "Hast thou heard from the Red Sweeney, yet?"

"Sweeney?" Jack said in irritation. "No friend of mine. He's one of your lot." With that, he folded his data-slate and stylus, tucked it under his one arm, and marched from the room.

When he was gone, the Fudir grunted. "There's your answer."

"Which one? That Jack didn't send Sweeney, or that he lies so well? I take it that the Dancer is gone. How can you be sure it's not hidden somewhere?"

The Fudir tossed his head toward the stairwell. "It was. That was the hidey-hole."

Hugh followed the Terran down the staircase. "You've been busy," he said. "Jack thinks you're looting."

"He thinks the Molnar left any loot?"

"It's not a joke." But the Fudir had pressed on ahead.

At the base of the stairs lay a broad room lined with shelves and storage racks that had been tumbled about. A contour chair, attached to a post embedded in the cork-soft flooring, had been slashed and the frame bent. It faced a wreath on the farther wall. Debris was everywhere. The walls were made of a spongy material through which ran twisting veins of pallid yellow. Cartons and strongboxes were cut or pried open, their contents vanished or smashed. The vault door at the far end of the room hung twisted on one hinge.

"They were thorough," Hugh said. Somehow the despoiling of the ICC vaults did not move him as much as had the destruction aboveground, though he knew some wealthy Eireannaughta had kept their valuables stored here rather than in Down Bank and Surety.

"I found Jumdar's aide-de-camp in the field hospital, the poor beggar," the Fudir explained. "He said they tortured her until she told them where the Dancer was; then they fashioned the Blood Eagle. They made him watch the whole thing—and burned his eyes out afterward so Jumdar's body was the last thing he'd ever see. He doesn't understand why they let him live." Fudir stepped into the vault and looked around at the empty racks and safe-deposit boxes. "That's because he doesn't understand the depths of their cruelty. He said Jumdar brought the Dancer down here personally. That was a mistake. People began to question her orders after that. Not the ICC folk, who were oath-bound; but the Volunteers, who thought their experience with assassination and mob violence gave them an insight on military strategy. Not that Jumdar was a military genius, and not that it mattered. They should be thankful—Voldemar and Jack—that the Cynthians hadn't come to *occupy* this world. Your guerilla campaign only worked on the Rebels because there were boundaries neither of you would cross."

Hugh stepped around a shattered wooden box lined with chesterwood and decorated with enough artistry that it might have been worth something in itself. He lifted a paperboard sheet. A pallet separator, he thought. "I didn't think there were too many boundaries left, at the end."

"Did either of you target women and children?"

Hugh looked up sharply, let the separator fall to the floor, dusted his hands. "No."

"Pull one of your ambushes on a Cynthian, they don't even try to track you down. The next day, they round up a dozen civilians and kill them. I take that back. They don't recognize the concept of a civilian. If you try again, it's two dozen. How long would you have pressed your campaign?"

"You know a lot about them."

"I looked them up in *Fou-chang's Gazetteer of the Spiral Arm* while *New Angeles* was coming downsystem."

"Why bother? They're long gone."

The Fudir came out of the vault. "Clean as gnawed bone," he said. "No question Jumdar gave it up. It's on its way to the Hadramoo."

Hugh had paused before a large sculpture attached to the wall. A wreath of ceramic composite tendrils that twisted and twined around one another in a complex pattern that his eye could not follow. He turned away and stared at the Fudir. "Oh, no. You're not thinking of chasing this fable into the Hadramoo, wherever to hell and gone that might be."

"North-by-spinward of the Old Planets, out near the Palisade," the Terran replied with a cheerful grin. "Don't worry. I wasn't thinking of a frontal attack on Cynthia. And you needn't come with me."

"Oh, needn't I? Thank you. I thought we were hunting the Dancer because it would help me restore the rightful government here."

The Fudir shrugged. "You never believed that. You told me so yourself."

"Yes. But I'd wondered if you believed it."

"By the time I can fetch it back from Cynthia, it'll be too late to matter much here. Beside," he added quietly, "there are other worlds needing their rightful governments restored."

And there always had been. Hugh did not voice the comment; there was no need to. It had always been a mistake to trust the Fudir. He'd never had expectations from this far-fetched scheme, so he ought not feel betrayed.

"The rievers didn't take everything," Hugh said, pointing to the wreath on the wall.

The Fudir, who had been standing with his head slightly bowed, looked up, blinked. "Yeah, I noticed it earlier. It's the Ourobouros Circuit—not the original, a replica. Too much trouble to rip it off the wall, I suppose; though not for lack of trying. You can see the marks from the lasers and the saws. Not worth stealing. Look, if you want to come with me to the Hadramoo, you're welcome."

The invitation startled Hugh and he cocked his head. "Why?"

The Fudir shrugged. "It's a barbarous region, and I could use some civilized company."

The harp thunders savage chords and the men and women in the Bar of Jehovah sing and roar with it. The harper has abandoned her table with the scarred man and resumed her place in the corner. Fists pound tables; voices join in chorus. She stops, and voices boil in protest. One more! Just one more! The Bartender watches with approval. This is more like it! Geantraí. Something glorious and triumphant to lift the spirits!

But, instead, she gentles them with suantraí; for a horse ridden hard must be cooled afterward by a hot-walker. Peaceful strains soothe excited nerves; tones of bliss bless dreamy joy. These, too, the Bartender regards with favor, so the harper improvises a transient motif from the goltraí solely to wipe his smile away with a finger's brush of loss and desolation. But it is a trick sorrow, not the real thing. The Bartender sees that it is a joke, and grins across the room. They understand each other. She closes with a rollicking march and once more the spacers in the Bar respond with stamping feet. But it is lagniappe and she has gentled them and now when she rises from her stool, they let her go.

The scarred man is waiting in his alcove with a smile she had not thought his face capable of making. "You know how to work them, darlin'," he says with admiration. "There is something of the Dancer in you, I think. You command, and they respond. Is that why you play? For the sense of power?"

"You confuse consequence with intention. My talent lets me pluck their hearts with my own nails, but I don't play to play with their hearts."

"I should hope not," says the scarred man. "Nails leave scars."

The harper turns and makes a sign to the Bartender. "I'll play once more before I go."

"Yes. It's hard to put the scepter down." He smiles as if at a secret joke: his lips stretch and his eyes turn inward.

The harper thinks suddenly that her companion might have been a handsome man in his youth, before what had happened happened, and that within this sour old man had once lived a sour young one. (Sweetness was something she would not credit.) Almost, she asks what tragedy had reduced his body to such ruin; and she forbears only because prowling old ruins can be dangerous. They are full of deadfalls and uneasy masonry; and wild things have crept inside.

"So the Fudir did believe in the Dancer, after all," she said.

"Why suppose he believed in anything?"

"No one chases off to the Hadramoo on speculation. I confess, I thought at first he wanted only high-level access on New Eireann for some criminal plan—a 'scramble,' they call it—and Hugh was his tool to gain it."

"And the legend was his tool to gain Hugh? No, the Fudir was as twisted as the Dancer, but in those days there were still a few things he believed in. If one belief was a mad fancy, what of it? Tell me you've no mad fancies. Tell me you'd no other motive in coming here than to pick the tale of the Dancer off my teeth."

The harper does not answer for a while and she brushes her strings gently with the back of her nails and they sigh in glissando. "And what of January," she says. "Surely, he had more right to the Dancer than the Fudir."

But the scarred man shakes his head. "What has

right *to do with any of it? If only they'd wondered about the chair; or if Hugh hadn't had, as the Terrans like to say, 'a big mouth.' "*

"What chair?"

The scarred man signals the bartender for another bowl. The harper is paying, so why not? *"One player is nearer his goal, at least,"* he says when the drink has been delivered.

The harper cocks his head. *"You mean Little Hugh?"*

The scarred man laughs.

SUANTRAÍ: DOG DAYS

You may recall, the scarred man says, taking up the tale once more, *that Fir Li had called to Hounds . . .*

. . . with the thought of penetrating the Confederacy, to confirm on that end what he had sent Greystroke to confirm on the other. But Hounds are few and space is large and travel through the creases sufficiently slow that in the three and a half metric weeks since he had sent the call only three Hounds had proven near enough to respond.

The first to arrive was Grimpen, who by chance had been passing through Peacock Junction when the swift-boat sang its summons. He was a large, rough-hewn man who resembled nothing so much as a nickel-iron asteroid garbed in colorful tunic and pantaloons. Yet he had remarkably soft and gentle lips and an easy way about him. His colleagues regarded him as "slow and ponderous," although he preferred the term "methodical." If Fir Li was a fleet wolfhound straining at the leash, Grimpen was more the St. Bernard: careful, helpful, resourceful, intelligent. Not the sort on whom to bet in a race—unless the race were one of endurance.

A few days later, Francine Thompson arrived from Wiedermeier's Chit, where she had just resolved a string of serial murders by a man calling himself "the Delphic." Breezy, and confident to the point of arrogance, she used the office-name of Bridget ban, and she strode the gangways of *Hot Gates* like the queen of High Tara. Her hair was red and her skin was gold and she was living proof that deadliness could decorate. She had a voice like the bursting sea—rushing and crashing and with just a taste of salt.

A week after that, Gwillgi passed through Sapphire Point on his way to the Lesser Hanse and, intercepting Fir Li's broadcast, decided to lay over and consider the matter. The problem that awaited him on Hanower was important, but not urgent, and might already be settled by financial auditors before Gwillgi arrived with Plan B. In either case, the suspect would be brought to accounts. Gwillgi was a banty man sporting a thin moustache, and seemed somehow to be wound from razor wire. He did not grow hair so much as bristles, and his eyes were a deadly topaz in color.

Fir Li did not think that any others would appear soon enough to matter, and so he called a pack meeting shortly after Gwillgi's arrival, sweetening the affair with a fine board of wines and fruits and dates and a main course featuring a roasted haunch of satin tiger, prepared after the fashion of Valency with a chutney of mangoes and chilies. The crew of *Hot Gates* gave the Hound's quarters wide berth, for much of what transpired within was not for outsiders to know.

In theory, they were a band of brothers, anatomy notwithstanding, but neither competency nor collegiality can entirely overcome ambition and human nature. The four Hounds who gathered in Fir Li's private suite after the meal respected one another and worked with one another, but they did not always like one another, and kept one eye focused always on their own advantage. They were reluctant to accept orders from a peer; so, Fir Li fell back on logic and reason.

Logic might have persuaded Bridget ban—she was the sort for whom a well-constructed narrative is worth a thousand detailed facts, and on occasion she was known to discard a fact or two to save the narrative; but Grimpen was a man unimpressed with theories. From any finite collection of facts, he was fond of saying, one may construct an infinite number of theories, and the probability approached zero that any one of them was true. As for Gwillgi, fact and theory alike meant nothing; the deed was all.

"Why don't you go in yourself?" Gwillgi asked Fir Li. But the dark Hound waved his arm broadly, encompassing *Hot Gates* and her squadron beyond the hull, patrolling the exit ramps of Sapphire Point.

"I would. But I'm committed to this duty. And I've been across before. Some there might remember."

"We all have duties," Gwillgi replied, "save Grimpen, here. He seems at liberty."

"We don't even know," rumbled the big man, "that your disappearing ships are more than a statistical anomaly." Having arrived first, he had already reviewed the data.

"I showed you the analyses," Fir Li protested. With his left hand, he crooked a finger and a junior Pup approached with a flagon of channel wine from Greatthorp. Fir Li held his cup out. Both Gwillgi and Bridget ban eyed the boy speculatively. Gwillgi ran a nail—it was very nearly a claw—along the lad's forearm as he passed. Fir Li, seeing this, chuckled. "You won't fluster him. I've taught him the falconer's art."

Topaz eyes caught the light. "You launch falcons aboard *Hot Gates*?"

Grimpen rumbled like an earthquake, signifying laughter. "He didn't say that." But turning to his host, he said, "You yourself admitted the conclusions were subject to an alpha risk of . . ."

"O! dear, large Grimpen," said Bridget ban, who drank nothing but water. "Were the world an equation, we'd ha'e solved it ere now."

"Nonetheless," Fir Li insisted after an appreciative sip, "we've reason to suspect that ships crossing into the Confederacy disappear too often. Now we've intelligence that the Confederacy harbors the same suspicions about ships crossing into the League."

"What of the second courier?" asked Grimpen. "I assume there was one."

Fir Li shook his head. "Hanseatic Point saw nothing unusual. I haven't heard from the farther crossings. If there was a second courier, he likely made the crossing as a crewman on a freighter, jumped ship once over here, slipped surveillance, and hijacked a small ship to use. I've sent out a request that any recent hijackings of personal yachts be reported to my office."

"If your fish was sent in order to be caught and spill disinformation," said Gwillgi, "why bother sending a second?"

"And why would they spread such disinformation?" Bridget ban asked. "I mean, that *particular* disinformation? Suppose we were to believe it. How does the Confederacy benefit?"

Gwillgi scratched his chin with his forefinger. "The ICC and the Chettinads and the rest grow spooked about crossing the Rift. Stop sending ships across. Fewer nosy strangers, hey?"

"Our trade ships may dock only at Gaphavn," Grimpen pointed out, "and their movements are tightly controlled."

Gwillgi struck the arm of his chair. "Then the Confederates are doing something at Gaphavn. Don't want us to know!"

"Then they've only to abrogate the Treaty," said Bridget ban. "They'd nae let our ships in aforetimes, and need no ruse to be keeping them out once more."

"Blather," said Grimpen. "It's pointless to speculate on Confederate motives for doing something before we're quite sure they're doing it. Either Olafsson's mission was genuine, or it was disinformation. Start from there and ask what facts you'd need to—"

Fir Li turned to his door, where stood Graceful Bintsaif, who was senior Pup now that Greystroke was on the scent. "Yes."

Bintsaif bowed. "Your pardons, Cuin," she said, and turning to Fir Li, "Cu, the commodore has asked for you. His pickets report the Cynthian fleet returning."

Fir Li cocked his head. "And this interests me, how? Must I listen again as the Molnar mocks the Ardry and the rule of law?"

"Cu, the commodore said to tell you that they number only half as many ships."

Fir Li drained his glass and placed it on the salver proffered by the junior Pup. "Now, *that* is interesting," he told the other Hounds. "A pirate fleet going and coming is no great thing in these wretched times; but a fleet going and half a fleet coming—*that* has a story."

Fire Control greeted Fir Li when he entered the command deck deep within *Hot Gates* by saying, "*Now*, can I take them? They've only ten corvettes, and each badly damaged."

"Not yet, Fire Control. Let's hear the story first."
He nodded to Commodore Wildbear, who had replaced Echeverria in the rotation. "Bring the alfvens
to standby."

"Cu?"

"Which word was unclear? Do it. Comm, compress this and squirt. *Cuin,* if you would, stand within
the field of view. Thank you. Record. 'Cynthian ships,
this is ULS *Hot Gates,* Cu na Fir Li commanding.
State your business.' End."

Several minutes went by as the message packet
penciled out to the Silk Road exit. Overhead, Traffic
Control displayed the positions of the ships as they
crossed the high system to the Palisades Parkway.
Red lights indicated the observed positions; green
lights, the projected real positions, corrected for vector and Newtonian light-lag. Fir Li told Fire Control
to show dead lines. "One for kinetic weapons; one
for energy beams. Localize to ship-centered coordinates, by ship."

Just in case. Fire Control grinned. Commodore
Wildbear scowled. Technically, the commodore had
operational control of the squadron, but *Hot Gates*
was Fir Li's personal property and he sometimes forgot the protocols, or pretended to.

When the reply came from the Cynthians, the Molnar put on a brave front. "Hey, doggy, you got yourself a reg'lar pack there. Just on my way home, now,
me. Don't want no trouble. You keep watching for
Confederates, okay? And better watch that Silk Road
exit, too—might be followed, me."

"So, your victim proved too tough a nut!" Fir Li
tried to show that he was trying not to smirk.

Lag-and-reply and: "New Eireann? Naw, they was
pussies. Like the sages say: 'The strong take what they

can, and the weak suffer what they must.' Was ambushed at Peacock Junction, Deceiver take 'em! Ever see a ship hit caltrops at high-v, you? Shredded my vanguard coming off the ramp. Took the damned Twister, after all the trouble we went through to fetch it."

This time Fir Li did not try to hide the smirk. "The strong take what they can," he answered philosophically. Gwillgi, behind him, began to laugh, but Fir Li waved him silent and awaited the Cynthian's reply.

"Don't be such a smart mouth. Fight anybody, me; and if I lose, I lose." He actually struck his chest. "Gods decide. But sneakin' *ambush,* that's no fight. Hey, doggy, they come through the Road after us, they make recycle outta *your* punky squadron."

And they would have the Twister. Fir Li pondered that for a moment before he formulated his next squirt. "Did they know about the weapon when they took it?"

"Weapon? What weapon?" The Molnar's replies came faster as his ragged flotilla approached perihelion with Sapphire. "Oh! Naw, that Twister was just some old prehuman rock. The ICC factor on Cynthia was fulla crap."

Fir Li relaxed, a movement undetectable to any but his colleagues and senior Pups. The idea of a new weapons system had worried him, but . . . Only an artifact. Valuable, to be sure, but *only* valuable.

Before he could respond, the Molnar added, "They musta had a spy in the New Eireann system what sent a swifty through the Road ahead of us, 'cause nobody else knew we even had it. They laid for us at Peacock, hijacked the loot, after *we* did all the work gettin' it! They took a whole treasure ship, doggy. Matched our course, boarded, demanded the Twister."

A bitter, sly look came over the Molnar's face. "Some-day, I find those hijackers, me. Then we show them Cynthian justice."

"Justice!"

"Yah, justice. That's where the boss gives everyone what they deserve; an' these hijackers deserve everything I'm thinking to give them."

Fir Li was astonished at the man's wink, as if he and Fir Li were partners complicit in the same enterprise. "And what of *the Ardry's* justice?" he demanded. "Should *he* give out what everyone deserves?"

The Cynthian ships were accelerating toward the Palisades Parkway, approaching the dead line for kinetic weapons. Fire Control turned with an appeal on her face.

"He can try," the Molnar told them. "A man has whatever power he can grab."

Fir Li said, "I will take your advice." He nodded to Fire Control, and the ships of the Sapphire Point squadron unleashed a timed barrage, each ship firing her kinetics so that all would arrive simultaneously on-target.

It was exquisite pleasure to watch the image of the Molnar khan Matsumo first puzzle over Fir Li's comment, then a moment later react to his watch officer's cry. "Oho! Doggy wants to bark," he said, and he ordered counter-battery fire.

The Cynthian fleet dispersed at high-v, adding jitter to their projected course. Targeting computers guessed at likely course alterations, compensated, and fired again even before new images had been received. Sensor images were seconds, or even minutes old, so Fir Li's ships had to fire at where the targets would be, based on glimpses of where they had been. Only ULS *Justiciar* was close enough to see the Cynthian corvettes in "real time," and flashes on the display showed where her weapons found the alfvens on two corvettes slow to maneuver. Crippled, the corvettes skated off onto the Newtonian flats at the system's edge, unable to grab space and slow down.

A third Cynthian jittered too much and entered the Palisades at the wrong angle. A hoop of false color on the overhead screen highlighted the Cerenkov radiation that marked its disintegration. A fourth Cynthian encountered kinetics loosed earlier by ULS *Victory*. "Cu," said the battle-space manager, "*Justiciar* has taken damage." Fir Li nodded. Close enough for precision fire, she had been close enough to receive it. Grimpen leaned toward him to whisper.

"What can we do for *Justiciar*?"

Fir Li said, "Nothing. Once the dice are cast, they tumble as they will. No one manages a high-v battle space."

Comm called out, "Cu!" and Fir Li saw the snarling face of the Molnar fill the screen. Behind him, his control room smoldered, alarums clanged, and men and women rushed to their tasks. "Now, doggy, you see how a *man* dies! Aye-yiii!" And with that cry, he cut communication. A minute later, Traffic announced that the Cynthian flagship had changed course.

And a moment more, the new course had been extrapolated. "He's coming directly toward us, Cu. He means to ram."

"So *that* is how a man dies," murmured Bridget ban.

Gwillgi grinned. "You have to admire his style."

"How long before he reaches our position?" Fir Li demanded.

"At that speed, he can't turn on a dinar," Traffic said. "He has to shed his tangential velocity. But once he's normalized, no more than twelve hundred beats. No, he's accelerating. Make that eight hundred beats."

Wildbear ordered *Hot Gates* to shift station, but

Fir Li countermanded the order. "Belay that," he told the helmsman. Wildbear spun to confront his commander.

"Are you as mad as they say? We have to jitter. He's got the gravity gauge on us."

"Which means, Commodore," Fir Li explained patiently, "that a small angular adjustment on his part will compensate for even a large shift by us. We must wait as long as we can before jittering."

"But . . . the inertia! *Hot Gates* wants time to move herself. We have to start acceleration now!"

"Thank you, Commodore. I was utterly unaware of that. Tracking, how long before impact?"

"Seven hundred, Cu, if he continues to accelerate at the present rate."

"Traffic, give me a deadline. Cuin," he addressed his colleagues, "the Molnar may have the gravity gauge, but we have topology. We know his starting position and we know his intended final position; namely, right . . . here." With his foot, he sketched an X on the deck. "Therefore, we know the sheaf of coordinates along which all his weapons must track. Shields, see to that. Kinetics will be coming in rather fast, and I'd rather they not swiss my ship."

Traffic displayed the deadline. "If the Cynthian passes these coordinates," he said, "we cannot move the ship in time."

"Aye," Fir Li answered with a fierce grin. "But if we shift much before he reaches that line, he can simply tap his helm and compensate."

"An exquisite problem in geometry," said Bridget ban. "I can see only one solution."

"Have you ever watched a bullfight on Riftside Andlus?" Fir Li asked her. "There is a maneuver called—"

"A Veronica," supplied Bridget ban. She stood with arms crossed and legs akimbo. Unlike Grimpen and Gwillgi, she had sought neither seat not handhold.

"You may want to strap in," Fir Li advised her.

"For such a closing speed? Sure, the straps must be uncommon strong."

Fir Li quirked a smile. "Weapons," he said. "Fire caltrops. Give him something to think about."

"At these speeds," Grimpen commented, "thinking isn't even in it."

"Even if we swiss him," Wildbear objected, "his ship's mass will continue on the same trajectory."

"Grapeshot off," said Weapons. "But his mag fields are up. He'll deflect most, and the ceramic ones will just glance off his glacis."

"Did I ask for an opinion, Weapons? The Molnar may have the faith in his defenses that others place in the gods, but he cannot help being distracted for a moment."

"A grossbeat," said Tracking. "Approaching deadline."

"Time flies," said Gwillgi, "when you're having fun." Fir Li grinned but did not turn to him. The point was to distract and not be distracted.

"Power, set alfvens for two leagues."

Wildbear reared up. "Alfvens? You *are* mad! We're too close to the sun!"

"Commodore, you are relieved. Gwillgi, would you indulge me and take custody of Hideo Commodore Wildbear?" The small, wiry Hound did not move, but grinned at Wildbear. The grin was sufficient hold, for the commodore glimpsed his teeth.

"Incoming kinetics," announced Counter-battery. "Engaged." *Hot Gates* shuddered as the fields absorbed the impacts and slewed them around the ship. A thud high above the command deck signaled an airtight door closing.

"Breech on E-17," said Damage Control. A ceramic striking at high-v had pierced the ship like a needle through butter. Muted chimes summoned the damage party to E-deck.

Fir Li said, "Power. At deadline, engage alfvens. Two-league jump, random vector outside the sheaf. Enter."

"Entered," said Power; and Ships rang the chimes that announced upcoming alfven yanks: short-long, short-long, over and over.

"If you knew more of Alfven Theory," Fir Li heard Grimpen tell Bridget ban, "you'd not be so calm." But he was answered with laughter like breakers on an empty strand.

The visuals had grown insensibly coincident with real-time positions. The "grab hold" chimes sounded and the alfvens snatched whole handfuls of the threaded fabric of space and yanked *Hot Gates* violently aside. Too late to compensate, the Molnar's corvette was past almost before they saw her coming and she dopplered downward into Sapphire Point itself.

"At that velocity," Traffic observed, "she can't vector aside before . . ."

The command deck fell silent, watching while the Cynthian ship fell toward the sun. She tried to maneuver, but the gravitational field of the blue giant pulled her insistently. For a time, it seemed as if she might make it anyway, perhaps only graze the photosphere. But then something happened—it was not clear what—and all attempts at maneuver ceased.

It was a long fall. Even at near-light speed, it was two more watches before the Cynthian ship had been finally engulfed by the blue giant, and another two before they saw it happen on the screens.

Long before then, Fir Li had left the control center, giving command back to Commodore Wildbear. "I'll expect damage reports for ship and squadron, and an accounting of the Cynthian ships as well. At least three succeeded in making the Palisades." As usual, he had been watching everything.

The commodore could not conceal his surprise at being returned to command, but before he could speak, Fir Li had spun on his heel. "Graceful Bintsaif."

"Yes, Cu."

"You know what to do."

"Yes, Cu."

And with that, Fir Li and his colleagues left the command deck, Gwillgi sparing one last smile for the commodore.

"What does Graceful Bintsaif know what to do?" Grimpen asked when they had returned to Fir Li's quarters.

Gwillgi answered in Fir Li's place. "Why, to take command of the ship should Wildbear show further weakness."

"He was only showing caution," Bridget ban said.

Gwillgi's laugh was like broken glass. "That's what I said."

Grimpen poured himself a tumbler of channel wine from the pitcher on the sideboard and drank it empty before pouring another. "A hard fate," he said. The others knew he meant the Molnar and they all glanced at the clock to see how much longer before Shree Newton accepted this new sacrifice.

"He loved it," said Bridget ban, "the Molnar did; or didn't you notice. When he turned to give orders to his watch, I saw that he was hugely aroused."

"He certainly tried to fuck us good," said Gwillgi.

"And it was a madman's chance," said Fir Li, who

had entered his quarters last of all. "That's why I knew he would try it, or something like it."

"Yes," said Gwillgi. "I noticed. You brought the alfvens online as soon as you entered the command center. You meant to destroy him from the first." Gwillgi approved, of course.

"And what you did *wasn't* mad?" suggested Grimpen. "There's a reason no one engages the alfvens this far down the gravity well. Can't you smell the burnt insulation, the tang of overheated ceramics and melted metals and plastics? *Hot Gates* isn't going anywhere soon."

Fir Li shrugged. "I hadn't planned on going anywhere. Damage Control is at work. If needs be, *Justiciar* can order materials and components. I'm sending her off-station for yard repairs, so she can carry any requisitions with her. But I hope our own stores and shops can repair things."

Gwillgi had drifted to the viewscreen and adjusted the coordinates until Sapphire Point seethed and churned in the center. "I wonder," he said. "At the speed he was going, he could be out the other side of the star before the temperature and pressure could matter."

Grimpen shook his massive head. "A star may be nothing but hot gases, but at those speeds, it would be like hitting a stone wall."

"A stone wall," murmured Bridget ban, looking upon some childhood memory. With a part of his attention, Fir Li caught that momentary lightening of her features, and would have thought nothing of it, except that she closed up immediately after.

"Radiation will have cooked him long before," Gwillgi said.

"Well," said Grimpen, placing his drink on the sideboard. "I'm off to the Old Planets."

Gwillgi turned from the viewscreen and cocked an eyebrow. "There, you think?"

The man-mountain shrugged. "Perhaps."

" 'Tis tae Peacock Junction, I'll be going," Bridget ban announced. "Someone thought enough of this Twister to be taking it from the Molnar; and the Molnar came all the way from the Hadramoo to fetch it off New Eireann. Perhaps I can catch the scent of this black fleet there."

"Yes," said Grimpen. "All the way from the Hadramoo."

He knows something, Bridget ban concluded. *Or he thinks he does. But we'll see who gets to the root sooner.* She gave Grimpen a pleasant smile and wondered if the other Hounds even knew the tale of King Stonewall's Twisting Scepter. They had been raised in the interior, not on Die Bold, as she had been; and stories about "the Folk of Sand and Iron" did not circulate that far into the Spiral Arm.

Fir Li turned to Gwillgi. "Then, that leaves only you to cross into the CCW and learn about the lost ships."

"Sorry, Dark-hound," replied the other. "Business on Hanower. Maybe, after. No rush. Ships've been disappearing for years, you say."

Seeing that his plans had come to nothing, Fir Li sighed. "Perhaps Greystroke will learn what I need."

Bridget ban realized that Fir Li did not understand the possibilities of the Scepter. He was too focused on the Rift, on the long-awaited Confederate invasion, on the mysterious disappearances. The Twister had in effect passed directly across his field of vision without once registering on his consciousness. All the better. There would be much honor at the Ardry's court to whomever brought the Scepter in. Better that it be Bridget ban than Fir Li.

If one fleet had thought to seize the Scepter, and

another fought to take it, it might be something worth the having. If nothing else, it would be a quest out of the ordinary. And if she found the Scepter, and if she could take it from those who had wrecked the Molnar's fleet, and if it had the powers that legend gave it, possession of it might give the Ardry at last the power to rule. That was a lot of "ifs," but she was a Hound.

Still, even should the Stonewall Scepter prove as inert as the Ourobouros Circuit, the Ardry would at least have another bauble for the Royal League Museum on High Tara. Tully O'Connor was an art lover, and fancied himself an amateur archaeologist. He would be pleased with whoever brought him such an artifact, and favor at court was not something to be shunned.

But it bothered her that she didn't know what Grimpen knew, or thought he knew.

AN CRAIC

And what is it you know, or think you know?" the scarred man asks, so suddenly that the harper at first does not realize that he had broken the thread once more.

"I am the one come seeking to know," she temporizes, and teases a tune from her strings. The scarred man watches her fingers dance for a time and waits for a true answer.

"You knew her then, this Bridget ban?" she says.

It is not an answer, but only another question. Yet, the scarred man treats it as an answer. "Of course, I knew her. How do you suppose I learned her part in it? I knew all of them, the gods' curses that I did; for the knowing of this tale has been a hard burden." The scarred man plays a little with his bowl, spinning it, and pushing it from hand to hand.

"And what of Bridget ban?" the harper insists.

The scarred man bows his head. "She was a witch-woman. She enchanted men and used them as casually as a workman uses his tools, and as casually puts them aside when the need is past. You could not measure the arrogance in her—nor could you notice it, when she chose that you did not. What you do with those strings, she could do with a glance and a gesture. Give me Gwillgi and his tight, explosive ferocity, or even Grimpen and his implacable persistence. No one will ever love them."

The harper is surprised to find genuine tears in the old man's eyes. She hadn't thought him capable of it. "And did she love as greatly as she was loved?"

"How much do you already know?" the scarred man asks again. "What was your purpose in coming here? She may have loved hugely or not at all. When one can feign love as well as she, who could ever tell the dross from the gold? That was the horror of it." He bows his head and dabs at his tears. The harper sees him tense, and a shudder like a small earthquake passes through his frame. His hands shoot out and grab the table's rim.

When he raises his head, she sees the same distant, mocking quality in his eyes as when she first met him. And there are no tears.

"Have you begun to see the pattern yet?" he asks with the old curl back in his lips. If a portion of him mourns the memory of Bridget ban, that portion has retreated out of sight for now. The glimpse of it had pleased the harper. It had proven him capable of feeling.

"*I've seen that two of the three who possessed the Dancer have died terribly,*" she says.

"*Is there another way to die? I hadn't heard. Who can face the endless dark and not feel terror?*"

"*The Molnar.*"

"*He never faced it. His madness was his blinders. It was those looking on who saw the face of it—the bright blue eye of Sapphire Point in the broad black face of the Rift.*"

"*There is another side to the Rift,*" she pointed out.

"*Take no comfort from flawed analogies. If there is another side of death, none have come back to tell us of it.*"

"*There are ancient legends that, once, someone did.*"

The scarred man laughs like broken glass. "*Are you one of them?*"

"*If one may believe one ancient legend, of a Twisting Stone, why not another, and more comforting one?*"

"*Because comfort is a lie.*"

"*But the Fudir seems to have been a clever man. He would have seen the pattern . . . Ah. Yes, he knew only of Jumdar's death, not of the Molnar's. Only a madman draws* kolam *from a single point.*"

"*And a man caught up in the immediacy of events may find it hard to step back and appreciate the pattern. That requires a distance that the Fudir did not yet have. Even the cleverest man may be blind.*"

The harper plucks a sharp chord from her strings. "*But two points make no pattern. Jumdar and the Molnar died for different reasons, not because they had possessed the Dancer. Jumdar may have been the modern, careful sort of soldier and the Molnar the ancient, careless sort, but neither of them could have supposed Death to be a stranger. Besides, January has not died, and he possessed it first."*

The scarred man smiles horribly. "All men die," he answered. "It is only a matter of when, and how."

GOLTRAÍ: THE LEAVING THAT'S GRIEVING

The Fudir became a momentary folk hero on New Eireann, the scarred man says . . .

. . . when the word went about that he wanted to go to the Hadramoo. Everyone assumed that it was to take revenge on the rievers, and while they thought it a mad idea, both madness and revenge are well thought of on New Eireann and they applauded the sentiment. It never occurred to anyone other than Hugh—and maybe January—that he might have any other motive, for people engulfed by their own tragedies presume that others are too, or ought to be.

But reaching the Hadramoo required first leaving New Eireann, and this was proving remarkably difficult.

The rievers had systematically destroyed the alfvens on every interstellar ship in or around Port Eireann, so the only vessel presently capable of leaving the system was January's *New Angeles*. Other ships would eventually appear—ICC freighters to service the orbital factories, tourist cruises to enthuse over the molten geysers—but none were expected soon. Cerenkov wakes had been detected out beyond the coopers, but they had been bound elsewhere and slid smoothly past New Eireann on the Grand Trunk Road, oblivious to the disaster below.

January's *New Angeles* could carry twenty people in reasonable comfort, and perhaps another ten or so in reasonable discomfort. Beyond that, as he smilingly put it, he'd arrive at Jehovah with a ship full of corpses. That was a great many fewer berths than there were people clamoring to have them, so naturally the prices rose. Most of those wanting off New Eireann were technicians and managers who had been working the orbital factories—those who had not been aboard them when the Cynthians struck. More than one such, asked to pay his passage out-system, denounced January as a "profiteer," by which they meant that they should be able to escape at his expense.

But *New Angeles* was not, as January pointed out, a subsidized charity, nor had he the deep pockets of the ICC or, indeed, of their own corporations. He had expenses to meet—fuel, port fees, rations, and supplies. The Laser Lift was out of commission, and he would have to boost into orbit by rockets alone. That required disposable boosters, also expensive. He took promissory notes in Gladiola Bills drawn on their employers—and redeemed those chits as soon as he could, exchanging them at a discount with Port Eireann for fuel and with local merchants for the food, drink, and air he would need to keep his passengers alive during the transit. The Port Authority and the merchants assumed the risk because Gladiola Bills were hard currency, and the sooner January reached Port Jehovah, the sooner word of the catastrophe could be spread and help summoned.

The Fudir found January in the freighter's control room, reviewing readiness reports with Hogan, Barnes, and Tirasi. The captain welcomed him with his usual rosy-cheeked smile and told him to go fuck himself.

"I'm not asking for one of the passenger berths," the Fudir explained. "I'll ship as an instrument tech. You still need one."

"Do I, now?" January remarked, as if in surprise. "Bill, do I need an instrument tech?"

Tirasi looked up from the screen he had been checking, glanced briefly at the Fudir. "Not while I'm aboard."

January smiled at the Fudir. "Port Eireann tells me, because I'm running an 'errand of mercy,' they won't insist on a full crew—not that they ever were sticklers like Port Jehovah."

"With me along, you won't have to work watch-and-watch," the Fudir pointed out.

Without looking up from her console, Maggie B. said, "We'll manage."

"Beside," said January, "your certificate reads 'Kalim DeMorsey of Bellefontaine,' and if I've learned nothing else since landing here, it's that whoever else you might be, you're not him." He picked up a thin-screen and began checking preflight items against his database.

"The name was a convenience," the Fudir admitted, "but the qualifications were real."

January glanced at him. "Were they. How do I know? Your word?" His tone implied what that word was worth.

"No, my work. On the trip out here."

But the captain shook his head. "If I took you on *knowing your certificate was false,* I could lose my own license. Hogan, have Chaurasia's technicians finished the quality check on our alfvens?"

"Not yet, Chief."

"Remind them they're under warranty from Gladiola yards. I know it wasn't ICC's fault that New Eireann's magnetic cushions were off-line, but I only want to know if my alfvens are still up to Yard specs after that emergency brake."

"Can you take me as a passenger, then?"

January seemed surprised to find the Fudir still in the control room. "A passenger? If you have the fare, I can put you on the waiting list. At number . . ."

"Fifty-seven," said Maggie B. "We can fit him into our third trip; but another ship will probably come along before then."

"You can have my wages back from the outbound voyage. I can pay you the rest when I get to Jehovah."

Maggie B. said, "You shore seem dang eager to run out on your buddy."

January shook his head. "Sorry. No money, no ticket."

"How am I supposed to get off this place, then?"

January grunted and frowned over his checklist, running his finger down the screen. He showed it to Tirasi. "You see there anything about helping an im-poster and petty crook back to Jehovah?" Tirasi shook his head. "No sir, I surely do not." So January shrugged and pointed, as if helpless, to the checklist. "Sorry, it's not my problem. Look, 'Fudir,' you and that 'Ringbao'—that O'Carroll—tricked your way on board my ship to come here and start that bloody civil war up again. I don't like being tricked and I don't like being used." He slapped the thinscreen checklist on his console. "Now, leave my ship before I call up Slugger."

The Fudir complained of this later in the office Hugh had appropriated in Cargo House. "He was playing with me. It's that eternal smile of his. He makes you think he's in on it, that he's on your side. Then—wham—he blindsides you."

Hugh made no reply and did not even look up

from the reports he was reading until the glaziers at work on the window began to put their equipment away. "Finished?" he asked them.

The senior glazier tugged his forelock. "That we are, O'Carroll. And bulletproof, too." A knuckle tap on the pane demonstrated this property. "No one'll be pot-shotting yer honor; not through this here window."

Hugh thanked the men and they left, and he stood and walked to the window, where he gazed down on the carpark, from which the wrecked vehicles had already been cleared. A bicyclist appeared, racked his bike in a row of other requisitioned bikes, and ran into the building. Another messenger, another report. Hugh hoped it was for one of the other ministers on the United Front.

Farther off, in New Down Town, repair parties were razing unstable structures with wrecking balls and dozers. While he watched, the Fermoy Hotel fell in on itself, raising a cloud of debris, gray and white and black, that seemed for a moment a smoky outline of the building itself, as if its ghost had survived the building's demise. *That's where the gardy first raised the Loyalist flag,* he thought. Work gangs spread out and began hauling the debris into wagons, some horse-drawn, others motor vehicles brought up from the relatively unscathed south. From this distance, the work gang looked like children at play.

"It's good to know," the Fudir said, "that when someone does pot-shot you, it will be through another window entirely."

Hugh turned from his melancholy survey to face the man who had brought him back to this. "You think January was putting on a happy face to fool you? I'd not expect *you* to complain of deception."

"I'm a 'scrambler.' Deception's what I do. January's supposed to be 'on the square.'" The Fudir joined him by the window. "I didn't think there was an un-broken pane of glass in all New Eireann."

"They came up from the Mid-Vale," Hugh explained, missing the humor. "Handsome Jack organized the plants down there that make the crystal tourist souvenirs to switch to window glass. There's a plastic plant in County Ardow doing the same." He rapped the new window with a knuckle. "Maybe this should have been plastic. But Jack and I agreed it was important that I do business with Mid-Vale suppliers, not only with the Loyalists in the Ardow."

"Politics," said the Fudir.

Hugh shrugged. "You say that like a dirty word. But—cut deals or cut throats. Your pick." He crossed his arms. "Who's on my list today?"

The Fudir had appointed himself the task of separating from the chaff of those eager to meet with Hugh the wheat of those who actually needed to. It was not a very arduous duty—it consisted mostly of telling people "no" without obviously telling them "no"—and if the Fudir was practiced at any one thing, it was at not being obvious. The work would keep him busy while he awaited a ship. He opened his notebook and toggled the calendar with his stylus. "Kiernan Sionnach, from the Reek Guides, is your ten o'clock. He wants to know how you plan to rebuild the tourist trade." He shook his head. "Sometimes, I think people have no sense of priorities."

"It's that politics thing, again," Hugh told him.

The window shook to a dull thud and both men looked up. Over Lower Newbridge Street, on the far side of town, a plume of smoke rose. Hugh sighed. "Another fine old building down."

But the Fudir frowned and shook his head. He laid his notebook on Hugh's desk and came to the window. "No. No, that was a bomb." Even as he spoke, the banshee wail of distant sirens arose and the gang dismantling the Down Hotel paused in their work and looked off to the west.

"A bomb . . . ?" Hugh said. "But . . . Who . . . ? Why . . . ?"

The Fudir crossed his arms and studied the ragged cityscape at the base of the hill. "There is a Terran saying attributed to the Auld Deceiver. 'Better to rule in Hell than to serve in Heaven.' Some people"—and he pointed with a toss of his head toward the black plume that now curled in the distance—"will first create the Hell over which they mean to rule."

That evening, a space yacht entered the Eireann-naughta system out of Port Jehovah. That meant a few more berths for refugees, and the Fudir was determined to secure at least one of those berths for himself. So a few days later, when the yacht had reached Low Eireann Orbit, the Fudir took a bicycle from the rack in front of Cargo House and pedaled down to the Port. Others on the street, assuming he was on some errand for Little Hugh—by now his close association with the Ghost of Ardow was common knowledge—made way for him. A few waved, and one wag shouted, "On to the Hadramoo!"

At the Passenger Terminal, he found several score out-system techs mobbing the newly repaired terminal doors, crowding and shoving, and waiting for the yacht's pilot to emerge. The Fudir continued around to the maintenance gate on the east side of the field. There, a large sign read ABSOLUTELY NO ADMITTANCE. WATCH YOUR STEP. He dismounted and chained the bicycle to the fence.

The Fudir exchanged friendly greetings with the watchman—he had made a practice of standing various low-level functionaries to their pints—and they discussed for a few minutes the latest lorry-bomb, which had demolished Handsome Jack's party headquarters. "Ask me," said the watchman, "that was Jack hisself done it. Settin' up Little Hugh as the goat." The man was a staunch Loyalist and when the Fudir pointed out that Hugh himself had given Jack quarters in Cargo House, answered, "The bitter to keep an oy an' 'im." The Fudir's policy was never to argue with a man you're going to ask for a favor, so he said that he had been sent to the Port to learn how many refugees the newcomer's yacht could take.

The watchman did not ask to see an authorization. "She's grounding in no more'n a dekaminute. Pilot-owner's name . . ." He checked his manifest as he swung the gate open. "Ah, his name's Qing Olafsson, sez here."

The Fudir paused as he passed through the gate. "Qing Olafsson?"

"Aye. D'ye know him?" The guard seemed to think that all off-worlders knew one another.

The Fudir shook his head. "No." But he frowned and fell into thought as he crossed the field to Inward Clearance.

A wooden bench had replaced the padded chairs in the waiting room at Inward Clearance and a clipboard with paper sheets had replaced the computer terminals on which tourists and businessmen had once registered their arrivals and departures. One smashed and blackened terminal bore a handwritten sign: OUT OF ORDER. The bench was empty and the Fudir set himself to await the pilot's arrival.

Olafsson Qing. He didn't believe in coincidence, bizarre or otherwise; not where *that name* was concerned. What business had *They* on a remote place like

New Eireann? *The Brotherhood should never have gotten mixed up with Them.* The Great Game was best appreciated from a distance.

A slim, sallow-featured man was standing at the kiosk filling out the inbound forms. The Fudir, immersed in his thoughts, had not noticed him enter. Now he rose from the bench. "Slawncha," he said, holding out a hand to Olafsson. "I'm from the 'Welcome Wagon.'" That drew a blank look—or a blanker look: the Fudir had never seen such an unremarkable countenance. "I've come down from Cargo House. I suppose you've learned about our situation here while you crawled down from the exit ramp."

"Yes," said the other. "Terrible tragedy."

The Fudir waited a moment for him to say something further, but Olafsson continued filling out the forms. If the name had suggested a possibility, the indifference confirmed it. Fellow feeling was not something looked for among Those of Name. It was a bad idea to bring oneself to their attention. Yet, the Fudir was in no position to be choosy about the rides he hitched.

"Then you ought to know we've got several hundred refugees who need a lift to Jehovah," he said, "although they'd accept a lift to New Chennai or Hawthorn Rose, if you're going that way." Actually, there was only one refugee that concerned the Fudir, but if Olafsson wanted to take others, that was no matter. There was safety in numbers.

But Olafsson shook his head. "Sorry. I've very little room on board, and I've only come here to pick up a friend." He had finished filling out his entry form and handed it to the clerk, who looked up startled from his damage lists and requisitions.

"Yer a quiet one," he said, squinting at Olafsson.

Then, noticing the Fudir also, he added, "Top 'o th' morning there, Fudir."

"And the rest o' th' day for yerself, Donal. This way," he said to Olafsson. "I'll take you out the back. The refugees outside the main terminal building will be all over you, begging for passage." He thought if he gave Olafsson enough assistance, the man might feel more inclined to take him along as a favor. "Maybe I can help you find your friend."

Olafsson glanced at the customs clerk, then at Fudir, and almost smiled.

They crossed town on foot, the streets being still too rubble-strewn for most vehicles. The Fudir walked his bicycle, explaining the delicate political situation, pointing out the progress already made. All this, the newcomer absorbed in unnerving silence. They had passed the shell of J. J. Brannon's Mercantile Emporium before the man spoke.

"You said you were from Cargo House," Olafsson said. "Do you work for the ICC?"

A peculiar and irrelevant question. "No, the United Front co-opted the building for its council. It was the only large structure still more or less intact. But the co-managers refuse to call it Council House. I'm taking you there to meet them."

"Co-managers," Olafsson repeated. "A tramp captain I passed coming in said there was a disputed leadership. Is this 'United Front' some temporary truce?"

"January's a born pessimist. We're hoping it proves more than that."

The business district had been badly mauled by the Cynthians. Now jackhammers shook the pavement. Timbers crackled and broke and fell. Work gangs hauled debris away. Straw bosses hollered out directions. One man, apparently tired beyond endurance, covered with the gray dust of demolition, had sat himself down on the curbstones and was quietly weeping. His fellows continued to work around him, affecting to take no notice.

"By the gods," Olafsson said after they had passed him by, "I could smash the bastards who did this."

The Fudir turned and gave him a twisted grin. "I'll keep that in mind."

The road turned right and climbed New Street Hill toward Cargo House. A young boy on a bicycle, with the plain green pennant of the Front snapping on an antenna behind his seat, came spinning down the hill crying, "Make way! Make way!" The Fudir and Olafsson stepped to the side of the road.

"They're gaining some of their spirit back," the Fudir said, watching the boy out of sight. "We arrived just after the raid, Hugh and I did. You should have seen these folk then. They'd had the sand kicked out of 'em. We barely missed it ourselves—the raid, I mean. They tell me an ICC courier boat did arrive right in the thick of it, the poor bastard."

Olafsson said nothing, and the Fudir thought, *You're a stunning conversationalist*. They walked together in silence until they came to a stretch of road just below Cargo House itself where there was no one about and no houses nearby. "So, who is this friend you've come to find?" the Fudir asked. "You can see things are all confused here, but the Housing Council may have some records of his whereabouts, if he's still alive."

"His name's Donovan."

The name was a blow in his stomach, but the Fudir did not allow it to show. "Donovan, is it?" he said breezily. "Can't be more than a couple thousand people with that name on New Eireann." There was still the possibility of coincidence. Somewhere in the Spiral Arm there must be ordinary men named Olafsson Qing who had ordinary friends named Donovan.

"This one lives on Jehovah."

"Ah. Does he, now? Then, I hate to tell you, but you've taken a wrong turn somewhere."

Olafsson shrugged. "I was given a channel by the Seven of Jehovah. Fudir, they said, and he has gone to New Eireann."

"They said that, did they? Well, not so many go by that name," the Fudir admitted. "All right. You want Donovan . . . What's your business with him?"

"For him to know," Olafsson said.

"He doesn't like me to . . ."

"Those of Name greet you, Fudir."

And there it was: the very thing he had dreaded since hearing the name of the arriving pilot. It was enough to make the Fudir believe in the gods, or at least in the crueler sort. He had been looking for a ship. Now a ship had come looking for him.

Be careful what you wish for.

"Why should they greet *me*? They know nothing of me. I don't work for them."

"From your lips to Donovan's ear. That makes you a proper object of Their attention. Come. I need only a name, such a little thing. The next link in your chain to Donovan. That is all. You betray no one. You need not even leave this place."

And what sort of assurance was that when leaving was the thing he desired most? But he looked off down the hillside to the wrecked city and listened for a moment to the sound of hammers and crashing masonry and wondered if that was true. Could he run out on Hugh in the midst of all this? For the first time in many years he was party to something worth doing and the problem was that it clashed with something else more worth doing. He had to follow the Twister, even if it meant running out on New Eireann. What was one man less in the Reconstruction?

He rested his body against the bicycle, gazing on nothing in particular. He thought of the intricate quadrille now taking place on New Eireann. Handsome Jack. Little Hugh. Voldemar and the Direct Action Faction. Now, Those of Name. The betrayals would have to be set up very carefully.

"The name?" suggested Olafsson with an air of tried patience.

The Fudir sighed. "I can't give you her name."

"I am grieved to hear it."

"Save your tears. I mean I *can't* give you her name. Donovan set things up so that if the wrong person makes contact, the chain breaks apart. They disappear into the Corner, and you'll *never* find them. Try it, and you end up in the lime pits on Dunkle Street."

"Then, you have a problem. I need Donovan, and that apparently means I need you on Jehovah to vouch for me. I'd rather not disrupt matters here, but shall I tell The Names you refused? There are other agents at large, this side of the Rift. They might be given other assignments."

The Fudir recalled that couriers were often sent out in pairs. He screwed up his mouth. "Like assassinating reluctant Terrans?"

Olafsson did not deny it.

Another messenger bike passed, this one pedaling uphill. The girl raised a fist and squeaked, "On to the Hadramoo!"

Olafsson raised an eyebrow after she had passed. "Surely, the Eireannaughta are not contemplating a reprisal against the Cynthians!"

But the Fudir didn't answer. Suddenly, he smiled. "You'll have to arrest me, Br'er Fox," he said.

"What?"

"Can you pretend to be a Jehovan proctor?"

Olafsson waved a hand. His pretenses ran wider and deeper than that. "Why?"

"No, make that a League marshal. Then they can't refuse extradition. Give me one day to make some arrangements here, then serve me with a writ. I'll give you the details later tonight."

"That seems a bit elaborate; or do you deceive as a habit?"

The Fudir closed his eyes briefly. "I don't want people here to think I've run out on Little Hugh."

"Why should you care what other people think when the Secret Name calls you?"

"Indulge me. You're getting what you want. Only don't tell Hugh until you actually 'arrest' me. He may try to stop you."

"He may try."

"Don't underestimate the Ghost of Ardow."

All that evening, as he met with the people he needed to meet with and made the arrangements he needed to arrange, the Fudir weighed the ulta-pulta, the yin and yang, the drivers and constraints.

On the plus side, he could leave New Eireann now, and resume his chase of the Dancer. On the minus side, he must go in the company of a dangerous man who expected a service that the Fudir was disinclined to render. There was something about the courier that was not right. Like a cracked bell, the tone was a little off. Something he had said . . . The Fudir did not know what it was; nor was he especially eager to learn. The greater a man's knowledge, the shorter his life.

He didn't care what the "Hombres con Nombres" wanted of Donovan. It was a distraction from the

Dancer, and he cursed Donovan for ever joining the Great Game. Over the years, as no assignments came, Donovan had gradually come to believe that They had forgotten him. He had pursued other avocations, and found them quite fulfilling. Had Those of Name somehow discovered his abdication? *Was the courier in fact an assassin?*

A bad thing, then, to lead such a man to Donovan. Yet, the Fudir couldn't very well refuse a direct summons. And Olafsson might be no more than he appeared—an ordinary courier with an ordinary message, requiring Donovan only to pluck some particular fruit from the tree of knowledge.

A man could live most of his life forgetting the Confederation or the League existed at all. Life's real problems ran far below that august level, but League and Confederation ground like millstones along the Rift; and now something of that abrasive emptiness had drifted down Electric Avenue and touched him. An ancient Terran god had once said, "You may forget about politics; but politics will not forget about you."

Yet the Fudir knew that he must follow the Dancer into the Hadramoo. As stolid and remorseless as were the oppressions of Dao Chetty, the wild cruelties of the barbarians of the Cynthian Cluster were worse. The Dancer might be no more than myth; but if there were the slightest chance that the old legends were true—and the experiences of January and Jumdar hinted that they might be—then at the least he owed it to the Spiral Arm to attempt recovery before the Cynthians discovered its powers.

Not that the Spiral Arm would ever thank him.

The next day, Olafsson strode into Hugh's office wearing what seemed very much like the undress uniform of a Hound's Pup and waving papers of official appearance "demanding and requiring" the person of one Kalim DeMorsey, d.b.a. "The Fudir."

Hugh was by turns startled by the intrusion, intent on the warrant, angry, saddened, and finally resigned. "It seems your sins have found you out," he told the Fudir. Then, laying the extradition papers on his desk, he addressed Olafsson. "These seem to be in order, but I would like to enter a protest—"

"So noted," Olafsson snapped, but then added more softly, "Don't concern yourself, PM. We'll send him back when we're done with him. He's a material witness, not a suspect."

The Fudir hadn't really expected the courier to follow through on that particular touch, and was pleased that he had. It would reflect badly on Hugh if he had been friends with a wanted felon. Of course, the Fudir was a wanted felon, but perceptions matter. So "material witness" was a small kindness wrapped in a greater cruelty. The Fudir would not meet Hugh's eyes, and hung his head as if in shame.

Olafsson took him by the arm. "Come along," he said. "There's a good fellow. No need for the shackles."

The Fudir turned to Hugh and said, "Just remember when you first met old Kalim DeMorsey."

Hugh nodded and said, "Amir Naith's Gulli. I owe you my life."

Olafsson did not handle him roughly, but did keep a firm grip on his arm as he guided the Fudir down the hallway. Handsome Jack Garrity came out of his office as they passed. The Fudir nodded infinitesimally to him, and Handsome Jack returned the gesture, and the Fudir continued under Olafsson's guidance, satisfied with this microscopic farewell.

Olafsson's yacht had carried a light ground car that could ride on surface effect, magnetic tramline, or inflated wheels, as circumstances required. Granted, it was not much of a vehicle. Made of "solid smoke" for lightness and jointed to fold compactly, it nevertheless worried the Fudir when he saw it. Confederate couriers normally traveled lean and swift; stealth was more their mode. Had Olafsson stolen a ship from someone else? And if so, what had he done with the owner?

The streets were encumbered with construction materials and demolition debris, around which Olafsson wove with patient skill. At the intersection of Port and MacDonald, one of the new gardies halted them for a time while he waved a debris lorry backward into the lot where a row of shops were coming down. The site contractor saw the Fudir and came over to the 'buggi waving a paper. "Tell Hugh," he said, "that the composites haven't come up yet from Fermoy for the Jackson Street reconstruction." The Fudir smiled and said he would.

Olafsson made no comment until the gardy had waved them through and they turned onto Port Road. "When did you plan to tell him?" was all he asked.

On the spaceport hard, the Fudir stood by Olafsson's yacht while the robot hoist folded the dūbuggi and raised it into the cargo hold, and the boarding stairs deployed from amidships. The Fudir chafed at the speed of it all, and glanced repeatedly toward the maintenance gate, through the maze of wrecked shuttles and lighters and bumboats that the Cynthians left behind. He was anxious to leave, but the timing had to be right.

"Expecting someone?" Olafsson asked. He had

been watching the hoist keenly, but the Fudir was not surprised to find him aware of the goings-on about him.

"I thought it might rain," he said, indicating dark red clouds gathering above the distant Reeks. The hot, violent updrafts on the other side sometimes created rains of gray ash over the Vale. Olafsson spared them only a glance.

"We'll be gone before then. It's the bicyclist that bothers me."

"Bicyclist . . ."

"It's your friend," Olafsson said a moment later as the approaching figure rounded a blasted ICC packet. "I hope he doesn't intend to prevent your leaving." He surreptitiously loosened the flap on one of his pockets.

The bike that O'Carroll had taken was too small for his frame and he appeared almost comical, an awkward set of pumping knees, as he rode between two shattered corporate shuttles.

"Climb the stairs, Fudir," said Olafsson, stepping between him and Hugh.

"That would be rude," the Fudir answered. "I think he's come to say good-bye."

Olafsson grunted, but made no response.

Hugh turned his bike into a tight circle and skidded to a stop just in front of them. Letting the bike fall to the ground, he strode up to the departing pair. "I finally remembered," he said, pointing a finger at the Fudir, "when I first met 'Kalim DeMorsey,' and I'm after wondering how this spalpeen knew of that name at all."

Olafsson may have been expecting a great many things, but this was not among them, and he turned to give the Fudir a puzzled look, for the Fudir had given him that very name to use on the warrant.

The courier had not shown many lapses of attention in the short time the Fudir had known him, but this one was all that Little Hugh needed. He tackled Olafsson around the chest, pinning his arms to his side and knocking the man to the ground. The Fudir was impressed. Hugh had to believe he was fighting a Hound's Pup; and that meant he had tossed both legal and physical prudence to the winds.

Olafsson appeared to no more than shrug and Hugh was thrown aside. Hugh rolled and rose—and Olafsson already had a weapon in his hand.

"Don't shoot!" the Fudir cried.

Olafsson cocked his head, but this time he did not take his eyes off the O'Carroll. "I didn't think there were more than five men alive who could have done what you did, and four of them are . . . I'm sorry, PM, but your friend really is urgently needed on Jehovah. Now, I'd suggest leaving as quickly as you came."

"Sahbs," said the Fudir. "Company."

A band of armed toughs had emerged from the two wrecked company shuttles and advanced now on the three men standing at the base of the yacht. At their head strode Voldemar O'Rahilly wearing a sleeveless vest and bearing the sweep-gun he'd been given by the ICC during the Cynthian raid. Hugh, unarmed, turned to face them.

The Direct Action fighters leveled their weapons; but O'Rahilly raised his left arm and patted them down. "There's no need for blood this day, boyos," he said. "Hugh and I, we've spilt too much blood together for me to be happy spilling his." Then, to Hugh, "But it seems to me only fair that if you arrived here with the Terran, you should leave with him as well." His bearded lips split into a red grin. "Symmetry's appealing, ain't it?"

"But the Cause . . ." Hugh protested.

"Will carry on widdout yez; as we did durin' yer exile. Come on, now, the both of ye, be boardin' the yacht."

The *both* of ye? The Fudir looked for Olafsson and saw him nowhere. Had he managed to slip unseen into his ship? But no, he spied the courier now, *in the midst of Voldemar's men*. And with a weapon in either hand.

The Fudir wasn't sure he liked the odds on that; but neither was he sure which way the odds broke. "Hugh, better do as he says."

The O'Carroll raised a chin. "And if I don't?"

"I said I wouldn't be happy wid it," Voldemar answered. "Never said I wouldn't do it." And with that, he aimed his sweeper directly at the Fudir.

As a way of not shedding O'Carroll blood, it was ingenious; but the Fudir wished O'Rahilly had picked some other way.

But Voldemar hesitated and the Fudir realized that Olafsson was now standing directly behind him and one of his weapons was shoved against Voldemar's spine. "I'd really rather you not damage my goods," the courier told the faction leader.

The Fudir saw a cloud of doubt pass across Voldemar's face and the two of them locked gazes for a moment. Then Voldemar shrugged. "What we got here," he said, "is what yez'd call a 'conundrum.' Ye can kill me, for sure—no boyos, hold off for just a wee bit and we'll see if we can't untie this widdout we all get burned, especially me. Ye can kill me, Pup; but ye'll only do it if I actually do damage to yer goods, so to speak. I gotta shoot first, right? It's what ye call a 'code of honor' or something. Now you wouldn't like that, and I wouldn't like that, and for sure old Fudir here wouldn't like that. So let's try something we can all like. All I'm askin' ye to do is take one more pas- senger. That's all. I mean, by the gods, man! Think of the mess we'd be after layvin' here for the mainte- nance crew!"

"I won't have it be said," Hugh announced, "that I ran out on my people."

"Oh, don't ye worry none about that. When the guard at the gate finally gets hisself untied, he'll let everyone know it was a shanghai job—by Jack's Reb- els! Man, you're a legend—*and I need that legend*— but I don't need *you*. Fact is, yez've gone soft. Cozyin' up an' makin' dayls wid Handsome Jack an' all. That ain't fookin' right. Yez're a traitor to the O'Carroll."

"To myself, ye mean?" Hugh said bitterly. Then he jerked when he felt Olafsson's weapon pressed to his side.

"I am persuaded by the man's rhetoric," the cou- rier said. "Also, I have counted his guns; and while there might be a certain philosophical satisfaction in letting things play out, I really do need to take the Fudir back unharmed to Jehovah. If your presence is the price, so be it."

Hugh's shoulders slumped. "If I'd brought my bodyguards with me," he said.

"There would have been a bloodbath for sure," the Fudir said. He had already taken two steps up the stairs. "Count your blessings. And mine."

Shoulders slumped, Hugh followed him up the stairs with Olafsson directly behind him. At the head of the stairs, and just before closing the airlock, the courier turned and faced the faction fighters. "I'm not sure how wide the blast circle is for these strap-on boosters, but I'll be lighting off directly."

The Fudir saw Voldemar and his men scrambling for the edge of the field before the lock had fully closed.

"I'll be back!" Hugh shouted through the closing crack. "I'll be back," he said again, after it had closed. And then, in a piteous voice, he added, "Oh, my poor world! My poor world!"

AN CRAIC

*O*h, *my poor world," the scarred man mocks. "And it wasn't even his own world! He was born on Venishànghai."*

"But he grew on New Eireann," the harper says, idly strumming a lament on her instrument. It doesn't sound quite right and she isn't sure why. "And where a person grows may matter more than where he sprouted."

"How did he 'grow' on New Eireann? He came there already a man."

"He promised he'd be back, but he didn't swear this time on his father's name. That seems like growth to me."

The scarred man smiles like a razor. "You noticed that, did you?"

"I did. I wonder if he did, at the time." Underneath the lament, she plucks out in a minor off the fourth mode the motif she had begun to think of as The Fudir's Theme, a twisting melody that never quite resolves. The scarred man surprises her by saying, "Yes. I think you've gotten it right."

"It must have been a schizophrenic voyage," the harper suggests. "Olafsson wants to go to Jehovah; the Fudir wants to go to the Hadramoo; and Little Hugh wants to go back to New Eireann. They're pulling three ways. The mean value is to stand still."

"Yes, standing still is a difficult means of pursuit. Although"—and here his gaze turns intently and discomfortingly on the harper—"there are times when it works."

The harper stills her strings and sets the harp aside. The Bartender has brought over two plates of stew, the hearty, plain sort consonant with Jehovah's austere nature. She recognizes carrots and onions and a stringy meat that suggests pastures rather than vats. Curious, she tastes it and finds it much like artifact meat, only different in texture. The great doors at the front of the Bar open briefly on some arrivals to reveal a night well advanced.

"Tell me," she says when she has swallowed. "I don't understand why the Fudir went through the charade of being 'arrested.' Why didn't he simply leave when Olafsson gave him the chance?"

The scarred man eats as if filling a pit with a shovel. "Because when history repeats itself," he says, without swallowing, "the second time must be a farce."

"What do you mean, farce? Voldemar's ambush—Oh."

"Yes. The 'arrangements' the Fudir made the night before. Considering how things ran out afterward, it was probably the best thing he could have done."

"What do you mean?"

"We have two theories. The one more favorable to the Fudir's character is that he had come to like Hugh, and New Eireann, and could not bear to see either ruined by the inevitable three-way struggle with Jack and Voldemar."

"You mean, better a two-way struggle?"

But the scarred man shakes his head and cackles with brief and unpleasant glee. "No," he says around another spoonful of stew, so that streamers of gravy dribble from the corners of his mouth. "He made more than one set of arrangements that night. Jack's men ambushed Voldemar as he was leaving the Port and cut the head right off the snake. So things worked out in the end. The Fudir left New Eireann with competent, undivided leadership, and saved Hugh's face by shanghaiing him. No one could say Hugh had run off."

The harper is skeptical. "And those were the Fudir's motives? They seem rather high for a man so low."

The scarred man looks into the darkness of his stew. "Perhaps those were motives he thought of afterward. But we can no longer ask him."

"He died then? So we don't really know what happened."

"Ah. The beginnings of wisdom." He applies himself once more to his meal.

"What was the second reason? You said there were two."

The scarred man shrugs. "He needed someone to watch his back."

"That's a less noble reason," the harper agrees.

"Yes. It is."

"There's a third reason."

The scarred man raises his face from his stew. He swallows and wipes his lips with his hand. "Is there?"

"Friendship. They were in the dance together."

The scarred man gives that some thought. "Maybe," he allows. "Sometimes you can triangulate what really happened from the testimonies of those who were there." His grin reveals ruined teeth. "But you don't have even that. You've only my account of their accounts."

"Do you embellish, then?"

He shrugs. "Even engineers prepare their plans and levels from more than one perspective. It's late, and *you've played three times tonight. Four, if you count our conversation. Do you have rooms at the Hostel?"*

"I thought I would stay here. They've rooms upstairs, you said."

The scarred man nods, but says nothing.

"Room 3-G, if it's available."

Another grin. "We might be a little snug, you and us."

The harper studies him for a long moment, and he simply waits her out. Finally, she says, "Another room, then."

The scarred man signals to the Bartender, makes a sign, and points to the harper. Shortly, one of the servants comes with a homing key and lays it on the table. "Compliments of the house," she murmurs, and her eyes caress in turn the harper and her instrument.

"You may want to consider what I've told you so far," the scarred man says. "It will give you something to sleep on, if not someone to sleep with."

"Will Hugh escape once they reach Jehovah and try to return to New Eireann? Will the Fudir slip loose from Olafsson and heigh for the Hadramoo? Will Olafsson find Donovan or will Greystroke catch up with him? And what of . . . And what of Bridget ban? What has she been doing in the meantime?"

"That," the scarred man suggests, "will give you something to wake up for."

*G*ood morning, harper," the scarred man says with malicious cheer when dawn has drawn a few hardy souls to the Bar. Praisegod is behind the counter—to all appearances, he might never have left his post. So, too, the scarred man, who sits once more in his niche. The room is redolent with the pasty odors of oatmeal and eggs and daal. "I hope you slept well," he says. "After a time, the crack of the overnight ballistic runs can grow quite restful and the morning cargo drops little more than a cock's crow."

The harper spares him a blurred look and asks Praisegod for a cup of something more lively than she is. She carries the coffee to the table by the niche and slowly puts herself outside of it. The scarred man's plate is heavy with daal and baked beans, with scrambled eggs and cold, fatty bacon, with sautéed mushrooms. She spares this feast no more than a horrified glance and notes that he seems in a good humor.

"Every day is a promise," he replies. "Compared to the night mare, we have an easy ride."

"And what nightmares visit your sleep?" It is an idle question—she is not yet fully awake—but the silence of his answer draws her from her drug. He dips a piece of naan into the daal and shoves it in his mouth. The sauces drip and pool in the upturned cleft of his chin. "None that you would care to ride," he says just before he swallows.

Silence then draws on toward the point of discomfort. But it is from a point of greater discomfort to one of lesser. The scarred man begrudges her: "Yet there are dreams that come during the day. Sometimes

I think you are not quite real, and I am speaking only to another part of my own mind. I'm not sure."

"Do you not know your own mind, then?"

A facetious question, meant for humor, the words push the scarred man deeper into his niche. "No," he whispers. "I do not."

Now the discomfort is real and the harper hurriedly excuses herself to visit the buffet table. Few are the guests who stay at the Bar, fewer still those who breakfast there; and so, few were the choices presented to her. She stares at the unsavory dishes. The bacon is cold and more fat than meat. The eggs have congealed into something resembling rubber. She settles finally on a bowl of oatmeal and some naan, a small glass of muskmelon juice. With these she returns to the niche and is only a little surprised to find the scarred man still there, and still gazing silently at his meal.

"When we parted last night," she prompts, "Hugh and the Fudir were sliding toward Jehovah with the 'Federal courier."

The scarred man says nothing and the harper fears she has stopped up the well with her remarks. Then he looks up and fixes her with his gaze. "What is your story? Perhaps you should be the one here telling tales."

"Every man, every woman, has a story. But some are less interesting than others. I've come to learn of the Dancer. My own tale is far less than that." *She does not ask about his personal story, although she suspects there may be a goltraí in it. She is not sure she would want to hear it; yet the question lingers unspoken in the air between them.*

Eventually, the scarred man sighs and begins the dance anew.

"Bridget ban," the scarred man says, "arrived at Peacock Junction . . .

. . . a world of lush colors and bubbling waters, and of careless men and women. There, the tropics run from pole to pole and the ocean currents are delightfully warm and languid. It is a world on which not much happens, and what does happen happens slowly. They have a Seanaid of sorts: garrulous old men and women who meet in an open amphitheater during the dry season, and not at all during the rains. Someday they may pass a law, but there is no hurry.

The universe is in motion: planets and stars spinning, galaxies swirling, starships sliding from star to star along superluminal channels in the fabric of space. There is no reason why any world in such a universe should be so much at rest as Peacock Junction.

But while Peacock has very few laws, she is rich in customs; and customs have the greater force. A law may be appealed; but from custom there is no recourse. When Billy Kisilwando killed his partner in a drunken fit, he was given one hundred days' grace. He set off into the Malawayo Wilderness with a rucksack, a hiking staff, and a small, but faithful terrier. He emerged after ninety-nine days, minus dog and staff, and reported to the District Head, confessed his sin, and prayed forgiveness from his partner's *manu;* and ever afterward he repeated his confession in the Hall of Remonstration to all who came to see him. Such is the cruelty of custom.

Compared to the great roundabout of luminal highways that converge on the worlds of Jehovah, Peacock barely deserves the name of junction. Route 66 splits off from the Silk Road and heighs off toward Foreganger and Valency, but that is all. In the early days of settlement, it was thought that proximity to the blue giant at Sapphire Point would endow Peacock with a great many roads; and much effort was spent on the survey of its approaches, but the tenor of scientific thought now runs in the other direction. And a good thing, too; for nothing tempts the highwaymen of the Spiral Arm more than a sun with plentiful roads.

Shalmandaro Spaceport was the primary STC repository for Peacock Roads, and so it was to this gracile orangestone tower that Bridget ban came on the trail of the phantom fleet. The tower was inlaid with gold and decorated with pastel murals of Peacock scenery and of those few 'Cockers who had ever faced anything requiring heroism. On the building's western facade, a bulbous extrusion eyed distant Polychrome Mountain and the tea plantations that tiled her slopes. There, trace elements in the soils and the artifice of bioneering gave the tea fields sundry colors and the mountain its name.

Despite the building's importance, there was no security screen at the entrance. Bridget ban was not surprised. It was of a piece with this lackadaisical world. But after she had passed through and was standing before the lift tubes in the great, multistoried atrium, she gave the matter a second thought. Indolent need not mean stupid. Indeed, indolence often required considerable ingenuity. So she returned to the vestibule and studied its walls with greater care, and discovered amid the wild swirls and colors with which the 'Cockers embellished any flat surface the lenticels and digitizers of various sensors. She nodded her approval at one camera eye, her opinion of the 'Cockers rising by a notch.

_____

Konmi Pulawayo was not in the Director's office when, thanks to typically vague directions from staff, Bridget ban had finally located it. The room did not strike her as very official. Offices ought to appear functional: with desks, storage drives, comm units, hard-copy files, and the like. They ought, in fact, to have walls. They ought not have a whispering water-fall and a glade guarded by colorful parrots and sweet larks. A parrot is not a receptionist; and a hammock is not an office chair.

"So where," she asked one green-and-yellow bird, "is your master?"

The parrot shuffled a bit on its perch, cocked its head, and squawked. "Whaddaview! Lookaddaview!"

Bridget ban snorted, turned away, then wondered if there was something more serious under this frivo-lous facade. The 'Cockers were famous across the Spiral Arm for their bioneering. Perhaps the parrot was a receptionist, after all. Yet there was nothing about the bird that suggested it was anything more than a bird. The skull was not of an encouraging vol-ume; its attention span fleeting. It glanced at the in-truder repeatedly, but that would be expected of any half-wild beast. Its exclamation was probably no more than a trained reflex.

But why train a bird to make *that* response to *that* question? Answer: the Director took his breaks in the viewing room she had noticed from the outside. She glanced at her watch. It was early for a break— unless, as she suspected, 'Cockers inverted the times devoted to work and leisure.

A passing technician, frail and featureless as an elf, bare-chested and wearing a tool belt over his "srong," told her the lounge was at the end of Redfruit Lane, and pointed to a bush growing along the side of the "corridor." Bridget ban thanked him and he nodded vaguely, plucking a "redfruit" to eat as he sauntered off. She wondered if he was on his way to repair something and how long that repair would await his arrival.

The redfruits wound through the seventeenth floor, intersecting at times with other winding paths marked by other bushes. There were no walls, but occasionally there were lines of shrubs or trees, or rivulets crossed by short footbridges, each evidently intended to mark the boundary of a "room." Not one was straight. There might not be a right angle in the entire building. She did see individuals working at screens and chatting casually to hologram images. It could not *all* be personal activity, could it? Somehow, cross-stellar and in-system traffic in the Junction was choreographed; somehow lighters and bumboats were lifted and landed. *Someone* out there must be working!

Eventually, curiosity—or surrender—overcame her and she plucked a redfruit for herself. Its skin was soft and plump and the texture, when she had bitten into it, crispy. The taste was succulent and sweet, suggesting both apple and cherry in its ancestry. She had to remind herself that she was inside a large building and the groves through which she wound were only clever artifacts.

The lounge was entirely transparent; even the floors and furniture. In effect, one seemed to be walking in midair, and Bridget ban could see past her boots the traffic far below. Only the people and a few other objects—brightly patterned cushions and the like— were stubbornly opaque. Directly ahead, Polychrome Mountain had been artfully framed between two other high towers so that it appeared larger and closer than it actually was. She wondered if the 'Cockers had erected those two buildings precisely to achieve that effect.

Bridget ban wore a green-and-gold coverall with the blue facings and collar pips of "The Particular Service." Above her left breast were discreetly pinned two of the twelve decorations to which she was entitled: the Grand Star and the Badge of Night. The Kennel called it "undress uniform," but she thought herself the most completely dressed person in the lounge, perhaps in the entire building. Some 'Cockers she saw carried casualness of dress to its logical, and ultimate, conclusion.

A few inquiries eventually led her finally to the Director. She had wondered from the name whether Konmi Pulawayo was male or female and, after having been introduced, continued to wonder. Most of the human race was bimodally distributed, but the bioneers of Peacock had achieved the bell-shaped curve, with most inhabitants clustered around a sort of genderless mean and rather fewer out near masculine or feminine extremes. Pulawayo might have been a fine-featured man or a boyish woman. Large, liquid eyes set in an androgynous face gave no clue. There was one way to be certain—and, judging by what she had seen so far, not a way entirely out of the question—but she was struck by the disturbing notion that lifting the Director's srong would not lift the uncertainty.

Tentatively, she designated Pulawayo as "she," and firmly fixed that pronoun in mind.

The Director called for tea. On Peacock, that was a foregone conclusion. The variegated flavors and fragrances unique to Polychrome Mountain constituted the planet's primary export, and drinking it was an act of patriotism.

Pulawayo had preceded her tea order by a slight cough, by which Bridget ban concluded that she was "headwired" and the cough was how she activated the link. While they waited, the elf regarded the Hound with a smile bordering on amusement and studied her with palpable interest.

"Zo," she said through near-motionless lips, "wuzzahoundoneer?"

The Peacock dialect ran words together and softened its consonants. Indeed, a common joke in the League was that on Peacock, the use of a consonant was subject to a heavy fine. Lazy speech for lazy lips, thought Bridget ban. Her implant sharpened the phonemes to Gaelactic Standard. *So. What's a Hound doing here?* the Director had asked.

In answer, she produced her credentials—by ancient tradition, a golden badge of metallo-ceramic that glowed when held by its rightful bearer. "I'm investigating the battle that took place here recently." It was more than that, of course. The phantom fleet had taken something from the pirates—a prehuman artifact of great value and possibly greater power. But such secrets were best held close, lest they pique greed and ambition.

The Director barely glanced at the badge. "Oh, that," she said. "No battle. Battle needs two sides. Ambushers caltroped the exit ramp and swissed whichever ships came out next. Good luck, they caught a pirate fleet with top booty and their shields down. Nuisance."

"Aye. Such lawlessness . . ."

But the Director had not been concerned about lawlessness. "Clean up the mess," she complained. "Sweepers *still* out there. Sent swifties down the Silk Road with warnings. Placed marker buoys. *Duchess of Dragomar* took damage coming off next day. Didn't want more ships running into shards. Bad for tourism."

As she spoke, she muttered under her breath, annoying the Hound. Bridget ban tried to make out what she was saying, but the subvocalization was too slight. Irritated, she said, "And have ye identified the combatants?"

"Pirates were from Cynthia, barbarians coming back heavy from somewhere—"

"From New Eireann. We know about them. The survivors reached Sapphire Point while I was there."

"Zo. Heavy with loot from this New Eireann place. Lost their vanguard on the caltrops. Other ships jittered. Two skated off on hyperbolic. One braked into elliptical. Saw Cerenkov flashes, so some ships reached the high-c's but missed the channel and grounded in the mud."

And those who escaped down the Silk Road had been destroyed by Fir Li's border squadron. "And what about the ambushing fleet?"

The Director held up a hand palm out. "One sec." Then she closed her eyes. "No, no, no, darlings. Move Atreus 9-1-7 into High 'Cock Orbit. Low 'Cock ICC 3-2-9-1. 'First come,' dears. Do *not*, repeat *not*, land lighters from *Chettinad Voyager* . . . Because *Heart of Oak* is still on the designated landing grid, that's why. *Where*," and this was said with deadly sweetness, "are the tugs?" A pause. "I don't care. *King Peter* is off the active field. *Heart of Oak* is still on it. I can't land *Chettinad Voyager* with the field cluttered up that way." Pulawayo sighed, rolled her eyes in mute appeal to beings unseen, and smiled at Bridget ban. "Sorry. New controller. Needed full attention." She stretched her arms over her head and arched her back.

"Ah, here's the tea. I asked for Wenderfell, a very nice blend with a spicy aroma and an aftertaste of clove."

The server who brought the tea on an elaborately chased silver platter was refreshingly thick-limbed and hairy. He poured a stream of iridescent tea into cups of near transparent china, painted on the outside with a colorful hunting scene from ancient times: an elderly guide pointing into the distance and a quartet of men in hip boots carrying double-barreled pellet guns. In the background, a flock of aboriginal ducks arched like a feathered bridge into the sky. On the other side, the cup bore a painting of a duck in flight, rendered in subtle colors. It was bleeding from a dozen wounds, and despair had been imposed somehow on its immobile features. The shimmering tea, swirling behind the translucent ceramic, gave it the illusion of desperate motion.

Pulawayo handed her the cup, contriving to touch hands as she did. Bridget ban took it and waited to see what all this portended. "You're paraperceptic," she said.

The Director seemed disappointed in the response. "Oh. Yes. Only duplex, I fear. Half my brain—the logical, calculating half, I hope"—she giggled—"is overseeing the space traffic controllers. The other half . . . Well, here I am. Do you like the teacups?"

Bridget ban thought there was also an element of calculation in the half-brain she was facing, but she said nothing. "Ye painted these cups yourself," she guessed.

Pulawayo waved a hand. "Oh, it's nothing. Just a hobby. You should see our export ware. But I'm such a silly. You were asking about the 'bushers. They matched trajectory with one of the treasure ships— and wasn't *that* a pretty piece of work at high-v?"

"I know *what* they did. I'm trying to find out who they were."

A blithe shrug. "They never said."

Suppressing an exasperated retort, Bridget ban explained: "The, ah, 'bushers ne'er passed through Sapphire Point, so they must hae gone toward either Jehovah or Foreganger. If ye've no idea o' their homeworld, at least tell me which direction they went."

The Director waved her hand. "Oh, surely you can't suspect Foreganger or Jehovah. Hijacking pirates isn't Foreganger's style, and Jehovah's a turtle—keeps its head tucked in."

"Of course not," the Hound explained patiently, "but the phantom fleet must hae *passed through* one o' them, and *their* STC could tell me where they went next. Now, I could be tossing a coin tae pick one, but I'd lose a fortnight running down and back, should I be guessing wrong. Those are twa of the busiest interchanges in this region o' the Spiral Arm, and that's a lot of straw to sift for one flotilla of needles. Unless," she added sarcastically, "the ambushers fight a battle at each interchange to draw attention to themselves."

The Director laughed. "Oh, of course. How silly of me. But . . . We don't know which ramp they came off. They must've entered under heavy traffic, hiding themselves in a forest of arrivals. No beacons sent ahead. Incoming's supposed to hail the port. Can't always see 'em at high-v, y'know." Pulawayo had reverted to choppy sentences, by which Bridget ban deduced that her paraperception was imperfect. When the Director split her attention and subvocalized, she could not frame complex sentences.

"Then, which road are they after *leaving* on?" the Hound asked with growing exasperation.

"Don't know. Swung around . . ." Pulawayo held a hand up, said *waidasec,* and stopped the alternate

conversation with a curt, *Handle it yourself, dear*.
Then, "They swung around grabbing space like that
ancient god, Tarzan. The aether strings are *still* rip-
pling out that way. We thought they meant to circle
around to the Silk Road entrances. But they never
showed. All that confusion—do you know how many
ships were in the sky at the time? And stealthed the
way the 'bushers were—well . . ." She shrugged. "We
lost them."

"Ye lost them," Bridget ban repeated. She could
well believe in 'Cocker sloppiness, but this beggared
the imagination. The Director was, as the Terrans
were wont to say, "blowing smoke." Bridget ban had
listened to evasions spun by the best of them, and
recognized all the symptoms. "I see. Is that a common problem around the Junction?"

The Director muttered, *No, no, no. I'm off-line*,
then, "What do you mean?"

"Losing track of the traffic out in the coopers.
Does that happen often?"

The elf's face hardened as much as elf faces could.
"We do well enough."

"Ye noticed the battle itself, I'm sure. Ye must hae
gotten *some* positional fixes. I can extrapolate origin
and destination from those."

"They changed vectors three times while we did
track them, and might have done anything while they
were in the black; so I don't think the fixes we did get
can help you."

Bridget ban spoke as if to a child. "I'll be judging
what I can and can nae do. I need to review your
transit records." She was already proffering a memo-
stick when the Director shook her head.

"Oh, dear. I'm afraid that won't be possible."

This was more than evasion. This was obstruction.
But the why of it eluded the Hound. Was Peacock

protecting the phantom fleet? She began to suspect that if she did not obtain the STC records soon, she never would. At least, not the original records. The Director was, as the Terrans said, "playing for time."

She flashed her badge once more. "I'm afraid ye've nae choice. League regulations. I 'demand and require' your information in the name o' Tully O'Connor, Ardry of High Tara and president o' the League o' the Periphery." Maybe the formal language would kick start the woman.

But the Director smiled sweetly. "And I'm *afraid* your 'high king' doesn't mass much here. Peacock's not a Member State."

Bridget ban reared back. "Nae a Member? Ridiculous . . ." But her implant shook hands with the library aboard her ship and confirmed the fact. No agreement was on record. Was her gazetteer deficient? "The Treaty of Amity and Common Purpose was submitted one hundred and fifty metric years ago."

"The Seanaid is still debating it. We don't rush into things here. Oh . . ." She waved a hand. "It's our *custom* to cooperate with the League. But we don't cooperate because we're *ordered*. We do it because we're nicely asked."

Bridget ban swallowed a sarcastic observation and forced a "please" through smiling teeth.

Pulawayo ran a finger along the back of the Hound's hand. "I said *nicely* asked."

Bridget ban finally understood what the Director wanted in exchange for cooperation. She was no stranger to bribery, even sexual bribery, but casual sex could still shock her. When she used sex, there was nothing casual about it. It was purposeful, deliberate, and well planned.

The Director misread the pause. "Are you exclusive

to men?" she asked. "Because I'm seeing my surgeon later today. I've been feeling very male lately."

Bridget ban greeted this announcement with astonished silence. She could not imagine this . . . *elf* containing a single manly impulse. One surge of testosterone and the vessel would shatter. For that matter, anything genuinely feminine would whistle through her as through an empty reed. Those who try to do two things at once, she decided, would seldom do either very well.

Foreganger or Jehovah? She could simply guess, but Jehovah was ten days' journey and Foreganger closer to twenty. Better an extra day on Peacock to make certain, even if that meant snuggling with Pulawayo. Yet, what guarantee did she have that, even after the bribe, Pulawayo would cooperate? She could imagine an entire series of such delays—always immanently cooperative, never overtly a refusal—until finally a well-doctored set of records would be handed over with great fanfare, cooperative exclamations, and calculated deception.

She wondered if they thought they could doctor the records well enough to deceive a Hound. There were rumors that captains carrying illicit cargoes could "launder" their transits through Peacock Junction, and could drop off radar screens when the need arose. A Hound's matter, if true, though not to her present purpose; but Peacock might well fear otherwise.

And so the Hound found herself at liberty until evening. The day was one of brilliant clarity. Polychromopolis, the planetary capital, lay in the monsoon belt and the dry season had just begun. The temperature was hot—at or above body temperature, and fans and parasols were common along the streets. Above, in a cloudless sky, a few high white streamers marked the tracks of jetliners and ballistic leapers headed for the antipodes. Below, the recently ended rains had painted the landscape in moist pastels. Flowers of brilliant yellow and orange and red lined the pedestrian walkways beneath the shade of broad, leafy trees. Some of the blossoms would have been known on Old Earth—assuming the origin myths were really true—but others were artifacts unknown to nature: exotic races of palm and orchid and rose and deodar, bearing those ancient names only through courtesy and the contribution of a few ancestral genes.

Passing her on the Embarcadero—the slidewalk from the Port into the main shopping district—were folk from all over the Spiral Arm. She saw pale, squat Jugurthans with their startlingly wide and out-turned noses; Chettinads in tartan kilts and turbans. There were sour-faced, girdled Jehovans muttering over their prayer beads; and gaudy trade-captains from the Greater Hanse whose jewels and rings and robes glittered in the late-morning sunlight. She heard the hooting accents of Alabaster, the flat twang of Megranome, and the nearly incomprehensible jibber-jabber of Terran pack peddlers. Peacock wasn't a great interchange like Jehovah, but many travelers stopped here for pleasure and relaxation. It was the preferred vacation spot for this region of the Arm.

She noticed how heads turned and eyes flickered in her direction. A Hound? Here? Why? It was the uniform, of course. The concept of a uniform was alien to 'Cockers, perhaps a little perverted. Pulawayo had asked her to wear the uniform tonight.

She stepped onto the Esplanade, a lateral slidewalk traversing the main Portside shopping district known as Rodyadarava. She had no eye for the clothing stores—the Rift would fill with stars before she would prance about in the topless srong that the elves of Peacock favored; and judging by a pair of Jugurthan women passing by, a few sagging tourists might have profited by adopting the same attitude. But a tea shop at the corner of Kairthnashrad caught her eye, and she entered on a whim to seek refuge from the heat.

Inside, she encountered a medley of odors: a hint of vanilla, a suggestion of roses, the unmistakable aroma of Abyalonic holdenblum. On the far wall of the shop, a rack of bins was filled with teas of various colors: blacks and duns and ochres, but also more exotic shades that nature had never intended.

What, she thought in a mood approaching panic, *if I only want a cup of tea?*

Small round tables had been set up around the shop and on the little plaza outside. Some were at sitting level; others were tall and people stood at them, drinking and chatting. At this time of day, about half the tables were occupied by a mix of sixty-forty, locals to tourists. Two Chettinad traders, in matching kilts and turbans, pondered over a game board. They whispered to each other as Bridget ban passed by.

"Ah, Cu," said the teakeeper behind the counter. "You have come for a cup of Pleasurepot? Our most famous blend."

Bridget ban studied the rows of teas. "I'm . . . not sure."

The teakeeper laughed. "A more meditative blend, then. I have Gray Thoughts, a private blend the Consortium makes for a colleague of yours; but I'm sure he'd not grudge you a taste of it."

The Hound had been curious where the teakeeper

had learned the form of address the Kennel used among themselves. She could also guess the name of the colleague: Greystroke would have found the name of the blend both amusing and irresistible.

The teakeeper went belowstairs and climbed back with a canister of plain metallic gray. Turning it, he showed her the embossing on the bottom: Greystroke's personal logo. At her approval, the teakeeper took a carefully measured scoop of the leaves; filled a small, perforated ball; and prepared an infusion—discussing all the while the physics and chemistry involved. Bridget ban only wanted a drink, but the teakeeper would not hand the cup over until a mandatory amount of "steeping" had elapsed. "It's different for each blend, you see."

She didn't see, and did her best to forget after she took the steaming cup away.

The Chettinads were playing shaHmat, and were in the mid-game. Some versions of the game were played in three dimensions. Some used computers and hundreds of pieces with fluctuating fighting qualities. Still others—called "chutes and ladders"—mimicked the superluminal creases of Electric Avenue and allowed game pieces to slipstream rapidly between designated squares. But the Chettinads were playing the true game, unadorned, handling finely carved wooden pieces across a nine-by-nine board of squares.

Red, whose turban was an intricate plaid of green, yellow, and red checks and lines, was engaged in Remour's Offer. His emperor stood unmoved on the center square of his home row while his minions had pushed forward in a complex arrangement of mutual support. The flanking councilors and leaping hounds were in play on the princess side, although the fortresses still anchored the two ends of his line. The princess was in midfield with a good chance to marry the opposing prince. If White allowed that, his prince would become powerless in any attack on Red. Hence, he was playing McDevitt's Refusal.

An unstable arrangement, she thought. Complexity upon complexity, and the least wrong move would send it all crashing into chaos from which only the most nimble thinker could pluck victory. White's prince was castled, refusing to meet the opposing princess.

After a time in which nothing seemed to happen, White picked up his teacup and sipped. He put it down again. Nothing happened some more.

Then, with a shrug, he sent a White hound leaping out.

A mistake! Bridget ban took a swallow of Gray Thoughts, and leaned forward a little to see how Red would respond.

Red barely noticed. He moved his prince forward one square. "These are bad times," he commented after a sip from his cup.

White's turban—richly green, shot through with ochre threads and golden bands—bobbed side to side in agreement. "The ICC grows bold and arrogant. They strut."

It was the custom of the Chettinad traders when in public to speak in allusions. "Three ships of Sèan Company passed through the Junction yesterday," said Red. "They paid no duties as poor Chettinads must pay. This was said by a customs officer far gone in her cups."

"'Drink makes truth.'"

"'Wise is the sober man.'"

"Would only that such wisdom extended to the movements of princes." White advanced a second hound on the other side of the field, threatening Red prince.

"'Long-lived are the fish that rise not to the bait,'" Red observed, shifting a minion laterally to take a

White minion. "Why do our cousins in Sèan Company preen? Strange words have been said. With the aid of sand and iron, they shall make the Ardry himself their minion." He raised his head from the board and met his companion's eyes. "Hard words, those; and what did the speaker mean by their saying?"

White shrugged. "It is not for poor Chettinad traders to know such things. To move excellent goods at fair prices is all they desire. The moods and wants of high kings are nothing to them. But what if their rivals should gain such power over kings?"

"Then woe to the poor Chettinad, and to his wives and children."

Bridget ban placed her cup on its saucer with a tiny click and said, as if to no one in particular, "The Ardry has ears everywhere, but knows not always the meaning of what he hears."

White bowed his head, and a small smile played across his lips. "May the wisdom of the Ardry increase—or that of his 'ears.'" Red grunted in amusement.

"The Ardry," said Bridget ban, "is the servant of the League and its Member States."

White cupped his chin and studied the board. "The Ardry may be a servant of the League, but he cannot wish to be a servant of Sèan Company." He moved a councilor down a diagonal.

Red made the sign of the wheel and touched his chakras. "May the Bood forbid such a thing."

Bridget ban returned to her hotel room and prepared for her "assignation" with Pulawayo. She stripped herself of the uniform, and showered the heat away. Afterward, she inspected the clothing she had brought, mentally inventoried that which remained aboard her ship, and sighed with frustration. Pulawayo had asked that she wear the uniform; but did she really care about the wrapping for the confection she desired? (*He,* she amended the thought. The surgery was done by now.)

She needn't worry about dressing seductively. The conclusion was tacitly agreed. So, comfort, convenience, and inconspicuousness were the order of the day. Something she could remove and don with relative ease, and which would not stand out on the street.

Which was sounding more and more like a topless srong in bright, gaudy colors.

She went to the 'face that sat on a desk by the wall and accessed the hotel's system, accepted a nuisance charge to her bill, and slid out into the information slipstream. She screened on the Director's name, found it moderately common, and fined up the mesh size with job position and hobby.

Teacup patterns. There! As she had thought, Pulawayo took enormous pride in her . . . in *his* hobby—*damned genderbending nuisance custom*—and had set up an information locus where people could see examples, comment approvingly, and even purchase complete tea sets. Hah. One commentator had written that the designs were insipid.

Well, there was more than one way to practice seduction. If the body's surrender was a foregone conclusion, that of the mind was not. And what the Hound wanted from the Director was not the body.

She downloaded the pattern for the teacup she had seen at the STC tower and extracted the colors from the duck's feathers. These, she entered into a drawing program and set it for smooth abstract shapes and long sweeping lines.

The result was a pattern that suggested the duck's plumage from the teacup without being a mere representation of it. Imitation was the sincerest form of flattery. Pulawayo might not consciously notice, but seduction need not be conscious and no one ever made an enemy of a parent by praising the child's beauty.

When the pattern had downloaded, she consulted *Benet's Sumptuary Guide to the Spiral Arm* until she found something she could reasonably wear as a top for a srong: a light poncho used by the Kushkans on 'Bandonope. It was short and made of diaphanous cloth. She entered her personal measurements.

Then she went to a drawer, pulled out two bolts of anycloth she had brought with her, and inserting the data-thread into the port, downloaded the design and the cut into the cloth. The micro-electromechanical weave shimmered and became . . . a duckwing srong and matching poncho top. The gaudy ensemble would win no kudos in the fashion houses of Hadley Prime, but it would pass for inconspicuous here.

The Director's home lay in the Nolapatady, a district of the capital easily reached on the maglev's Sandpipe line. The house proved an oval building of intricately carved dark wood that encircled a central courtyard open to the sky. In the courtyard, interlocking fishponds were fed by an elaborately decorated terracotta rain-catcher and cistern. Planters, atria, and the artful placement of furniture served in lieu of internal walls, so that from any point around the orbit of the house, one could cross to any other point. Overhanging eaves and runnels in the courtyard prevented rainwater from entering the residence itself.

Pulawayo met all of Bridget ban's fairly low expectations that evening. She—now *he*—proudly displayed the results of the surgery, and panted and pawed and squeezed and made numerous exclamations of what were apparently intended as signs of masculine appreciation and pleasure. Bridget ban made a few comments herself; but they were planned, and intended to achieve a certain rapport with the Director. She had earlier applied a numbing agent so that she would not be distracted by untoward sensations at crucial moments, but in retrospect she thought that she needn't have bothered.

There was a Terran proverb she had heard: *Practice makes perfect.* But Pulawayo had not spent enough continuous time as either man or woman to get much practice at either.

She was slightly nettled that the Director had not noticed the effort she had put into her outfit. The deliberation was not supposed to be noticeable, but some comment would have been welcome. Instead, the Director had pouted a bit that she hadn't worn her uniform, and the Hound wondered if this indicated some need for dominance. So she took the upper role, told him exactly what to do, praised him when he did it right, slapped him when he didn't. She could not help thinking of how one trained puppies.

She had worn a crystal pendant—a product of Wofford and Beale on New Eireann—and as she moved rhythmically above him, it swung to and fro, catching the light from the foyer. She murmured to him in a low monotone, at first using standard terms of endearment and pleasure, but after a time shifting to suggestions of sleepiness and fatigue. *Are you tired? You can't be tired already. You can hardly keep your eyes open . . .*

Soon, aided by the physical release, Pulawayo lay in a drowsy, hypnotic state upon the cushions and silks that 'Cockers used for beds. Bridget ban softly dismounted, pulled a sling chair to the side of the bed, and set to work.

It did not take long to learn the pass codes and the location of the hard key to the STC database. Suspecting that the 'Cocker love of indolence meant a great deal of telefacing from home, she tried the keys and codes on Pulawayo's home 'face, and was gratified to find her assumption justified.

She used the data-thread to download the information into her clothing. The database was rather large, and she could leave nothing but the "duckwing" outfit in active memory. That was chancy. One system crash, and she'd be wearing two gray towels around her waist and shoulders.

When she was finished, she erased all memories and logs from the 'face. She had been wearing fingercaps, so no genetic information was on the keyboard, and for any genetic traces found elsewhere, she had established a reason that any 'Cocker would readily accept.

A moan escaped from the bed area. Bridget ban frowned, because Pulawayo should not be coming out of the hypnosis on his own. She dashed across the courtyard, around the fishponds, and between two thick pillars carved to resemble tree trunks, coming to the mound of cushions and drapes on which the Director lay.

Pulawayo was still under, but his mouth opened and closed slackly and his throat, loose in sleep, struggled to form sounds. *Talking in his sleep,* she thought. *He must be dreaming.*

But the 'Cocker dialect was built of lazy lips and throats, and Bridget ban's implant began to make sense out of the moans, helping her to hear them in Gaelactic.

"Where did you go?" the Director said. "Why did you leave me?"

Bridget ban had been leaning over the bed to hear better. Now she stood straight in alarm, thinking furiously. He *couldn't* have come out of it. "I needed to use your facilities," she temporized. "Go back to sleep now."

"He *is* asleep. Why did you ask him about the access codes?"

Him? It was eerie enough to be conversing with a sleeping man. To hear him speak of himself in such a detached fashion reminded Bridget ban of old Die Bold tales of "spooken" that could take over your body. Each New Year's Eve, with other Die Bold children, she would dress in terrible and frightening costumes, pretending to be already possessed and trusting to professional courtesy. The practice was taken less seriously than in Settlement Days, but the recollection came on her so suddenly and so completely that for a moment she almost ran in terror from the house. Only her iron control kept her at the bedside long enough to realize what must have happened.

"He was going to give me that information in the morning," she said. "Hush. You sleep, too. That was quite a ride we had. You must be tired."

"*I'm* not tired; but, oh, you were so good. And your clothing—that was a nice compliment. I don't want them to hurt you."

"No one's going to hurt me."

"They'll be waiting outside, on the street to the maglev. *He* suggested it. He said the secret was worth the risk."

"What secret?"

"Oh, *I* don't know. I'll remember when he wakes up, I suppose."

Of course. The paraperception. Awake, both halves of the brain would be cross-talking. Right now she was talking to Pulawayo's emotive-perceptive half, but naturally they gave both hemispheres access to the speech center.

Note to self: when interrogating a paraperceptic, be sure to hypnotize both halves.

Gently, she calmed the frightened half of the brain. Then, speaking into the right ear, she told the other half that he'd had a confused dream, and he would forget it when he awoke. She described their lovemaking as more passionate than it had been, and played to his fantasies by telling him she *had* worn her Hound's uniform and they *had* played dominance games. She told him that she had left an hour before the current clock time. She told him they had kissed at the door.

There. The memories most easily recalled are the ones that we wish we'd had. If he remembered from his other half that she had left the bed during the night, he would ascribe that to her female needs.

Then, surrendering to an impulse, she pulled up the right eyelid.

The eyeball was rolled back in its socket, moving in a slow rhythm.

She pulled up the left eyelid.

And it was looking right at her.

"Good-bye," she told the left ear. "You were wonderful. I shall never forget you."

It was a small lie, and she needed the gratitude and cooperation of that half.

It was night and the street was shrouded in darkness broken by the pools of light created by the lamps. Most of the houses were dark blocks set into the night. A few, at this late hour, showed pale lamplight behind shades and curtains. A distant hiss marked the Hilliwaddy River where it spilled over the rocks in its descent from Polychrome Mountain. The wind stirred the trees into whispered excitement.

She had reached the corner and had turned onto Olumakali Street leading to the maglev station when she smelled them.

Two of them, waiting in the shadows between two of the houses. Under that tree.

(Is that her) she heard one whisper.

(She's a tourista, in't she?)

(But they said she'd be wearing some kinky sort of clothing. A "uniform.")

She was passing by them now, pretending she couldn't hear or smell them. She remembered the brawny 'Cockers she had noticed now and then. Peacock was ruled by custom, not laws. They didn't have policers. They had enforcers.

She wondered if they knew what a Hound could do? There were only two of them.

Or were there?

She continued to listen as she drew away.

(That wasn't her.)

(Wait. She's passing under the streetlight. We'll get a better look.)

(Red hair. That's her alright. Call Kerinomata and tell them to come up the street. We'll follow her down.)

They came out of the shadows with a silence remarkable for their size. She did not turn around to look at them. Four, she supposed. Two behind, two ahead. That made the odds not quite even. But she ought not simply kill them. She had come to Peacock Junction to track the phantom fleet, not to create a diplomatic incident between Peacock and the League. On the other hand, if she let them attack her, every Hound who heard of it would come straight to the

Junction, and there would be no stone left atop another.

(Here comes Kerinomata. We got her . . .)

"Hey! Where'd she go!"

In the lightless interstice between two streetlamps, Bridget ban had leaped aside, leaving a pair of sandals standing in the walkway behind her—as if she had simply evaporated in place. Wooden soles would make noise when running and silence now was worth any price. Fleet as a whippet, she sprinted between two darkened dwellings into a shared greenery behind: trees, a fishpond, several beds of colorful flowers, a stone garden. As she ran, she gathered her srong up and tucked it into her waistband. Now, it was a short skirt, and her legs were free. She bounded over the pond, ran a few steps along a bench, and—up!—over a hedgerow of fat-leafed oily plants.

And down—in another back garden, again shared by several houses. She crouched, knees bent, fingertips lightly touching the grass like a runner poised for the gun, and listened. A whistle in the distance, on the block she had come from. Was this a world where people pulled the shutters closed when they heard such sounds at night? Or one where they ran to their windows and spied on the dark with comm units clutched in hand?

Long hours in the training room now returned interest a hundredfold. She sprinted out to the next street, where she paused, sniffed, listened, looked. Nothing. *Across the street,* and repeat the process over to the next street. Could she run fast enough to put herself outside the radius of what they would consider a reasonable search area? How far to the next maglev station?

No. Forget that. They'd be watching the maglev stations.

She paused, panted, looked around the neighborhood.

A large hulk of a building stood in midblock, like a rock among soap bubbles. The walls were rough, unfinished granite and bore in front a colonnade whose pillars seemed the least bit too wide and short. It appeared more lasting than the evanescent homes around it; more serious than anything the frivolous 'Cockers would build. Its stolid facade bespoke an earlier epoch in the planet's history. If other buildings of this ilk had ever squatted along this street, they had long since been demolished and replaced.

An official building, then; dark, unlikely to be occupied at this hour. Perhaps it was a library, or a meeting hall. Was it open? Locked? Alarmed?

By now, her description was abroad. There would be someone waiting in her hotel room. Her ship would be guarded. (She hoped no one was so stupid as to try to break into it. The ship's intelligence frowned on such mischief.) They would be expanding the search, block by block.

They had been fools to send only four men to arrest her. She could not count on them remaining fools. If they had woken Pulawayo by now—likely— he would tell them she had left his home an hour earlier, and that she was wearing her Hound's uniform, as they had expected. This would confuse them for a time. Were they chasing the right person, or another redhead tourista coincidentally in the same neighborhood?

Either way, they would want to find her.

She found a back door to the building, where she could work unobserved in the dark. Her night vision was very good, at one with her enhanced smell and hearing. She studied the walls, saw no wires, no receptors. She paid particular attention to the mortared crevices between the great stone blocks. If she were to insert a monitor into the walls, *there* would be a good location . . .

Nothing.

Remembering the vestibule at the STC tower, she leaped to no conclusion, remained crouched there, pawed a little at the door, snuffled. It was hinged to open inward. A lever latch. She pressed it down.

No alarms. This far from the tourist areas, the 'Cockers did not fear unauthorized entries. Among themselves, custom was a stronger bar than locks and alarms. Those who found trespass unimaginable would find it hard to imagine trespassers. Briefly, she wondered what it might be like to live in a society that did not bar its doors.

Her implant returned the datum that buildings of this style were called *remonstratoria,* or Halls of Remonstration. They were thought to be either law courts or temples, but no off-worlder had ever been inside one, and what rites were performed within remained a mystery.

Wonderful. She could add sacrilege to her list of offenses.

The door swung noiselessly inward, revealing a darkened corridor. She stepped through, closing the door softly, and found herself in a rough basement. She squatted there, panting from her run, and sniffed. A harsh chemical odor stung her nostrils. It might mask the odor of a human being—a custodian or night watchman.

But listening, she heard nothing save the creaking and settling of the building itself. This was an old building. She could smell the age in the dank stone, in the seasoned wood. The years had soaked into them and settled there.

Old buildings are sacred in societies ruled by custom.

Sacred because it was old or old because it was sacred, it made no difference. But how could she enter such a building and not explore? Hounds are, by their nature, always sniffing around.

She picked out a flight of old wooden steps twisting up a narrow stairwell. The runners had rounded dips in their centers, worn by countless feet over countless years. She thought the building might predate the Reconnection, when some of the Diaspora worlds had recovered the ability to slide between the stars.

Stairs are meant for climbing; and so, she did.

She paused again on the main floor to sniff and listen. The chemical scents were stronger here, but the silences remained as profound. Light glimmered through shutter slats covering the windows. A tree must have stood between the window and the streetlamp because the light flickered irregularly as the branches outside wavered in the fitful night breeze.

She made out row after row of racks reaching nearly to the ceiling and arranged in rigid precision from the front of the room to its back. The severity of the geometry was at one with the architecture of the building—and very unlike the free-flowing, unwalled improvisations of modern 'Cockers.

A library, she thought, *or possibly an art gallery.*

Drawing nearer, she discerned solid objects mounted to the walls. Sculpture, perhaps? If so, sculpture of little variety. Equally spaced in rigid rows, each seemed roughly the same size as all the others. Well, sonnets were all the same "size," yet each could be an exquisitely different work of art—for the greatest art,

Die Bolders believed, lay in "achievement within re-
strictions," just as accomplishment in sport required
hurdles and nets and balk lines.

Brief bursts of dim light alternated with closeted
darkness as the leaves fluttered in front of the window. Bridget ban stepped into an aisle to get a better
look at one of the sculptures.

*And came face-to-face with a wide-eyed, grim-
lipped elf with wild, frizzy hair.* It required all her
Hound's training to stifle the cry that climbed up her
throat.

Discovered! There had been a watchman, after all.

But the elf said nothing. The eyes did not blink.
The mouth did not part. A disembodied voice spoke
through sewn-still lips. "I am Billy Kisilwando. I
killed my partner in a drunken fit . . ."

And the horror of discovery gave way to the discovery of horror.

It was a head, carefully preserved by the taxider-
mist's art, eyes replaced by glass, lips stitched closed,
mounted to a wall bracket. Beneath was a plaque
bearing a name, an offense, and a date. Evidently, if
someone stood for a time before a particular head,
an intelligence would play that person's last words.

*When Billy Kisilwando killed his partner in a drunken
fit, he was given one hundred days grace to set his affairs in order and to meditate, which he did. He set
off into the Malawayo Wilderness with a rucksack,
a hiking staff, and a small, but faithful terrier. He
emerged after ninety-nine days, minus dog and staff,
and reported to the District Head, confessed his sin,
and prayed forgiveness from his partner's manu. Then
they cut off his head, preserved it, and mounted it in
the Hall of Remonstration, where it is admired by all
who pass through the Nolapatady District on their*

*journeys. And forever after he repeated his confession
to all who came to see him. Such is the cruelty of custom: not that a man be given the grace to contemplate
his end; but that he feels bound to honor its expira-
tion.*

Bridget ban contemplated the head of Billy Kisilwando, and passed judgment.

"Now, *that's* different," she said aloud.

She wandered fascinated through the hall, and
found aisle after aisle of stuffed and mounted heads.
The panels near the street entrance were newer; those
near the back or in side chambers were older, more
severe in their lines, with classical moldboards and
trim. The older plaques bore dates in the former "Peacock's Era." The newer plaques bore Gaelactic dates,
but with the Year of the Peacock noted parentheti-
cally underneath.

There were fewer elves in the back rooms, and in
one especially dusty room, the only heads were iden-
tifiably men and women. These older displays were
crowded closer together, and the heads were tattered
and moth-eaten. As the displays grew more recent, the
heads converged toward the androgynous average.

On the newer walls, brightly painted in the exuberant pastels of modern Peacock, were mounted among
the elves the heads of others: pale, flat-faced Jugurthans; golden women from Valency; thin-featured
Alabastrines with skin like night; even a Cynthian
warrior's head, dripping with jewels, cruel arrogance,
and barbaric splendor—and hard must have been the
severing of *that* neck. The off-worlder faces all bore a
look of immense surprise; as if they could not credit
what was being done to them; all except the Cynthian, who managed somehow to sneer even in death.
Curious, she waited until it spoke its confession.

Eat my dick, the head whispered, and an involuntary smile caught at the ends of Bridget ban's lips. One thing you had to grant the barbarians of the Hadramoo: they died in style.

A Hound can construct marvels out of odds and ends, and in the *remonstratorium* she found all she needed. The preparation rooms downstairs contained a dye with which she darkened her entire body from gold to brown, save on the palms and soles. She had known Megranomers who styled their bodies so. A knife in the same room cut off the longest part of her hair, and a thong bundled the rest of it atop her head. A bit of charcoal from the machine shop added lines to her face and aged her appearance in subtle ways, and two small coins found in a drawer and pressed into her nostrils altered the shape of her nose.

Finally, she wound her srong about her waist. It was possible that the enforcers had gotten a picture of her clothing. But she had been in the dark between two lamps when she slid away, and they had been sauntering complacently behind, thinking themselves clever and undetected. At best they might recall the srong having "many iridescent colors," which would narrow the sartorial odds not at all. She dared not try to alter the pattern, because she had purged the cache and most of the memory in the fabric was now taken up by the STC database. She contented herself with turning the fabric the other way out, which reversed the pattern and presented a slightly more muted version.

Ponchos, however, were not native to this world and they would notice hers immediately. She could not discard it, since part of the copied database resided in its mems; but she did manage to tighten the neck hole into a headband—the old-fashioned way:

there was needle and thread in the prep rooms—and she wrapped the whole thing above her head in a fair imitation of a Chettinad turban. This served the double purpose of concealing the remnant of her red hair.

She still looked like an outworlder, but she might be an older Chettinad or a Megranomer or at any rate not the fleet young golden Hound who had fled from them the night before. "Ah aim abutt mahyō bizz," she said aloud, practicing a Megranomic accent from the Eastern Isles. Best not lay it on too thick. The idea was to be unnoticed.

Finally, it could not be good for any outworlder to be found too near the *remonstratorium*. So, as the eastern sky grayed just a little, she worked her way through still, silent gardens toward the maglev line. There, she found a copse in a public park and concealed herself. Outdoors, the waning night was chilly and she wrapped her arms about herself, wishing she hadn't had to disguise the poncho.

In the morning, as people began to gather at the Uasladonto Street maglev station for the ride into town, Bridget ban spotted a mixed trio of touristas. She slid from concealment and crossed the walkway so as to come smoothly into line with them. As she expected, they were delighted to find "another real woman," the man in the group being especially appreciative. He was from High Tara itself, and sported checkered kilts, a fringed cloak, and an admiring glance. The Jugurthan woman with him was robust of physique and carried an umbrella matching the pattern of her srong. She introduced a Valencian woman she had met in a nearby restaurant.

And so, in this chatty company, to all appearances boon traveling companions, Bridget ban sauntered past the weary enforcer standing by the entry with a digital image in his hand and the upcoming shift change on his mind. He was looking for a younger, more athletic woman, traveling alone.

Entry to her ship was simple. She contacted the intelligence over her implant and the guards that had been placed about the ship were knocked out by a sonic burst from the ship's defenses. She then slipped aboard, locked up, and let them wake up naturally. Later, she would call the hotel and have her belongings shuttled over, tell them she had spent the night aboard "on Hound's business." If the events of last night were brought up, she would profess ignorance. Yes, she had been wearing her "undress greens," because Pulawayo had seemed much taken with her uniform. Yes, she had left Nolapatady at such and such an hour: they could ask Pulawayo. With only a little luck, they would feel so foolish at chasing some other red-haired tourista through the streets of Nolapatady that they would not press matters further. That would only attract the interest of the League and, more dreadfully, of the other Hounds. There would be no trace of her download of the STC database, and the Director would corroborate all the important details.

They might wonder what had happened to the other redhead, but everyone would pretend to believe a story that held together so wonderfully.

In the meantime, the data in her anycloth had better hold a damned good secret to make the whole effort worthwhile. What reason could Peacock have for protecting the phantom fleet that they would risk attacking a Hound?

She pulled off her srong and turban and linked them into her shipboard 'face, gave the intelligence the local dates for the ambush of the Cynthians, and asked it to track the ambushing fleet forward and backward. Then she showered and restored her appearance, produced a fall to complete her hair. When she returned to the 'face, the analysis was finished.

She studied the results. Then she asked for similar traces on *all* traffic, deleting first local in-system traffic, then traffic on the Silk Road and Route 66. Finally, she highlighted the points of origin and termination.

The results made her whistle.

The sky was full of holes.

AN CRAIC

You have to admit," the scarred man says, "to an element of farce to all this. The Hound had come sniffing after one secret and flushed out two others quite by chance."

The harper plays with her strings, tuning them for her first set. Her head is bent, her ear close to the clairseach. She plucks an A, listens, turns a key to tighten the cord. "That's the way of it among secrets," she replies without looking up. "One thing leads to another. The secret of the Dancer to the secret of the phantom fleet to the secret of Peacock's hidden holes. Sometimes I think there is only one secret, and all others are but manifestations of it, and if only we learned what that one secret is, we would know everything."

The scarred man screws up his face. "That's too mystical for me. I prefer the irony of chance to the certainty of myth. It was luck, not fate. When you have your eye fixed on one thing, it's easy to stumble over others."

The harper sets her harp aside. "The 'certainty' of myth?"

"Of course. You can have supreme confidence in a thing only when you don't quite know what that thing is."

"Really." The harper considers that: what it may say about the universe; or at least about the part of it the storyteller occupies. "I'd have thought the opposite."

"No." The scarred man grows animated. His hands accentuate his words, fluttering, chopping like a meat cleaver on the tabletop, causing the morning bowls to dance. "The more you know a thing, the more you know how it can fail you. That's why we fall in love with strangers—and grow estranged from our closest companions. 'Ignorance begets confidence,' an ancient god once said, 'more often than does knowledge.' "

The harper shows her teeth. "You seem very confident of that."

The scarred man's laugh is like the rustle of ancient, long-dried leaves. "Very well. Let us leave the issue uncertain, and at least smile that Bridget ban struck a goal at which she hadn't aimed."

The harper brushes a glissando from her strings. "At least she struck a goal." This, she punctuates with a single plucked note, high at the end of her harp. It lingers in the air between them.

"But later," the scarred man foretells, "she lost what she had loved and the tragedy is that she never knew it."

The harper's smile fades and she lifts the harp to her lap and plays aimlessly for a time. "Why did they try to kill her?" she finally asks.

The scarred man studies her. His lips work as if tasting something. "Five uncharted roads on Electric Avenue? Unknown rivers of space leading to . . . Where?

New worlds? Shortcuts to old ones? It was a secret worth killing for."

"Provided you aren't on the sharp end of the knife."

He waves a hand, conceding the point. "What sacrifice goes willingly to the altar? The 'Cockers were terrified. Let word of such a prize leak out and every would-be highwayman in the Spiral Arm would cast his die to seize it. Perhaps even the Elders of Jehovah would stir at the thought of a rival so nearby. Certainly, the People of Foreganger would. The 'Cockers are clever and subtle and even dangerous in their quiet, treacherous way, but the 'strong right arm' is not their play and the wise man bets on the larger fleet. Who knows how many heads in their Halls of Remonstration once let slip the holes in Peacock's sky through the hole in their face. Loose lips are best sewn shut forever."

"There is not enough thread in the Spiral Arm for such embroidery," the harper objects. "How many smugglers did they move over the years through those hidden channels? And none of them ever mentioned the clever way in which they laundered their cargo?"

The scarred man shrugs and looks about the Bar, where men and women laugh and trade stories and withhold secrets. "One hears a great many tales from captains in their cups. The stories move at a discount. But, no, the 'Cockers did the laundry themselves. Smugglers came to them, turned over their cargoes, and were paid 'on the barrelhead,' as the Terrans say. They might suspect a secret channel—most captains know of some here and there—but they would not know the currents, directions, loci, entry ramps, all those things needful for finding and using them. That was why Peacock could not let a Hound see the STC records. She'd learn not only that the roads existed, but also where they were."

"*Then it wasn't the phantom fleet they were protecting, at all.*"

"*Not as such. I suspect they were surprised—and maybe even frightened—that the strangers knew one of their secret shortcuts. The 'Cockers told no one— but they forgot that holes often have two ends.*"

"*But why not lie? Tell her the fleet had come out of Route 66 or off the Spice Road from Jehovah. Then she'd leave and . . . Oh.*"

"*Yes. 'Oh.' She'd reach Foreganger or Jehovah and find that no such fleet had passed through there. There are nodes where trans-cooper traffic is not well tracked and passersby go unrecorded; but not at those two suns. She'd've been back in a fortnight or two, and not in the best of humors.*"

"*Then they ought to have had a false record already prepared against the day.*"

"*But they were 'Cockers, and forethought is not their métier. The need for a 'second set of books' was never urgent until it was critical. And then, when they were faced with it, they doubted their ability to fool a Hound. A quite reasonable doubt,*" the scarred man adds with a smirk.

The harper finds a menacing chord and plays out, in theme and variations, the grim array of severed heads, stretching back and back into the dawn of the Peacock's Era. Their world might be accounted a paradise, but paradises have always been bound by strict rules, the breaking of which means exile or death. But she follows it with a jaunty, triumphant strain as Bridget ban leaps though the backyards of Nolapatady. "*So, she left Peacock Junction and followed the phantom fleet down a secret hole. But I had thought . . .*"

"*What?*"

"*That she and Hugh . . . and the others, of course . . . joined forces.*"

"*Because it would make a better story?*" The scarred man rubs the side of his nose with a forefinger and works his lips. He looks to the side, as if he studies the scene, as if he sees it in his mind's eye. "There is a move in shaHmat in which an opponent's princess is blocked and each of her replies ends badly. Having asked for the records, Bridget ban could not now say, 'Never mind,' and leave. They would know she'd gotten the intelligence some other way, and the planetary defense batteries would take her out before she reached low orbit. She was clever and her ship was quick, but the god Newton is cruel, and they would pot her on the rise. Of course," he adds cruelly, "she could not wait too long, either, or they would wonder at her patience. She was pinned like a butterfly on the Spaceport Hard. She dared not leave."

"*They would dare a Hound? Would panic overcome their common sense?*"

The scarred man spreads his hands wide. "They have an excess of the former and a deficit of the latter. It is a world where impulse rules thought."

"*No matter,*" the harper says, her fingers entangling an intricate and triumphant strain. "*She was too clever for them. She will find a way.*"

"How can you be certain?" he mocks. "Two of our players are already dead."

But the harper makes no answer. The scarred man studies her closely. His eyes narrow and he allows himself a moment of wonder . . . But his uisce bowl is empty and the hum in the Bar is rising to midmorning volume. "Consider, then," he says, "how suited she and Peacock were for each other."

The harper arches an eyebrow in lieu of the question.

"Each one beautiful on the surface; each one deadly underneath."

SUANTRAÍ: THE SPEED OF SPACE

If a story begins in many places, the scarred man says, *it will also continue in many places. Little Hugh and the Fudir, on their unwilling way to Jehovah, were caught up in a web of lies and deceits and, worst of all, of truths.*

Little Hugh was a romantic, but only when it suited. When the circumstances warranted, he could be as cold-eyed a realist as anyone. Hadn't he proven as much in the Glens of Ardow? It was only through the tear of sentiment that his vision blurred. And hadn't he proven that, too, in the Glens of Ardow? If anyone could be called a cold-eyed romantic, it was Little Hugh O'Carroll. So his kidnappers took him farther and farther from New Eireann in more ways than one. His tenure there seemed to grow unreal, like time spent in Faerie, and his sulks gradually dampened, although what replaced them was not at first evident. It was better to dwell on the exigencies of the present, the realist in him declared, than on the injustices of the past; and he came to this epiphany while the sun of New Eireann was still visible to the ship's telescopes. He borrowed a kit from Olafsson, and the ship's intelligence even tailored him a set of coveralls. Thereafter, he began to explore the boundaries within which he had been so suddenly and involuntarily circumscribed, and that included the human boundaries.

The Fudir, he thought he had plumbed, but the doubts were always there, beneath the surface, for the Fudir was a doubtful man. The Terran seemed genuinely pleased that Hugh was aboard; but did the pleasure grow from friendship, or from something else? It

was hard to tell. With him, there might be no difference between the friendship and the something else.

But Olafsson was another matter. He was the anti-
Fudir, as displeased with Hugh's presence as the Fudir
was pleased; as remote as the Fudir was companion-
able; as simple as the Fudir was complex. And where
the Fudir was a petty criminal, with all the scrambler's
swagger and carefree independence, Olafsson was a
lawman, single-minded in his duty, humorless in its
execution.

There was some game about between Olafsson
and the Fudir. Hugh caught enough snatches of conversation to know that the Pup was interested in a man
named Donovan, perhaps the man at whose trial the
Fudir was to testify. But the Fudir contrived always
to have Hugh about when Olafsson was present. This
made the one reluctant to ask, gave the other an excuse not to answer, and produced no little unease in
the heart of the third.

The Pup conducted a fine simulation of hospitality,
and was so unobtrusive that half the time Hugh hardly
knew he was about. Yet, he had shown himself on
Eireannsport Hard capable of sudden and violent action. That made more sense than Hugh liked. As the
Ghost of Ardow, who knew better how deadly the
unnoticed man could be? Therefore, Hugh slept but
lightly as the ship crawled toward the Grand Trunk
Road. The airlock was uncomfortably close by, and
the solution to "three's-a-crowd" stunningly obvious
to anyone sufficiently ruthless.

It was not until two days out of New Eireann that
Hugh and the Fudir found themselves for the first
time alone. They were in the refectory breaking fast
when Olafsson was called to the saddle to deal with

the entry onto the Grand Trunk Road. The Fudir had programmed the *kuchenart* to produce a vile Terran sauté of rice, potatoes, onions, green chilies, mustard, curry, and peanuts whose pungent odor the air filters struggled to overcome.

Hugh began to say something about the Dancer, but the Fudir cut him off with a sign. He fingered his ear and rolled his eyes toward the pilot's room. Hugh nodded and brushed his lips.

Sighing, he rose from the table and went to the sideboard to brew more tea. The Fudir seemed disinclined to discuss either the Dancer or their current predicament, at least while Olafsson might be listening—and Olafsson might be listening at any time. "Did I ever tell you," he said, "that for my first seven years I didn't have a name?"

The Fudir grunted and looked up from his breakfast. "And now you have too many of them."

Hugh took that as a sign of interest. "I was what they called a *vermbino*. I ran the streets with a gang of other boys, stealing food or clothing, dodging the *pleetsya* and the *feggins,* searching out bolt-holes where we could sleep or hide. The shopkeepers had guns, and we were nothing to them. Worm-boys. Now and then, they'd form . . . hunting parties. Oh, it was great fun dodging them, and the prize for winning was that you got to live and do it again the next day. That's why Handsome Jack could never find the Ghost. Not when being found has been a death sentence almost from birth. I grew pretty good at it. Not all of us did."

The Fudir shoveled a spoonful of the *masala dosa* into his mouth. "Did you ever know your parents?" he asked around the potatoes and onions.

"Fudir, I didn't even know I *had* parents. I didn't know what parents were. Then, one day—there were only three of us left by then in my . . . my pod—I tried to rob a man in the market along the Grand Canal. He was a lean man and carried a purse that he wore on a belt around his robe. So, I ran past him, slicing the belt on the fly, and grabbing the purse as it dropped. I was halfway to the alley when he called after me. He said . . ."

Hugh paused over the memory.

"He said, 'Wait, you did not get it all.' I turned and stared and he was stooped in the street, gathering some ducats that had spilled from his purse and was holding them out to me. Well, as I learned to say later, 'time was of the essence.' There were several people on their handies calling the *pleetsya,* and two others who had pulled knives of their own, though whether to restore the money to its owner or take it for themselves, I don't know."

"The nature of every animal," the Fudir said, "is to seek its own interest; and if anyone or anything—be it mother or brother, lover or god—becomes an impediment, we will throw it down, topple its statues, and burn its temples. I don't understand the man with the purse; but I understand the men with the knives. It was a mistake to stop and turn. You lost lead time."

"Yes." Hugh dropped into silence and studied his past as if from the outside, trying to recognize the *vermbino* as himself. He seemed to float in memory above the scene on the Via Boadai, looking down on everything: the men with knives, the passersby frozen in anticipation, the robe with his hand outstretched, most of all the *vermbino* poised in flight. "I don't know why," he said. "To this day, I don't know why. But I ran to him, to the robe, I mean; and he threw his arms around me, warding off the two knife-men, and he said . . . He said, 'Would you like to have a name?'" Taken by surprise at the immediacy of the recollection, at the echo of that voice in his memory, Hugh turned away.

"And that was your first name. What did he call you?"

"Esp'ranzo, the Hopeful One. I thought he must have seen something in me to give him hope."

"Your initiative," the Fudir guessed. "Your daring, your survivability. He may have been a priest of the Darwinists, naturally selecting you because you had survived."

"No, I asked him once, years later when I brought him a *beneficio* from my father; and he said that he had the hope before he had the boy."

"And your father was della Cossa."

"Della *Costa*. Shen-kua della Costa. He came to the home where the robes kept several boys like me and he lined us up and walked back and forth in front of us, and then he crooked his finger at me. He took me to the family compound, and they dressed me up in red quilted clothing, put golden rings on my fingers, and had a feast where they toasted me with wine and tea, as if I had just been born."

"And so you became Ringbao della Costa. And later . . ."

"There were office-names. Those, I usually chose myself. I was Ludovic IX Krauzer when I was deputy finance minister on Markwald, Gessler's Sun. I was Slim—just 'Slim'—when I was education minister on Jemson's Moon, Urquart's Star."

"And now you're Hugh O'Carroll."

He didn't answer the Fudir, and the silence lasted while he steeped the tea ball. He waited for the Fudir to make some reciprocation, but the Terran had evidently not had a childhood, or at least not one that he wanted to talk about. Finally, the urgent call of the boiling water drew him back to the sideboard, where he prepared a cup. "Olafsson's taking his time," he said over his shoulder, but the Fudir made no reply.

The odor of the steeping tea was quite savory. The Eireannaughta were great tea-drinkers when not on the creature, but this smooth and fragrant flavor was something Hugh had not encountered before. Surely these leaves had been born on Peacock Junction or at least on Drunkard's Boot. He brought the cup to his companion, who took a sip and scowled.

"It isn't the real thing," he said, indicating the cup with his hand but the passage to the pilot's room with a toss of his head. "It smells funny. Why don't you watch what you're doing?"

Hugh nodded. Message received. Olafsson wasn't a real Pup, and Hugh should be careful around him. The Fudir had hinted early on that the ship might not be Olafsson's. He returned to the sideboard and made a cup for himself, using the last of the leaves in the canister. Of all his names, he decided, he liked Esp'ranzo the best.

He wondered what had led the Fudir to suspect Olafsson's authenticity. Did he know Pups so well as to sniff out a false one? And what sort of person would dare such a pretense? Someone well north of harmless. Yet, the Fudir had gone with Olafsson willingly, so it must be something he had learned since boarding.

But if Olafsson was a fraud, there was no trial and the Fudir too was being abducted—for what purpose, the Terran either did not know or would not say.

Good fortune, then, that Voldemar had decided to press Hugh on board. The Fudir at least had someone with him to back his play.

When he upended the canister to tap the last of the leaves into the tea ball, Hugh's fingers discovered an embossing on the bottom. Perhaps the logo of the tea-smith? Idle curiosity revealed a blank shield with a broad diagonal brushstroke across it. In ribbons above and below, writing that he could not make out. He turned the canister to catch the light at an angle, and the Fudir, attracted by the action, left the table and joined him.

The writing was Gaelactic. *An Sherivesh Áwrihay.* "The Service Particular." Underneath the shield, a motto: *Go gowlyona mé.* "I would serve." Hugh shook his head, and when the Fudir reached for the canister, he relinquished it.

"Well, I'll be damned," the Terran muttered; then continued in a whisper. "The Particular Service is the Kennel, the Ardry's dogs."

"So," said Hugh aloud. "Then the blend *is* what it appears to be?"

The Fudir tossed the empty canister back to Hugh. "Either there's more like that in stock, or that's the end of it."

Either Olafsson really was of "the Particular Service," or his masquerade ran to such fine details as this. Hugh grunted. His companion was given to fits of subtlety; but the simplest explanation was that Olafsson really was a Pup.

What bothered the Fudir the most and, in more reflective moments, amused him the most was that it had been at his own suggestion that Olafsson had masqueraded as a Hound's Pup. It had been meant only to make his removal from New Eireann more palatable—to Hugh, to the Eireannaughta, not least to himself. Now, it seemed, the Confederate agent pretending to be a Pup was likely a Pup pretending to be a Confederate agent pretending to be a Pup. Oh, there was recursion for you!

Now that he knew, much of what he had noted in

passing made sense. He had thought this ship a hijacked vessel; but that it was in fact a Pup's field office was the simpler explanation. And Olafsson's evident sympathy for the Eireannaughta ... A true servant of the Confederacy would have felt indifference, or perhaps a mild satisfaction at a Member State's misfortune.

The real question was whether he was better off in the custody of a false Pup or of a genuine one. The Kennel was reputedly less ruthless than Those of Name; but that did not make them especially merciful, and it seemed to him that a Hound's Pup would take a dimmer view of someone who had served the Names than a 'Federal courier would.

But Olafsson, genuine or not, wanted Donovan— and the Fudir was inclined to let sleeping Donovans lie. He was afraid, a little, of what might happen should the long-dormant agent be aroused. But so long as he was aboard Olafsson's yacht, he was safe. Whether League Pup or Confederate courier, Olafsson needed him, and needed him agreeably hale—at least, until they reached the Corner.

After that, his options would open up.

Greystroke did not mind the Fudir's evident complacency. The traitor knew he was in no immediate peril. Donovan was a door, and the Fudir was the key and, like all keys, must be kept carefully, at least until the lock was turned. Once Greystroke had learned from Donovan whether CCW ships had also been disappearing in the Rift, he could decide what to do about both men. There was some benefit to allowing a known agent to remain in place. Much could be learned by observing who he met and what he did. But there were advantages also in cauterizing a wound.

It was his other passenger who puzzled the Pup.

O'Carroll, having shaken his initial distress, had resigned himself properly to the Fates, and seemed now to watch his companions with detached amusement. Greystroke did not know the reason for either the amusement or the detachment. There was, to put the matter Eireannically, something funny about his amusement.

One evening, as the ship slid down the Grand Trunk Road, Greystroke tracked O'Carroll to the library and invited him to spar in the exercise room. O'Carroll put the book he had been scrolling on standby. "I doubt I'd be much of an opponent," he replied.

"Really? I was told you were a fighter."

"Not that sort. Turn your back, and I can cold-conk you with the best of them. But I don't brawl."

"Hmm, yes. A guerilla fighter. Major Chaurasia told me you conducted a brilliant campaign against the government of New Eireann."

"He lied."

"It wasn't brilliant . . . ?"

"It wasn't against the government. *I* was the government; Handsome Jack was the rebel. You shouldn't listen to Chaurasia. When the ICC showed up, they took the rebel side. And their factor was hip deep in the original coup."

"Ah. They do play a rough game."

"History is written by the winners," O'Carroll said. "Isn't that what they always say? New Eireann never had a history before. I hope she never does again."

Greystroke understood what he meant, but it was his intention to probe at the secret that the Fudir and O'Carroll so evidently shared. And for an introspective man like O'Carroll, that meant putting him on the defensive. "Washing your hands of it, eh? I don't blame you."

Anger flickered briefly on O'Carroll's face. Or was it a grimace of pain? "I used to think it was important that I won," he said. "Then *I* could write the history. After all, from a cosmic perspective, my position was *right*."

"And 'right makes might'?"

A brief smile—and that *was* a grimace of pain. "You'd think so. It certainly makes you unwelcome. But the gods don't care. No, what it comes down to is this: Handsome Jack was shady and he wanted to dip his beak in the revenue stream and the Clan na Oriel ran an honest administration. But down in the bone, the difference between Jack and me was not worth the life of a single Mid-Vale farmer."

"Whereas between either of you and the Cynthians . . ."

"Oh, gods, yes! *That* was a fight worth making—if there'd ever been a chance to make one. Nothing like slaughter to lend perspective."

Greystroke reached for another chair and sat down across the reading table from O'Carroll. "So, you don't want to spar?"

"Not that way."

Greystroke started and recalled that the younger man had been trained in reading people by the famiglias of Venishànghai. He decided to try another angle. "What book is that you're reading?"

"*Fou-chang's Illustrated Gazetteer of the Spiral Arm.*" Hugh turned the screen so the Pup could see.

"*Tribes and Customs of the Hadramoo,*" Greystroke read the chapter title. "They're a nasty lot," he agreed. "So, what will you do now?"

O'Carroll turned both hands palm up. "Contact

the Home Office, I suppose, and see if they have a position for me. That's if they haven't torn up my contract. Always opportunities for a Planetary Manager."

"Or for an experienced guerilla leader."

O'Carroll laughed. "Yes. Well, they're both interesting work, though the retirement plan is better in the one."

"You don't sound very confident. About getting your contract renewed, I mean."

"By now, The O'Carroll Himself—she's a hard woman with no sense of humor—will have gotten the quitclaim from the ICC and vacated our contract rights. I wish I knew why it's called a *golden parachute.*' The Fudir tells me it's from an old Terran language, but he doesn't know what it means, either. Well, legal documents are full of terms from old dead languages. But the Home Office can't have been pleased with me fighting the hostile takeover. So, maybe I'll find myself 'at liberty,' and go off with the Fudir to the Hadramoo." He laughed a little bit at that.

Greystroke did not so much as blink. *Off to the Hadramoo!* the passing bicyclist had cried as Fudir had led him up New Street Hill. He glanced again at the screen O'Carroll was reading. No, the man did not expect renewal. Off to the Hadramoo? Were they mad? Or planning a career move . . . ? He tried to imagine the two men as pirates. Fudir, he thought, could pull it off, but not Hugh. Piracy required a certain degree of thoughtlessness. "Yes," he ventured, "Fudir said something about that."

"He told you, did he?"

"Only in passing. He said that once he's done giving his testimony, he plans to go to the Hadramoo and . . ." By artfully slowing his cadence, he left a hesitation at the end for O'Carroll to fill.

"And get that fool statue back from the rievers." O'Carroll laughed and shook his head.

Greystroke concealed his satisfaction. His perplexity was another matter. "You didn't reach New Eireann until after the Cynthians had gone. How could they have taken his . . ."

"Oh, it wasn't *his*. He went there to get his hands on it, but the pirates beat him to it. He was going to smuggle me back on-planet, and I would get him into Cargo House. That was our quid pro quo. He's a romantic; a believer in fables."

Greystroke recalled what he had overheard when he met with the Committee of Seven on Jehovah.

Perhaps the Fudir was right about the Twisting Stone . . .

He understood now. The Fudir had been planning to steal this statue—the Twisting Stone?—to sell to some wealthy art collector on Jehovah who had commissioned the theft. Such petty criminality was hardly worth a Pup's effort but, technically, inter-system crime fell within the Kennel's jurisdiction, and who knew? Shake a tree, and low-hanging fruit might drop in your lap. Greystroke had been born on Krinth, where Fate ruled all, and the random concatenations of the universe always worked to an end. As a youth, he had thrown the yarrow stalks, rolled the urim and the thummin, cast the horoscope, spattered the rorshacks, and always the runes had yielded a meaning—or could have a meaning read into them—but what it came down to in the end was that if you didn't shake the tree, you'd never get the fruit.

"A believer in fables . . . ?" he prompted.

"Oh, the statue is a prehuman one, and has a tale associated with it."

"They all do. It must be very valuable."

"Sure, and it was. January—he was the tramp captain we shipped with. He found it way out in the back of beyond, if you can believe him—oh, maybe a dozen fortnights ago. But he had to trade it to Jumdar in exchange for ship repairs and a percentage of the eventual price. The barbarians took it from her."

"Are the Kinlé Hadramoo art lovers, then?" Greystroke asked.

O'Carroll flipped his hands. "They do love splendor; but from what I've been told, this Dancer is not very splendid. January said it looked like a sandstone brick, when it wasn't twisting itself into a pretzel." O'Carroll laughed. "There was a replica of the Ourobouros Circuit in the vault—a much prettier prize, if you ask me, though a man might get dizzy looking at it—but the rievers didn't take it."

"Well, a replica isn't valuable like an original. The ICC must have adopted the Circuit as a corporate symbol. I've seen copies of it in several of their facilities."

"Considering what they paid House of Chan, they had to do *something* with it. Isn't Lady Cargo a collector of prehuman artifacts?"

"I've heard that she has a private museum on Dalhousie Estates." And Greystroke suddenly flashed on the Molnar, garish in his jewels and mascara, repeating the ICC factor's boasts. They "would settle things in Cynthia, now that they had the Twister." So the barbarians had not grabbed the statue in passing. They had gone to New Eireann *intending* to snatch it. The Molnar had thought it a weapons system, and must have been greatly disappointed to find only a statue, and an unlovely one, at that.

Yet, why should the ICC factor have made such a boast? Greystroke could not imagine that the unruly clans of the Cynthia Cluster would submit to ICC dictates simply because Sèan Company held an impressive art collection.

The mystery deepened that evening, when the intelligence alerted him to a whispered argument between the Fudir and O'Carroll. It had begun in the library and resumed when the Fudir had followed the younger man to his room. There, he had turned on the player, setting a round of Drak choral singing to high volume. The intelligence dutifully subtracted the music, and though it was unable to reconstruct most of the argument, the fragments it did recover were enough to reveal the gist of it. The Fudir was angry that O'Carroll had mentioned the Twister to Greystroke, and O'Carroll seemed amused at the anger.

'Tis but a fable, the Oriel manager had said.

We can't take that chance. If it's true, and the Cynthians learn—

—a matter for the Hounds—

And *No!* the Fudir had cried, incautiously overriding the intricate motet with which he had tried to blanket the words. *Olafsson's no Pup. He's a Confederate agent! If this fell into Confederate hands, it would doom the League.*

Greystroke considered that comment—and the Fudir's loyalties—for some time before retiring.

The next day, Greystroke hosted a meal for his two passengers, during which he laid some of his cards on the table. The meat was a filet of Nolan's Beast, a form of bison peculiar to Dangchao Waypoint, a dependency of Die Bold, and simulated by the intelligence from the protein vats. But the savor of any meat lies in the sauce, and that Greystroke had prepared himself from a roux of elderberry and mango from his own reserve. He served a black wine with the meal—Midnight Rose—and offered with it a toast: "On to the Hadramoo!"

The Fudir did not lift his glass. Instead, he gave O'Carroll a venomous glance. "Hadramoo's not the healthiest place for travel," he grumbled.

"Perhaps not, but certainly a place from which to recover stolen goods."

The Fudir indicated O'Carroll. "He told you about January's Dancer."

"Some. The ship's library filled in a bit more. King Stonewall's Scepter. Do you really think it confers the power of obedience?"

"*He* does," said O'Carroll, hooking a thumb at the Terran.

"But if it *is* true," Greystroke said, fixing the Fudir with his glance, "it's too dangerous to remain in the hands of the barbarians. Sooner or later, one of them may read a book."

"Small risk of that," said the Fudir, "but even more dangerous for *you* to have it."

"Meaning the Confederacy. Have you forgotten your duty?"

The Fudir drew himself up stiff in his chair. "Dao Chetty oppresses my homeworld. I don't want your reach to cross the Rift. Does that sound foolish and sentimental to you, Olafsson? Well, I'm foolish and sentimental."

"He is," agreed O'Carroll, but the Fudir stifled him with a glare.

"It does sound foolish," Greystroke admitted, "to say such things to my face."

"I might have led you to Donovan," the Terran continued. "He dropped his coat years ago, but I might have led you to the man who could have led you to . . . But no matter. Whatever business you had with him, I will *not* permit you to go after the Dancer."

Greystroke had relaxed into his seat at this tirade; now he permitted himself a smile. "You will not *permit* me? Do you think your permission would mean much to Those of Name?"

"Well," said O'Carroll mildly, "he'd have my help."

Greystroke blinked at him, then allowed himself a hearty laugh. "All right," he said when he had wiped the amusement from his eyes. He was satisfied now about the two men. "Let me ease your mind." And he reached into his pocket and brought forth his badge. The opal glowed a bright yellow.

The Fudir gave it only a glance. "I know a tinsmith in Bitterroot Alley who can cobble a better badge than that one."

"May I?" said O'Carroll. Greystroke allowed him to handle the badge and the opal faded to a smoky gray.

"By the Fates," Greystroke said, "the criminal mind is a slow one! Didn't you wonder how I could masque myself as a Pup so quickly?"

"My mind was paralyzed," the Fudir confessed, "at the terror of the Names." Hugh choked on a swallow of wine and coughed it out. He handed the badge back to Greystroke. "I believe him," he told the Fudir. "I think he really is a Pup."

The Fudir pursed his lips. "You were very convincing," he told Greystroke, "as a Confederate agent . . . Alright, so you're a Pup. What should we call you? Not Olafsson, I hope."

"My office-name is Greystroke."

"So. And what happened to the real Olafsson?"

"Does it matter?"

"Not really; but what about the Other Olafsson? They travel in pairs, I've heard."

"I've been watchful. There's been . . . little sign of him."

"Probably won't be more than that until it's too much."

"I'll be careful." Greystroke finished his goblet of black wine and set it down. "I have a proposal to make."

The Fudir, who had not touched his meal for some minutes, picked up his fork. "And what proposal is that?"

"I go with you to the Hadramoo, and you help me take the Twisting Stone from the Cynthians."

Hugh choked again on his wine. "Three of us," he said when he had recovered, "against an entire barbarian horde?"

Greystroke considered the matter. "We could use one or two others," he admitted.

The Fudir grinned around a mouthful of food. "No, the Pup's right, Hugh. We'd never take it by main force. We'll have to go by stealth and trickery. And who better than a thief, a guerilla, and the man that no one sees?"

At Jehovah, Greystroke left his ship in parking orbit and he and his two deputies took the bumboat planetside. There, he sent them to secure lodging at the Hostel while he reported to the Port Captain.

Because they were on the Pup's ducat, Hugh took a three-room suite at the Hostel, and he and the Fudir spent an hour preparing lists of supplies they would need for the Hadramoo venture. Hugh laid out a work structure breakdown and schedule with budgets and resources. He calculated the demand rate of three people for water, food, air, and other necessities, multiplied by the likely lead times for resupply at various ports of call, and applied a safety

factor. He even included reasonable stocks of weap-
onry and ammunition. They planned to talk their
way in and talk their way out, but it was just possible
they might have to fight their way one direction or
the other. He was in his milieu, and the Fudir was
impressed.

"I was being groomed for a planetary manager
position," Hugh reminded him, "long before I took
up the guerilla's trade."

When they were satisfied with the plan, the Fudir
told Hugh to head over to Greengrow Street. "That's
where the wholesalers and outfitters have their en-
trepots. Do you know how to find it? Get a positioning wristband. No, don't depend on the 'rickshaw
drivers. They'll take you three ways around the barn.
Don't worry about the cost. The Kennel has deep
pockets. But don't buy anything until I get there. These
Jehovan *dukāndars* will cheat you blind and short
you on your change just for the practice. You may be
an assassin, but you're too honest a man to deal with
the likes of them."

Hugh saved the list and slid the stylus into its
sheath. "And what will you be doing the while?"

"I've business in the Corner to attend to, for the
Pup."

"He trusts you not to run off on him?"

"We've an understanding. Apparently, ships have
been disappearing in the Rift. Greystroke's boss
thought the 'Feds were impounding them for some
reason. Then they learned from a courier that the 'Feds
have been losing ships, too, and wanted this Donovan
to investigate."

"That's all?"

"The courier may have been a ruse. Greystroke
wants to find out if they really have been losing ships
or they just want the League to think they have. He

needs Donovan to decrypt the data bubble and he needs me to find Donovan."

"It all sounds . . . complicated."

"Agents don't walk around announcing themselves. It's what Greystroke plans to do with him afterward that might make Donovan uneasy about surfacing. He dropped out of the Game years ago."

"Now you're going to pull him back in. A friend of yours?"

The Fudir made a face. "We've shared a room. Listen, you have two ears too many, and too much in between them for your own good. Sometimes it's better not to know things. Wait for me in the lobby. I have to dress proper for this venture."

Hugh had purchased a wristband from the Hostel's notions shop and had just shaken hands with the positioning network when the Fudir stepped out of the lift tube. He had changed into a dhoti of pale blue checks and stripes and had smeared across his forehead a broad band of charcoal and, above it, a tripunda of bhasma. The desk clerk called out, "Hey, you! Boy! What you do up in residence? You fella no mess voyagers! Prenday?" The Fudir turned a cold eye on the man, but Hugh intervened, saying, "It's all right. He's with me."

Whether that raised the clerk's estimate of the Fudir or lowered it of Hugh was a fine point. After they had exited the Hostel, the Fudir said, "You big man, first chop. Make poor chumar-man pukka." Hugh turned a puzzled eye on him, and the Terran switched to Gaelactic. "I don't need your endorsement to be a man."

"Should I apologize, then?"

The Fudir's jaw clenched. "No," he said. "But it grates. Let's go. Chel-chel."

They parted company at Greaseline Street. The Fudir crossed the street and slipped into the Corner, while Hugh continued toward Greengrow, where he made the rounds of the portside outfitters. He noted the goods available against his list, and jotted down the nominal prices and the sources. At Shem Kobaurick and Son, Armorers, he found a display of crescent-shaped ceramic knives with micron edges, imported all the way from Raven Rock, and he paid three-quarters the asking price for it. It was more than he ought to have paid—as a onetime economics minister, he had some grasp of markups—but he was content. It was not the *dukāndar*'s tale of his crippled daughter that swayed him, but that he wanted the knife and wanted it badly, and the merchant knew this the way he knew his own heartbeat. Kobaurick threw in a scabbard for the knife that fit snugly under the armpit. A hideaway *sica* would not make one spit of difference if it came to the touch in the Hadramoo, but he felt infinitesimally more confident knowing that he had it.

The Fudir met him by Undercook's Emporium, looking somewhat the worse for having passed through the Corner. He explained the cut on the cheek as a difference of opinion regarding the possession of certain shekels entrusted to him by the Seven. The jingle of coins in a purse can be heard at greater distances and by keener ears than physics and biology presume, and while the Memsahb had sent Bikram and Sandeep to escort the money, the scuffle had been a near-run thing. "But that dacoit-chief," the Fudir said, "he got his feet all tangled up in a bhangī-man's broom handle." He laughed. "Oh, that was a pinwheel! The boys and I stripped him naked and split his purse three ways to teach him how fleeting are the wages of theft. And I shoved—Let's say I left him the broom handle so he'd watch his step more carefully in the future." He clapped O'Carroll on the shoulder. "Chop and chel, boy! Let's fetch those supplies. I love it when me spend other man his money—and the Kennel, he have deep pockets."

Afterward, Hugh and the Fudir repaired to the Bar to wait for the Pup. Praisegod, cleaning glasses and trying in a desultory manner to proselytize an Alabastrine woman standing at the rail, saw them enter and his eyebrows rose incrementally. "So," he said when the Fudir had ordered two long ales, "the sinful universe wouldn't have you?"

"I've been sent back here to do my penance," the Fudir admitted. "But don't worry. I'll be going to hell shortly."

"A journey so long in progress deserves at last to find its end," Praisegod allowed. "How did you find New Eireann?"

"Same as always. One week down the Grand Trunk Road, just past Gessler's Sun." But then, on second thought, he dropped the banter and told the Bartender how things stood on that unhappy planet.

The Bartender grew solemn at the news. "May God turn His merciful face toward them."

"Better his face," said the Fudir, "than what he's been showing them lately."

"I'll hear no blasphemy, friend. I'll beg alms in my Brotherhouse and urge other houses and the Sisterhood to do the same. Thus shall the glory of God shine forth from our hearts and become a beacon to others."

The Fudir turned away, but Hugh laid a plastic slip on the bar. "Here's my personal chit. Throw it in the pot with the rest. They need building materials and tools, not food. Craftsmen, they have, but willing hands will not be turned away. Clothing, too. Don't send money. Without goods to chase, the money inflates."

The Bartender did not look at the amount before the chit disappeared. "God bless you."

Hugh took the two ale-pots from the Fudir's hands and carried them to a table near the back wall, where there was a sort of niche. He did not look back to see if the Terran added a contribution of his own.

"It was the least you could have done," the Fudir said when he joined him a moment later. "After all you've done *to* 'em, you may as well do something *for* 'em."

By now, Hugh had gotten used to the man's provocations, and he tried not to let the barb affect him. Yet the sharpest barbs are those that have a point; and he drank from his ale in silence for a few minutes. When he spoke, it was deliberately to another subject. "Did you finish your errand for Greystroke?"

The Terran nodded. "Aye."

"Will you be taking the Pup to Donovan before we leave for the Hadramoo?"

The Fudir made a face. "Finding the Dancer is more important."

"I'm rather inclined to think you're right," said Greystroke, who was sitting at the table's third side.

The Fudir shook his head. "I wouldn't mind learning how you do that."

Greystroke spread his hands. "There are disadvantages. The waitress doesn't seem to know I'm here."

"The question of the missing ships is important, but not urgent," he continued while Hugh waved down a passing server. "I'll explain to Fir Li when we pass through Sapphire Point. As for Donovan, I can find him whenever I want."

The Fudir pressed his lips together. "Can you?"

Greystroke pulled a silver shekel from his scrip and tossed it off his thumb to the Fudir, who caught it in midair. He looked at it, looked at the Pup.

Greystroke said, "You gave that shekel to a one-eyed beggar by the Fountain of the Four Maidens."

The Fudir studied the coin, rubbed it between thumb and fingers, then slapped it on the table. "You're robbing beggars now?"

"I *was* the beggar. Profitably so, I must say. You Terrans are generous to your own, I'll give you that. I was a sweeper, too—though I lost my broom later in a scuffle."

A server came with a pot. Greystroke took it from her, and picked the shekel off the table. "No change," he said, handing it to the server, and indicating the Fudir with an inclination of his head, added, "He's paying."

"I thought you had business with the Port Captain," the Fudir said.

"Oh, that was just a formality. All the data was in the hailing drone. I was in and out before you two had reached Greaseline Street. You'll be glad to know," he said to Hugh, "that Jehovah's preparing a relief armada. Two Hanseatic Liners are in port and their captains volunteered to evacuate the stranded tourists and orbital workers. A cohort of Jehovan rectors will be sent to police New Down Town until League militia arrives. Odd thing is, they should already have . . . Yes, madam, what is it?"

This last was addressed to a tall, full-faced woman of light peach complexion and short silver hair who had approached their table. "You're Kalim DeMorsey," she said to the Fudir. "You shipped out in *New Angeles* when I took sick. The Alabastrine woman at the bar pointed you out to me."

The Fudir blinked and remembered. "Micmac Anne," he said, introducing her to the others. "January's First. How is the old bastard? I thought he'd turn straight around and go back for another load of refugees."

"That's what I came to ask you. When I saw you, I figured he was back. How is the ship holding up? Maggie B. didn't let it go to pot, did she?"

"January left New Eireann several days ahead of us," the Fudir said.

Micmac Anne shook her head. "Then he would have been here by now."

"And the authorities would already have known about New Eireann," said Greystroke. "That's what I was starting to say. Maybe he went somewhere else instead."

"No," said Anne. "He'd have come here. He'd have come for me—and maybe for Johnny, too. But he'd have come *here*."

"Maybe he was delayed," said the Fudir. "New Eireann was pretty badly wrecked. If some of the food he took on turned out to be bad, he may have had to turn aside at Gessler's Sun or . . ."

Anne shook her head. "That old ship is always breaking down. He'll show up sooner or later, and Hogan will have a big mouthful of excuses. Gessler's Sun Cut-off is a one-way slide down to the Lower Tier. He'll be *months* coming back the long way round. What's this about New Eireann?"

They told her about the Cynthian raid and the devastation they had left behind. "We're planning to chase after them," Hugh said, earning disapprovals from his two companions.

But Anne treated the comment as a joke. "You won't have far to go," she said. "*Xenophanes,* out of Foreganger, came in, day before yesterday," Anne said. "Her captain told me that a Cynthian fleet was swissed in an ambush off Peacock Junction, oh, a fortnight ago."

"A fortnight . . ." Hugh exchanged looks with the others.

"The timing's right," the Fudir said.

"And how many Cynthians fleets can there be?" asked Hugh.

"More than you might think," said Anne. "There's always a couple of them out cruising; though they don't normally venture as far as the Grand Trunk."

After Anne had gone, Greystroke pursed his lips. "We'd have to pass through Peacock Junction anyway."

The Fudir frowned over his balled fists. "Seems someone else wants the Dancer."

"Not necessarily," Greystroke said. "The ambush may have been fortuitous. No one around Peacock would have heard yet about the rieving of New Eireann."

"Don't jump to a conclusion, Pup," the Fudir said, "You know how those people like to brag. Someone could have known of the Molnar's intentions beforehand. Another Cynthian clan, maybe. They let him do the hard work, then waited on his return path to seize the fruits."

Greystroke nodded. "In which case, they have the Dancer now. But it's more likely the Dancer is flotsam out in the Peacock coopers."

"That's not even a needle in a haystack," said Hugh.

*T*he scarred man smiles. "What a hopeless search that would have been! Needles and haystacks ain't in it. And yet they set off with a will." He holds his bowl out to be filled.

The harper knows some wonder that a man could drink so much yet show so little of its effects. "But of course the scepter was not tumbling about in the Peacock coopers. The ambushers seized it with great deliberation. We already know that."

"Aye, but they did not."

"It is too close in here," she says. "The air grows oppressive. Perhaps we could take a walk outside. I need to see there is still a larger world."

The scarred man smiles. "But in here we have travelers from every corner of the Spiral Arm and—who knows?—perhaps even from the Central Worlds? And what world could be larger than that painted by our words. In our stories, we span all times, all places, all people. Out there . . ." And he gestured toward the Great Doors. "Out there, you will find only the prosaic world of shippers and merchants. In here live heroes and adventures. Here, failure can really matter."

"It always ends in failure. You told me so yourself. An' if it always ends in failure, how can it matter at all?"

"Because it matters how you fail," the scarred man says, and in so bleak a voice that the harper cannot answer him. Instead, she plays aimlessly for a time, improvising a lament.

"What happened to January?"

The scarred man shrugs. "Sometimes ships never show up. No one knows why."

"*Everyone else who possessed the Dancer died.*"

"*Do you* really *believe in curses?*"

"*They are easier to believe than coincidences.*"

"*Then believe in possibilities. January isn't dead until you open the box and look. An odyssey grows crowded unless you leave some folks behind.*"

"*Then let's see what folks are ahead,*" she tells him when the music has warmed, a little, the winter in his soul. "*It will be on Peacock Junction where the princess of Hounds will meet the exiled prince at last.*"

The eyes of the scarred man are hard, and so it is difficult to note them hardening further. "*There is a word for a female hound. Why you think her a princess, I cannot fathom. I knew her. And as for exiled princes, she will have three to choose from, for each of the three is exiled in one way or another.*"

"*It was the one way that I was thinking of. And she will choose* him.*"

She does not expect a response, for the scarred man has made an art form of avoiding response; and so she is startled when he says, "*She chose each of them, and none of them.*"

That answer, unlooked for, stills the strings of her harp. "*Oh?*" she says. And then again, in a smaller voice, "*Oh.*"

The scarred man allows her the silence. Perhaps he even gloats. But eventually he teases at her. "*Is the pattern complete yet? Is it a song? Each time the Dancer changes hands . . .*"

"*. . . it moves closer to the Rift. A curious coincidence.*"

"*I thought you didn't believe in those. All things move toward their natural end, but 'end' can be spoken of in three ways.*"

"*What!*" cries the harper. "*First you tell me a story*

with too many beginnings? Now it is to have too many ends!"

The scarred man grimaces. "No, these are different kinds of ends. The first, and simplest, is simply the terminus, where action stops, because there is no more potential for further action. 'The End,' as we like to say when a story comes to a stop. As if any story ever truly came to a stop. There's always an 'ever after,' isn't there?"

"I've heard it said," the harper responds dryly. "But it's life that goes on; the story stops."

"And so all of life is a dreary sequel once the climax is past?" But the sarcasm dies on his lips and his eyes turn inward. "Why, so it is," he whispers in surprise. "So it is."

"And the second way? Surely, your story has not come to a termination!"

But the scarred man does not answer.

GOLTRAÍ: DOWN THE RABID WHOLE

In the thirteen metric days since her acquisition of the STC records, the scarred man says when he resumes the tale, *Bridget ban's ship had become something of a convent,* from which she spurned the enticements of the profane world and within which she had busied herself with conventional duties. There was never a shortage of administrative tasks. Her report on the Delphic was still unfinished and there were one or two other matters of a similar nature. Now and then, she prodded Pulawayo about the STC records, to maintain the pretense that she did not already have them. Still, the stall could not be prolonged forever. What she needed was a plausible reason to abort her search for the phantom fleet, and she sat tight in the hope that something would come up.

Instead, something came down.

Bridget ban did not expect her dilemma to be so neatly solved by a *deus ex machina,* but it was not the *deus* that surprised her. It was the *machina.* The Spiral Arm is vast and the Kennel thinly spread. So when her communicator announced the arrival in Peacock Roads of a ship of the Service, she did not at first believe the machine. Yet, surely it was beyond the skills of the 'Cockers to emulate the Blue Code; and it was this that finally convinced her. Greystroke, the beacon informed her—Fir Li's chief apprentice, sent to seek a Confederate Agent on Jehovah—returning now, she assumed, with the intelligence desired.

She decided to use this unexpected crowbar to pry herself from the surface of the planet.

She sent a message in the Red Code telling him to pretend that he had come with a new assignment for her and, in case he had heard of it on Jehovah, warning him *not* to make that assignment the Cynthian ambush.

The Pup's response was as minimalist as the Pup himself. It read: "?"

This led to a series of time-lagged exchanges, in the excruciating course of which they laid out a plan. Bridget ban learned to her astonishment that Greystroke, too, was in search of the Twisting Stone and had come to Peacock Junction holding the other end of the same tangled skein of events.

The coincidence did not astonish the Pup. "It was fated, Cu. You followed one end and I followed the other. The Friendly Ones used the Molnar as their woof to weave this rendezvous; but we never see their tapestry, save in hindsight."

"The past is always inevitable," she grumbled. "I'll believe in yer Fate, when ye know of it aforehand."

Peacock STC could not be unaware that deeply encrypted communications were flowing between the two ships of the Service. So Bridget ban called Pulawayo at STC and, when the elf's visage had appeared on the comm, told him—or her—that there'd been a change of plans. "Greystroke's brought a new case. He and I are tae rendezvous at Lunglopaddy High an' discuss it. So I'm needing a traffic window as soon as yer folk can arrange it."

Pulawayo made a pout. "I thought we might have another rendezvous of our own," he said. If he meant to lure her into another ambush, it did not show on his face.

"Oh, darlin', I'd hoped so, too," Bridget ban replied with all the feeling she could fake. "But, Hound's business, ye know. I've been tied up here with admin work on four cases while I waited . . . Which reminds me . . . Hae ye no got the STC records, e'en yet?"

The Director appeared both devastated and embarrassed. "No, they're in *such* a mess. Heads will roll over this, dear, I promise."

Bridget ban repressed a shudder, suspecting the statement as more than a metaphor. "Well, there's nae time for it the now. The ambush is bumped tae a lower priority. Greystroke an' I are for Xhosa Broadfield—and I cannae say more o' that—but I'll be back when we've finished our business there—say, in two or three metric months. Ochone! We gang where the Little One sends us, but the trail will wax muckle cold by then.

I imagine ye'll have the information properly organized before I return." The last, she said in a chastising tone.

Pulawayo nodded, puppy-eager. "Oh, yes. Surely. Yes. By then. We must look like such sillies, to let our database grow corrupted like that, and the bureaucratic confusion—not to mention the diplomatic implications. We *are* an independent state, you know, and we can't just turn our records over to anyone who asks."

"Silly" was not the word that occurred to Bridget ban. She brought the conversation to a rapid and superficially friendly close before Pulawayo could lay any more excuses on the barricades. Shortly after, she received her clearance to lift for the geosynch station. Even if the 'Cockers remained uncertain about the night of her visit to Pulawayo, they would dare nothing with Greystroke now watching from the high ground. A Pup's field office was no battle cruiser, but it had more than enough firepower to avenge any treachery.

Never had a departure so pleased her as her departure from Peacock Junction. Hedonism, incompetence, and treachery made a deadly mix, for each quality led inexorably to the next. Just before breaking the connection with Pulawayo, the limpid eyes of the gentle boy-girl had hardened for a bare instant into black adamantine, and she had glimpsed the viper coiled within the paradise.

Lunglopaddy High was, for obscure reasons, called a "twenty-four." It circled Peacock in a geosynchronized orbit midway between Shalmandaro and Malwachandar Spaceports. Bridget ban arrived first and waited for Greystroke in the Dapplemoon Lounge, where she watched the ballistic ships through the broad view-window. It was an early hour in the station's cycle and the Lounge was nearly empty, which in theory should have ensured attentive service, but did not.

Several ballistic ships had decoupled from the passenger dock to fall toward the atmosphere when the Hound became aware that the Pup was sitting at the table with her.

Greystroke smiled. "Have you been waiting long?"

"A couple of hektominutes."

"Newton is a cruel god." He snagged a passing attendant by the sleeve and ordered a pot of tea. "Chanterberry Lace," he said.

"Order it 'to go,'" said Bridget ban.

He raised an eyebrow. "It's been three and a half weeks since the Cynthians were ambushed. The trail is as cold as space. What do a few minutes matter?"

"It grows a mickle colder."

"Hah. Did you know that 'weeks' and 'months' are old Terran tempos? The 'month' is how long it took their moon to make one complete circuit."

"A month is forty metric days. What moon was ever turned in so neatly divisible a manner?"

"Fudir says the metric day is a little shorter than his Earth's day, but that the one was based on the other, back in old Commonwealth times. The Terran day was divided into twenty-four 'hours' instead of the ten horae we use now, and their week had seven days."

"A *prime* number? Awa' wi' ye! And why not a nice divisible ten?"

Greystroke shrugged. "Or twelve, like they use on the Old Planets. Fudir said there were seven moving lights in the skies of Old Earth. Each one was a god, so each one was given a day in his or her honor."

She thought a chance assortment of planets a

foolish standard against which to mark the passage of time. Too many suns crossed too many skies to privilege the motion of any one of them. "Ye ken a muckle o' glaikit knowledge today, Grey One."

"Oh, Fudir is the fountainhead. He can be entertaining when he puts a hand to it. And more entertaining still when he doesn't."

"An ye bear a regular geggie o' folk wi' ye."

"Cu, you're challenging my translator's tolerances. Can we use Gaelactic Standard? Ah." This he added to the attendant, who had brought a teapot and cup. "Thank you, old 'Cock."

Bridget ban sighed and spoke to him, this time in the Yellow Code. "He of Fir Li and I are not rivals. He seeks no place at the court; and the God Alone knows I seek no place by the Rift. And even were we rivals, our interests converge the now on this strange scepter. Ye serve him better by joining me."

He smiled. "You are even more attractive than the stories pretend."

"And you, even more drab. Shall we pass over my beauty for more weighty matters?"

But Greystroke shook his head. "I never said you were beautiful." He poured a cup of tea and, placing a lump of honey-sugar between his teeth, drank the hot liquid. "Shall we continue this conversation in your office?" he said when he had set his cup on its saucer. "I've asked my deputies to join us there."

"Deputies! A geggie I said, and a geggie, I mean. Next, an' it mought be stray cats yer takin' in. I'll be speaking tae each of them before I agree tae travel wi' 'em. Send them to my office. Then go and see about the supplies we'll be needing."

Bridget ban called her ship *Endeavour* and unlike Greystroke's wildly exuberant interior, it was a model of form and function, the one following the other in orderly fashion. There were no beasts on her control knobs, thank you very much, nor even much in the way of adornment, although the few pieces that were displayed might have been revealing to anyone perceptive enough to read them. She had a custom of keeping some memento of each case that she worked.

She had donned a dinner jacket of pure white in which to conduct the interviews. On it, she wore beside the insignia of the Particular Service only the Badge of Night. It pleased her that Greystroke was taken aback by the sight of it, and by what it said about her and what she was prepared to do when necessity had won the field.

Someday, she thought at him, *you may earn this badge yourself, and wish you hadn't.*

Little Hugh O'Carroll proved a well-built young man: self-confident, and with an easy smile. He had been forced upon Greystroke at Eireannsport, but the Pup had kept him on when he could have left him on Jehovah. The Pup was much given to whimsy, and one never knew what would catch his fancy. Bridget ban had supposed that it was only because O'Carroll had become Sheol to the Fudir's Jehovah—a satellite carried along by its primary. The Pup was not about to let the Terran go until he had been led to Donovan, and that meant keeping O'Carroll, too.

But Hugh was certainly a potential asset to the team. His skills in the deadly arts were useful, but his tactical sense and his ability to marshal and organize resources could prove invaluable. No one rises to assistant planetary manager without considerable talent in those fields.

His air of patient competence reminded her of a jaguar lounging on a tree limb. He was not a schemer,

to arrange circumstances to his own advantage, but
he was ever aware of what those circumstances were,
and could spring quickly and unexpectedly when an
opportunity appeared among them.

"What do *you* think we should do with the Dancer?"
she asked him at the conclusion of their interview.

"Me?" he said. "Frankly, I never believed the old
legend. The Fudir was only a way to get back to New
Eireann. Now . . ." He shrugged. "If the Dancer is
just a funny brick, then this whole expedition is a
fool's errand. But if it is what the legends say . . . I
didn't like the idea of the Cynthians having it. Still
less, whoever had the stones to take it from them."

"You don't want the Dancer yourself, then, to regain control of New Eireann?"

O'Carroll threw his head back and laughed. "No."

He said it far too easily, given that he had waged a
guerilla for just that purpose. "You've kept your
office-name," she pointed out.

"It was the name the Fudir met me under, and
Greystroke, too. Why go back to my base-name?"

"Because it's your true name?"

He looked away a moment. "That, it is not."

At first, the Hound had thought to use O'Carroll's
friendship with the Fudir as the handle to control
him; but she had seen in certain glances he had sent
her way during the interview that there was an older
and far more reliable handle for that.

It would be only a matter of providing the right
opportunity for him to seize.

The Fudir was in many ways the more intriguing of
the two. In her private bestiary, she labeled him a
"fox." She suspected from his conversation that he
was a clever man. From his silences, she knew he was.
Indeed, she thought he might be the cleverest one on

the team. Certainly, *he* thought so, and that could be used against him, should the need arise.

"So," she said. " 'Twas yourself who started all this."

The Fudir sat at ease, with a small tight smile lightening his otherwise morose face. His eyes had fallen on her badge, and she saw in the briefest of flickers that he had recognized it for what it was and that, in some fashion, he approved. "I wouldn't say I started it," he said. "Maybe King Stonewall started it millennia since. But the quadrille was already spinning before I heard tell of it. January had consigned it to Jumdar, and the Cynthians had seized it from her before I even reached New Eireann. So I arranged for Greystroke to take me off New Eireann—"

She interrupted. "That's not the way he tells it."

Again, that taut smile. "He has his perspective and I have mine. Greystroke is good, but I'm glad you're leading this team and not him."

"You think him deficient as a leader?"

"It's not that. Men can't follow a man if they lose track of him too often."

Bridget ban could not prevent the laugh.

"To lead," the Fudir volunteered, "a man must inspire, and to inspire requires a certain vividness, wouldn't you say? Now, yourself . . . Well, vivid is too pale a word. Men would follow you into the coldest parts of Hel." His smile broadened and his expression lost some of its habitual furtiveness. "You'd warm the place up nicely."

"Awa' wi' ye," she said, reverting to her native accents. "Ye'll turn my head."

"And why not turn it? Your profile is a fine one."

Bridget ban continued to smile, but no longer laughed. "Don't be too clever. The blarney will nae get ye snuggled wi' me . . ."

"Why, thanks for the offer, but there are women

a-plenty in every port of the League, and their price isn't near as high as the one you'd extract."

Bridget ban, who had been about to put him off as a first step to reel him in, was slightly nettled by this preemptive refusal. "So, ye'll follow me, but nae too closely? Is that it?"

"Cu, you listen to what people say. That's a rare gift, and it more than compensates for the nose."

Her hand had started involuntarily toward that member before her training stayed it. Instead, she drummed her nails on the desktop. "You think a great deal of yourself."

"And everyone else thinks little; so, it averages out."

"Yes, and that works to your advantage, doesn't it?"

The Terran smiled mockingly and spread his hands palm up. "In my work, it pays to be underestimated."

Bridget ban leaned forward over the desk. "That is not a mistake I will make. Tell me. What do you propose we do with the Dancer, once we've obtained it?"

The Fudir chuckled and wagged a finger. "That's another thing I like about you. You don't use that awful word."

"What word . . ."

"'If.' Let me turn the question ulta-pulta. I suppose *your* plan is to give it to the Ardry. Tell me why."

"You saw New Eireann. And you must know of the Valencian Interregnum or the awful line of Tyrants on Gladiola. There was a terrible rieving two years back on Tin Cup, not by pirates, but by the People's Navy in a dispute over an uninhabited system that lay between them. If the Ardry had the Twisting Stone, he could put an end to that."

"Could he?" the Fudir asked. He sat back and crossed his arms. "How?"

"How? By using the power of the stone."

"You disappoint me, Cu. You are so entranced by the *idea* of the Dancer that the details escape you. But that's where the Devil lives. The scepter may confer the power of obedience, but how far? The Reck Guides on New Eireann never succumbed to Jumdar's charms because, living the Simple Life, they never heard her broadcasts. Text doesn't carry the . . . the manna; only the voice. And how far does that cover? A single system, at best, if you narrowcast to the farther stations and allow for the light-lag. But broadcast 'frog' to the nearest star and years would pass before they'd jump. So, in practice, the Ardry could bend the Grand Seanaid to his will and tighten his grip on the capital. But a good Ardry can do that now—if he has stones of another sort."

Bridget ban scowled, aware that the same thoughts had been niggling at her hindbrain. Grimpen had always told her that she leaped to conclusions, though it wasn't the leaping so much as the distance leaped. "He could travel the Avenue and carry the scepter with him," she said, but she already saw why that would not work.

The Fudir nodded. "Right. The Ardry would carry a sphere of obedience wherever he went; but whenever he left—"

"—Matters would eventually revert."

"Aye. As happened to January's crew and to the Eireannaughta. And how could Ardry Tully have stopped the Cynthians from rieving New Eireann? By the time he heard of it, it would already be over. No, Cu, there's but one way to use the scepter to the League's advantage."

Bridget ban cupped her chin in her hand. "And what may that be?"

"Entrust the Dancer to me, and I'll have Terra in

rebellion *with* the garrison on our side. Four years later, the Century Suns will join us; and in ten years, Dao Chetty herself will fall."

"But you said . . . Ah."

"Aye, Cu. Those suns lie close to Terra, and our broadcasts will crawl through Newtonian space and reach their ears. A slower, but less bloody conquest than sending out an obedient fleet."

"Surely. Ye'd not dare leave Terra, lest they all come tae their senses. The legend on Die Bold was that after the Earth was cleansed, it was resettled with people from the Century Suns, the Groom's Britches, Dao Chetty herself. Maybe it was once your folk's world, but others have lived there for an old long time, and they'd nae take kindly to all of the 'Sons and Daughters of Terra' coming back."

"Everyone's a son or daughter of Terra," the Fudir said. "It's just that some of us haven't forgotten."

"Then what difference does it make who lives there? You maun be wary o' dreams, Fudir. They're like rainbows."

"Pretty."

"An' only fools chase them. But there are some few things about the Twisting Stone legend that puzzle me." She rose and walked to the sideboard, where she poured a fruit nectar for herself and her guest. In the burnished metal that framed the sideboard, she could see the Fudir's eyes caress her and knew that he had lied about his desires. About how much else he had lied, she was not certain. A blow struck into the very heart of the Confederacy? The plan might work—*if* she could trust him. "The version I heard as a wee bairn told of a great struggle for its possession between Stonewall and his rivals; and in the end, Stonewall was imprisoned by the victors in a crypt deep within the earth and guarded by monstrous horses. But if the scepter compels obedience, *how could anyone have struggled with him?* And if its power is limited by the crawl of light, why would anyone have bothered?" She handed him the nectar.

He took a long swallow. "Pears!" he exclaimed. "I've always loved the nectar of pears. Cu, that a legend contains a *core* of truth does not mean that all its *embellishments* are true. On Terra, we have many legends of ancient rulers who sleep beneath mountains. Holger Danske, Barbarossa. Arthur sleeps on the Blessed Isle. Philip Habib slumbers in a cave within the cliffs of Normandy. Our Dark Age ancestors applied some of those same themes to the prehumans. As for the struggle for the scepter, don't expect logical coherence from myth. Heroes behave as their stereotype demands." He handed the cup back to her and contrived to touch hands as he did. "Alla thankee, missy," he said. "Nectar good-good."

"We ought to talk o' this further," said Bridget han, "but the team's tae meet in a few minutes and, after, ye'll fare on the Gray One's ship." She favored him with an appraising look. "I'd rather ye fare wi' me, for I'd fain know ye better, but . . ."

". . . but Pup hold leash tight-tight," the Fudir said, miming a grip around his throat with both hands. "No let go poor Terry, now he got 'um. Too bad. You-me samjaw."

"No, you're wrong. You-me don't 'understand' each other. I don't know, for one thing, why you tint your hair gray."

The Fudir passed a hand along the side of his head, brushing the wild curls flat. "O Missy! Old man, he harmless. Get close-close sliders, clean 'um pockets good."

The Hound shook her head. "And yer lying the now. Ye never pulled a con so low as that. It's the high line for you or none at all. Someday, ye'd maun tell me the sooth ahint that little show on Eireannsport Hard. 'Twas too well choreographed, I think. Ye cozened the Memsahb. Ye cozened Hugh. Ye cozened January. Maybe ye even cozened Greystroke. But don't think you can cozen me."

The Fudir placed his left hand on his heart and raised his right. "Of all the things I might dream of trying with you, I would never include lying!"

Bridget ban wondered at his inflection. She could take "lying" two ways. The great gengineers of ancient legend—had they ever crossed a fox with an eel? For the Fudir was as slippery as the one and as clever as the other. "Tell me," she said. "When this is o'er, will ye really lead Greystroke to Donovan as ye promised?"

Eyes wide, the Fudir said, "Greystroke-me, samjaw. Follow me into Corner, him. And what I owe Donovan or his Confederacy? I spit on they. Ptooey!" He mimed spitting. "We Terrans have become wanderers," he said, reverting to Standard, "living everywhere; at home nowhere. Our holy cities—Mumbai, Beijing, and others—are home to people to whom they mean nothing. We were tossed into the sea of stars and—as the stone said in the proverb when tossed into the ocean—'After all, this too is a home.'"

At Hugh's request, they first reviewed everything they knew, from the old legend to the present circumstances, while he took extensive notes in a pocketbase she had lent him. The Fudir told the story he had heard from January about the discovery in Spider Alley and the transfer to Jumdar at New Eireann. Greystroke told of the Molnar's first transit of Sapphire Point, and Hugh and the Fudir filled in the details of the resulting raid and the plundering of the

ICC vault. Bridget ban related the Molnar's Last Stand and what he had said of the ambush at Peacock Junction. Finally, she described the uncharted roads in Peacock space.

"So we chase this phantom fleet of yours down an uncharted hole," said Greystroke.

"They've got the Dancer," she pointed out. "What other choice do we have?"

"Follow their mind," suggested Hugh. "If you know which way their thoughts run, then you know where they're bound. Then you get there before they do. During the Troubles, I once ... But you'd not want to hear that, and I don't see how we might get ahead of them. Not if this uncharted road *is* a short-cut to the Old Planets."

The others turned to his end of the table. "The Old Planets?" asked Bridget ban.

Hugh gestured to the pocket-base he'd been filling. "The ICC runs through this like the drone of a bag-pipe. They took the Dancer from January with little more than a promise. An incautious remark by one of their factors sent the Molnar on his doomed quest. They refurbished the engines on January's freighter, and now he's vanished. The Chettinads told you of incautious remarks they overheard. Either your phantom fleet represents a new player entirely, or the ICC recovered their stolen property—and the god Ockham prefers the latter. Who else but the ICC would have known why the Molnar left the Hadramoo, *and* been in position to intercept his return?"

"Grimpen!" said Bridget ban.

The others looked at her blankly, thinking it another of the odd words in her dialect. But Greystroke said, "What has Large-hound to do with this?"

"After the fight with the Molnar, Grimpen said that he was going to the Old Planets. He's a methodical sort, not given to sudden flights of fancy. But what nugget of thought did he pluck out of the Molnar's tale?"

The Fudir spoke up. "Chop and chel, folks. First first," he said. "Alla bukkin where hole *goes*—bhōlā. Big dhik, miss *front* end. Alla blink-blink."

"A pity," said Hugh, "that translating implants are so expensive."

"They're no great edge when it comes to Terran," the Hound said. "The patois is a pidgin of a dozen languages. But you're right, Fudir. If we cannae go in the front end, we'll ne'er come out the back. So let's cover that first. Look here." She activated a lenticel in the conference table and projected the chart she had recovered from Pulawayo's files into a cubic that hovered above it. "People," she said, "if you would come around to this side, please? Thank you. This is the point of view from Peacock at this time of their year. These stars I've highlighted in red form the constellation they call The Assayer; and this nebula is the one they call His Tail. D'ye see them?" They all nodded, Hugh and the Fudir with agreement; Greystroke because he had navigated through these skies many times.

"*Here* is where the phantom fleet disappeared. Peacock claims they lost track of the fleet, that it had entered a segment of sky that they did not monitor, or that their equipment failed, or that their STC controllers were distracted by the havoc on the Silk Road."

Greystroke looked up. "Well, which was it?"

"It was hard to keep track o' the excuses as they flittered by. Now, *here* are the tracks of a couple of dozen freighters over the past hektoday. As ye see, and correcting for sidereal drift, they all vanish or appear at the same locus."

"Not too many points off the entrance ramp for

the Silk Road if you take your heading off the Greater Fops," said Greystroke.

"Aye, and that works tae our advantage. We can heigh as if for the Rift—Xhosa Broadfield lies off the Palisades—but turn aside before the final approaches and pull for the farther point."

Greystroke pulled his lip. "And if you're wrong, and we try it, we're all blinked. Your STC records show us where the entrance *was* and a certain amount of calculation can approximate where it's gone; but 'approximate' isn't good enough. Sidereal drift is sensitive to initial conditions and the equations have no analytical solution. 'The Ricci tensors are all agley,'" he added, imitating her dialect.

"A ramp acts as a gravitational lens," the Fudir pointed out. "You can pinpoint its location without an ephemeris by checking for parallax shifts and the doubling of background stars behind it." When they all turned to look at him, he shrugged. "I really do hold a rating as an instrument tech."

"Then after we're in the groove," Bridget ban added, "we maun track the phantom fleet from their fossil images, to learn where they turn off. Who knows how many side channels this road has?"

Greystroke knew which ship had the better imaging equipment. The Fates were subtle indeed, for they had led him to take up the hobby years before in preparation for this day. "Then I take the point, and Fudir stays with me," he said.

Bridget ban agreed to take Little Hugh O'Carroll with her, and she tried not to smile at the prospect and made sure that Hugh saw that she had tried not to smile.

During the long climb toward Electric Avenue aboard the Hound's ship, Hugh amused himself by preparing lists; and Bridget ban by preparing him. While he tabulated and crossreferenced everything that the team had learned about the Dancer, she tabulated in a more quiet way everything she learned about him. It was far too easy. She saw that in Hugh's sometimes self-conscious behavior in the confines of her ship. All that wanted was the right moment for him to seize, and she set about providing it.

Their first day out did not bring them together until dinnertime. Bridget ban stayed in the control room coordinating the magbeam booster schedule with Peacock Roads Traffic and fine-tuning the ship's onboard power reception. Later, she went belowdecks to the power room and ran the readiness tests on the alfvens. She emerged finally to find that Hugh had prepared a dinner for the two of them.

Nothing exotic: a type of fish called a "colby," found in the great freshwater sea on Dave Hatchley. He had assembled the filet from the vats, coated and broiled it, and served it with an assortment of familiar vegetables. Like her, he seemed to prefer the plain and simple.

"I don't know why you bother going down to the power room to run the tests," he said when they had settled to the table. "Can't the intelligence run them for you?"

Bridget ban separated the flakes of the colby with her fork. "This will be a tricky approach. There are no marker buoys, no quasar benchmarks to steer by; so the engines must be as finely tuned as possible. The intelligence knows only what the instruments tell it. It can nae ken if the instruments are agley." She waved the fork. "Always run the standards," she admonished him.

"I shall," he said, "should I ever grow daft enough to try for astrogation."

Bridget ban laughed more than the wit warranted and touched him briefly on the back of his hand. She made careful note of how he responded to the touch and on what his eyes involuntarily fell. By the next day, she had programmed her anycloth to accentuate those areas, arranging everything a little tighter, a little higher, and a little lower.

At his request, she pulled up a map of the South Central Periphery and displayed it on the holowall in the conference room, which consequently took on the aspect of infinite depth. She also gave him access to the ship's open-source databases. "Just be careful," she said, rapping her knuckles on endless space, "not to walk into the wall."

He chuckled. "It does look real. Can I shift the point of view?"

She moved inside his personal space. "Just tell the ship the origin and direction of the view you want. For fine-tuning, use this glove and watch where its icon appears in the wall. Then, push or pull on the image. When you shift your point of view, the stars change to account for light-lag, up to my last gazetteer update. Here, do you see that star?" She touched it with her virtual finger. "Watch what happens when I zoom toward it." She curled her finger and pulled the view forward and they seemed to race through Newtonian space faster than the speed of space. Hugh staggered a little, his balance confused, and Bridget ban placed her left hand on his waist to steady him. "It takes some getting used to," she said, meaning the cascading stars, not her hand. Hugh opened his mouth to say something—and the star suddenly blossomed.

What had been a red pinpoint became unbounded fury as the star tore itself apart. For a moment, it was as bright as all the other stars combined. The interstellar gases glowed as they were swept along with the wave front.

And then they were through the shell of expanding gases and where the star had been there was nothing but a carbon-oxygen white dwarf. Hugh blew out his breath. "Quite a ride!"

There is a trick well known to those who practice it, of invading another's "personal space" like a smuggler nestling into a friendly cove. She stood very near to him, not quite touching, and told him, "The supernova is out past the Jenjen, in the Roaring Fork nebula. It appeared five years ago in the skies of Hanower and the intelligence back-dates everything from that; but it won't be visible from Peacock for centuries. If you watch the backdrop under 'hyperfast evolution,' you can see the spiral galaxies age and spawn seyfert pairs and the seyferts spit out matched quasars. It's quite beautiful, the underlying structure and design. There"—she pointed again, leaning a little across him—"that's Andromeda, our mother galaxy. There's a twin Milky Way on the farther side, so the legends say. Andromeda spawned us as quasars when she was a mere slip of a seyfert . . . And that is Virgo, our grandmother. The sky is our family tree."

She stepped away, then, but he contrived to let his hand brush against her, and she pretended not to notice.

One element of the art of conversation is to ask the other about himself. Since this is often their favorite topic, or at least a topic on which they are reasonably well informed, it seldom fails to draw them out and put them at ease. It was over a game of shaHmat that Hugh told her of his terrifying childhood on Venishànghai and Bridget ban nearly wept to hear of it.

"They *hunted* you?" she said in disbelief. "The shopkeepers *hunted* you? Like animals?"

"But never alone," he said with his teeth, but Bridget ban thought it was a false grin, or one of pain. "Understand. We used to vandalize their shops and rob them. I can't say they'd no reason to hate us."

"But still . . ."

"And it did school us in agility and quick-wittedness, and that stood me well in the Glens of Ardow. I was accustomed to being stalked. But, sometimes . . ." He paused and fiddled with one of his hounds, moved it, changed his mind, and restored it to its position. "Sometimes I wonder how long I could have kept it up. Not in the Glens; in New Shanghai. There were no *old* vermin-boys."

"You shouldn't call yourself that. Look at what you've accomplished. You're a certified planetary manager. You've run entire government departments and, from all I've heard, run them well."

He smiled thinly. "And I ran a *guerilla*, too. Don't forget that. There is a part of me that knows what I've accomplished. But there's one small sliver of my brain—somewhere back here in the old cerebellum—that still thinks those shopkeepers were right. It's not something you can hear for years and years when you're young and ever entirely forget. And what was my *guerilla* but another and vaster case of vandalism? That's why I'm fit for—" But he stopped then, and did not say what he was fit for. Instead, he smiled. "And you, *a vawn Chu?* I've told you my base-name." He managed to bow sitting down. "Ringbao della Costa, *bēi rén.* How did you become Bridget ban? Was it your childhood dream to go to the dogs?"

"Are you going to move that piece or not?"

Hugh looked in surprise at his hands and saw that

he was playing idly once more with the princely hound. He replaced it on its square and moved a councilor up the white diagonal. "Sorry," he said. "We should concentrate on the game."

"It takes the mind off . . ." She bit her lip as he looked up.

"Off what?"

"Off entering an uncharted road."

"Greystroke knows what he's doing. And the Fudir's a licensed chartsman."

"Aye . . ." Bridget ban blocked his councilor by advancing a minion. "But, well . . . Alright. My base-name is Francine Thompson. There's no secret in that. I never wanted to be a Hound, though. Oh, I read all the stories growing up. About Efram Still or Moddey Dhu and the others. But I never wanted to be one. I only wanted to be regular Francine Thompson. You see, I grew up on Die Bold, and the most important thing in the world was to be 'regular.' At least in the Pashlik of Redoubt, where we lived. All I ever heard was 'communal solidarity' and 'the fingers work together make a fist.' Things like that. So I studied for my assigned career and worked at perfecting my character for it. I was to be a nurse-practitioner in the Kentwold Hills. It was a good assignment, one worth doing. The hill towns are scattered far between and don't see a medico very often. But . . ." She watched Hugh slide a fortress slowly up the leftmost file, as if doing it surreptitiously. But she had expected the move and immediately castled her emperor. Hugh frowned over the board.

"But try as I might with the character-building exercises," she continued, "I couldn't enjoy nursing or, more importantly I think, I couldn't do it well. So, I thought there was something wrong with me, that I lacked the plasticity to mold myself to the type that society needed me to be."

"And what was it," Hugh asked, "that you most loved hearing about in those days?"

Bridget ban closed her eyes and became young Francine Thompson, sitting before the televisor in the block community center. There had been a terrible arson in Ark Alpikor. Two hundred people had died. "When the public inquiry agents caught the bastard who did it, everyone was pleased to hear it; but I was . . . 'ecstatic,' I suppose is the word. After that, it seemed that every time I opened a newscreen or picked up an idle book at the center library, it was something about policefolk, and more often than not it was a story about one of the Hounds. It was almost as if the *idea* of being a Hound was tracking me, hunting me down."

"Not all policers are worth the aspiration," Hugh told her. "The People's Police on Megranome wouldn't have cared if the man they caught was the true arsonist or not. And if I'd fallen into the hands of the New Shanghai *pleetsya*, I wouldn't be here today." As if to underline the point, he took one of her minions with a counselor and swept it from the board.

"That might be the other question: What did I most *hate* to hear of? It wasn't anything like the arson itself. That was only tragedy. They rebuilt the dormitory, named it 'The House of Sorrow,' assigned new families to live in it, and life went on. No, what I hated most was when I read of innocents wrongly prosecuted."

"You should have been a Robe, not a Hound. They were always on about 'justice.' So when did you— Pay no attention to the counselor. He's innocent and you're wrongly prosecu—Damn." Bridget ban had sent one of her hounds leaping across the field to take the piece. "You weren't supposed to see that line of attack."

"If you don't want me to see your line of attack, you shouldn't pursue it. Unless you want to play in the dark," she added in a playful voice. "What was I . . . Oh. When I was fourteen, local, the County Planning Board sent me to a medical school across the border in the Kingdom."

"The Kingdom of what?"

"Just 'the Kingdom.' The odd thing is that they don't actually have a king, just a regent. The story was that they'd had a king once who had been so just and wise a ruler that no king after could hope to measure up. So after he was gone, they set up a regency to await his return. The Kingdom's medical technology was more advanced than Redoubt's; so I was supposed to learn what I could and bring it back to the Pashlik. But after a month at the Université Royale, I asked for asylum and was granted it and I transferred my major to criminology. And then one day while I was walking past the Eglantine Traffic Star to my classes, I passed the League Consulate and, purely on a whim, I walked in and asked them how I went about becoming a Hound."

"And what did they tell you?"

"'If you have to ask, you'll never be.' I don't think they really knew and were just brushing me off. So I insisted they send an inquiry to High Tara." She smiled in self-deprecation. "Obstacles harden my whims. Well, I didn't think much about it afterward, but a couple of doozydays later, when I was sitting under the great fir tree in the university Green, a shadow fell across my textbook—and there stood Zorba de la Susa, the greatest Hound of them all. He had come personally to evaluate me. Yes, of course I recognized him. He could have become the Little One Himself, had he wanted the post, but he preferred the field. 'The Spiral Arm's a more spacious office,' he used to say, 'than the Little One's palace suite.' He examined me, ran me through a battery of tests, and must have seen some hope, because he made a place for me at the Kennel School."

"'He must have seen some hope,'" Hugh repeated, as if to himself.

"I was nineteen, local. I didn't know if I could ever measure up to the likes of de la Susa or na Fir Li."

Hugh laughed. "And now you're almost single-handedly chasing an entire battle fleet down an uncharted hole because of a fanciful legend."

She had made sure that they exercised together in the fitness room, running in tandem on the slidewalk, spotting for each other on the mass machines, and afterward sitting side by side on the floor mats. The day before they were to enter the uncharted road, he asked her what her most difficult case had been.

"I can tell you what the most frightening one was. I've never been tasked with governing a planet or with disaster relief like Black Shuck carried out on Kamerand. Those would be frightening, but in a different way." She described her escape from Pulawayo's house, her discovery of the monstrous exhibits in the *remonstratorium,* and the artful disguise she had used to elude the guards at the maglev station.

"So there I was," she said, laughing, "striding proud as ye please along Uasladonto Street with my breasts stuck out for everyone to see."

Hugh could not help but drop a glance toward those now-concealed treasures and said, "I wish I could have seen that." He laughed a bit to show he had meant it as the sort of light double entendre that was almost mandatory after a story like that. She laughed back at him and laid her hand *for just a moment* on his and said carelessly that she wished he could have seen it, too.

That evening, she left the door to her quarters ajar just a wee bit and waited until she heard Hugh's footsteps in the hallway before she began disrobing for sleep. The footsteps halted and she knew he had noticed her reflection in the mirror, visible through the crack in the door. How could he not? She had aligned everything with the utmost care. She paused awhile after removing the blouse, as if in thought, and then stepped out of his view.

She wondered if he would barge into her quarters after that. It was not unheard of for men of his age to lose all control of themselves under such circumstances. But the Ghost of Ardow had not survived as long as he had by losing control under any circumstance. There was no doubt in her mind that he would "seize the moment," but he was, to use a term lauded on some worlds but derided on others, a man of honor. She found, in spite of herself, a certain admiration for him.

That was the problem with using affection as a weapon. Like a knife, it cut two ways.

She had orchestrated the finale for the very day they entered Electric Avenue.

They had fooled Peacock STC for a while, sending swifties down the Sapphire Point ramp as if they were hailing drones. In fact, they were reports to na Fir Li informing him of what they had found and what they intended, as well as more routine reports to be forwarded to the Kennel archives on High Tara.

But Traffic Control had been screeching at them for three days running that they were approaching local-c far off the proper bearing for the Silk Road. Bridget ban did not think that any secret could be kept by a large number of people, and so most of the pleas directed at them were genuine concern and panic. The Border Patrol cutter that altered course to intercept them clearly had a more malign intent. If no one else, those who had dispatched it certainly knew by then where the two Kennel ships were actually headed. They could project a course as well as anyone.

Cutters were fast, but Kennel ships were faster, and it could not catch them before they reached the ramp. If they missed the entrance, however, and braked before they blinked, the cutter would make sure they had no second try.

Now, Bridget ban had never been as nervous about the attempt as she had led Hugh to believe—that had been intended to trigger his protective reflex—but there was always the possibility that measurement error really had mislaid their trajectories. So when they entered the ramp successfully and slid into the Krasnikov tube it was with a sense of genuine relief and when she emerged from the pilot's saddle, she and Hugh embraced in delight.

And then, as sudden as the shift to superluminal, they delighted in the embrace.

There is a certain jadedness that comes with the considered use of one's affections. It is not that they lose their edge, but the edge cannot help growing a little dull. She had been prepping him for days during the crawl up to the coopers. With carefully chosen stories, with carefully calculated touches and glimpses, she had readied him, body and mind, for this precise moment. Yet she found his caresses welcome; and later, considering how long he had been celibate, she found him gentle and unhurried. Even so, while they played with each other, she could sense him straining at the leash. But the Glens of Ardow had taught him control.

(But the Glens had taught the Ghost of Ardow many more things than patience and control. He had been schooled in realism, too. He knew when he was being stalked, and could recognize the signs of a well-laid ambush. He was not such a fool as to expect a Hound of the Ardry to kick up her heels for a chance-met stranger; but he tolerated the ambush for the sake of being well laid. Don't look so shocked, harper. Her actions were calculated; but the Ghost as well knew how to add two and two.)

The two ships proceeded down the road at a moderate pace so that Greystroke's instruments could tease out fossil images from the shoulders and track the phantom fleet. The shoulders grew narrow along one stretch. Skewing out of the main channel would not put them into the mud; it would smash them against the cliffs! Bridget ban spent many hours in the pilot's saddle taking bearings, and pricking off the qualities of local space on her charts. Greystroke was undoubtedly doing likewise; but better there be two such charts. Just in case.

The cliffs, however, explained why the road had not been discovered early on. Who knew how many ships had entered it, only to smash upon those steep gradients? And when success finally came, Peacock had seen more safety in secrecy. Too many roads in their system and the 'Cockers would become a target for every planet and pirate in the region.

It was not until the shoulders had flattened out that Bridget ban could relax and leave the steering to the intelligence. Hugh helped her relax, though where he had learned the art of massage he did not say. If only intelligences had *judgment,* she told him; and he recounted the Fudir's tales of ancient Terran triumphs, the fanciful hyperbole of which amused her.

And so day followed day. A strange road requires close study, and Bridget ban spent more time in the saddle than on more familiar routes. Occasional messages drifted back from Greystroke. Several times, the shoulders flattened out into ramps, but each time the images of the phantom fleet continued past them. What unknown stars lay at the ends of them?

To maintain the charade of affection for the remainder of the transit, neither Hugh nor Bridget ban could plausibly deny a kiss or a casual touch to the other. But there is this strange property of a simulated affection. Continued long enough, it becomes real enough. There were certain sympathies of character that lay between the Ghost and the Hound that eased the transition and made it all but insensible. Bridget ban discovered herself looking forward to his attentions, which were not by any means entirely sexual. He was, she learned, a literate man, widely read and well spoken, and as attentive as only an assassin can be.

There came a day at last, nearly two metric weeks after they had entered the road, when Greystroke warned that the laminas were broadening once more but that this time the images of the phantom fleet had blue-shifted, which meant they were preparing to exit.

She hurried from the pilot's saddle to tell Hugh and came to the conference room to find him standing hipshot before his "wall of evidence." He had one arm across his chest with the other nestled elbow-in-palm and with his hand along his cheek. A tight wrinkle marked the forehead above his nose and his lips were pursed and . . . She came to his side and he absently draped an arm around her, and the comfort she felt at this small gesture disturbed her greatly.

Hounds sometimes took companions. Most did not last the rigors, but Hugh might be one who did, and the Little One Himself would almost surely have given his grace. She might have chosen Hugh, did she not already love another.

"We've come off the ramp," she said, and he nodded.

"Among the Old Planets," he said.

"Aye, you guessed that part right."

"I didn't guess." He rapped the surface of the holowall with his knuckle, striking Old 'Saken, and Die Bold and Friesing's World, knocking on the doors to Waius and 'Bandonope and Abyalon. "Which one?" he asked.

"The intelligence has recognized the Lizard and Winking Arnulf. We've come out in the coopers of Die Bold."

He turned to her and smiled. "Welcome home."

AN CRAIC

Wait," cries the harper. "Wait!" Her harp is stilled and she has half risen from her seat. "What do you mean she already loved another? Who was it? Why have I heard nothing of him? She always said that—"

She stops abruptly, but the scarred man seizes upon the caesura. "She always said?" His voice rises from his gravelly whisper to a growl. He is a sleeping predator surprised in his den. His age has not stilled his joints and as fast as a black mamba striking *he has* seized her wrist and holds her tight against her flight. "How do you know what she 'always said'?" His eyes pin her as the snake pins a bird, his face as hard as flint.

Until flint cracks into shale and slides.

"Oh, by the gods! Oh, by the gods, you are her daughter! You've lied to me this whole time!"

His rising voice has turned a few heads in the broad common room of the Bar. A man in the uniform of a Gladiolan "cop" sees how he holds her restrained by her wrist and, scowling, rises from his seat. The Bartender reaches under the bar and something black and metallic emerges in his fist.

The scarred man sees all this, as he sees everything but the woman before him, with only a part of his attention. He might almost welcome their assault, so ready is he to fight the world over this latest of betrayals. But in the end, and this end takes but a moment to achieve, he releases her.

And she does not run. He has not answered her question.

"I've not lied to you," she tells him.

"Your silence was your lie. Be gone. Go. The story's ended."

But she does not move. "There are three sorts of ends, you told me; and this seems like none of them."

But the scarred man is not to be comforted from his rage. He shoves the table violently aside, toppling goblets, shrieking its legs against the flooring, and he bolts from his niche in the wall. He moves swiftly, half bent over, and he passes like a ghost through the crowded room. The Great Doors swing wide, and he is gone.

The harper hurries after, but when she emerges onto Greaseline Street, there is no sign of him, not northward toward the spaceport, not southward toward

*the Hostel. Then she turns and looks past the Bar's
rooftop where the ramshackle Corner of Jehovah and
its tangled warren of alleys clutter the slopes of
Mount Tabor.*

AN SOS

*B*ut a woman who has in her something of the
strider does not hesitate at the brink. What chasm
can be crossed in *two* steps? She enters the Corner
and immediately it is as if the world has changed. The
paving grows irregular, then crumbles, then ceases to
exist at all. Streets become alleys and gullies, some
too narrow for vehicles, or even for fat Jehovah merchants. Stairs clamber the sides of Mount Tabor.
Most of them switch-back to take the bite out of
the pitch, but many others are an undaunted climb
straight up the slope. The different ways the scarred
man might have gone increase like loaves and fishes
with every stride she takes.

She comes at last to a sort of plaza—if such a broad
and open term does grace for such a constricted
space—and here she stops. The plaza is bordered by
gloaming buildings, each four or five stories high,
some with windows, most presenting blank backs to
the outer world. They are the color of sand and dirt,
and indeed many of them appear to have been built
from that most common of materials—and are now
reverting to their original state. It is more like a close
room than a public square, and lacks only a roof to
complete the illusion. In the center, a fountain gur-
gles. The water is nearly the same color as the surrounding buildings, and has left brown stains in the

stone of the basin. Water drools like venom from a stone cobra's mouth, lacking the pressure head for any more vigorous jet. The cobra is erect and flaring, and on his coils sleeps a recumbent man cut from the same dull stone.

No less than seven exits cleave the wall of buildings, ranging from pedestrian walkways wide enough for two men to pass each other to narrow cracks between the buildings through which most men might not pass at all. Each path is of rammed earth; each is accented with raddī-piles of rubbish and flat pans of cracked mud where the heat has sucked fetid pools dry. She goes to the mouth of each in turn and finds no sign that the scarred man has passed that way.

In despair, she returns to the fountain. She had let her tongue slip its leash. Now, whatever the scarred man may think, there will be things to her forever unknown.

There is no one about to ask, even assuming Terrans would answer a stranger's queries, or answer them honestly. It is midafternoon and the plaza is deserted. She had not expected sunlight in the secular world. The Bar is timeless, and had promised night outside. The Corner, too, is timeless, but in another sense, for here the Past never dies, while in the Bar, the future never comes. But the deserted quality of the early-afternoon plaza is unnerving and she imagines a faerie host, lurking just out of sight, and watching. She does not know the Terran custom of vatyum, the *sesta*, or sixth "hour" of their day.

Yet not everyone slumbers during the heat of the day, and there are always some who really do lurk and watch. These idlers had faded into byways and gullies at her approach. Who knew who this confident strider might be? Better to avoid trouble by avoiding contact. And so, emptiness had opened before her path as the waters part before the bow of a swift ship.

But let motion cease and the waters close in.

A furtive shift in an airyway; a shadow down a dark colonnade. She senses them gathering at the borders of her vision. Beggars, thieves, urchins, those who for one reason or another find sleep discomfiting and so haunt the afternoon.

The harper slides her case from her shoulder and eases herself onto the flat stone rim of the fountain. The slabs are rough and cool; at her back the turgid waters mutter. A man in a kaftan stands at the mouth of one of the gullies. It is one that doglegs a short distance in, and there might be an army of such men just past that concealing corner. An old woman leans two-handed upon a stout walking staff in a doorway that had seemed closed. Someone whistles two or three notes, like a signal. Unseen feet scamper down an arcade. The harper bends and opens her case and sets the harp upon her lap.

Three small children, pale-skinned beneath the grime of the streets, have come out of the narrow arcade, and they bend and whisper to one another, lifting their heads in her direction now and then. The oldest, a tall, skinny boy of perhaps thirteen metric years, towers above them. He slaps one of the younger on the side of the head and the smaller boy grins at him.

The harper tunes her strings to the Descending Doric mode. In the gully, the kaftan man uses a knife to slice a guava and lifts the piece to his lips on the blade. He has been joined by a second man, this one clad only in a light blue checkered dhoti, which displays thereby a torso evident of a sensual life, for he is soft and fleshy and his pendulous lips quiver as they watch the harper. The man with the knife pays him no mind, but cuts another slice off the guava while he watches her.

No one has yet made a sound, and so the first chords the harper plays explode in the silence. Heads half-tucked jerk up. The children—five now—unknot themselves and face her. A shutter on an upper-story window creaks open a crack. She plays the hexa-chord to limber her fingers. The man in the dhoti wanders casually into the plaza, pointedly looking everywhere but at the harper. The man with the knife follows him. A rheumy-eyed beggar walking with the aid of a wooden crutch hobbles from the shadows in a corner of the square. He holds his bowl before him, shaking it so she can hear that it does not rattle. Three men variously dressed in Terran "business suits" squat along one of the buildings and confer in low whispers with one another. One of them laughs.

She plays the Dancer theme that she developed on the first day. It is more fully realized now, less uncer-tain. But it starts quietly and most of those in the plaza do not yet hear it. The adolescents nudge one another and finally push forward one of their num-ber, who stumbles a little in the harper's direction, looks back over his shoulder, then approaches, his hand thrust deeply in a pocket of his robe. He fingers something, and the harper notes from the drape of the cloth that it is shaped like the barrel of a gun.

The music builds in volume and tempo. The stately quadrille begins to break into wilder beats: a gallop below which her thumb strikes a thumping bass of thunder. More windows have opened on those facades possessing them. One of the men squatting against the wall—he has a face like a vulture—has risen, and he comes to stand beside her, but a little behind, just out of her vision. "Sweet," she hears him say, but whether sincere or sarcastic—or even whether directed to the music—she does not know. The man with the guava cuts a final slice and wipes his hand on his shirt and his sleeve across his lips. He studies her and gauges the clothing, the harp, the scrip belted to her waist.

The pock-faced youth before her pulls the tube from his pocket. Her fingers falter just a moment and for the first time in many years she strikes a false note. But the boy has pulled out a Terran *tinwissle*—a simple tube with finger-holes and a whistled mouthpiece—and after a moment's further hesitation, he begins to play against her, picking up the dance as it whirls into a reel, pulling it up above her register and spinning it free. He is not a terribly good player and his fingers often hold a note rather than dare dance it in thirty-seconds, but he stays close to her—and he has heard the tune only once. His friends cheer him and he blushes and loses the tempo, pauses, then picks it up again.

The vulture-faced man tosses a few coins into the open harp case.

More upper-story windows are open now, and in one of them a blowsy, large-breasted woman leans on the sill, listening. The children, the ones who had pushed the piper forward, are dancing now, ring-a-rosie. A few people jostle and shove in the small crowd that now surrounds the harper. Now and then, a coin rings in the harp case. Not all smile. Some eye her with suspicion, or even hostility. One man, seizing the advantage of the sudden audience, juggles balls in the air by the arcade; another, seizing the same opportunity, moves about, lightening purses until an onlooker on a balcony spies him and raises the hue-and-cry, and the man plies swift heels for the nearest airway with others in hot pursuit. The harper mocks his flight with galloping strings before resuming the geantraí.

She shifts tempos abruptly, confusing the dancing children and the piper, who takes his whistle from his lips and listens to the new melody, nodding his head to the beat until he can pick it up once more. She plays January's Song and then the Lament for Little Hugh. The latter stills the jostling crowd, and the piper trills a high sweet melody of his own above the weeping strings. The harper finds his melody attractive and brings it down to a lower register with intricate glissandos and grace notes, runs some variations on it, then, with a nod to the boy, gives it back to him, its sweetness now shaded with poignancy. When she segues to Death in the Gully and introduces The Fudir's Theme, she uses a mode beyond both the piper's kenning and the bore of his whistle. It is a minor key, and he has not a second pipe. His high, pure piccolo notes still, leaving only the darker thrumming of the clairseach's metal strings. It is only coincidence that clouds pass before the afternoon sun and cast a sudden shadow on the square.

No one dances now. Few dare breathe.

A man with a tabla has pushed through the press and sits now at her feet, with his hands poised over the drumhead; but he dares not strike, for such a melody flows beatless toward a distant ocean. It is not the *alap* with which he is familiar, but the long line of an ancient poetry in a forgotten country of green downs and chalk cliffs. It is a murmur of their spirit that has survived the ages.

The harper whispers *sixteen to seven* to the tabla man and *dee* to the young piper and, at her nod, tin whistle soars and hands patter in *drut-laya* and the dark thrumming strings burst into sunshine. *Triumph!* The treacher tricked! The audience cannot restrain a shout and the children leap and clap and pick up their dance where it had fallen. The vulture-faced man nods, as if passing judgment. Yes, it is exactly right. Nothing has ever so sweet a taste as after despair.

She will not take them further, not to the desolation of the Rift or the Rieving of New Eireann, not to the hall of heads on Peacock Junction. It is too bright an afternoon for that. She gives them a sample of Bridget ban's theme—it is not yet fully realized—and allows the music to fade into the mysteries, into diminished sevenths, before stilling her strings.

The tabla man grunts with satisfaction and the young piper grins. The crowd murmurs its satisfaction—it is not their way to clap hands—and they begin to break up. The young boy holds his *tinwissle* up to her in both hands and the harper, remembering a story she once heard from a Terran "saxman" on Jenjen's Khōyāstan, takes it in her own hands and gravely kisses it before giving it back to him. The boy backs two solemn steps away and then boyishness triumphs and he turns and rushes to rejoin his companions.

The harper has thought that in such a mood the locals might answer her questions, but when she mentions the scarred man, they turn away and begin chattering among themselves. The *sesta* is past and the plaza begins to fill with the usual late-afternoon bustle of people busily going nowhere in particular.

"I take you, missy."

It is the jowly man in the blue-checked dhoti. His smile is oily; his lip wet with perspiration. "Scarhead, me, goombah. I take you him." His eyes are harder than his smile and they smolder. The harper hesitates. "Chel, Memsahb," he says. "He no long one place."

"Give me one minute." The harper bends to put the harp back in its case and notices with no surprise that the modest pile of coins that had gathered there is now gone.

But when she straightens, harp case now slung over shoulder, the man in the dhoti stands with a fixed, glassy smile, looking past her. "No, missy. So sorry. Not know him, scar-head." He turns and walks away and the man behind him, who had eaten the guava, now puts his knife away. He bobs his head to her. "We watch 'um, such men, no touch women. E'en so, eetee woman."

Then, he, too, turns and walks away.

The harper sits suddenly on the edge of the fountain.

"We don't know how you came this far," says the scarred man, who is sitting on the other side of the fountain, his back to her. He rises and comes around to sit beside her. "That was a fool's play. How did you ever hope to find us?"

"It can't be so foolish as all that, seeing that I have."

The scarred man grunts. "He heard you playing *that* theme, and we knew you'd stuck your head in the lion's mouth."

"That's why I played. You can't catch a man by chasing him. Better betimes to remain still, and he will come to you."

Several loiterers had edged closer to them and the scarred man jumps suddenly to his feet and cries, "Yo, skevoose! Go see where you gotta be. Scat, before I give you leather in the kuli." They slink off and he resumes his seat. "Pay the illiewhackers no mind." He strikes his fist into his palm and rubs it. "Why did you come after me? What is it that she wants?"

"She?"

He turns red-rimmed rheumy eyes on her. "Your mother. The witch."

"She didn't send me."

"No?"

"I'm chasing her, too."

The scarred man digests that a time in silence. "I see," he says at length, "that is the 'One Thing' that you have loved and lost."

"Not a thing, a person."

"And there's no music for that, is there?"

"Your story's not at an end yet. And at the end of your story I may hope to find the beginning of mine. What is the second way? In what other way may we speak of the story's end?"

They sit side by side now, no table between them, but neither do they face each other. "An end," the scarred man says. "There are qualities each story must possess, and when it has them it has been perfected. However good or bad the story may be, when it has all the qualities it needs to be itself, what can change accomplish but to lose one of them, and so become something less." He inclines his head toward the harp case, which she has once more slid from her back. It rests now between her knees. "What you played here this afternoon . . . You will never again play it without remembering this day, without comparing it to this day, and it will never sound half so fine on your fingertips as it did here in a dusty, closed-in plaza of the Corner of Jehovah. You and others may play it from now until the Heat Death, but in that way, it has come to its end. From now on, it will always be a reprise."

In answer, she recites a proverb: "'A tune is more lasting than the song of the birds.'"

Perforce, he must complete it: "'And a word is more lasting than the wealth of the world.'"

"What are those words, seanachy? Your story has yet to perfect itself."

"What has she already told you?" he asks. "How does *her* version run?"

But the harper only shakes her head and stares silently at the windowless building before her. Eventually, the scarred man grunts. "I've never seen any reason for self-deception," he says. "But she spent her whole life deceiving people. Why should she have exempted herself?"

"You don't know that," the harper says without looking at him. "I knew a different woman, sweet, gentle, but always with a sadness beneath her smile. It was a wan smile, the ghost of a smile. You had to look twice to see that it was there. But once you saw it . . ."

The scarred man nods slowly. "Aye. I knew her long ago, and what man or woman is only one man or woman? She had a god who was supposed to be three without being more than one; but she put her god to shame with the multitude *she* comprised." He turns his head and his eyes pin her. "Are you certain you want to know how this ends?"

"It's why I came."

"It may also be why you go."

She thinks for a moment, then nods her head slowly. "It may. But the question is: To where?"

GEANTRAÍ: THE CALL OF DOOTY

Die Bold, like the other Old Planets, is a place where the future was born but whence, like an ungrateful child, it has departed to seek its fortune elsewhere on the Periphery. The Old Planets have been left like aged parents in an empty nest, remembering what things had been like when the future was young.

Like any whelping, the future had been delivered amid pain and blood and cries of anguish, despite it

having been, in some sense, a Caesarean birth. In
those days, so the stories ran, they really had been
Terrans and really had remembered Terra herself, and
not just, as now, the memory of that memory. Cast
across the Rift, mingled with strangers, they had hud-
dled and despaired and fought with one another and
slowly built something new from what wreckage
they had saved.

Die Bold was old enough to have a history. Scattered and quarrelsome refugee camps had grown into
cities, burned in civil wars, grown again upon the
ruins. Conquerors came and went; old arts informed
new renaissances; knowledge lost was rediscovered—
or its merest memory vanished forever. Archives con-
served by loyal priesthoods were cracked and archaic
tongues deciphered, and humanity cruised once more
along Electric Avenue. Die Bold explorers arrived at
Abyalon. A ship of Old 'Saken encountered one from
Friesing's World already in orbit at Bandonope. Megranome found bustling industry on Waius; suste-
nance farmers on Cynthia; and naught but desolation
on the nameless worlds of the Yung-lo Cluster.

Ships went forth to terraform and settle. New
worlds incubated, farther from the menacing Rift:
Jehovah and Peacock and New Chennai; High Tara
and Hawthorn Rose; Valency and Alabaster and far-
off Gatmandar.

Until, after a thousand years of splendor, a millen-
nium of effort, the Old Planets settled back to enjoy a
well-earned rest.

And so there was in the spirit of each Die Bolder
something of the refugee's despair, something of the
youthful rush of rediscovery, something of the queru-
lous satisfaction of old age; and something too of the
insecurity of the epigone. Visitors from the rawer

worlds of the League often perceived in them a false humility; but there was nothing false about it. Behind their every triumph lay the suspicion that it had been surpassed in the old Commonwealth of Suns, and that they were at best only second best. It took something of the heart out of everything they did and put something heartfelt into their humility.

It was four days inbound from the coopers to Die Bold itself, during which time the Hound and the Pup agreed not to announce themselves officially, nor even to admit they were traveling together. They did not know that the phantom fleet had been bound here, nor that the fleet would expect pursuit, but until then Greystroke would be a merchant from Krinth named Tol Benlever and Bridget ban would be Julienne Melisond, a lady of the court. And because Hugh would be more convincing as Greystroke's factotum, Bridget ban took the Fudir to play the role of her manservant. The two swapped ships during the layover on Jewel-of-the-Giantess, a trans-shipment station orbiting the second gas giant in the outer reaches of Die Bold's system. There was sufficient bustle and coming-and-going so that no one noticed that some people left in a different ship than brought them. Julienne Melisond stopped for the spectacular view of the double rings that the Jewel provided, while her man, "Kalim," chatted with the servants and kitchen staff. The Krinthian merchant was little seen, as befitted a merchant prince, but his representative, "Ringbao," was everywhere, discussing trade opportunities and inquiring after recent events with other traders and with Die Bolders outward bound.

That night Bridget ban told Greystroke that she planned to send the Fudir into the Corner of Die Bold once they were down. "Terrans are everywhere," she said, "and what one knows they all know; but they'd sooner spit than trust an 'eetee.'"

"An 'eetee'?" Greystroke asked.

"It's what they call anyone who is not a Terran."

Greystroke propped himself on his elbow and ran his hand along her flank. "Do you trust him to come back?" he murmured. "I'd hate to lose him, now that I have him."

"He wants the Dancer as much as you and I. Beside, I've programmed *aimshifars* into the livery I gave him. If he bolts, we can always find him through the anycloth."

Greystroke chuckled. "Using a bolt to find a bolt. Droll. Very well, Cu. I cannot deny you."

Aye, thought Bridget ban sadly, drawing him close. *Ye cannae.*

Èlfiuji was capital of the Kingdom and the largest city on Die Bold, a soaring metropolis hard by Morrigan's Ford on the River Brazen. The ford had given the city its original rationale, but had long since faded to irrelevance. Thopters and whirlies now buzzed between the towers and the New Royal Bridge arced across the treacherous currents, indifferent to the age-long absence of royalty.

Hugh made the rounds of the traders' clubs near Port Èlfiuji in the Mercantile Loop, where he engaged in idle chatter over light snacks and strong drinks. Merchants, he found, came in three sorts. First, there were the fat, confident ones, comfortable in their wealth, who enjoyed the pleasures of the flesh and for whom no contract was so dry or so technical that it could not provide an occasion of sin. The second sort, more vulpine, were those on the make. They were all in the air, for all their wealth was in the venture itself, and their first failure would be their last. Since "Ring-bao" lacked the standing to speak with the "merchant princes," and the "paper tigers" could spare no time to speak with him, he sought out the third sort.

These were the "reps," and gossip was their stock in trade. They came to buy and sell—mostly to sell—but they also knew when and how to turn off and simply chat with chance-met strangers. Not that selling was ever far from their minds, but men and women of their school believed that "establishing a relationship" was the key to selling, and they never blew another off as of no account. "You never can tell," they would tell one another, "when a shabby stranger might prove a wealthy customer."

Krinth was outside the immediate region, off to the Galactic West, where the suns packed closer and the night cast shadows, and so as a rep for "Tol Ben-lever," Ringbao attracted considerable interest. What had Krinth to offer that might sell dearly here? What did Krinth desire that might be bought cheaply here? Hugh had been thoroughly prepped by Greystroke and what he didn't know, his implant told him; and what his implant didn't know, he simply made up.

"I hear it's dangerous out there," said a rep for a Gladiola firm that made entertainment simulations, "and a man's life isn't worth a demi-ducat."

"No more dangerous than it is here," Hugh replied, seeing an opening. "On Jehovah, I heard that some planet out that way had been attacked by barbarians."

He was sitting in a high, wing-backed chair, facing three other reps around a low table of hors d'oeuvres. A woman representing Obisham MC, and feeling very good about herself for having already met her quota, said, "New Eireann, I was told."

"The bandits, they came outta the Cynthia," added a thin man with a Megranomic accent.

"There," said Hugh, "you see. I heard Die Bold itself was scouted by a fleet of warships no more than four, five metric weeks ago."

"When was that in local time?" asked the Obisham rep. "Waiter, how long are four metric weeks here?"

The man replenishing the tray of cold meats and cheese shook his head. "Please, got no head numbers, missy, please. I ask."

"Terrans," the woman said as the man scampered away. Hugh wasn't sure what she meant by that. It wasn't as if *she'd* known the conversion factors.

"For all I know," he said, "that fleet is still around, maybe waiting for a fat merchant to waylay. Think they're the same bunch as hit New Eireann?"

The thin man waved a hand, which held a wedge of some dark, grainy sausage impaled on a wooden pick. "Naw," he said. "Them Cynthians is more disciplined than that bunch was. Couple of the ships fired on each other, can y' believe it! I was inbound transfer at the Giantess when they passed through. And didn't that startle the traffic folks up yonder! Die Bold's JPCG cutters—that's Joint Planetary Coast Guard, babe," he added to the Obisham rep—"they can take the price of a raid out of your hide, so mostly the pirates lay off the Old Planets. But still, JPCG was taken by surprise, and didn't like it one stinkin' bit."

"If the fleet's not still lurking up in the coopers," Hugh said, "where'd it go?"

Shrug complemented shrug.

"I think it broke up," the fourth man said. He was a man of ruddy, almost orange complexion, and wore his hair lime-white and pulled into spikes, a fashion popular on Bangtop-Burgenland, although he himself repped for Izzard and Associates out of the Lesser Hanse. "I heard that some ships took the Long March down to the Cynthia, some took the Piccadilly to Friesing's World, and the rest went the other way round the ring to Old 'Saken."

"Was the winners heighed for Old 'Saken," the thin man said.

"Didn't one stay behind?" the woman asked.

"One of its officers, I heard," said the Gladiolan. "A Gat. He asked for asylum or something."

"If it please, missy," said the waiter, who had returned. He looked at a sheet of scratch paper on which some figures had been scrawled. "Is four metric weeks one-*punkt*-six case doozydays. Which be thirty-eight days straight up." He bobbed several times and scuttled off.

"Doozydays," said the Gladiola man. "Why can't the Old Planets use metric days like everyone else?"

The Megranomer grinned at him. "Why cain't the rest of the Periphery use doozydays? Twelve makes more sense than ten. More *divisible*, d'ye see."

The woman for Obisham Interstellar frowned. "What did he mean—'thirty-eight days *straight up*'?"

Hugh hid a grin. The waiter had meant Terran days, but he saw no reason to enlighten his chance companions.

The Fudir had not been to the Corner of Èlfiuji in many years and found that he did not know it as well as he once had. The patois was a little different; and the smells and foods and noises, a trifle exotic. Much depended on the mix of ethnicities that had been settled here during the Great Cleansing. There was more wealth here than on Jehovah and the people moved with less of the edginess that marked the Jehovan Corner. Yet one hand knows the other and a few grips were enough to gain him access to the Brotherhood's clubhouse where he met with Fendy Jackson.

"Had I known thou wert coming, Br'er Fudir," the man said, "I had prepared a finer welcome." He was tall, with a vulpine face and a wiry beard that covered all and fell to his chest. "How fareth our sister, the Memsahb of far Jehovah?"

"She doth well, Fendy." The Fudir and his host sat on soft hassocks in a richly carpeted room draped in gossamer curtains of red, gold, and black. To the side, a servant prepared tea and a bowl of chickpea paste. "And happy she was to see the back of me."

Fendy Jackson struck his breast with his fist. "May her loss be my gain. What service dost thou ask of our fellowship, Br'er Fudir? What hath brought thee to my miserable porch?"

"A complex story, I fear me. But at the end of it lieth the Earth, free once more."

The Fendy paused with his teacup half raised to his lips, and the servant, too, in the act of handing a second cup to the Fudir. "Is't so?" the Fendy asked. "A tale long told, but with no such ending yet. But there stood once a city there that it is in me to visit. It is an obligation that my grandfather's grandfather longed to meet. How might we see such an end?"

"It is a matter of utmost delicacy that must be plucked from any number of grasping fingers. Thou knowest the story of the Twisting Stone? There may float a bean of truth in the pot of legend."

"'The man one day older is a man one day wiser.' The prehumans left much behind them, though more in fancy than in fact."

"Thou hazardest nought. I risk the search. If nought lieth at the end of it, how art thou diminished?"

The Fendy considered these words while he tore off a piece of bread, dipped it in the hummus, and handed it to the Fudir. "How might our brothers and sisters aid thee?"

"There is a man," the Fudir said around the mouthful. "In himself, he is nothing. But some few weeks ago a fleet passed through Die Bold. Seven ships, we believe. Perhaps eight. They fought. Who they were and where they went are matters of interest. But it is said that one ship remained behind, or perhaps only this man; and him, we seek."

The Fendy ate for a time in silence while behind him a monkey screeched in a brass cage. Then he inclined his head and the servant hastened to him and they bent their heads together in whispers. A wave of the Fendy's fingers sent the man from the room.

"I have put the question out," he said. "An answer may return on the echo. Meanwhile, be thou my guest and I shall call in women who know a little of the *rock sharky* and we shall dine on sweetmeats and dates." He clapped his hands. "I am miserable that I cannot offer thee better than these poor inept dancers; but they do not oft stumble, and should one catch thy fancy . . ." He made a fig with his fist.

The Fudir bowed where he sat. "Thou art too generous, Fendy. I deserve not such largesse, but will for thy honor accept it; though from the dancing women's comfort, I beg exemption."

The Fendy's thick red lips split his beard in laughter. "Oh, ho! Oh, ho! That madness cometh betimes to all men. May thou regainest soon thy sanity!"

While they dined, they spoke of matters affecting Terrans. Those of the Kingdom fared moderately well compared to some worlds. "But in the Pashlik, Fortune turned her face from us. The last Pash but one— Pablo IV Alqazar, that was—seized all the wealth of the Corner of Chewdad Day Pashlik to pay off his debts—and he was a man of costly habits. Then he expelled all our people, lest they demand it back. The son discovered that money was not a thing to have, but a slave that one sends forth to labor. Hah-hah. Now, the grandson seeketh to woo us back, and some hath chanced it for the sake of the dime; but for the most part their children have found a home with us here."

"We live on the sufferance of others," the Fudir said. "Never will we be safe entire 'until the lions ride back on the wave,' and we have our own world once again."

The dancing girls, as promised, did not stumble much, although considering in how many directions they shook their bodies, it was a marvel that they did not. The Fudir wondered in which cultures of ancient Earth their dance had originated.

Most likely, he knew, it was an amalgam of several. During the Dark Age, the songs and legends of the Vraddy, of the Zhōgwó, of the Murkans and others had been blended by folk themselves deliberately commingled. Only the most painstaking scholars could tease the threads apart, and even then not to their certain knowledge.

Yet, the dancing was sensuous and rousing, and the sweetmeats and caesodias pleasing to the palate. The dancers wore petal skirts and halter tops, midriffs ill-concealed by sheer taffeta veils—except for the boys, of course, who wore only white cotton sirwals. The Fudir found his pulse quickening to the rock beat, the tinkling zills, and the undulating bodies of the dancers, so different from the syncopated and coordinated vradanadyam on Jehovah. One dancer in particular swayed around his hassock, plucking a date from the salver and placing it between his lips, only to whirl away laughing.

The Fendy's servant returned several times during the dance to kneel and whisper in the Fendy's ear. That worthy would stroke his beard listening and nod and the man would scurry off once more. The Fudir did not grudge patience. The phantom fleet had a long head start and dashing off at random with incomplete information would not close the distance.

When the dance was ended and the pipes had stilled and the panting dancers had departed, the Fendy, with a gracious wave of his hand, turned over to the Fudir a flimsy bearing the notes his man had collected from the whispers of the Corner. "This one," he said, gesturing with a nail, "may be he whom thou seeketh. But there be further news, O Seeker, to interest thee." A smile emerged from the forest of his beard. "Know that thou art also sought. One hears the Fudir of Jehovah asked for in low places about the city, in brothels and in bars."

The Fudir grunted. "They know where to look for me, then." He thought Hugh or Greystroke might be trying to get in touch.

"Ah, thou art the soul of wit," said his host. "She soundeth quite anxious to find you." Again, he allowed the smile to show.

Bridget ban? Images of flesh and petal skirts whirled in his mind.

"Ah surely, the madness has you." The Fendy laughed. "May fortune fly with you on your quest. On *each* of your quests, haha! You could have had a dancer here tonight; but perhaps you will find another Dancer later. You and this Alabastrine woman."

The Fudir had already joined his host in the laughter; but the last comment brought him up short. An Alabastrine woman?

Hugh took the Tigrine Avenue tube to Alkorry Street, where he departed the capsule to find himself in a neighborhood of narrow buildings and narrower byways. Most of the windows were dark or dimly lit through yellowed shades, and Alkorry Street itself lurked in permanent shadows. The Tigrine Line was elevated in this part of the City and so the rows of apartments had that look of dimness that evenfall only accented and daylight could not dispel.

On Venishànghai, people lived on the outside—the evening *pramblo* around the streets, greeting friends and neighbors, the dining 'frescos, the liveliness of the *pyatsas*—and went home only to sleep. Here, everyone seemed to huddle inside, like they were hiding, like the whole planet was a planet of vermin-boys. They must emerge sometimes, he thought, but only to work, not to live.

He shouldn't judge everyone by the standards of his homeworld. Die Bolders might live as lively as anyone—but indoors; though "lively, but solitary" seemed a contradiction to him. Yet, if he had not spent so much of his childhood in hiding, would Die Bold strike him as grimly as it did?

He consulted his wristband. The Mild Beast was around the corner on Raggenow Way. According to the Terrans, their quarry could be found there almost every night. A Gat, they had said, and was that not a stroke of luck, for Hugh had heard the unmistakable Gatmander accent in the Hatchley Commonwealth years before.

He wondered what else the Terrans told the Fudir. He had seemed troubled on his return.

Raggenow Way was a gloomy side street lined on both sides by redstone apartment buildings whose sameness was only heightened by the small tokens of differentiation. Each was precisely five stories tall; each possessed a broad stone staircase leading a half flight up from street level to the main entrance. Each had a passage under the staircase to a garden-level apartment half a flight below street level. But the moldings and cornices were slightly varied in pattern: geometric here, floral there; and the stairs were flanked by different cast-stone beasts perched on their concrete newel posts: lions, eagles, bears, and so on. Hugh wondered why they'd bothered.

The buildings were separated by narrow airways. Reflexively, Hugh glanced down each as they passed, and noted iron grates blocking them. Back gardens, he thought, or car parks in the rear.

Stolid. That was the word to describe Die Bolders. They were not going anywhere, at least not anymore; but neither would they be moved from where they were.

He stopped before a wooden sign bearing the likeness of a Nolan's Beast. The "blackface" bull wore a wreath of flowers girdling its horns and a look of unlikely benevolence on its features. The public house—they called it a "local" here—occupied the garden level and the entrance was underneath the main stairs. On New Eireann, the pubs had flaunted themselves. But then, if this were a local, the locals undoubtedly knew how to find it.

Inside, the taproom was low-ceilinged and raftered with black oak; but whitewashed between the beams, so the overall impression was not as oppressive as it might have been. The musty smell of beer mixed with the sharp metallic tang of whiskies. The haze of various leaves and smoldering lemongrass dubars hovered cloudlike just below the ceiling. On the farther side of the room, four men around a manual piano were singing something about "The Brazen Boatman." They had not agreed upon a key beforehand, but such an agreement was of obviously little concern.

A few heads glanced his way when he entered, but only for momentary scrutiny. *Yes*, thought Hugh, *a very private people, even in public*. He found an empty table and sat there until a barmaid came by, cleaned it, and took his order. The men's choir shifted to a different song, this one involving Dusty Shiv Sharma, "the best Beastie boy o'er all the High Plains."

Hugh settled in, watching for anyone with the bearing of a ship's officer and the peculiar rhythm of Gatmander speech. He saw a plaid-turbaned Chettinad sharing a booth with a local businessman and two capable-looking hired women. Shortly afterward, a tall, thin Alabastrine woman entered from the street and took a position foot a-rail at the bar. Everyone else had that dough-faced, rather wistful look of the Die Bolder born. Hugh drank his stout with some satisfaction. A Gat would stand out in this crowd.

Two mugs later, a short, burly man entered the Mild Beast and received a few nods of recognition from others. His skin had the appearance of leather, both in color and in texture and his clothing had the nondescript look of castoffs, but Hugh could see the darker spots on the fabric where insignia had once been sewn. Hugh's suspicions were confirmed when the newcomer faced the barman and said, "With regard to the rum unto me, there is an occasion of thirst."

Without turning, the Gat lifted a glass of rum high and said to the room at large, "Die bold!"

The locals lifted their own drinks in turn and "Live bolder!" rumbled in a dozen throats, above which the Alabastrine could be heard piping "Leaf boolder!"

Hugh emptied his mug in a single long swallow and carried it to the bar. Hugh could see that the Gat watched his approach in the mirror, and his hand crept near the open flap of his jacket. Hugh placed the mug on the bar. "Draw black," he said. When the barman had filled it, Hugh lifted the mug to the stranger. "Far Gatmander."

The Gat looked him over and the skin of his face

tightened. "Not far enough." He shot back the rum and thrust the empty glass straight-arm to the barman, who filled it without taking it from the spacer's fingers.

"Not many outlanders here," Hugh said. "Would you like to join me?"

Leather-face grunted. He shifted the glass to his left hand and held the right out as before, beckoning with his fingers until the barman put the rum bottle in their grip. "The invitation as it regards myself is acceptable," the Gat said.

Hugh led him back to the table. "My name's Ringbao," he said, not entirely lying.

The Gat gathered glass and bottle into his left hand and held out his right, which Hugh took briefly. "The name as it pertains to me is Todor," he admitted, taking his seat. He poured another glass and lifted it to eye level. "It shows a pretty color. And"—he sipped—"a prettier taste."

"What brings a Gat all the way to Die Bold?" Hugh asked.

Todor gave him another look and let the silence lengthen before he said, "A ship," in front of another sip of rum. This time, he set the glass down on the table half empty. "With regard to the years upon me, there have been many," he said.

Meaning he wasn't born yesterday, so get on with it. Hugh nodded. "We heard you were with the fleet that passed through Die Bold a month ago."

The other grunted again and wiped his mouth with the back of his hand. He looked around the table. "We," he said.

"Myself and a few friends."

Another sip. "And regarding the information, what will be paid by you?"

"What is your price?"

The Gat drew in his breath. "A ticket. Passage to Gatmander."

Hugh knew that the Kennel had deep pockets, and passage on a Hadley liner would not be the greatest expense the team would incur. "Done," he said.

Todor sighed and looked down at his large, gnarled hands, which played with the glass of rum. "On Gatmander, far Gatmander," he sung, more off-key than even the quartet drinking around the piano, "on the very edge of skies . . ." He blinked and looked away for a moment. Then he added, "And maybe it lies far enough. Aye, far enough. Beyond the reach of Radha Lady Cargo."

Hugh nodded. Suspicions confirmed. "Company cops after you?"

Todor glanced briefly at the door. "Soon enough. There was a bauble she wanted and the thought was in me that she oughtn't have it. There was talk, there was black mutiny, and ship fired upon ship. But as regards the commodore, there was an occasion of success; and obedience and remorse overcame the unruly, save only those ships that severed all communication and fled. The commodore's ship was wounded, but the prize was his, and perhaps by now, Lady Cargo's. Here's to hope," he added, raising his glass, "that the ship of the commodore foundered on the 'Saken road."

Hugh reached out a hand. "Come with me. My friends need to hear this, too."

Todor drew back suddenly and stared at him narrow-eyed. One could almost hear the creak of leather in that squint. "And for why with respect to you should there be unto me an occasion of trust?"

"Because we mean to take that 'bauble' back."

"Do you?" Todor drank a swallow directly from his rum bottle. "Against Cargo House itself?"

"We were ready to take the Hadramoo," Hugh said mildly.

The Gat shook his head. "As it pertains to you, there is an occasion of madness. By now it's too late, and a man ought to increase, not decrease, the distance to Old 'Saken. Not that it will matter in the end."

"Oh?" said Hugh. "And why not?"

Todor laughed. "The best-kept secret in the Spiral Arm . . . All right. As regards myself, what matter whether you command or Lady Cargo—when Gatmander ears lie far from your voice and hers alike? For the price of the transit, the story will be told. And well damned be all of you." He stood again and Hugh stood with him and they left the Mild Beast together, climbing the short flight to the dark, deserted street.

Hugh paused to consult his wrist strap for directions and Todor seized the moment to lift the rum bottle to his lips.

The bottle exploded, and for a mad instant Hugh thought, *That is powerful rum!* But his instincts preserved him and he dove for cover behind a dustbin, pulling Todor to the ground with him, just as a second shot struck the bricks. "It wasn't a trap," he said to the Gat. "I swear I didn't lead you into a trap." But he saw that, as regarding Todor, there was no occasion for assurance. The bullet that had shattered the bottle had continued into the mouth and out the back of the head, and amid the blood, brain, and bone that spattered the wall where he had stood was whatever else he had been prepared to tell.

A third shot struck the dustbin, penetrated, and rattled about inside. Hugh wanted to shout that he was not one of the ICC renegades. But he knew the assassin would take no chances. Whatever secret Todor had been killed to preserve might easily have been revealed already to his companions. Hugh shivered.

It had taken weeks for the assassin to track his man down. Those companions could include everyone inside the Mild Beast.

Hugh pulled from his jacket the knife he had purchased on Jehovah. The *sica* did not seem much. It was an assassin's weapon, not very useful for defending a position; but it was all he had. He frisked Todor's body and found a small caliber handgun. He weighed it in his hand, thought about it, then he pressed it into the dead man's hand, curling the finger around the trigger. He found a trash bag that had missed the dustbin and propped the arm on it so that the gun could be seen around the corner.

He peered into the darkness, seeking the sniper's position. Todor had stood *thus,* had lifted the bottle *so,* and the bullet that had killed him had come from . . . He saw the building across the street, the slight flutter of drapes, the open window on the second floor. . . . *from there.* But the killer had most likely shifted. An assassin who stays too long in one place is a fool . . . usually a dead fool.

Hugh put himself in the assassin's mind. He must make sure of Todor and his companion, but he wouldn't come out the building's front entrance. Hugh had no gun, but the assassin wouldn't know that. So, he'd go out the back to the alley behind. The airyways were blocked, so he'd have to go to one corner or the other. Not to Alkorry Street, which was farther and brightly lit, but to the left. And coming around that corner would give him a clear shot into the space behind the dustbin.

Now the only question was whether the sniper would expect astuteness of his quarry and so outguess the guesser. But one could reason oneself into paralysis in that manner, and paralysis, he knew, was the one fatal strategy.

There is this paradox of those who live on the edge, and that is that one may keep his life only by putting it at hazard. He must, as an ancient maxim had it, "desire life like water and yet drink death like wine." Or, in the words of an older maxim, "He that would lose his life, the same shall save it."

He was already running on cat feet across the empty street when he heard the shot whine off the paving. It had come from the direction of the main street. Hugh hunched over, dove for a shadowed airyway, and vanished into it. *Stupid!* he told himself. There had been two of them. The first to cover the Mild Beast; the second to block the way to the transit station. But he was sure there was no third man. Anyone positioned at the other end of the block would already have had a shot behind the dustbin. He listened, but heard no footsteps. The second man was either uncommonly silent or he was maintaining discipline.

The airyway was blocked like all the others. Hugh studied shadows, saw a deeper darkness in the ambit of the stairs, and melted from the airyway to crouch in its protection. From there he could slip through the garden-level passage under the stairs and up the other side. That put a stone staircase between him and the second sniper and he could move, with care, to the next building. Then, down again through the passage, and up, and that put him just at the corner.

There, he waited, either for his quarry to come or for the second shooter to move into a better position.

He listened.

The breeze was steady, channeled by the rows of buildings on either side of the street, but not strong enough to lift more than dust. A stone rattled from a careless kick. Hugh smiled grimly. The assassin likely thought he faced only a couple of drunks from the Beast, one of them—if he were in communication with the second man—last seen cowering in a blocked airway two doors up the block.

He felt a presence approaching: stealthy, but not too much so. He readied himself, exhaled softly, emptied his mind, waited for the moment. A figure stepped around the corner with an air rifle already shouldered, a bead already hunting for the space where Todor lay with gun extended, and Hugh sprouted from the very pavement like a *spartos* from a dragon's tooth, inhaling broadly as he did. He seized the gunman's mouth in his left hand and ran the *sica* across his throat with the right, then pushed him forward to stumble and fall onto the street.

Hugh reached for the air rifle, but a bullet sang on the paving and he withdrew once more into the shadows. The second assassin was coming—he could hear the soft, rapid footsteps—and he had no intention of allowing Hugh to get to the fallen weapon. Of little use, now, his *sica*. He would get one throw, but the curved blade was not a good throwing knife and was unlikely to deal a death blow.

Then he heard the distinctive pop-pop-pop of a handgun followed by the clatter of a weapon sliding along the cobblestone paving. He risked a look and saw the other shooter sprawled in the center of the road and, in the stairwell to the Mild Beast, the Alabastrine woman checking the load in her weapon.

"Coom," she called in a loud whisper, "my goon is noot so soondless as theirs. Roon."

And so, they did.

Neither of them spoke until they had reached the transit station. The Alkorry Street platform was nearly deserted and here, well above street level, the breeze flowed unimpeded. Three young men dressed with feathers in their hair had congregated at the east end trying alternately to look tough and to keep the feathers from taking flight. Two hired-women stood by a kiosk near the center of the platform discussing in low tones their clients of the night and advertising for additional sales. Both groups eyed the newcomers—possible customers, possible prey—but one look was all they required to keep their distance.

Hugh regarded the ebony woman warily. He distrusted coincidence. What usually popped out of the *machina* was seldom a *deus,* and in his line of work surprises were seldom welcome.

Yet, the woman had saved his life.

"I didn't have time to thank you, back there," he said.

"That's ookay," she said, smiling like a skull. "I have my dooty, as do you. I have a message that you moost take to the one who calls himself Tool Benlever and to the Foodir. 'Patience wears theen waiting for your dooty.'"

Hugh shook his head. "I don't understand."

"It is noot needful that you do. Joost tell them what I have said."

"Who are you?"

"You may tell the soo-called Tool Benlever that my name is Ravn Olafsdottr, and that name is surety for what I have toold you. Now goo." She pointed west with a toss of her head. There, a string of lights foretold the arrival of a train of capsules. When Hugh looked back, the Alabastrine was gone. He shivered. The Other Olafsson had appeared at last.

When the train pulled up he entered an empty capsule and keyed in the address of the hotel where "Benlever" and "Melisond" were staying. The system would shunt the capsule to the proper lines and bring it to the nearest station. The doors hissed closed and the train slid forward gathering speed. Through the window he saw the hired women welcoming two men who had stepped off another capsule. Then the train was sliding high over the rooftops with nothing but the night beyond them.

AN CRAIC

Evening has come to the plaza in the Corner and the stones of the fountain have grown chilled, for the blank-faced buildings have tossed their shadows across the square and pinched the sunlight into streams pouring from the narrow passageways. Down those arcades and alleys, plaster and stucco walls glow a golden red, as if they led to fabulous palaces just out of sight. The scarred man grunts and, leveraging himself on his knees, pushes to his feet and offers his arm. "Come," he says. "The Corner is not a good place to be at night." As if to underline his point, the harper hears the sounds of shutters closing, of locks tumbling, of bars sliding into place.

"I will buy you a dinner," she says. "At the Hostel."

But the old man shakes his head. "Such fare's too rich for the likes of me. I'll dine one day at the frozen center of Hel, and I'm saving up my appetite."

She slings her harp case over her shoulder and takes his arm. "No," she insists. "There is a meal I've always wanted to buy, and I'll not be denied."

The scarred man says nothing and the two walk slowly down Merry Weather Alley, toward Grease-line. After a moment, he pats her hand gently. "Thank you," he says. "We've always wondered what came of it in the end. Whether it was all worth it."

The harper fears to respond. Matters are too deli-cate; the most hesitant of touches could shatter them. Instead, she returns to the story. "Your Other Olafs-son was too fortuitous. I thought her appearance bad art."

"Oh, her appearance was bad enough without bringing art into it. There was nothing sudden to her. She's been there all along, lurking in my prepositional phrases and subordinate clauses. It's not that you haven't been warned. She'd been to see the Commit-tee of Seven; she followed Greystroke into and out of the Corner. She directed Micmac Anne to the Fudir's table. She has loitered now and then in the back-ground of my tale."

"I don't understand why she saved Hugh from the ICC assassins."

The scarred man chuckles. "Oh, listen to the sound of your assumptions rattling! Your head is like a cas-tanet. You've forgotten that she and Qing were sent with a mission. She wanted to remind her colleague about that mission, and the sniper threatened to dam-age the medium she planned to use for the message."

"She didn't know Greystroke was Greystroke?"

A slow shake of the head. "We think not. But she is the one player in that dance that we've never spoken with, so who knows what she knew?"

"But why so roundabout? Why not approach Greystroke—Qing, as she thought—directly?"

"Because her task was to kill Qing if he failed in his duty. That is an intimate relationship, and like the bride and the groom, it isn't seemly for the one to see the other before the day of consummation."

"But . . . Donovan's task was routine. An investi-gation of cross-Rift traffic. Next to the Dancer . . . Ah. Ravn didn't know about the Dancer."

"Or she didn't care. Couriers are remarkably focused. She must have known from her own visit to the Seven that the Fudir was the key, and the Fudir had gone to New Eireann for his own reasons. So she didn't worry when 'Qing' also went to New Eireann. She waited on Jehovah, knowing he'd be coming back with his quarry. But then, instead of forcing the Fudir to take him to Donovan, 'Qing' hared off to Peacock Junction with him. That didn't add up—unless Donovan had also gone to Peacock—so she followed them on what you might call 'yellow alert.' Then when he continued on to Die Bold, it began to look like he was shirking his duty. Hence, the reminder. A courier doesn't jump to conclusions. It might be that the best place to learn about cross-Rift traffic was near the Rift, and Donovan might have gone there ahead of them."

"Wouldn't Ravn be suspicious that 'Qing' was associating with a Hound?"

"Again, it's hard to say. She followed 'Qing' but may have reached Peacock Junction after the two had conferred. So all she saw was a Hound's ship following Qing onto an uncharted ramp."

"And so she followed. That must have taken nerve."

"Nerve has never been short rations among that lot. Here. Let's go down these steps. There's a restaurant at the edge of the Corner, on Menstrit. They serve a delicious chicken tikka. If you want to buy us a dinner, it's cheaper there than at the Hostel."

"The cost doesn't matter."

"Good. Then you won't mind spending less. Perhaps there we can bring this squalid tale to an end."

The harper laughs. "In what way?"

"What do you mean?"

"You said there are three ways in which a thing may reach an end, and so far you've mentioned ter-

*mination and perfection. What is the third way?
Surely, the story has not perfected itself! Too many
pieces are yet missing!"*

"Ah. The third kind of end is purpose."

"You mean the tale must achieve a purpose, a
moral."

"No, that a teller may have a purpose in telling it."

SUANTRAÍ: GRASS PYJAMAS

Greystroke was a virtuoso in the use of anycloth.
By cleverly manipulating its pattern against his backdrop, he could make himself seem from a distance to
be fatter or thinner than he was. He could break up
the contours and outline of his body. He had spent the
day as a fly on a great many walls; not, indeed, in solitary corners or in shadows— for no man is so conspicuous as a man alone—but in convivial company at
those taverns and restaurants where ICC personnel
gathered after work. He could, when he wanted, look
like someone else's friend. And in the whirl of aimless
chatter an anonymous question at just the right moment could, like a seed crystal, condense conversation around a particular topic.

All in all, a good day's work. A good day and half
the night! (Die Bolders no longer spent long hours at
work, but they invested considerable time in its aftermath.) It waited now only to find what Hugh had
learned from the officer who had jumped ship. And
what Bridget ban had discovered, using her own less
savory methods on the ICC factor.

The Crown Royal Hotel, on the west side of the
Place of the Chooser, by Ferry Street, was not the

most sumptuous hotel on Die Bold, but was suited to the station of such well-to-do travelers as Julienne Lady Melisond or Tol Benlever. The staff was attentive to their needs, but not so attentive as to inhibit their activities.

Greystroke stepped out of the lift tube and by habit walked close to the wall. His clothing took on a color and pattern that complemented the wallpaper without becoming too obviously a camouflage. He was halfway down the hall when a door opened, and he sidestepped without thinking into the alcove leading to the darkened concierge's lounge.

It was the Fudir's room that opened, but it was Bridget ban who emerged in a long, sheer robe the color of her hair. The Fudir, also in a robe, stood in the doorway. He looked younger than he usually did and his smile was that of the cat who drank the cream. Bridget ban ran her fingers through the Fudir's hair and gave him a small, quick kiss before turning toward her own room. Greystroke's jaw clenched, but only for a moment. Why blame the Fudir for taking the bait when it was offered to one and all?

The Fudir's door closed and Greystroke stepped from the alcove as Bridget ban passed him, taking a position in her blind spot. When she opened the door to her own room, he stepped in behind and moved around her when she turned to shut it.

Most women would have started, perhaps cried out, to find another unexpectedly in the room with them. Bridget ban merely regarded him for a moment before proceeding into the parlor of her suite. Greystroke followed.

"You should nae use those tricks of yours on our own," she said.

"I could say the same of you."

Bridget ban did not ask what he meant. She crossed

to a stuffed, high-back chair and crossed her legs. This allowed the flap of her dressing gown to fall open, revealing golden brown thigh up to the hip. "Poor gray man. You can nae help wonder how you might compare to our Fudir."

"Pfaugh. I know your tricks. Like that one." He waved a hand at her exposed leg as he took a seat on a sofa opposite. "And knowing them for artifice, I'm not affected."

"Aye," she said. "That's why I can relax with you, and be only myself." She pulled the edges of her robe together, concealing her limbs.

"You were going to interrogate the ICC factor; but instead you wasted your time with Fudir. Were you unable to find go-Hidei? Unable to seduce him?"

Her smile was a little puffy, her hair somewhat tousled. She tossed her head and the tangled red tresses waved. Her robe, neglected, parted once more as she shifted position. "Or was he nae so time-consuming a man. Men o' his ilk dream o' beautiful strangers seducing them for nae reason at all, and seldom question their good fortune. 'Twas child's play. An' mickle return for mickle effort. He knows nothing and, worse, knows he knows nothing. He was nae told o' the fleet or its mission, and resents being, as he put it, 'out of the loop.' He so wanted me to pity him. He wanted, I think, his mother."

"And he got you. Cu, I think it coarsens you."

She turned her head away. "Can the berating nae wait on the morrow? The night is gae late, and I'm for bed."

She moved as if to rise and Greystroke said tightly, "I would think that you'd been in enough beds for one night."

Her eyes widened. "Why, ye're jealous, Pup, aren't ye?"

Greystroke examined his conscience. "I'm afraid so. A small bit. One cannot help one's enzymes. It's not me you should worry about."

"The Fudir, then? The Fudir is a man of parts."

"And I'm not?"

"Tae each man, his gift. Yours is simplicity. Ye ha' nae parts, but are a seamless whole. Ye'd nae could do wha' ye do without that true simplicity. As for the Fudir, I find him . . . engaging."

"And what am I?"

"So. You do want to know how ye compare tae him."

"It's always a means with you, and never an end. 'Business before pleasure,' as I think the Terrans say."

Sudden tears started in the eyes of Bridget ban. "An' d'ye despise me so!" She stood and turned away from him, hiding her face. "But that dart can nae hurt," she added in a low, sad voice, " 'less it finds its mark. Ye're right, Pup. Aye, ye're right. It does coarsen."

Greystroke stood, too, and took a step toward her. "That needn't be true, Francine."

She turned a tear-tracked face to him.

"Cu . . ." he said.

"Come to me."

Later, he said, "This can't possibly mean anything to you."

And she answered, "Anything is possible."

Little Hugh returned within the hour, banging on hotel doors and calling the others out in a variety of dishevelment to tell them what had happened. This could not wait until morning! Bridget ban concurred and soon everyone was gathered in her parlor.

The assassination of the Gat was ominous enough, they agreed. How much did the ICC know? But the appearance of the Other Olafsson was as alarming as a scorpion in a picnic basket.

"And she gave me a message to deliver to the two of you," Hugh told Greystroke and the Fudir.

"I don't want to hear it," said the Fudir.

"Bad luck for you, then," said Greystroke. "I'll be harder for her to track than you."

"The Fudir no work CCW," insisted the Terran. "I no their bhisti."

Greystroke's smile was not kind. "You know that, and perhaps I know that; but if she apologizes to your corpse afterward, what difference to you? You thought to play at the margins of the Great Game and not get taken? The more fool, you."

"I don't think she knew about the Dancer," Hugh said before the argument could more than blink. "She wanted you to focus on your original assignment."

Greystroke laughed. "*My* original assignment was from Fir Li—to find Donovan."

"So was Olafsson Qing's," Bridget ban reminded him. "But that mission must wait for the non. 'Tis the Dancer that matters, not the Dark-hound's statistical anomalies. I'm more concerned about the assassins. The ICC does nae do such things. That men are greedy does nae make them murderous."

The Fudir waved his hand. "Es mock nix," he said. "Most ICC oakiedoke, yes. But how many bad to make big dikh? You say, factor, he no know nothing."

Bridget ban nodded slowly. "Nothing about the fleet, which I suppose means 'nothing about the Dancer.' "

"At least some in the fleet learned what the Dancer is," said Hugh, "and mutinied to keep it from Lady Cargo. There may be a civil war within the ICC itself. But if the commodore had the scepter, how could anyone have gone against him?"

"I could guess," said Bridget ban.

"Guesses!" said the Fudir.

"Hear her," said Greystroke. "Her guesses are more solid than most people's evidence."

"No one in the phantom fleet knew what it was they were supposed to seize. 'A prehuman artifact,' they were told. They were but recovering property stolen from the ICC on New Eireann. Can ye imagine Radha Lady Cargo entrusting anyone else wi' the possession of Stonewall's Scepter? Hardly! But a muckle o' ICC's household troops come from the Old Planets, and the behavior o' the artifact—its slow stone dancing—would ha' reminded some of the ancient legend. Perhaps there was a struggle for its possession; perhaps some, like Todor, fought to keep anyone from possessing it. But once the commodore realized and gained hold of it, resistance evaporated, save those ships that severed communication with the flagship. You can nae obey a voice you can't hear."

"But Todor wanted to go home," said Hugh, "not wherever his ship was headed, so they dropped him on Die Bold. Why did he wonder if Gatmander was far enough from 'Saken to escape?"

Greystroke spoke up. "Does anyone know if a *recorded* voice would have the same effect? No? If it does, Lady Cargo could record commands to submit and send them out to every world in the Spiral Arm, even far Gatmander."

"And why bother," asked the Fudir, "to send a kill team to track this Todor down? If Lady Cargo does have the Dancer, everyone will know it soon enough. And those within reach of her voice won't even care."

"'The best-kept secret in the Spiral Arm,'" Hugh remembered.

"Does Lady Cargo knows there's a Hound on her trail?" Greystroke said. "If she had eyes and ears on

Peacock, they would've sent word the moment you came asking about the phantom fleet."

But Bridget ban shook her head. "I don't think the 'Cockers knew anything. They were protecting their secret ramps, not the fleet. I think the fleet worried them, too."

"Though not worried enough to cooperate with you," Hugh pointed out. He rose and went to the kitchen to brew tea for everyone.

"No, they're nae good at thinking ahead," the Hound answered. "The fleet triggered their paranoia—and I was the immediate threat."

When he had filled the hotel's flash-boiler and set the tea ball in the samovar, Hugh returned and stood behind his chair. "How long before the Other Olafsson figures things out?"

The others fell silent and looked one to the other.

"She was in the Bar when January told the story about the Dancer," the Fudir ventured. "She'd heard something about a 'Dancing Stoon,' but no details. She's not stupid and the 'Feds have their own stories about the prehumans. If she hasn't figured it out by now, it shouldn't take her too much longer."

"She knew who you were," Greystroke remembered. "She pointed you out to Anne."

"Ja, and she knew I'd gone with January to New Eireann, and what name I'd used."

Greystroke nodded. "And she'd met with the Seven before I got there. She knew Qing's assignment and learned you were the link to Donovan. But she stood by protocol. She waited until I showed up, and stayed on Jehovah until I returned with you in tow. Heighing off to Peacock must have puzzled her; so she followed. But was she at Peacock long enough to learn about our interest in the phantom fleet? Or that the fleet had taken the Dancer from the Cynthians? No, I don't see how she can piece it together."

"Not until after she does," the Fudir commented. "Then you'll see it."

Hugh looked at the clock on the wall. "Morning news feed," he said. "I'd like to know what they're saying about the killings at the Mild Beast. We may have to duck the Die Bold bobbers if we're to get to 'Saken."

Greystroke spoke while Hugh fiddled with the 'face on the wall, bringing up the news feed to the hotel's screen. "If Lady Cargo has the Dancer, going to 'Saken may not be our best move. One word, and we'd be her adoring slaves. And if I'm to be any woman's adoring slave, she'd not be my first choice."

"It wouldn't be *your* choice in either case," said the Fudir, glancing at Bridget ban.

Greystroke bristled and made to rise, but Hugh hushed everyone. "It's cycling into the city news now."

The others turned to the screen on the wall. Bridget ban said, "Do you think anyone saw you?"

Hugh raised his brows. "A deserted street, late at night? Of course, someone saw us. There were a lot of window— Hush. That's Alkorry Street."

Another Killing in Crossford District, the news-reader told them. *Three dead, all outlanders. Rifle duel in Alkorry Street leaves both dead. Bystander killed while leaving local. Bad timing, eh what? Your comments on our site. Does allowing outlanders to come and go freely put our citizens at risk? We Want to Know. Robert seeking two witnesses. Sketches from residents.* <Pop-up window shows police sketches.> *Call Robert with information.*

"Ravn was a lot thinner," Hugh said of one of the police sketches, "and her hair was bright yellow. They *might* identify us from those reconstructions, but . . ."

"Wisht!" said Bridget ban, and she pointed to the screen.

A pale, fleshy dough face was displayed there, one with an ingratiating smile, shown among a festive crowd.

Rough Love Tryst Gone Awry. Go-Hidei Kutezov, ICC factor on Die Bold dies in S-M bondage ritual. Kinky secret life. Neighbor says, <Pop-up window shows a matronly woman with bewildered eyes.> *"We had no idea he was like that." A lesson for all. Robert finds secret cache of pain-love instruments.* <Second pop-up shows bracelets, leather mask, spiked glove.> *See here, go-Hidei at Klabarra Day party, Regent's Palace. Actress Jo-wan Venable on arm. Is she rough-sex partner? She says no. Robert seeking information. Your comments on our site. Is Jo-wan telling truth? We Want to Know!*

The news then shifted to sports and Bridget ban said, "Off," to the screen. In the short silence that followed, Hugh said, "Who's Robert?"

"It's their name for the metropolitan police department," said Bridget ban. "The founder, I suppose. It's why the agents are called bobbers."

Greystroke turned to Bridget ban. "You never mentioned you killed him, Cu. But I can't say I blame you, if he was like that. Duty, and all that; but there are limits."

"Fash it! I did nae sich thing! Believe me, Pup, I'd hae known were he that sort o' man! An' he was nae."

"Ravn was a busy little girl last night," said Hugh. Greystroke looked at him. "You think it was her?"

The Ghost of Ardow shrugged. "Call it a hunch. If she was curious what Qing was up to, she had to be even more curious what the Hound following Qing was up to. She may realize by now that you're working with her."

The Fudir cackled. "'In cahoots,' we say."

Hugh made a long face. "Treason, *she'd* say. Excuse me. The tea is ready. I'm thinking to do a systemic risk analysis on our next move."

"We know what the bleeding risks are," the Fudir called after him.

Hugh stuck his head back into the room. "It isn't the risk categories," he said. "It's how they impact one another. There's a portfolio of risks to consider, and their causal chains. It may be more important to manage the causality of the relationships than to manage the risks themselves."

When he had disappeared again into the kitchen, Greystroke said, "Is he serious? We're about to stick our heads into the mouth of a Sable Tiger, and he thinks we need to *enumerate* the teeth in its jaws?"

The Fudir pursed his lips. "Well," he said. "Something *could* go wrong."

Later that morning, as the posse checked out of the hotel, the Fudir contrived to be in the same ground car as Little Hugh. When they stepped from the colonnade to the line of spaceport shuttles, the Fudir carefully scanned the windows of the hotels bordering the other three sides of the Place of the Chooser. As these were also for the most part hotels of many stories, that meant a lot of windows to study.

"Don't worry," Hugh told him. "She's gone on ahead to Old 'Saken. The best way to follow someone is to learn where he's going, and then get there first. She's not ready to kill you or Greystroke yet. Not until she's certain that 'Qing' is derelict in his duty or has joined forces with the enemy. Besides, it's Donovan she wants—to give him his assignment. You she'll only torture until you tell her what she needs to know."

"That's a relief. How do you know she's gone to 'Saken?"

"It's what I'd do."

"Uh-hunh."

"Well, we both think like assassins."

"Usually, when I get 'two,' I have a couple ones around somewhere."

"So. She must know by now that we're tracking the phantom fleet. If she didn't learn it from the 'Cockers, she learned it from our attempt to contact Todor. So, that's one. And then because your *buddy* Greystroke was *palling* with a known Hound, she tracked Bridget ban to the factor's home and then . . . One beautiful woman seduces him, and right after she leaves, a second one comes to his door. He must have thought he had died and gone to heaven."

The Fudir grunted. "Well, he was half right. Okay. 'Qing is following the phantom fleet' plus 'the fleet is from the ICC' equals 'next stop Old 'Saken.' Where'd you pick up Terran words like 'buddy' and 'pal'?"

"Where do you think? Give me a couple months more, and I could pass for Terran."

The Fudir showed what he thought of that possibility. When they reached the cab line, the Fudir told the luggage cart to stop and he loaded the coffers into the lorry's boot while the driver held the door open for Hugh. The shuttle was large on the inside, with plenty of headroom and legroom. The Fudir climbed in beside him, noticed the driver had gone back to his seat, and reached out to swing the door closed. Hugh stretched his legs out straight. "This is so much better than those auto-rickshaws on Jehovah. You'd think nobody there grew to nineteen hands."

The Fudir told the driver to take them to the number two beanstalk. The driver blinked and looked to Hugh for confirmation. "You heard him," he said in his manager's voice. The Fudir shut the partition with more force than required, but Hugh said nothing about the driver's snub. That would only further irritate the Terran.

"Now what's all this about risks?" the Fudir asked. "I know what we can do about Lady Cargo and her irresistible commands. There's an old Terran story that covers it. But what else were you thinking of?"

"You want the Risk Management Lecture?"

"No."

"Pity. It's one of my better ones. All right. We know what failure is. Lady Cargo imposes her iron whims on Old 'Saken. More so than she already has, I suppose. And maybe on Die Bold and Friesing's World, since they're only one day's streaming from one another. That's not really as bad as the Cynthians, when you stop to think about it. The Molnar would have carried it with himself on every raid and induced surrender from every planet he attacked. I can't see old Lady Cargo riding a circuit. But now there's a chance the Confederates will try to get hold of it. If Those of Name . . ."

"I thought about that when I thought Greystroke was Olafsson Qing. They make the Cynthians look like fluffy bunnies."

"Agreed. But there's another problem. What is success?"

The Fudir did not answer for a space. Hugh watched him stare out the cab's window at the rows of stores along Èlfiuji's main business street. "Success?" he said finally. "Success is making all that not happen."

"Aye, but who gets the Dancer afterward, Fudir?" Hugh asked softly.

"You still planning to rule New Eireann with it?"

"No, and I'm not too worried about Bridget ban. She thinks the Ardry should have it, and I suppose that's harmless enough as long as I stay away from High Tara and Tully King O'Connor doesn't. But Greystroke . . ."

"Ha! I'll tell you what Greystroke would do with it. He'd command Bridget ban to love him."

"Aye. And you'd rather that she love you, is that it?" He kept his voice easy, but the Fudir must have heard something in it, because he turned and stared at Hugh.

"You, too? Oh, she's got the three of us wrapped around her finger, hasn't she? She's a cold-blooded witch. I think that's what bothers Greystroke. He thinks she's forgotten how to love."

"And he can *command* it otherwise? He's a lot to learn of love, then. Does he know he'll do that with the Dancer?"

The Fudir thought about it, then bobbed his head side to side. "Not yet. But it *will* occur to him, by and by. Give him credit, though. He'll do it for her sake, not his own."

"The excuse of every despot, especially the most sincere. And what about you, Bre'er Fudir?"

"You-fella no call me so. You no pukka fanty, sahb. Only Brotherhood use 'um 'bre'er.' "

"Fudir, if you and I are not brothers by now, there is no meaning to the word. Do you want Bridget ban's love, too?"

"No. I can buy *that* product in ever port in the Spiral Arm. I'd like . . . I think I'd like to have her respect, and I'm not sure I can have that while she's manipulating me through my trousers. Although," he added thoughtfully, "I can't say I dislike the manipulations."

Hugh shook his head. "She isn't really that beautiful, you know. Not in an objective sense."

"There is no objective sense to beauty. A *knockout*

on Jugurtha is a *plug ugly* on Megranome. But she knows how to listen and how to speak. There's a Terran legend about such a woman, named Cleopatra."

"There's a Terran legend for just about everything. But now you know why the chance of our success worries me almost as much as the chance of our failure. I wish . . ."

The Fudir cocked his head. "You wish what?"

"I wish it was still just you and me attacking the whole fookin' Hadramoo."

"You do? Why?"

"At least then we had a chance."

AN CRAIC

The restaurant itself is only a shed with an open front and a service bar in the back and three or four rickety tables. The cooking is done in the back by a wide-bodied woman named Mamacita Tiffni who smiles a lot and speaks an unintelligible patois. The harper eyes the place with instinctive distrust, but the chicken tikka proves excellent and is served in the traditional "tortiya" with "fresh fries." She wonders why Terran food is not more widely popular. Mamacita carries plates in from the back in an apparently endless series. Not only the tikka, but roganjosh and hodawgs and sarkrat. Now and then Mamacita swats the scarred man playfully on the back of the head, calling him "Old Man," and it is the first time that the harper has ever seen a genuine smile on what remains of the scarred man's lips.

When dessert is served—it is called a rasgula—the

harper feels full to bursting and waves the balls of iced chocolate milk off.

"We should have met here from the beginning," she tells him. *"It is a better venue for the story."*

But the scarred man shakes his head. "No, this is too bright and open a place for the darker passages."

It is not bright. The sun has gone down and the only illumination is from strings of small electric lights that outline the shed and dangle in loops from the nearby trees. A short distance away, ground cars hurry past, as many west as east, and the harper wonders where they are going. It seems that if everyone would only move to the other side of town, there would be no traffic at all. "Shall we conclude the tale, then? How did the posse manage to take the Dancer from Lady Cargo?"

"Why do you suppose they did?"

"You jest. We would all be ruled by the ICC."

"How do you know we aren't? That we aren't may be a dream we've been commanded to have. The gift to command has many facets. Do this. Do that. But also, forget this. In fact, we were once given that command."

"By Radha Lady Cargo?" The harper is suddenly appalled that everything she has ever known has been a lie. Then she relaxes. "That is what you meant, wasn't it, when you said the moment before the Dancer was discovered was the last sane moment in the universe. Because there could never be any certainty afterward."

"Only the mad are certain," the scarred man says. "And sanity is a precious thing. Law of supply and demand."

The harper laughs at the jest and at that the scarred man stiffens and his eyes go wide. "No!" he cries.

"Not now, of all times and places!" He stands in a violent motion and the table slides, toppling ceramic mugs with smiling solar faces and sending balls of kulfi to the wooden floor. Mamacita dashes in from the back and wrings her hands in her apron while she stares. Two skinny men at another table rise just as abruptly, reaching for their belts, but they relax on seeing who it is and only laugh.

The harper wants to call to him, to say something to soothe his evident agony. But she realizes that she does not know his name. "Old Man!" she cries, using Mamacita's name for him. "What is wrong?"

"It is fit, lady harp," says Mamacita. "Is come on him some time. You!" she hollers at the two skinny men. "Be gone! No mock him! You go, meal free; you stay, price double! Harimanan!"

At her call, a giant of a man rises from the shadow under a tall palm tree where he has been resting. "Hey, boys," he tells the two, "no dikh. You go jildy. Hutt, hutt." He hefts a stout billet of wood in one hand and the harper sees tucked into the waist of his dhoti a teaser of an old and obsolete model. One question is answered. How does a woman operate a cash business safely on the edge of a high-crime neighborhood?

When the mockers have been expelled, the harper turns to the scarred man, who stands at the rail that marks the entrance to the shed. Both hands grip the rail and he stands half hunched over. The harper places a tentative hand on his arm, and he shrugs it off with an abrupt, hard motion of his shoulder. "You want the ending, harper? Are you quite certain you want the ending?" He turns and impales her with a single eye.

The harper takes a step back, wondering if she should flee. But the scarred man blocks her way and, with a grip that surprises her, guides her back to their table. "Go on, sit," he says. "You've heard this much. You'll hear the rest."

The harper looks to Mamacita, who nods her head ever so slightly, and taking comfort at this signal, she resumes her seat.

The scarred man drags a second chair to him and uses it to prop up his right leg, although it takes him two tries. "Let's see if you've been paying attention," he says, easily and cruelly. The harper wonders what has become of the man she shared time with on a fountain basin in a small square in the Corner. Yet, she has seen this once before, in the Bar, and more often, she now realizes, in a more attenuated form.

She reaches for her harp case. "Shall I play it back to you?"

"A parrot can do that much. Have you given any further thought to January's initial mistake?"

"His initial . . . Ah, you mean upon his escape from Spider Alley. Why surely, that is too obvious to remark. The Irresistible Object was the Dancer, not the terrible storm."

The scarred man leans forward and folds his arms on the table, which leans from the weight. "And if it was so irresistible, why did he give it up so easily to Jumdar? Every other time, it was violence that pried it from one grip to another; yet January gave the scepter to Jumdar for nothing more than ship repairs and the promise of a cut."

"Nothing more? A tramp captain would not think that so little. But I'll give you an answer. In the normal course of affairs, January would go no nearer the Rift than Jehovah Roads, while Jumdar would send it to Old 'Saken."

"Enter, the Cynthians," the scarred man prompts. "They would have gone all the way to Sapphire Point on their way home."

"Aye, into the hands of na Fir Li."

"Too simple. There's another reason."

The harper thinks about it, then shakes her head. "No, that cannot be it."

The skull beneath his skin leers at her. "Can it not? I've all but told you."

"Then why"—she slaps the table—"not come right out and say it?"

"Why else but that the story achieves its end."

GOLTRAÍ: HOWLING, IN THE WILDERNESS

*O*ld 'Saken! the scarred man says. The very name is magic. Here was the world at the end of the ancient Via Dolorosa, where the bewildered detritus of Terra was cast off to live or die as best they could in the collapse of the Commonwealth of Suns. In the tumultuous and despairing first generation, the ultimate decision had been to live, and that had resulted in a certain lack of sentimentality. "Whatever it takes" was the motto of the first dynasty of presidents. In her long history, 'Saken's refugee camps came under rough bosses, gave way to city-states, then organized in leagues and empires and shattered in civil wars. Her rough-and-tumble traditions linger in her civic religion, but the bond of fractious solidarity that arose among the exiles resulted finally in the largest world with a single planetary government. The Forsaken, as they call themselves, have a motto: "I against my brother; my brother and I against our cousin; my cousin and I against the world."

Other worlds were settled by successive waves of deportees: Waius, Damtwell, Die Bold, Bandonope, *and the rest, and some prospered (like Friesing's World) and some did not (like the derelict worlds of the Yung-lo), but 'Saken always held to pride of place. That their ancestors had been the first deported argued that they had been especially important in the old Commonwealth. At least, the Forsaken argued so. If Jehovah is unworldly and Peacock indolent, if Die Bold suffers ennui and New Eireann desperation, a certain whiff of satisfaction, of even arrogance, has settled over Old 'Saken. In the heart of every Forsaken man and woman rests the suspicion that they were just the least bit better than those upstarts on Die Bold or Friesing's World.*

All of which could be very problematical when it came to tourism.

People across the Spiral Arm came to visit Old 'Saken. Obstreperous boozhies from the Greater Hanse; pesky Megranomers and their peskier children; Chettinads in their ridiculous garb; yokels from Jehovah; rubes from Gatmander; even jump-up so-called royalty from the so-called capital world of High Tara. They all wanted to see the First Field, where the landings had been, and other sites associated with the early days: Kong Town, Elsbet Bay, Raging Rock.

So there was a great deal of traffic on the Piccadilly Circus and it was not impossible, nor even very unlikely, that a trader or tourist chance-met on Die Bold would show up also on Old 'Saken. So the posse would, Bridget ban insisted, maintain the same identities, just in case.

The transit took only a single day, but the traffic on the ramp was heavy and intricately choreographed by local STC. After that, the magbeam network caught the two ships and gentled them down toward the legendary world where the Human Diaspora had begun. During the crawl, Bridget ban and the Fudir studied maps of Chel'veckistad, searching out the best and most plausible routes from the spaceport to the Dalhousie Estate in the Northbound Hills where Lady Cargo lived. "She'll have it with her in the estate," Bridget ban had said. "Question is, do we enter the grounds openly or secretly?"

"Or both," suggested the Terran.

Greystroke and Hugh in the other vessel had agreed. A Krinthic merchant prince might have probable cause for calling on the chairman of the ICC and just enough social standing to pull it off. Hugh was able, after some research, to craft a plausible RFP involving a shipment of crater gems for Dalhousie Dew. The latter was an especially fine touch, since the hybrid fruit grew only in the soil of the Northbound Hills under direct control of Lady Cargo's estate. The pricing was inevitably months out-of-date, but the proposal would at least get them a hearing with the estate manager and the master vintner.

"She will almost surely try to influence the terms of the deal with the Dancer," Greystroke said. "Ringbao will use Fudir's plan and we'll compare notes afterward."

The Fudir had suggested aural implants that would block Cargo's direct voice, while repeating the sense of the words via simulation. He called it the "Odysseus Strategy," after an ancient Terran god. Hugh had thought of a number of other possibilities—the actual vibrations in the air might carry the effect, the sense of the words might carry the effect despite the buffer—but as no one could see a way around those objections, they had decided to go ahead with the plan.

"If ye agree to a muckle bad deal," said Bridget ban, "we'll know the buffers are no help."

"What matters," the Fudir interjected, "is to scout out the security inside the grounds. We need to know where she's keeping it, and what we'll have to bypass to get to it."

"Teach a Peacock pleasure," Greystroke retorted.

"I don't know why ye bait him so much," said Bridget ban after the connection was broken.

"Getting him to react is the only way I know he's there," the Fudir grumbled. "He's my jailor, gods take him. How should I feel about him?"

"Enough o' that, now," said the Hound. "Let's go over the topography again. There's a ravine near the north end o' the estate that might provide an entrance."

They were a day out of High 'Saken Orbit when Bridget ban picked up a Hound's beacon.

"Yes, Grey One," Bridget ban told the Pup when he had called with the same information. "We're hearing it, too. Yellow Code. A ship in parking orbit. Fudir's trying for a visual right now. I think it must be Grimpen. He told us at Sapphire Point he was going to the Old Planets. Wait, here's the image. Aye, that's Grimpen's ship, alright, the muckle great wean. No, no answer yet . . . Give it a minute for the time lag."

"According to the intelligence," said the Fudir, "the other ship's intelligence is on standby. Answers politely, but won't comment on the owner's whereabouts. Won't even acknowledge that Grimpen's the owner."

"No, it would nae do so . . ."

"Cu," said Greystroke. "Grimpen must have gone planetside. Ask his ship when he'll be back."

"Nay, the Grimpen is senior tae me, and his ship'll nae accept my override. Yes, *Rollover?* Yes, I'll leave a message. Tell your master that Bridget ban and Greystroke want to meet with him. Greystroke, if Grimpen came directly here from Sapphire Point, he's been here for a metric month. Unless he stopped at Abyalon, or took a side trip to the Cynthia Cluster."

"Which means he's on the scent of something."

"He was on the scent of something when he left Sapphire Point. But not the Dancer."

Early the next morning, the Fudir put *Endeavour* into High 'Saken Orbit not too far off the Chel'veckistad beanstalk. From parking orbit, they could see the two other beanstalks peeping over the horizon. Bridget ban admired the flame-red aspect of the distant Kikuyutown-Chadley Beanstalk, which was just catching the sunset. "They've been around a long time, the Old Planets have. Someday Jehovah, Peacock, and the rest will have them, too."

"Old Earth," said the Fudir, "had a dozen of them. They were like a wall around the world. Twelve-Gated Terra, she was called. People came from around the old Commonwealth just to see them from space. It's said that Earth's day was lengthened more than a minute by the conservation of angular momentum. No one knows how many tens of thousands died when the Dao Chettians scythed them down. Now your oldest planets have two or three apiece, and you think it's a marvel of science."

"It's not *science*," said Bridget ban. "It's *engineering*. Ancient superstitions have nothing to do with beanstalks."

"And where do you think those engineering formulas came from? Someone had to think them up in the first place, right?"

"Losh," said Bridget ban, "I'll ha' nae religious arguments here."

The posse contrived to meet as if by chance in the Great Green Square, where Congress Hall and the PM's Residence were must-see attractions. Both had been built over the course of several generations in the early years of Chu State, although they served now for the planetary government. They featured the tall, ornamented towers of that age. Giant mosaics of colored tiles, cleverly laid to use the angle of view from street level, turned the sharp-slanted roofs into murals. One showed an eagle fighting a snake; another showed a horseman charging across a snow-draped plain. There were spots on the Great Green, marked by low, railed platforms, from which each mural appeared as three-dimensional. Admission was monitored by a sullen young woman from Megranome, since no Forsaken would accept such a menial job.

Hugh took his turn and was delighted to see how the artist's use of forced perspective caused the horseman to appear as if riding out of the very roof itself. He asked the guide how it was done and the Megranomer replied in a dull monotone that "tile-artists of the Cullen Era were masters of the geometry of optics" and that the horseman was "Christopher Chu Himself bringing word of the Brythonic attack to Boss Pyotr." Hugh gathered that he was not the first ever to ask the question. Hugh wondered briefly who Christopher Chu Himself was before the girl called time on him and he stepped down from the platform to encounter "Kalim," the manservant to "Lady Melisond."

O happy chance!

Of course, it has all been carefully choreographed ahead of time; but Hugh had already encountered two other people he had met on Die Bold, so the usefulness of the charade was beyond question. "Reggie, meechee!" he cried for the benefit of onlookers. "I thought Lady Melisonde was going to Friesing's World. I must tell *my straw* Benlever and we will have lunch together. Have you seen the tiled rooftops? An effect of the most amazing!"

The Fudir glanced at the galloping horseman on the roof of the PM's Residence. "I wonder if he had his treachery already in mind."

"Who?"

"Chu. You know this peninsula was called Chu State in the early days. There were four or five refugee camps here, south of the marshes."

"Unified by Chu?"

"No, by someone called Bossman Sergei. There was a whole dynasty of 'Bossmen,' and the Chus were their majordomos."

"You mean, like a *tainiste*?"

"More like glorified butlers. The story there"—he nodded to the rooftop—"is that Bossman Pyotr wouldn't believe Chu's warning about a winter attack; so Chu improvised a hasty defense along the Challing River and repulsed the Brythons. Afterward, the people demanded he become the new Bossman."

"And it wasn't like that?"

The Fudir shrugged. "It's the official history, so it's probably wrong. I don't know that Chu planned to seize power from the beginning; but . . . Ah! Here's Lady Melisonde." He bowed from the waist. "Lady, see who I've found."

Bridget ban wore an ankle-length gown of emerald-green edged in gilt geometries, and a matching pill-box cap with a half veil hanging across her face. She offered her hand, saying, "Ringbao! Top of the morning to ye!"

Hugh bowed and pressed the hand to his lips in the High Taran fashion. "And the rest of the day to yourself," he replied, repressing his instinct to reply in the more vulgar Eireannaughta fashion.

Shortly, Tol Benlever had joined them and Kalim led them to the Green, where they claimed a table. Lady Melisonde ordered drinks from the dumbwaiter— four Ruby Roses—and shortly a machine of some sort rolled up to their table with flute glasses inserted in matching sockets.

They each took one and Melisonde said, " 'Saken mechs are quite clever, don't you think? They employ these automated servants for all sorts of menial tasks."

"Whatever will the Terrans do for jobs," murmured Kalim.

"Well, they don't speak out of turn," said Tol Benlever, with a significant glance at Kalim. When Lady Melisonde said, "Go," and the autoservant left, he chuckled. "And they listen better than Terrans, too."

"Ah, but a human waiter can anticipate your needs," Ringbao pointed out. "I suspect that autoservant can only do what it's told. And before you jape on that, *my straw,*" he added to Benlever, "may I remind you that cunning is to be prized wherever it is found."

"Granted," said the Krinthic trader. "Say, have any of you seen that nice Alabastrine woman we met on Die Bold? I think she was coming here, too."

Three shakes of the head. " 'Tis a grand, big planet, Tol, darling," said Melisonde. "I much suppose we'll run into her by and by." She raised her glass. "Our mutual successes."

They all drank. Hugh found the liqueur thick, almost syrupy, and with a distinct cherry aftertaste. "Not bad," he said. "Though I'd not drink it in quantity."

"You couldn't afford it in quantity," said Benlever.

"It's one of the 'padded wines' they make in the Dalhousie Valley here," he added for the others' benefit. "I'm to meet with their master vintner tomorrow to discuss a trade deal. We may sample enough there to satisfy even Ringbao's refined taste. Haha!" The others chuckled and pressed him for details, but he smiled and touched the side of his nose to indicate that those details were a trade secret.

"What of your brother," Kalim said to his mistress. He meant Grimpen. "You thought he might be here."

"I've seen no sign of him, I fear. I wish that omadhaun had left word where he'd be staying. At least he didn't do anything boorish to get his name in the news feeds." She meant that Grimpen had not openly named himself a Hound to the authorities. Yet if he was "flying low," he might be very difficult to find, nor desirous of being found.

"I can ask around," said Kalim. "I have friends here. They may've seen him." He meant the Terran Corner of Chel'veckistad.

Lady Melisonde nodded. "So long as you are back in time for my country drive. I do so want to see the Northbound Hills."

They ordered a lunch of quagmire soup—a chowder of corn and seafood similar to the *chow pinggo* that Hugh had grown up with—and thick "glutton" sandwiches of fried black bread filled with fish, sausage, cheese, and tomatoes. To accompany the meal, they ordered a local beer called Snowflake. Then, having established for anyone listening their companionship, they broke up. Hugh went to arrange fallback lodgings under different names. Greystroke vanished into the crowd on the Green to look for signs of a populace already ensnared by the Dancer. And the Fudir slipped off to change clothes and plumb the

Corner while Bridget ban set out to look for her "brother."

The Forsaken Archives on Udjenya Street, two blocks off the Great Green, was an impressively large building and bore a motto across its facade in a script and language that Hugh did not recognize—most likely one of those tongues, now forgotten, spoken by some of the original deportees. He supposed the motto was imposing and inspirational to anyone who could read it.

"I'm working for Kungwa Hilderbrandt, the Valencian historian," he told the senior archivist, showing him some official-looking papers that Greystroke had printed up on board *Skyfarer*. But the archivist barely glanced at them. He didn't care about outworlders, not even famous outworld historians. Still, one must be hospitable. So he put on what Hugh supposed was meant as a welcoming face and waited.

"Scholar Hildebrandt is tracing the genetic versions of the prehuman legends, and—"

"What the devil is a genetic version?"

"Why, as surely you know, different versions of the prehuman legends are circulating on different worlds. Scholar Hildebrandt believes these are all 'descended with modifications,' as he puts it, from original versions. For example, there is a version of the Tale of the Two Toppers on Megranome that he has shown to be elaborated from a passage in the Tale of the Awkward Kitchen-maid."

Hugh had managed to glaze the archivist's eyes. However much he did not care about outworld scholars, he cared even less about their research. His job was to preserve and protect the documents and media in his care. About their contents, he did not give a fig.

"And so, I would like to read the oldest compendium of tales in your collection."

"Oh, would you?" the man asked, so loudly that others in the vestibule turned and looked. "What is it with you outies? One after another, you come parading in here; and do you want to see the Articles for State? No. The Trans-Oceanic Pact? Couldn't care less. The Collected Letters of Genghis John Chu? No, you want to read old fairy tales. Bozhemoy! You expect us to let you handle the oldest and most fragile papers we have? No one touches those. No one. I don't care how big you are!"

Somewhat startled at this tirade, Hugh said, "No, no, goodsir. I don't need to handle the originals. I'm only interested in the matter. Surely you have scanned images . . ."

"*Of course,* we have scanned images. We're not a bunch of noovos, like some planets I could name, but won't."

"And I'm not really very big." Hugh said this with his most disarming smile. He knew that his musculature, toughened by the hard months "in the wind" on New Eireann, made him seem bigger than he was.

The archivist grunted. "No, not you. It was the first one. He was a regular Nolan beast. Sign here." He handed Hugh a light pen and Hugh entered his supposed name and homeworld and scribbled a signature. There had been seven individuals in the past month who wanted to view Document 0.0037/01. "Which was the big guy?" he asked curiously. Only two names were off-world: Elriady Moore of Ramage and Keeling Ruehommage of Wiedermeier's Chit.

The archivist sniffed and looked at the screen. "That one," he said, tapping Moore's name. "Why?"

"He's a field researcher for a rival scholar. I bet I

can describe the other outworlder for you. Coal-black skin, bright yellow hair, blue eyes. Thin as a rail."

"A-yuh. That's her. Sweet young thing, too."

"Alabaster accent?"

"Alabaster? Nah. She's from the Chit." He pointed again to the screen, as if he had never heard of false names and feigned identities. "They sound like Megranomers."

Hugh thanked the archivist, who gave him a code and directed him to a reading room. On the way there, Hugh pulled a disposable handy from his pocket, called the base-camp number, and said, "Look for a large man named Elriady Moore." Then he dropped the handy into a shredder and continued to the reading room.

"For all the good it did us," he complained later that night to Greystroke. "The oldest versions of the pre human legends. *Handwritten,* if you can imagine it, on paper. The annotation states that they were collected by a self-appointed commission during refugee times. Oh, that must have delighted those folks who had lost their homeworld! Academic researchers!"

They were in Greystroke's hotel room at the Hatchley, several blocks off Great Green, and Greystroke had ordered up in-room meals. Hugh had plugged his memo stick into the hotel room's 'face to show them the download that was the fruit of his labors. "It may have been a way to keep sane, by continuing the routines of their past lives."

Greystroke grunted. "No, the camps needed sanitation, not sanity. I begin to wonder if Fudir's Commonwealth was worth saving, if that's the way their exiles behaved." He walked over to the screen as he ate. "Funny-looking squiggles. We should've known they'd not have used Gaelactic back then. What language is it?"

"I didn't want to ask the archivist. I was a scholar's field researcher. I should have known the languages. I downloaded a copy, thanked him, and left. The Fudir looked at it before he and Bridget ban went off for their drive. He thinks it may be Brythic or Roosky. Those were two of the groups that were settled here. He says the Vraddy and the Zhõgwó used very different writing systems. He'll take a shot at reading it when he gets back."

"Well, getting more background on the Stonewall mythos may be useful, but it needn't get in the way of our main task. Bridget ban followed up on your call. Grimpen was staying in Eastport near the beanstalk base. And Fudir's friends around the Corner said he went camping in the hills. Bought a full rig at an outfitter's—thermal bag, tent, cooker, maps, and compass—the works."

"Question is," said Hugh. "Did he find what he came for and decide to take a little vacation; or was he still looking when he drove to the trailhead?"

The Fudir had pulled the ground car off to the side of the road, where there was a scenic overlook, and now stood beside Bridget ban while she studied the valley below with a pair of high-resolution scanning binoculars. The Fudir tried to keep a map of the Dalhousie Valley spread flat on the ground car's hood against the blustery winds that blew on the hilltops. Open beside the map was an ecological gazetteer of the region that he had found in a second-hand bookstore in Chel'veckistad. Now and then, for no particular reason, he would point to a passing bird and then flip through the book and Bridget ban would pretend to follow its flight with her binoculars. They operated on the theory that if they could see the Dalhousie Estate from here, the Dalhousie Estate could see them. For the same reason, the Fudir really did annotate a small notebook with avian observations. He recognized some of the birds from Jehovah and other worlds he had been on, but there were some that seemed unique to this world. All part of the grim carelessness with which these worlds had originally been seeded. He wondered if the Yung-lo worlds had failed because something vital had been missing in the original terraforming.

Bridget ban turned away from her study of the estate. "There is a steep ravine on the northeast side," she said, "which they don't seem to watch carefully."

The Fudir shrugged. It was a wealthy estate, not a prison. The guards were to fend off importunate visitors, not a determined infiltration. There would be fences, burglar alarms, possibly patrols and surveillance cameras. There were unlikely to be trip wires, dead lines, or even motion sensors. The guards would not want to scramble after every fox or rabbit that ran across the grounds.

"There's an interesting bird," said the Fudir. "A double-bellied nap-snatcher."

Bridget ban turned her binoculars on the approaching ornithopter. Two guards in gray uniforms.

"Twenty-four minutes response time," said the Fudir with a touch of contempt.

"Try to be polite. We don't want them to make any special note of us."

"Yes, yes, missy. No more'n they already have. Remember, this road is outside the estate bounds. We've every right to be here."

Bridget ban said nothing to answer the obvious.

She lowered her binoculars and waved at the approaching guards. "Tally ho!" she called. The Fudir shook his head.

The ornithopter set down a dozen double paces off, on the road. That this would block any traffic coming up the mountain from either direction seemed not to bother them at all. There were certain advantages to working for the biggest corporation on the planet, if not in the entire Spiral Arm. The ICC did not own the government of Old 'Saken, but it might fairly be said that they rented it.

"The top o' the marnin' to ye, darlings," Bridget ban said to the two men who approached. The senior—he had stripes on his sleeve—lifted his cap just a little. It was more like pushing it back a little on his head. His partner, a shorter, darker man, remained a step behind him and kept an eye on everyone. *He's participated in too many simulations,* the Fudir thought.

"May I ask what you are doing here, ma'am?" the senior guard said.

"Why, birding, to be sure, Sergeant."

"Corporal, ma'am," but the Fudir could see he was a little pleased at the virtual promotion. "Why the interest in the estate?"

"What estate?"

The Fudir thought that might be carrying innocence too far. "The Dalhousie Estate, ma'am," the Fudir said, pointing to the map. "You remember I told you. The wine-makers."

"Oh, losh, Reggie. I've no interest in *architecture.* You know that." She glanced into the valley at the complex of buildings. "Which one is it? The whole thing? My. Not as big as the palace complex on High Tara, but a nice enough country lodge."

"And you would be . . ."

"Julienne Lady Melisonde," said Bridget ban. "I'm Second Assistant Lady-in-Waiting to Herself, the Banry Keeva of High Tara."

The corporal was writing in a small notebook with a light pen. "Uh-hunh. Sounds real important." He looked at the Fudir.

The Fudir jerked a thumb at Bridget ban. "I'm with her."

The guard gave him a suspicious look. "You're a Terry."

"Yeah, but I'm housebroken."

The guard turned to Lady Melisonde. "You gotta watch letting them run their mouth, lady."

They showed him their identification cards. The guards had probably seen High Taran cards before, however little importance the court was given this far from the center of the League. If he was impressed, he did a good job concealing it. He tried to look at the bird book open on the ground car's hood without being obvious.

"I heard on Die Bold," Lady Melisonde said, "that the Friesing's woodleafsinger had recently been introduced here, quite by accident. I was wondering if you had seen one."

The guard's face showed that he did not know one bird from another, but he answered politely enough. "No, ma'am, I have not. But you might want to try the Rolling River Nature Reserve, out on the peninsula." By which he meant, far away from the Dalhousie Valley.

As the two guards returned to their ornithopter, the shorter one, who had remained mute until now, said to the Fudir, "You pukkah fanty, sahb?" And he made a Brotherhood sign with his fingers that the Fudir recognized.

The other guard swatted him on the arm. "What I

gotta tell you about bukkin that lingo, pal? You speak Gaelactic when you're on duty."

The next morning, Greystroke and Hugh went to keep their appointment with the master vintner to discuss the proposed contract. In the ground car along the way, Hugh mentioned that the deal could be a profitable one if it ever were carried out. Greystroke reminded him that it was only a ruse to gain access to the estate. Hugh sighed. "I know. But it really is a sweet deal."

A half league past Chel'veckistad city limits, they left the traffic grid and switched over to manual control. Hugh, who was driving, fussed a little bit with the unfamiliar control panel and at one point swerved into the opposing lane. "Sorry," he said. "On New Eireann, we used the other side of the road."

The countryside was a pleasant one of gently rolling hills terraced into vineyards. The landscape was open, warm and dry in the soft morning sun. The land rose, and the road switchbacked up to the crest of Moaning Mountain and down the other side into the Dalhousie Valley. Hugh whistled at the sight of the cliffs and the distant bright blue flashing river. Greystroke made no response and Hugh glanced to the passenger seat on his left, just to assure himself that the Grey One was still there.

A few moments passed, and Greystroke said, "You couldn't possibly have thought I jumped out the window on one of the turns."

Hugh grinned and said nothing.

The estate entrance was an elliptical arch made of granite and shuttered by a wrought-iron gateway. The old Dalhousie corporate logo carved into the keystone was still used by the ICC for their wine-and-spirits division. They showed their passes to the guards, who wore the uniform of the 17th Peace-keepers, ICC Civil Police company.

"Take the first right-hand turn, honored sirs," the guard said. "The winery is the large stone building at the end. Yellow granite. You can't miss it."

They thanked him and drove through. "I don't get it," Hugh said. "If Lady Cargo has the Dancer, why does everything on 'Saken seem so normal?"

"Two reasons," Greystroke said. "One: you can't improvise your way into power. There are logistical details to work out. Sometime soon, I expect, the ICC will buy commercial time for a 'must-see' spectacular show. They'll want as many ears as possible listening at the same time up front. Remember, if someone out of earshot—maybe across the sea in Sinkingland or up on Jubilee Moon—learns what's going on and dis-approves vehemently enough, they could lob a missile directly on old Lady Cargo's head. I don't care how persuasive that stone is. It can't sweet-talk ballistics and a targeting computer."

"What's the other reason?"

"Why bother? If the ICC and its policies are al-ready well thought of here—the government's not exactly in her pocket, but they do snuggle closely—why impose your will? To tell everyone to eat their vegetables? I understand power corrupts, but I hardly think Lady Cargo cares what simulations people ex-perience or what they cook for dinner."

Hugh nodded. The reasons made sense, but it seemed to him that Cargo had had the Dancer long enough that some move should already have been made. "Pup?" he said.

"What?"

"Suppose there *has* been a broadcast of some sort, and we listened to it, and we were ordered to forget we had heard it. How would we ever know?"

They pulled into the visitor lot by the winery and Hugh deactivated the motor, which spun down with a slight whine and the ground car settled onto its pylons. Greystroke opened his door. "We wouldn't," he decided.

The negotiations with Bris Dent, the winery's business manager, were tough but straightforward. Naturally, Dent proposed terms more favorable to Dalhousie Wines. "We expect price of our wines, which are unique in this quarter of Arm, to rise on Krinth and so shipment will be more valuable relative to crater gems. Krinthic crater gems to be dropping by two percent."

Tol Benlever waved his hand. "You cannot possibly know that, 'Spodin Dent."

"Our economic models best in all Spiral Arm. Find case where we are being wrong more than one, two points, Acts of God excepted. These price movements almost certain. You still make good profit when you resell wine on Krinth."

Hugh said, "Then you'd not object to making those terms a futures option rather than a straightforward price."

"No, not at all."

Eventually, they shook hands all around and Dent said that the contracts would be sent around to Benlever's hotel by the evening for his legal staff— meaning Hugh—to look at. Afterward, they were given a tour of the winery—except for the padding room, where the proprietary paddings, or "blends," were added to "thicken 'er up."

When the tour was drawing to a close, Benlever said, as if in passing, "I was told that Lady Cargo has the most extensive collection of prehuman artifacts this side of Jehovah."

"Oh, perhaps in whole Spiral Arm," said Dent.

"Is it open to the public? I was told in the City that she sometimes hosts viewings."

"Once a month . . . Ah, that is being local month by Splendid Moon, roughly one case of days."

Hugh leaned toward Benlever and murmured, "A case of days in dodeka time is just under three metric weeks." Benlever nodded.

"Next viewing on Thirdsday," Dent said helpfully.

"Pity," said Benlever. "I've business on Abyalon that will not wait."

"Business involving Hollyberry jellies, let me guess," said the vintner.

"Is my business so transparent, Ringbao? Haha. I don't suppose, since I'm here right now, I couldn't get a peek at them? I recently acquired a prehuman artifact myself, and I'd be interested in how it prices out."

"Is specialty market. Would you like to speak to Lady Cargo herself?"

"Is she in residence?"

"*Soglass*. I take you to her." Dent turned and Greystroke and Hugh followed him along a crushed stone path to the rear of the Big House. Hugh leaned close and whispered, "Is this too easy?"

Greystroke nodded. "Be alert."

Radha Lady Cargo was a short, wizened woman who wore a wraparound dress of bright patterns that left one shoulder bare. Hugh guessed her age at a hundred and twenty, past her prime, but holding up very well. But what he noticed most of all was not the mature body, but the intelligent eyes. He had looked into enough faces to know when there was someone looking back.

After some polite introductions, she bowed

graciously and personally led them through the room she had set aside for the artifacts.

"There is simply no price on such things," she said as she showed them from case to case. "This item, found on Megranome, seems to be part of a control circuit; but what it controlled, who will ever know? See the corrosion here? Not even the prehumans built forever." Greystroke asked some questions about provenance and Hugh made occasional notes in his handy. He was surprised at how the old woman's eyes lit as she described her collection. She really took joy of it. He had imagined someone grimmer, more jaded.

"What of the Ourobouros Circuit?" Greystroke asked. "Your most famous acquisition."

"Yes," she said. "Poor Chan was never able to make it work; and yet it seemed to be whole." Her lips curled a little at that and Hugh wondered at her brief and secret amusement. *There's something there,* he thought. *Something important about the Circuit. And then . . . They couldn't have gotten it working, could they? That would be the biggest news the League ever saw.*

Or "the best-kept secret in the Spiral Arm."

He glanced at Benlever to see if Greystroke had noticed that smile; but the Pup's face betrayed no sign of awareness.

"We keep that in its own room," said Lady Cargo and she spoke into her wristband. "Visitors coming." Hugh pondered that, as well.

There was a large man standing outside the door and Lady Cargo paused a moment to ask him some inconsequential question about household maintenance. Hugh noticed that the discussion lasted long enough for a discreet light inset into the woodwork of the door to change from red to green before Lady Cargo said, "This way," and led them into the room.

It was a broad room with perhaps a score of people working at desks. Interfaces winking and scrolling, low susurrus of voices over headsets. Lightboards on the wall with commodity prices from a hundred worlds flashing in turn. Among them, Hugh thought, must be the forecasted price of padded wines and crater jewels. In the center of the room, a chair fastened to the floor faced down a broad aisle clear of all obstructions to the famous Ourobouros Circuit. In form, it resembled a wreath, the wires twisted and twined around one another in a complex pattern incomprehensible to the eye.

"They say," Lady Cargo informed them, "that a part of it wraps through a dimension that we cannot sense. It never seems the same twice."

"I'm surprised you keep it in a working office," said Tol Benlever, glancing around at the muted activity in the room. "This is your trade desk, is it not?"

"One of them. We maintain such rooms on numerous worlds. There's no secret that I plan to adopt the Circuit as a corporate symbol—the ungraspable intricacies of trade networks connecting the worlds of the Periphery. Fitting, I think. So there's no reason why my people cannot enjoy the sight of it. 'Spodin Della Costa, would you take a seat?"

She meant Hugh. He lowered himself into the chair, shifted his weight. "Quite comfortable," he said.

"Now stare at the Circuit. Try to follow the twists and turns of the wiring." Some of the traders had paused in their work to watch, with grins on their faces.

Hugh shrugged and focused on the wreath. He picked an arbitrary starting point and tried to follow the path of the Circuit.

Benlever asked, "Are they optical wires?" But his voice seemed to echo from far away.

The wreath started to spin. Hugh blinked.

"Optic," he heard Lady Cargo say, "ceramic-composite, metal. It's a chimera, of sorts."

The wreath seemed to approach him and the light blue wall, visible through the center of the wreath, receded into the distance. The lighting seemed to change. The wall acquired a reddish tinge while everything in the foreground, illuminated by an unreal ghostly glow, lost all depth. A two-dimensional figure moved across his field of view and Hugh felt his shoulder violently shaken.

He moved, and colors, shapes, lighting, and perspective snapped back to normal.

Now the people at the trade desks were laughing and even Lady Cargo smiled openly. "A fascinating illusion, isn't it?" she said. "It was the one thing Chan Mirslaf learned before he gave up. It's almost hypnotic. We find it useful for meditation. It relaxes."

Hugh blew out his breath. "The far wall seemed to be twenty leagues away."

Lady Cargo straightened and her smile vanished. "Please don't touch it, '*Spodin* Benlever."

Greystroke had gone to the back wall and was bending close to the artifact. In answer to Lady Cargo's command, he held his hands up and away from his body. "Fascinating, indeed," he said, turning away. "Well, I don't want to keep your people from their work. Unless, it means I receive a better quote from Vintner Dent, haha!"

Lady Cargo led them from the Trading Desk to her own private office, where she offered both a glass of padded wine and dismissed her aides, who had followed along like a cloud of gnats.

"Well," she said, putting her now empty glass back on the sideboard. "Do you have it? Have you got it?"

Greystroke held a hand up to forestall any question from Hugh. "You mean the artifact I obtained?"

"Don't play foolish games. I appreciate your effort, and you were quite right to bring it to me. But please don't try to extort a price. You're entitled to a generous finder's fee, of course, and compensation for your troubles; but I do have legal title to it."

"What makes you believe," Greystroke said carefully, "that the artifact I obtained is the same one that you have apparently lost." And Hugh thought, *She doesn't have it, after all!* But he kept his face controlled.

Lady Cargo pointed at Greystroke. "You, sir, are a Krinthic merchant-trader—my people have checked your bona fides with House Kellenikos—but this man . . ." And now the bony finger was aimed at Hugh. "This man, you hired elsewhere. On Die Bold? Let me suggest to you that it was Ringbao della Costa who presented you with the artifact."

Greystroke bowed, extending his arm gracefully. "You are wise beyond your years, lady." Hugh, thinking furiously, wondered what was going on. The Pup was improvising over this unexpected development.

"You took it from Gronvius, didn't you, Ringbao? No need to prevaricate. Gronvius was a traitor, and deserved to die. But what you took from him—or what he sold you—was my property."

Hugh thought, *Gronvius?* Aloud, he followed Greystroke's lead. "I did not know him by that name."

"It doesn't matter what Todor Captain Gronvius called himself. He was a renegade. You see, when I said prehuman artifacts are priceless I didn't mean you couldn't sell them. Oh, no. They can command stiff prices in the right places. This temptation proved too much for Captain Gronvius and others in the squadron escorting the artifact. He mutinied, and fled with the statue. He tried to hide on Die Bold, but our detectives tracked him down. Witnesses described his two companions. One of them was you." She produced a printout of the Die Bold police sketches.

"Hardly a companion, lady. Chance-met drinkers in a bar."

"No, his quarters were thoroughly searched. His movements were carefully backtracked. There is no hiding hole; no safe-deposit box. He must have had the Twisting Stone on his person; and you took it from him when he was executed."

Hugh did not think "executed" was the proper word. The assassins had also tried to kill him; but he did not bring it up. "And how do you know that this . . . Gronvius, you said? How do you know that Gronvius had your artifact?"

"Bakhtiyar Commodore Saukkonen was in command of the squadron. He escaped the mutiny and told us what had happened."

"Ah," said Greystroke, his head bobbing. "Yes. Certain matters now become clear. Ringbao, you were less than forthcoming with me about that odd little brick, and you've put me in an embarrassing position respecting our hostess; perhaps even damaging the compact we recently entered into. We'll speak about this tonight. 'Spozhá," he added, "you have but to name a fair price and we will bring the artifact to you tomorrow. I will accept a draught for the finder's fee in Gladiola Bills or in Krinthic 'owls.' If your people could have that ready by seven tomorrow, I will provide you with an affidavit showing provenance, sworn and notarized. And the unsavory business on Die Bold should only add to its allure."

"Yes," said Lady Cargo distantly, "art loves a scandal."

In their ground car, after leaving the estate, Hugh took a deep breath. "I hadn't expected that."

"That Radha doesn't have the Dancer, after all?"

"That, too. I meant that we would leave the estate alive."

"Ah. Well, I wouldn't worry too much. It was easier for them to let us fetch the Dancer than to torture its location out of us."

"As long as it was easier . . ."

"By the way, just so you know. I have a little appliance here that neutralizes listening devices like the one they planted behind the sun-shield."

Hugh blinked, turned down the sun-shield, and saw a small scorch mark the size of a pinpoint. He flipped it back up. "Neutralized, alright. They'll probably follow us."

Greystroke looked in his mirror. "Yes, I expect so. Old habits. They think we'll lead them to the Dancer and save them the cost of a finder's fee. Not worth the effort. Once she has the Dancer in her hands, she can simply tell us we've already been paid—or that no payment was promised—and we'd believe her. But there's the slight chance that we may abscond with the statue. She doesn't think we know what it is; but she's certain we can get a better deal from any other collector in the Spiral Arm. Greed and power make people stupid."

"I'll try to remember that, if and when."

The Pup snorted. "Yes. She should have offered us payment enough that we'd be sure to bring it. Well, when we check the car back into the agency, it shouldn't be beyond the skills of the Ghost of Ardow to blend into the crowds and disappear. Buy a disposable handy, call the others, and tell them to abandon our rooms, and fall back on the secondary reservations.

Lady Cargo knows the names we rented under, and it doesn't take much for the ICC to call in a favor or two from the government of 'Saken. You know the code word?"

"The Fudir told me it was 'skedaddle.' "

Greystroke shook his head. "Terrans."

"You know, Pup, unless Todor was lying in the Mild Beast . . ."

"Yes. This Commodore Saukkonen must have the Dancer. Once the officers in the fleet learned what it was, the temptation proved too great. Why turn it over to the chairman when you can keep it for yourself?"

"Some tried to stop him."

"The ones who had no chance of gaining it for themselves, excuse my cynicism. But it no longer matters one way or the other. Saukkonen knows logistics, and has probably been making preparations for his coup. But I noticed something interesting in the tangle of the tale. The Dancer's powers have limits . . ."

". . . Or else Lady Cargo wouldn't still be so eager to obtain it. I saw that. Saukkonen could have told her to forget the whole thing—stone, legend, everything. I wonder if she does remember the Stone's powers, or only that she wanted desperately to obtain it."

"In either case, there are some things—deep desires, perhaps—that the Dancer cannot edit."

"There's your answer, then."

Greystroke turned a questioning look on him.

"We have to make sure that recovering the Dancer is our deepest desire."

The Pup shook his head. "I don't think it works that way."

Hugh had purchased new clothing, discarded his identifications, and was walking through a narrow alley between two warehouses on his way to their fallback hotel in a run-down part of the City when he sensed another man walking close behind him. He began to consider his options. He hadn't been such a fool as to take a weapon to the Dalhousie Estate, and that meant the only weapons he now had were those he could improvise from the materials in the alley. Of course, the Glens of Ardow had taught him improvisation.

"Rest easy, friend," he heard a voice say. "I followed you because no one can follow *him*."

Hugh danced a few paces ahead and spun around. The man who had accosted him was unshaven and wore stinking rags. His fingernails were black with dirt and grime. But most of all, he was large. Hugh, not a small man, came only to his shoulder. He looked up.

"Hello, Grimpen."

When he reached the hotel, the others were already waiting. Hugh stepped inside, leading Grimpen. He looked at Bridget ban. "He followed me home. Can we keep him?"

"I cannot tell you," Grimpen said later, "how much a hot bath and a change of clothes mean to me. There is no greater pleasure in life. Well, perhaps one." He had but lately emerged from Bridget ban's refreshing room, now groomed, shaven, cleaned, and wearing a nondescript "shiki" favored by residents of the Fourteenth District. He stretched, and the space he occupied doubled. Then he looked about the dayroom of the apartment.

"You, I know," he said to Bridget ban. And to Greystroke, "You, I know of. And you—Hugh, is it?—have been traveling with Greystroke; but I don't know you and I don't know your friend."

"Och, Large-hound," said Bridget ban, "is there no end to the catalogue of what you don't know?"

"You," Grimpen said to the Fudir, "are a Terran, or I miss my guess."

"Is that important?" the Fudir asked him.

"To you, I suppose." He looked at his colleagues. "Is he alright? A Terry? Confederate ties?"

"Enough Confederate ties to make a fancy bow," said Greystroke, "but he works for himself."

"He's the one," said Hugh, "who got us on the trail of the Dancer in the first place."

"Dancer?"

"Oh. You'd know it as the Twisting Stone."

"Oh, that. What's your interest in that?"

The others looked at Grimpen in astonishment until Bridget ban spoke. "Why hae ye come here, then, if nae for the Dancer?"

Now it was Grimpen's turn to look astonished. He pointed to Greystroke and Bridget ban, in turn. "You, Fir Li sent to track down Donovan. You went off after the phantom fleet. I went to learn how the ICC knew so much so soon. Yet, here we are, all together. It's enough to make me think there really is a purpose to the universe. Or at least a punch line. Why don't we take turns explaining how we all wound up here in this cockroach heaven?"

The briefing took them into the night. Grimpen listened carefully, took notes, asked penetrating questions. He was merciless in undermining their assumptions, pointing out alternative explanations for each of their conclusions. But in the end, he had to admit that the legend of the Twisting Stone seemed to have some substance to it. "Though I'd be wary of putting too much faith in the details."

"Then why did you consult the Book of Legends in the Archive?" Hugh asked.

"I lost a day and a half on that," Grimpen complained. "My ship's intelligence had trouble translating it . . ."

The Fudir told him it was because the refugee camps in this region had been settled by a mix of people called Brits and Rooskies and the language was an amalgam of their two tongues. Grimpen smiled and said, "That's nice. But what I didn't know was what I was looking for in that manuscript."

"Then how," said the Fudir, "did you know when you found it?"

Grimpen smiled and pointed a finger at the Terran. "I like you. You're funny. No, I knew the *kind* of thing I was looking for."

"Which was . . ." Greystroke said.

"The Cynthians knew too much, too soon. When they came through Sapphire Point the first time, they said they'd tortured the factor on Cynthia over some slight of etiquette and he warned them that the ICC had the Twisting Stone. They came back later—you'd already gone by then, Grey One—and they'd gone to New Eireann to get the thing. But, d'ye see, they left the Hadramoo before the word could have reached them. It's six or seven metric weeks from New Eireann to the Hadramoo. As near as I could tell, they'd set out to seize the stone no more than a week after the ICC laid hands on it in the first place. And that meant . . ."

"The ICC has some way of sending messages faster than courier ships." That was the Fudir. "Well, it makes sense, now that the Big Fella here has pointed it out. They always seem to know where the prices were best and what was selling well on which planets."

Hugh began to curse. "Then Jumdar didn't come to New Eireann by chance, either. I'll bet a shiny ducat that Nunruddin called for troops as soon as the coup went bad. And when the Cynthians came, she had plenty of time to warn her superiors so they could intercept the rievers at Peacock Junction."

Grimpen nodded. "If the Dark-hound had spent as much time analyzing ICC activities as he did Rift crossings, one of us would have tumbled to this years ago. I suspected they had something; but I didn't know what. A swifter swiftie? A secret shortcut, like you found at Peacock? I was reasonably sure it wasn't a new invention—'There's nothing new under the suns,' right? But maybe, just maybe, a prehuman technology that they had stumbled on. So I translated the titles of the old legends in the archive, looking for anything relating to communication. I found five that were suggestive. One was the Tale of the Calling Ring."

Hugh remembered the chair facing the Ourobouros Circuit, remembered too a similar arrangement in the ruined vault on New Eireann, and suddenly he knew. "The Ourobouros Circuit! It's a communicator."

Grimpen growled. "The sketch in the manuscript looked like a torus—a ring, not a wreath."

"A case for the Circuit," Greystroke suggested. "Now lost."

The large Hound's brow knit. "As might could be," he said, "or I'd've realized sooner. I scouted the ICC facilities, here in the City and out in the Hills for some sign where the communicator might be. Kidnapped one of their security guards out at the estate, and babble-juiced him. He didn't know anything, but he thought there was secret stuff going on with the Trade Desk. So I snatched a trader out of a bar in the City, ran the usual roster, and hit pay dirt. Sent a swiftie to Fir Li. But somehow they got wind of me and I had to go to ground." He looked at Greystroke and smiled. "Not as easy for me to hide as you. I had to find a bigger tree to duck behind." His laugh was like a fault line splitting under the earth.

Greystroke nodded. "The Circuit was warm when I got near it; so I *knew* it had been doing *something,* but I thought it might have been, oh, a quantum computer or some other magical instrument. Something they used to project the markets with such uncanny accuracy."

"I'm thinking," said Hugh, "that they stumbled onto the secret when they were building a duplicate. Once there were two of them, that 'infinite depth' illusion turned into a channel. I'll bet that it bores a Krasnikov tube somehow between two wreaths."

"And now we know, *meegos,*" the Fudir said, "why Lady Cargo was so anxious to have the Dancer. I never saw the sense of it, myself. With it, she could control a single system—one that she already effectively controls—and maybe dominate systems close by. For this, she sends a flotilla to tangle with Cynthian pirates? But the Dancer *and* the Circuit, ah, that's another kettle of soup entirely. Her voice could be heard on every inhabited world, as near to simultaneous as matters."

"Except, it's the commodore, not the chairman, we have to worry about now," Hugh said. "And it occurs to me that a naval base might be tougher to enter than Dalhousie Estate."

When the Fudir awoke in the middle of the night, he saw Bridget ban sitting in a soft chair across the room. The night lighting from the baseboards gave an odd sort of blue-white insubstantiality to her upper body. The shadows were cast upward, like spirits freed of the body.

"What's wrong?" he asked.

He could see the head shake briefly, but her face was in shadows and he could not make out her expression. "How could I have missed it?"

"The same way we all did," he told her. "We see the world through our assumptions; and when we don't know what those assumptions are, they can trap us. Sometimes, it's only possible to see the truth in the right moment of time. In the ancient legends, the god Darwin prophesied in a world in which tradesmen struggled in competition. The god Newton appeared in a world that had discovered machinery; the god Einstein in an age when . . ."

"Awa' wi' ye and yer gods. I don't think they were gods at all, but only Terrans that the One God gifted with wisdom."

"The One God?" The Fudir had always imagined the gods as beings much like men, but with powers beyond those even of the Hounds, and with an ability to act unseen greater even than that of Greystroke. As Newton controlled the motion of stars and planets, Maxwell and his demons shaped and moved whole galaxies and the electric roads that entwined them. And the quarrel between them could not be resolved even by the god Einstein, who sought a rune that would join them. The idea that there might be only one god astonished him.

"Och, list' tae me loshing. I said there'd be nae religious arguments, and here I am starting one myself."

"I never argue about the gods," the Fudir said. "It leads nowhere, and can only irritate them."

Bridget ban laughed at that, and they spoke a little more of inconsequentials. "Och, yer a comfort, Fudir," she said just before falling asleep. "There's nae denying it."

"Am I?" the Fudir asked the night when she was breathing softly.

In the morning, when Bridget ban awoke, the Fudir was gone.

*A*nd so you see him," says the scarred man, "for the treacherous bastard that he was, and why this quest of yours was always a waste of your time."

The harper says nothing but toys with her now-empty plate. She looks around for Mamacita, but the wide woman is gone. Darkness has fallen outside the shed and only the string of decorative lights provides an island of illumination. The busier sounds of the City seem distant, and the lamps along Greaseline Street and the Bourse are like the suns on the far side of the Rift, blurred and indistinct. The harper wipes at the corners of her eyes and hates the scarred man for the mocking grin above which he watches her.

"Let's finish this," she says harshly.

"We'll warn you. The finish is no better."

"But there must be an end of it. You said so yourself."

"You shouldn't listen to everything we say. He's been known to lie."

She stands and slings her harp over her shoulder like a carbine. "Will you at least escort me back to the Hostel?"

"Why not?" says the scarred man. "I'm in a hostile mood." He grins at his own pun. "I hate them all. The pompous Grimpen. The priggish Greystroke. The cocky Hugh O'Carroll. The ice-cold witch-woman."

"Men are more than adjectives. I find that I have come to love them all. What of the Fudir?"

"Him, I hate the most, for he betrayed all the others."

It was not easy to surprise the Fudir, the scarred man says, but Little Hugh O'Carroll managed it now and then. In that early hour of the morning, he managed it for the last time.

Hugh was sitting on the stoop just outside the ragged hotel tossing nuts to the equally ragged birds. The Fudir froze at the sight of him. Hugh looked up.

"Ready?" he said.

The Fudir pointed to the nuts. "You give them those things and they'll come to expect it. They'll circle the doorway waiting and shit on the people going in and out."

Hugh looked along the street. "And that would be different?"

"You sit out here alone and you're bait for every thief in the Fourteenth District."

"It's too early for thieves. They like to sleep in. How do you plan to get into Watkins Naval Yard?"

The Fudir ran his hand along the fringed anycloth he wore, took a tassel between his fingers, wondering what to do about this latest complication. "What were you waiting for out here?"

"You. I know you haven't given up on liberating Terra. But now the Kennel folks have a new reason to give the Dancer to the Ardry."

"By me, a new reason to keep it from him. I like his reign; I wouldn't like his rule."

Hugh nodded. "And that means you have to go in without the others."

"'Others.' That would include you. But I don't think you've given up on your own plans."

Hugh shook his head. "I'm not going back to New Eireann."

"That wasn't what I meant."

Hugh stood and brushed at the knees and seat of his trousers. "Let's go and save the galaxy. Unless you want to eat breakfast first."

"You've grown a bit since we first met."

"I'd hate to think otherwise. Only the dead never grow. You and me, Fudir, we've been through a lot since Amir Naith's Gulli. We were in this together almost from the beginning. It's only right that we're together at the end. Just you and me."

"I know. That's what makes this so hard."

And with that, *like a black mamba striking,* he poked Hugh in the brisket with his bunched fingers, bending him double, and followed it with a blow to the side of his head.

Hugh collapsed and the Fudir caught him before he struck the steps, eased him back to a sitting position, and replaced the bag of nuts into his hands. He felt the neck for a pulse. He stood and studied the unmoving figure bleakly. It was difficult to know how hard to strike.

There was a man watching from the pedestrian walkway across the city rail that ran down the center of the public way. He was slouch-shouldered, with a hangdog look. His clothing seemed slept in and none too new before that. "You mess this man," the Fudir told him, "and some people in that building will hunt you down and kill you. That's if you get away from me."

"I believe you," the man said, holding his palms up. "Just minding my business, me. You got a ruby or two? I'm powerful thirsty."

The Fudir studied him. "Don't go anywhere yet."

When neither Hugh nor the Fudir appeared in the morning to plan their infiltration of the Watkins Yard, Bridget ban went to fetch them.

"They're nae in their rooms," she reported.

The three Kennel agents looked one to the other. Grimpen said to Greystroke, "You trusted him."

Bridget ban said, "They may only have stepped outside for the air."

"Air's worse outside," Grimpen said. He rose like an uplifted mountain range. "I'll look."

When Large-hound had left the room, Greystroke turned on Bridget ban. "What was the purpose of all that cuddling if not to keep his leash short?"

Bridget ban had no answer. She turned away and looked into a corner of the room, her thoughts all in turmoil. "Maybe Hugh went looking for the Fudir," Bridget ban suggested.

Grimpen came back in carrying Hugh over his shoulder. "If he did, he found him."

The others jumped to their feet in alarm. "Is the wean a'right?" said Bridget ban.

Grimpen deposited his burden on the sagging couch and straightened his limbs. "He's not dead, but he's taken a bad blow to the head. He'll have a headache when he comes to."

"He'll have more than a headache," Bridget ban told him. "He liked the Fudir. He thought he was a nice old man, underneath that bitter act."

Greystroke's face was grim-set. "The bitterness was no act. The nice old man was. The Terran word is 'bonded.' It's something to beware of, Bridget ban."

"Aye? An' ye've lost yer lead to the Donovan, haven't ye?" Then she straightened. "The Other Olafsson! Maybe she snatched the Fudir so *she* could find Donovan and carry out the mission."

But Greystroke said, "No. Hugh would have tried to stop her and the Ravn would have killed him. The Fudir *is* Donovan. I suspected it when he didn't keep the sex straight of his next contact. After I followed him into the Corner of Jehovah, I knew. And *he* knew I'd puzzled it out. But he wanted out of the Great Game. He'd been hiding from the 'Feds, hoping they would never call on him. We had a silent agreement."

"Wonderful," said Grimpen. "The problem with silent agreements, Pup, is that they're no different from silent disagreements."

"I'm no fool, you great lump of flesh! The Red-hound and I programmed *aimshifars* into the clothing we gave him. We can track him through the anycloth. Bridget, where is he now?"

Bridget ban had already been studying her wrist strap. "Nearly out of range o' this mickle thing. Let me . . . Ah, there I have it. Sou'-sou'west. Half a league."

Grimpen grunted. "Not much of a head start, then."

"Not heading toward the Navy Yards," said Greystroke. "Nor the Corner. I thought he would have bolted there like a rat to its hole. What's his plan?" He activated his wristband. "Synch with me, Bridget. I'll find him and bring him back. No, both of you stay here. It was my error; it's my corrective action." He checked the charge on his teaser and tucked it into his waistband.

Greystroke hurried through the streets of the Fourteenth District wondering how he could have miscalculated so badly. What would Fir Li say when he graded the exercise? It was no excuse to say that the stakes had escalated from the routine task he had originally been set. *He had failed at that, too.* He should have minded his own assignment, left the Dancer problem to Bridget ban, and taken Fudir prisoner back to Sapphire Point. He had allowed ambition to seduce him.

The wristband told him that the Fudir had gone to the right, and he slipped around the corner onto a street even less inviting than the one the hotel was on. The morning sun barely warmed him, as if it too avoided these decaying tenements.

Few people were about. Lost souls with nowhere to go, and no idea how to get there. He paid no attention to them, or they to him. If they noticed him at all, they saw another early morning wraith living out his defeat.

As he passed an alleyway, the direction indicator on the wristband flipped. Greystroke drifted back to the opening and looked down a dead-ended cobblestone passageway lined with trash barrels, dustbins, and odds and ends of discarded appliances. Drainpipes ran from roofs five stories above to gurgle their burdens nowhere near the sewer grates. But the weather had been dry this season, so the pools of water were small and survived largely because the sun did not venture into this narrow lane.

Greystroke moved silently down the alley, looking behind each dustbin and trash can as he passed. The *aimshifars* reported that the Fudir was deeper in, but Greystroke did not discount the possibility of a confederate—or even a Confederate.

But there was no one. And when he came at last to the spot where the locators in the anycloth proclaimed the Fudir to be, he found a smelly, ragged man wearing clothing far too good for him, who was slug by slug putting himself outside of a bottle of white spirits. When he saw Greystroke suddenly before him, the derelict shrieked and raised his hands, saying, "I never touched him! I swear it! I never touched him!"

Few organizations are sufficiently feudal as to subsist in complete self-sufficiency, and this is especially so for those that are themselves military service organizations. External suppliers can be increased or decreased as the volume of business requires; whereas the same functions performed by cadre would require full-time expensing and general administrative overhead.

And for the most menial work, who better than Terrans? They work cheap, when they work at all, and with sufficient supervision will actually get the job done. That is because they are paid for performance rather than for their time. Slacking off only delays payment.

One service farmed out by ICC Peacekeeping Navy Yard Number Three—called Brisley Watkins Yard, after some forgotten hero—was victualing, for which Heybob Brothers—a local Terran firm—had low-balled the bid with the usual financial cunning of their people. At least, so the Yard Captain had reasoned. The Terrans, for their part, saw an opportunity for an easy ruby. If the prices they charged Watkins Yard were low, the cost of the provisions were lower still, and a dip of the beak went, as it always went, to the Terran Brotherhood—for the good of the Corner, the eventual liberation of the homeworld, and the more comfortable lives led by the Vanguard of the Struggle.

One way to keep costs down was to hire laborers by the day in the morning call-out at the hiring hall. Drivers and other skilled workers must be lured with wages and benefits, and were permanent employees; but day labor did not carry overhead when there was no labor that day.

The Fudir who presented himself at the Hall did not appear nearly as old as the Fudir who had traveled all the way from Jehovah. Certainly, he had no problem lifting the heavy sacks of potatoes and rice and beans. Besides, a particular hand-clasp and the passage of a wad of rubies had ensured him a spot with Heybob's morning victualing run—along with a promise to Himself and the Forsaken Committee of Seven that nothing ill would rebound on Heybob from whatever scramble the Fudir planned to carry out.

If there were anything known as "base security," it had been largely forgotten by the guards at Watkins Yard. The routine is the ally of the unexpected, and it had been a long time since there had been an enemy of the ICC on Old 'Saken. The goods lorry pulled into the Yard with a wave of the hand and the driver parked behind the Yard Refectory. The Terrans "schlepped" the vegetables into the storerooms, singing a work song about carrying sheaves that the Chief Victualer and his petty officers thought wondrously droll. "I hain't rejoicing, was I doing *that* scut work," the Fudir overheard one of them say.

Nobody at the gate bothered to count the number of laborers in the goods lorry when it left, let alone compare it to the number who had entered.

Terrans go everywhere and no one makes much remark. Thus, the Committee of Seven had a decently accurate map of the Yard from the observations of those who had previously been inside. The Fudir had memorized this map and knew exactly where Commodore Saukkonen had his office. The next problem was to transform a ragged Terran laborer into someone who looked like he might actually belong in a Navy Yard. For that, the Fudir slipped into a supply shed and emerged wearing a maintenance coverall of dull black, and carrying under his arm a "cliputer" and a paperboard tube such as those in which engineering flex-screens are kept. Armed in this fashion, he could go almost anywhere on the Yard without being questioned.

He paused and slipped into his ears a pair of the buffers that Greystroke had fabricated en route from Die Bold. The theory was that he could still hear what was said, but the voice would be so distorted by the micro-intelligence that the Dancer's effect would be nullified.

The theory had yet to be tested, of course.

Walking across the Yard, he traced out the cables linking the buildings with the practiced eye of an instrument tech. Those would be the secure channels, less vulnerable to intercept. Private voice calls and proprietary data went by "hard wire." He whistled the song about the sheaves as he located the bundle from 3rd Fleet HQ, narrowed it down to the commodore's office, and followed it to a junction box. Waiting for a moment when no one was nearby, he unscrewed the cable and let it dangle so that the contact was intermittent.

He returned to the headquarters building at a slow hurry and walked boldly inside. "This where the comm link complaint came from?" he asked the petty officer at the desk. He waved the cliputer at her. "Got a 'right-now-and-I-mean-it' repair order while I was heading for the mess. Says . . . Commodore's office. That's 145?"

"Right down the end of the hall," the young woman told him. "Wait. You have to sign in. Security."

The Fudir kept a straight face while scrawling a randomly chosen name into the register. "What time you off-duty, ma'am?"

"You're a bold one," she answered with a smile.

"'Bold knaves thrive without one grain of sense,'" he told her, "'but good men starve for want of impudence.'"

She laughed. "I don't expect *you'll* starve," adding, "I'm off in nine ares."

The Fudir did not miss a beat. 'Saken used dodeka time, and an are was forty-eight minutes Earth-standard, or slightly more than a half hora in metric time. He gave her his best smile. "Maybe I'll see you then? By the Refectory?"

The Fudir proceeded down the hall, content that the receptionist harbored no suspicions. *Bold knaves thrive indeed*, he thought.

The plaque on Room 145 read BAKHTIYAR COM-MODORE SAUKKONEN, VANGUARD SQUADRON, 3RD PEACEKEEPER FLEET. Following the protocols he had observed earlier, he knocked once, opened the door, and stepped inside.

"Sah!" he said, touching his cap. "Is this where . . ." He pretended to consult his cliputer. "You have an intermittent system connection?"

Saukkonen regarded him with calm, liquid-brown eyes. He was a broad man, wide in the shoulders and with large hands. His desk was a marvel of disarray. It was foolish to form an opinion of another man, especially a man of power, from a single glance; but the Fudir thought that, under other circumstances, he might have liked Saukkonen.

Of course, if he wanted to rule the galaxy, that would count against him.

The commodore's gaze shifted over the Fudir's shoulder. "Is that one of them?"

And the Fudir heard a voice say, "He is; and my particoolar prize."

The sentence was not even completed before the Fudir had run to the door; but two black arms wrapped around him like iron bands. "Noo, noo," whispered Ravn Olafsdottr, "do noot flay so soon after we meet."

The Fudir relaxed in her grip and waited his moment. "So," he said to the commodore, "you've sold out to the Confederacy!"

The commodore smiled like a bear. "Hardly. Which is he?"

"He calls himself thee Foodir," said Ravn.

Saukkonen reached below his desk and his hand emerged with a sand-colored brick. It was bent into a quarter arc, like a live actor taking a bow.

"Listen to me, Fudir," said Saukkonen. "You are a bold and competent man, and I need bold and competent men, so I am asking you to throw in with me and work in my Special Squad."

The Fudir felt no desire to do any such thing. He smiled broadly and said, "Of course, sah."

But Saukkonen frowned and shook his head. "You hesitated. Ravn, check his ears."

The Fudir felt his head turned roughly and the buffers plucked ungently from his ears.

"Now," said Saukkonen, "let's try that again. Fudir, will you join me on my Special Squad?"

"Of course, sah," the Fudir said, surprised that the commodore would even ask. Even as he spoke, a part of him knew he had been compelled. Yet he felt that his agreement was entirely rational and the use of the Dancer wholly unnecessary, almost an insult. He favored his new boss with a questioning look.

"Oh, yes," Saukkonen said. "It's more seamless when the subjects don't know. Then, they only think they've changed their minds. Leftenant Olafsdottr, for example, does not approve of my plan, but she will help me carry it out with every fiber of her being. Won't you, Leftenant?"

"With every fiber, sah!"

"You see? I haven't sold out to the Confederacy. I've only recruited a Confederate to work for me. Oh, don't worry, Specialist Fudir. You haven't become a zombie. You still have your own will. It's only that you also have my will. Where there's a will, there's a way, but there are no two ways about this! Haha." He hefted the brick. "Together, we can move with the same purpose, with a minimum of debate and compromise."

The Fudir nodded. It made sense. "And what is that purpose, if I may ask, sah?"

The commodore stroked the Twisting Stone, which now had the aspect of a screw. His smile bespoke contentment. "The Periphery grows weary of the constant vigilance needed against the Confederation. It is time we put an end to it, so the children of the border—of Abyalon, of Megranome, of all the Old Planets—may sleep peacefully at night. I will take the Mighty 3rd across that trackless waste and strike Those of Name and Bring Them Down!"

The Fudir's heart swelled with those words. He could fairly see the ships lifting, the Names cowed, Terra free! "Yes!" he cried. Terra free. How absolutely marvelous that this man would lead the charge!

Beside him, the dreams of Lady Cargo paled. Yet, this was far too grandiose for military contractors. Peacekeepers were usually hired to separate belligerents, interdict aggressors, patrol an exit ramp, or maintain order in the aftermath of catastrophe. Seldom could they go up against a planetary government, and never at any sort of profit. Saukkonen, of all men, should know how mad a scheme it was. Even with the Ourobouros Circuit, how did he imagine the "Mighty 3rd" would fare against the entire might of the Confederation of Central Worlds? He had barely escaped from his own flotilla when they had cut communication with the flagship.

"I'm a humble man," Saukkonen said. "I have always followed my orders honestly and to the best of my abilities. But lately, it has grown on me that this is not enough. Honor and ability demand more of me than that."

The Fudir saluted him. "Yes, sah!" And in a flash, he *knew.* And he knew what he must do.

And he dreaded it almost as much as servitude.

He turned to Lieutenant Olafsdottr. "What say you, Ravn. Will you help our Leader destroy you own Confederation?"

"Of course."

"But you don't like it."

The Confederate shrugged. "We do what we must, not what we like."

"I know how you feel," the Fudir said. "I'm also of two minds about the project. Do you understand me? But the Fudir is utterly convinced."

He saw the light in the Ravn's eyes, the understanding that she was free to act where the commodore's instructions ran not to the contrary.

"*Hear me, Donovan,*" she said in the harsh birdsong of Confederal Manjrin. "'*Your duty past is your duty now.*'"

Donovan grinned at her. No matter how enslaved the execrable Fudir may have been to the commodore's will, the slumbering Donovan had not been affected. He turned to Saukkonen and said, "I'm ready to do my duty, sah!"

As Saukkonen briefed him regarding the proposed raid, Donovan found himself falling more and more in sympathy with it. He had never had much love for Those of Name and thought bringing about their downfall a good thing. *Saukkonen has not reduced Donovan to obedience,* he thought, *but that does not reduce the persuasive power of his voice.* He knew he must act quickly, without warning, lest he soon

become a willing ally on this gallant but foolhardy
mission.

His chance came when Saukkonen asked for suggestions. Ravn told him the Confederate fleet dispositions and suggested alternate routes into the Central
Worlds, but the commodore disagreed. "Sapphire
Point, it must be." And Ravn and Donovan assented.

"But, Bakhtiyar," Donovan said, "if you take the
entire fleet across the Rift, the 'Feds will shoot first,
not open a discussion. Missiles will be launched before you can win over the master of each enemy corvette, and you cannot persuade shrapnel."

Commodore Saukkonen pursed his lips and cocked
his head at the Dancer, which he held cradled in his
arm. "True," he said. "True. What do you propose?"

Donovan rose and began to pace. "One may succeed where many fail. A small courier ship may slip
across the Rift and escape notice. Is that not right,
Ravn?"

"Obviously," the blond woman said without now
a trace of accent. "I've done it myself."

"And if this courier carried the Twisting Stone with
him, he could undermine authority on selected worlds;
soften them up for the Mighty 3rd. Then, when you
swoop in to disarm them, they will be agreeable. Is
that not a better plan?"

Saukkonen's brow knit and his eyes lost their limpid clarity. "It sounds . . . I think . . . Yes. It may be a
good idea, at that."

Ravn nodded enthusiasm. Donovan's own heart
swelled with pride that his commander had so com-
plimented his proposal. Quickly now.

His pacing brought him behind the commodore's
chair and *fast as a black mamba striking,* Donovan
reached over his shoulder and seized the Dancer,
which slid like a bar of soap from the man's fingers.

He nodded to himself. Another suspicion confirmed.

"Don't move, Commodore," he said, and with those words he felt the power course through him. Saukkonen sat back in his chair, his eyes full of fear and bewilderment.

"Don't worry, Bakhtiyar. I bear you no ill will. I only need your service. As you've already agreed, I will invade the Confederacy for you. A fleet is too big a thing for an invasion; but a single man . . . Yes? Call the field and order a courier ship fueled and provisioned for me. The swiftest ship you've got. Survey class alfvens. Supplies for a seven-week journey. Will you do that for me?"

"Of course," said Saukkonen, already reaching for his comm. "Why wouldn't I?"

In a sane universe, Saukkonen could have suggested several reasons why he shouldn't agree; but the universe hadn't been sane since Maggie Barnes shifted the backhoe on a nameless world off Spider Alley.

While Saukkonen gave brisk orders on the comm, Donovan took Ravn aside and spoke so the commodore could not hear. "I will take the Stone across the Rift to Those of Name. Along the way, I will investigate the reasons why our ships have disappeared there. When you contact your handler, you may tell him that League ships have also disappeared and they suspect the Confederacy of seizing them."

Ravn nodded her head once, sharply. "Yes, they would readily believe that."

"Tell them it may be a wise thing to call a joint commission to discuss the issue."

"Excellent," cried Ravn Olafsdottr. "Our master will be pleased with you."

"Don't be too sure of that," Donovan told her, "until you're sure of who our master is."

Donovan found it quite eerie to cross the hard to the ship that had been readied for him. Everyone he encountered bent immediately to do his bidding. Some indeed because Saukkonen had given orders obeyed in the normal course of naval affairs. But also 'Saken STC, which agreed without question when he asked for an immediate lift window and priority scheduling for the microwave boosts. It would be a long, hard crawl to the Abyalon Road. After that . . . Well, Hanseatic Point was closer, but he knew he would go to Sapphire Point for the crossing. He wondered why he should attempt the more closely patrolled crossing. Then, he remembered that Grimpen had informed Fir Li of the ICC's trans-stellar communicator, and laughed.

He also found it exhilarating to be free of the muddled cocoon of the Fudir. He had worked long and hard to build that persona, to make it more than a mask. But he had learned that while he might forget about the Game, the Game would not forget about him; and the life of a petty thief and scrambler in the back alleys of Jehovah, while it did have its charms, was rather more circumscribed than Donovan was used to. *Sleep well, Fudir,* he said. *Until I have need of you again.*

In the run-up to the Abyalon Ramp, when 'Saken had red-shifted behind him, his thoughts drifted to the Fudir's quondam companions and he wondered, though only for a brief moment, what had become of them.

"Perhaps I should have tracked them down and told them to forget everything," he said to the Stone. (Well, it would be a long transit, and he needed *someone* to talk to.) "But that would have been very hard. If they forgot the chase for the Dancer, they would have wondered how they wound up together in a seedy hotel in Chel'veckistad.

"I know," he told the Stone. "It would have been easier to tell them to kill each other. Maybe I should have done that, but . . ." But all those years wearing the Fudir had softened him. He would miss Bridget ban tonight. He would miss Little Hugh's companionship. He would even miss sparring with Greystroke. It bothered him that he would have killed them, had that been convenient. Killing strangers was far easier.

Saukkonen and the Raven had taught him a little of the limits of limitless power. If someone *knew* the Stone was being used on him, it was more difficult to impose one's will. One must guide the conversation in such a way that commands not only seemed natural, but seemed the subject's own ideas.

"That must be why the legends persisted," he told the Stone. "I could have told Saukkonen to forget he ever had you; but I could never track down everyone who had ever known he had it. Even if I had the Ouroboros Circuit, I might cover ninety, ninety-nine percent of them. But there would always be a few who were missed. And they would remember, and they would write down the legends."

The days ran by and he entered the Abyalon Road at last. There had been a few radioed messages. From Saukkonen, he thought; perhaps from Bridget ban, or Hugh. But he had not responded to them. Now that he was off-planet, his control was weakening. The commodore, in particular, must be wondering what madness had come over him. Perhaps he was begging in these messages that Donovan not start a war with the Confederacy. Ravn—had she escaped the Yard or not, once her allegiance to Saukkonen had faded? If she had, she would be confident that Donovan was doing the right thing, because it was what Donovan would have told her whether he had the Dancer or not. And if she hadn't escaped, then it didn't matter.

"Bridget ban knows how the game is played," he told the Stone. "If her own weapon was turned against her, she'll learn to live with it. And perhaps be less vulnerable the next time. And Hugh . . . Well, it was time he grew up some more."

Yet he could not conjure their faces without seeing a look of betrayal on them.

It was not until he was in the groove—"in the fookin' groove," he heard the ghost of Slugger O'Toole say— on the Palisades Parkway, that he sat down to have a serious talk with the Stone.

Behind him, on Old 'Saken, the ICC household troops turned out in such numbers that even the For-saken Planetary Manager took alarm and called out the civil police. "We can't have private justice, now, can we?" he asked in those oh-so-reasonable tones with which the Forsaken irritated the people of Die Bold and Friesing's World.

Killers fleeing Die Bold justice, the tellies cried. But they had only crude sketches of Hugh and Ravn to go by, and Hugh remained secluded in an insect-infested hotel in the Fourteenth. Lady Cargo had a vague recollection that "Ringbao" had been accom-panied by another man but she could not for the life of her recall what he looked like.

They were aware of Grimpen, too; but again, ex-cept for his size, his particulars were not specific, nor were they entirely sure he was connected with the oth-ers. ICC detectives rousted a great many large men in Chel'veckistad, and some of those large men did not take the rousting well. There was a near-riot in the fashionable Third District, and that is what triggered the PM's intervention.

The shootout on the Great Green with the willowy blond-and-black woman left three dead, none of them the suspect, and opened the civil police to charges of recklessness. Greystroke believed that Ravn had deliberately fired behind her to create civilian casualties that could be blamed on the police; but he could not prove it, then or later, and in any case the 'Fed agent disappeared.

Once, while shopping for groceries, Bridget ban encountered one of the ICC guards who had questioned the Fudir and her on the hillside overlooking Dalhousie Estates. There was nothing to connect her with the Die Bold killings, but the ICC was now suspicious of anyone who had been near the compound.

But it was the subordinate, the Terran, whom she ran into. She saw that he recognized her, and her arms full of groceries at the time. But he only shook his head and said, "You were with him," and passed on by. After that, however, only Greystroke ventured forth from their rooms.

The waiting game grew tedious, especially for Hugh, of whose face a rough approximation had been broadcast planet-wide. But even Greystroke and the Hounds found themselves chafing after two and a half weeks.

There was a common room at the hotel, and it had a 'visor for the use of the residents. Bridget ban and her people had been avoiding it, for fear of being influenced by the Dancer. But after they had read of Saukkonen's firing by Lady Cargo and his consequent defiance, it became clear that neither of them had the Dancer. The Fudir must have carried it off to liberate Terra. They were discussing how they might penetrate the Confederacy, when another resident pounded on the door of Bridget ban's room and hollered, "Ya gotta see this!"

It was not a ruse. Most residents of the Fourteenth

were themselves people who did not want to be found, or who had simply lost themselves. Strangers in their midst were carefully ignored.

The 'visor was broadcasting a continuing story—"breaking news," in the local dialect—and it was not clear at first what had triggered "the emergency cabinet meeting" or "the order to all vessels to stand down" or even "the hope for a peaceful resolution." Surely, no rievers would ever dare a planet like Old 'Saken! Perhaps it was Megranome? There were small systems in contention among the Old Planets. Piracy, raids, annexations, coups de main, but there had not been a trans-stellar war since the affair between Valency and Ramage on the far side of the Silk Road.

"Here are the visuals once again," the newsreader announced. "The ships emerged from the Abyalon road at are-four, Chelvecki time."

Against the stellar backdrop, cameras on revenue cutters hunted and tracked and locked on.

"Ah," said Greystroke. "That's *Justiciar.* And *Victory.* And, and *Argos.* And—" He could not contain himself and whooped for joy. "And that's *Hot Gates* herself!"

The cutter's angle of view widened, jittered, then adjusted for the relative velocities of the tracked ships. It was the entire Sapphire Point Squadron.

Bridget ban could not believe it. Fir Li had abandoned his station!

Grimpen smiled. "I'm glad Dark-hound reads his mail."

"It's time," Donovan told the Twisting Stone, "that you and I had a heart-to-heart talk. Should I call you 'Stonewall'? It's the name we best know you by. You're no scepter, are you? You are the Big Cheese himself."

The Stone made no answer.

"How long were you imprisoned before January's ship happened to break down? Not as long as the legends say, that's for certain. But then, you—or your rivals—had a hand in those legends. It was your folk who uprooted the old Commonwealth of Suns. Dao Chetty never had the bones to do something like that. You told us, and we believed it—only you couldn't get that elusive hundredth percent.

"It must have been a long, tedious wait for you. How many other ships have slip-slid right past you? But then, how can we measure the patience of a rock?

"Excuse me, of a 'silicon-based lifeform.' Not that there's anything wrong with that, but I think carbon has more fun. We certainly get around more."

He looked at the courier ship's calendar. "I suppose Sapphire Point is unguarded by now. To secure a trans-stellar communicator? Yes, even Fir Li would take that chance. Did Grimpen notify Fir Li on his own, or did he come within your range during one of his jaunts? No, sending notice was proper Kennel procedure. You're just taking advantage of it. Hanower and her partners are still patrolling Hanseatic Point. Too many questions, and I don't have the paperwork.

"This way, we can slip right across St. Gothard's Pass, no questions asked. Into the Rift. That must have been one honey of a war, Stone, to have wiped out so many suns. I hope none of them were Commonwealth Suns. I don't mean to sound testy, but I hope they were all yours, or your rivals', and you were all pretty much wiped out.

"But there must be something left. Something in the Rift, or you wouldn't be trying so hard to get back there. And no ships would be missing.

"Well yes, it was obvious you were trying to reach the Rift, that you were the prime mover in all this. Do you know when I was certain? Not when January gave it up to Jumdar so easily. Oh, I can see now why he did. January wasn't going toward the Rift, and Jumdar would have sent it straight to 'Saken, so you, hmm, 'nudged' him. It can't be easy for a rock like you to work your will on the old carbon-based noodle." He tapped himself on the head, and wondered if he was altogether himself. "You can nudge us, but you haven't the words to command us."

That struck him as funny. He would have to ask the Fudir about it the next time they met.

When he had grown serious once again, he said, "No, what convinced me at last was how easily Saukkonen let me have you. You realized that I had a better chance in a monoship—not of entering the Confederation, but of being ambushed and taken by your friends. So you 'switched horses.' "

Donovan paused and shook his head. "The more I don't want to do this, the more I know I must." He placed the Stone in the copilot's chair and sat facing it, not touching it. "I can't let you do it, you know. I can't let you bring it all back. The old legends are fun to read, but they would have been a horror to live through."

Donovan left the Stone where it was—it was not, under the circumstances, a flight risk—and climbed belowdecks to the equipment locker. Old King Stonewall was trying to drive him crazy, but he didn't know if any part of the courier ship was out of range.

He should just give up and take the Stone into the Rift. That would be the path of least resistance.

Until, *something* came out of the Rift. The people of sand and iron. Weaker maybe, but with undivided leadership this time. No rivals to kill each other off, or imprison each other on far-off planets.

He sighed and climbed back up the ladder to the

flight deck. Perhaps if he didn't actually touch it. There seemed to be some need for organic contact. Perhaps they could only work *through* organic beings. Wasn't there an old legend about Anteus and Hercules? But the touch of the Stone was so soothing.

The irresistible object, he reminded himself. *It's trying to seduce you.* "I've been seduced by prettier ones than you," he told the Stone.

He found a manipulating arm in the cargo bay. It was not a very large one of its kind, and he spent several hours—having grown unaccountably clumsy with the tools—to detach the outer portion. Then he carried it back to the flight desk.

He checked the settings on the pilot's console.

Still right in the groove.

Unless that was only what King Stonewall wanted him to think.

He used the arm extension to pick up the Twisting Stone.

It was extremely valuable. There were collectors who would pay him handsomely for it.

He carried it to the airlock and set it inside.

It was a priceless relic of a long-gone people. Hell, it *was* a long-gone people . . .

The folk of sand and iron.

He closed the inner lock. Hesitated. Began to open it again. Then, with a curse, hit the pneumatics.

The pins shot into place and the air pumps began to evacuate the chamber. Donovan aborted the cycle. He wanted the chamber full of air.

When the outer lock swung open the air puffed out, taking the Twisting Stone with it.

"After all," said Donovan, "this too is a home."

It was two weeks down the Palisades Parkway from Hanseatic to Sapphire Point. For most of that time,

Donovan watched the Twisting Stone tumbling away from the courier ship, maintaining the same forward velocity, but now with a lateral component. Now and then, he kicked up the magnification to keep it in view.

Donovan was traveling well under local-c, so the Stone passed through the first few lamina with no ill effect. But then it hit a layer of space whose local-c was less than its net velocity and in a wink it was gone. The ripple in space-time was minor. The next ship to pass would not even notice it.

Donovan continued to stare at the viewer, long after the impact site had fallen behind his craft. Then he resumed the pilot's seat, checked that he was still in the groove, and wept.

AN IARFHOCAL

And so it ends on a geantraí," the harper says. "A joyous triumph after all."

They have reached the bridge over the Bodhi Creek. The bridge is high-arched, and well known from souvenir art; but it is late and it is dark and no one is on the bridge but the scarred man and herself.

"Is it?" says the scarred man. He has stopped and has leaned his arms on the bridge's rail looking down at the gleaming black water. A streetlamp is reflected there, like a drowned moon. "How do we know that Donovan 'scuttled' the Stone? How does Donovan know it? It may be only what the Stone wanted him to believe."

"It's been years since all that happened."

"Stones are patient."

"Then at least let's enjoy this interval before the People of Sand and Iron come again."

"Unless they already have, and this is only what they want us to enjoy."

"No," says the harper. "I would know."

The scarred man shrugs. "That's the end of my story. It all happened long ago, and maybe it never happened at all." He looks at her. "Have you found the beginning of yours?"

"Maybe. What became of them in the end?"

"Those are other stories, and they require other prices."

"But surely you have some news of them. You told me that they had come here, to the Bar. Much of what you told me, you could only know if they had come back."

"Perhaps I made those parts up."

The harper shakes her head, but not in disbelief. "What about Hugh? Did he and Bridget ban not have an adventure together?"

"Did she tell you that? Then, they must have." He looks at her carefully. His gnarled hand reaches out and takes her by the chin. "And then one day she never came back," he says, reading the auguries in her face. "That's your quest, isn't it?"

"There was another, as well." She returns his gaze— and he is first to turn away. "And Greystroke?" she asks.

The scarred man shakes himself. "No one has seen him lately." And he laughs.

"The Fudir, then. Tell me more about him."

"Donovan, you mean. He continued on into the Confederacy, because he did not know what else to do. His struggle with the Stone had drained his entire will, as if he were a battery completely discharged. The Secret Names questioned him, with their wonted gentleness. Then they did something terrible to his mind. They diced it and sliced it until there was no 'I' remaining, only a 'we.' Fudir and Donovan and . . . others."

The harper sucks in her breath and she looks at the scarred man with pity in her eyes. "That sounds like a terrible story," she says.

"It is." He stoops, picks up a smooth, round stone and hurls it out into the waters of Bodhi Creek, whence returns a distant splash. "But it is a story for another day."